2-

THE BOYFRIEND AGREEMENT

St. Mary's Academy Book 1

SEVEN STEPS

Seven Steps Publishing

Edited by **Angela Campbell**
Proofread by **Genevieve Scholl**

Cover Photo provided by Shuttershock

Proudly Published in the United States of America

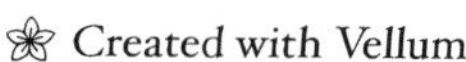

ALSO BY

Adult Contemporary Romance

Peace in the Storm

New Adult Romance

The Last Rock King

St. Mary's Academy Series

The Beginning of Forever

The Boyfriend Agreement (Book I)

Chasing Mermaids (Book 2)

The Golden Boy (Book 3)

Stealing Hearts (Book 4)

The Secret Lives of Princesses (Book 5)

Kissing Frogs (Book 6)

The Boyfriend Agreement

St. Mary's Academy

Book 1

❧ I ❧

I am invisible.

I eat, sleep, go to school. I even manage to strap on my running shoes from time to time and race around my lower middle-class neighborhood in Brooklyn NY, just one subway stop away from Manhattan. It's an ill-advised pastime, really. According to Maria Jimenez on the six o'clock news, criminals are no strangers to Briar Hills, Brooklyn. Let's just say that the neighborhood watch around here has a way different meaning than in nicer places. Still, no one has bothered me yet. It's as if they don't see me. Like I'm a single ray of sunshine on a clear day. Unheeded and hardly noticed.

Like I said. Invisible.

One would imagine that being invisible would be fun. It's not. It's less like a superpower and more like drowning in a glass tank in the middle of a crowded room. I hated it. At best, people looked through me instead of at me. At worst, my existence was completely forgotten. I knew this because when people got around to noticing me, it was always with a surprised expression.

"Hey. I didn't see you there."

"When did you get here?"

"Have you been here long?"

Being invisible sucked. I wanted to be seen. To be acknowledged. For someone to say, 'Nice outfit, Bella' or 'I love your hair, Bella' or 'What do you think about that, Bella.' But for someone like me, getting a compliment was like finding a yellow thread in a haystack. Impossible.

And so, I had no plans on being seen at school that morning. A fact that I flaunted by not washing my super curly hair and wearing old jogging pants with a hole in the knee. St. Mary's Academy didn't have a dress code for Juniors or Seniors. They called the policy progressive. Really, it was so that the junior and senior fashion club, of which the principal's daughter was the president, could showcase their latest designs. Nepotism at its finest.

Ms. Mitchell, my English teacher, walked between the classroom desks, a faded copy of *Shakespeare*'s *Much Ado About Nothing* in her hand.

She read the words reverently, as if Old Bill were writing them just to her.

"I do love nothing in the world so well as you. Is that not strange?"

The words pulled a sigh from me, and I slowly turned, looking for the boy that I always looked at when I thought of romance.

Jake Winsted.

I had been in love with Jake since the ninth grade. It wasn't just his looks, though his blond hair and blue eyes were the definition of gorgeous. It wasn't just his super-hot football player body, or his laugh that started deep in his belly and shook the walls whenever he released it. It was the quiet moments. Like, when something caught his interest and his whole body leaned forward, totally engaged. It was the way everyone looked up to him. He was the most popular boy in school, and yet I'd never seen him bully anyone. He wore his power with confidence and ease, wielding it sparingly and always for good.

Ms. Mitchell—Leah, to me—closed the worn book, slipping one slim finger between the pages to hold her place.

"It's often said that the simplest words hold the most power. You, my little birdies, are going to give me your simple but powerful words in project form."

A collective groan rose from my fellow students. I, however, gave a little cheer. I know it's weird, but I actually liked projects, and I loved school. My dream was to graduate valedictorian of my class. Considering that I had the second highest GPA in the school, that dream might actually become a reality.

"This project consists of two parts." Her red t-strap heels tapped against the polished wood floor as she continued her journey up and down the aisles. In the course of a class, Ms. Mitchell would walk down each of the four aisles at least a dozen times, her heels making short taps against the floor like some weird, slowed down version of Morse code. All that exercise must've contributed to her figure that I would best describe as lithe.

"You will write me a ten-page summary of the Shakespearian work of your choice."

Easy peasy, rice and cheesy. I could write essays in my sleep.

"The second part of this project will be a group aspect. You will be partnered up with a fellow student, and the pair of you will compose a short, dramatic play based on your chosen work."

I sat up straight in my chair. Partners? My mind raced with the possibilities. Who would be my partner? What if it was Jake? Could such a wonderful thing even happen?

Gooseflesh skittered across my upper back. I was suddenly very aware of my body. My outfit (homeless chic, at best), my greasy, puffy hair, my non-name-brand, red sneakers. I was a complete and total mess. I couldn't be Jake's partner wearing something like this. He'd probably take one look at me and barf. I know I would.

"The partners will be announced on Monday, and the project will be due two weeks after that."

She leaned on her desk, crossing her ankles in front of her. Ms. Mitchell was beautiful, in a librarian sort of way. Her wardrobe consisted of dark blazers with short skirts, white shell tops, and red t-strap heels. For the most part, she kept her hair up in a French twist, held in place with pearl chopsticks. Red cat-eye glasses dangled from a black strap around her neck. Reading glasses.

Ms. Mitchell and I were in a very exclusive book club together. So exclusive, in fact, that there were only two of us. Twice a month, we decided upon and read a teen-appropriate romance novel, then two weeks later, we'd meet up during her lunch break and my study period to discuss it, carefully picking apart each simile and metaphor. Every line of prose and allusions to theme. Every bit of dialogue that made us laugh or cry. There were bookworms, and then there was Ms. Mitchell and I. We didn't read books. We devoured them, brought them back up, and digested them again. We were like cows. Really cool, totally not fat, book cows.

Ms. Mitchell pointed to the back of the room.

"Yes, Cole."

"Will this project hold the same weight as our midterm?"

My back teeth clenched. Just the sound of Cole's voice made me curl my hands into fists.

Cole Winsted was one third of the Winsted triplets. Jake was obviously the hot triplet, Regina was the crazy one, and Cole was the smart one. I had the second highest grades in the school because Cole had the highest, and it rubbed me like a cheese grater. It wasn't his intelligence that bothered me. It was the fact that he was a jerk about it. He threw out facts and figures like the popular kids threw around their parents' annual income. His favorite pastime, aside from football and student council, was to throw it in my face that my GPA was one tenth of a point lower than his. Mine was 3.8. His was 3.9. One lousy tenth of a point. But to hear Cole tell it, I was half way to remedial classes.

Like I said. Grade A jerk.

"It will hold equal weight as your mid-term. Meaning, if you do not pass this project, then you will not pass this class."

Cole squinted in confusion.

"What does that mean? Not pass a class? I'm sorry. I don't understand. Is that an actual thing?"

A few kids giggled, mostly Cole's football teammates.

Ms. Mitchell didn't roll her eyes, but I could see that she wanted to.

"Yes, Cole, we know that you are the king of class passing. But that's a solo activity. Let's see how well you do with a partner." More giggles and catcalls erupted, and Ms. Mitchell's cheeks turned a deep shade of pink. Mine did too and I shifted in my seat.

She pressed on, despite the double entendre that now hung in the air like a humorously-shaped cloud.

"This project will hinge on two people working together. Meaning that both partners must contribute equally. If both partners do not participate in the dramatic reading, you will fail the project. So, no doing all the work and putting two names on it, Mr. Winsted."

Cole smiled innocently, his pearly white teeth gleaming.

"I wouldn't dream of it, Ms. Mitchell. My moral compass would never allow me to commit such an unspeakable act."

I snorted and Cole glared at me. I'd been in this school for three years and somehow, Cole and I were always rivals at something academic. If I scored the highest math grade in the class, he would say it was a fluke. If he scored the highest grade in chemistry, I would announce that he paid off the teacher. And so, back and forth we went, every year, every class, every day. It was a super annoying part of school life that I'd learned to live with.

Ms. Mitchell gave Cole a half smile and turned back to the class as the school bell rang overhead.

"Start thinking about the book you'd like to work on and the dramatic piece you'd like to do!" she called as everyone rose to leave.

I slung my book bag over my shoulder, rushing out to discuss this new and potentially life-changing event with my two best and only friends, Ariel Swimworthy and Jasmine Patel, when I crashed in to a wall.

A human wall.

I looked up, right into a set of eyes so blue that they'd put the clearest sky to shame.

Jake's eyes.

"I, uh, I..." My brain turned to mush. I couldn't think. His eyes were so beautiful. So perfect. I saw my future in those eyes.

"My bad," he said, giving me a half smile.

Lungs tight, I froze in place while Jake gave me a quick once over. Then, without another word, he moved on.

Jake Winsted looked at me. After two years and two months, he finally looked at me.

I could scream. That was, if my lungs didn't feel like they were in a vise. My feet rooted me to the floor, long after the class cleared. My heart raced.

Jake Winsted looked at me.

My mouth broke into a smile, happiness infusing every pore. After being in the shadows so long, having his eyes on me felt glorious. They were so blue. So beautiful. So perfect.

He was perfect.

"Is everything all right?" Ms. Mitchell asked from behind her desk.

"Yes." The word left my mouth in one long breath.

"Are you sure? You've been standing there for a while. You look kind of ... pale."

"I'm fine." I was more than fine. I was euphoric.

She paused, and I finally turned to look at her. Her red glasses were perched on the tip of her nose. Her brows were furrowed in concern.

"Okay," she said, her word sounding unsure. "So, I found a new book for our next book club meeting."

She reached in to her desk and pulled out a paperback. I was immediately drawn to the pastels and big, white, jagged letters on the cover. I read the title out loud.

"My Favorite Forever by Tabitha Browning."

I pulled my slipping bookbag strap higher on my shoulder.

There were three things one had to do when introduced to a new paperback book.

First, you had to touch the cover and notice if the print was raised or not. This part was very important, since raised text always meant better books. This book's text was raised, and my heart flipped in excitement.

Second, you had to sniff the pages. I raised it to my nose and took a deep whiff. It smelled like paper, ink and awaiting adventures. A beautiful, new smell. Not like the books in the library that smelled like fingerprints and mold.

Third, and this was the most important step, you had to hear the spine crack. I opened the book and the spine cracked hard, like there were actual bones in it. I smiled. Every book cracked a little differently. I liked to think of the cracking as the first word in the story.

I sighed. Today was turning out to be amazing. I really should have washed my hair.

"It looks fantastic," I said, turning it over and reading the back.

She grinned. "I know, right? I love *Tabitha Browning*."

I'd never heard of her, but I took Ms. Mitchell's word for it. She had excellent taste in books.

"Same time in two weeks?" she asked.

I nodded, my eyes still skimming over the words. "Yeah. Same time."

Not only had Jake looked at me, but I had a fresh book in my hands, ready for me to devour. This was the best day ever.

I thanked Ms. Mitchell and flew from the room, ready to take on the world. That was, until I passed under the class doorway.

"So, Bella French."

Cole stood outside of the door, leaning carelessly against the painted yellow wall. If Jake was an angel, Cole was, well, the other thing. Dark hair. Olive skin. They did share the same athletic build and blue eyes, but while Jake's wardrobe was straight off the runways of Paris, Cole's style was simple. Dark jeans, dark shirts, hoodies. Today, he wore glasses without lenses just so he could look smarter than the genius he already was.

"Not now, Cole," I replied, anxious to share the news with the two people that I knew would care to know.

"Just wanted to let you know that if you need anyone to proofread your project, I am open to tutoring."

I rolled my eyes.

"I can proofread my own project, thank you very much."

"Are you sure? Because, based on your 3.8 GPA, I would imagine that you would need a little help."

A growl escaped my throat. How could one person be so infuriating?

He ignored my anger and smiled wider.

"From you? The guy who is three A's behind me in English? No. I don't think so."

His smile dropped into a frown and my mood lightened.

"Everyone knows that you're Ms. Mitchell's favorite student. That's why you score so high in her class."

"I score high because my work is superior to everyone else's, including yours. Maybe you should be the one asking me to tutor you. The answer is no, by the way. A big, fat no."

"I would never ask you to tutor me."

"And I would never agree. Now that we have that settled, I have to be on my way."

"Still chasing Narcissus?" His eyes held mine, darkness infusing his gaze. The same darkness that always appeared when he spoke about his brother.

I rolled my eyes and crossed my arms over my chest. I didn't need to explain myself to anyone. Least of all, Cole.

He mimicked my stance and continued.

"If you catch him, be sure to keep him out of the bathroom. You know, in case he falls in love with his reflection in the toilet."

I gasped. "That's a sucky thing to say about your brother."

He shrugged. "That doesn't make it any less true."

"Jealous, much?"

"Of Jake? You wish."

I didn't bother hiding my knowing smile.

"You are, aren't you? You're jealous that he's popular and the girls like him, and here you are, all alone in a hallway, your sole joy in life teasing invisible girls like me. It's pathetic, actually."

He bit the left side of his bottom lip, his cheeks reddening.

I gushed with pleasure as he squirmed at my words. "Did I hit a nerve, Cole?"

"You're naïve."

"And you are turning green with envy."

"Whatever."

He glared at me, pushed off the wall and stormed away.

I smiled wickedly. Score one for me.

Cole was pretentious and a jerk. He deserved a reality check. I was more than happy to give him one.

Satisfied with my win and Jake's newfound, though brief, attention, I practically skipped to fifth period lunch.

2

Jasmine and Ariel are invisible too, though for very different reasons.

Jasmine is the only Indian girl in our mostly white, super exclusive, super rich school. Anyone who says racism is dead is lying. Her father owns a pharmaceutical company based in New York. She has amazing grades and is on student council. Despite overwhelming evidence to the contrary, some jerky kids still assume that she doesn't speak English. I want to kick those kids in their stupid faces.

Ariel's father holds the leases to at least a hundred buildings in Manhattan—including the lease to our school—and she still can't get a seat at the popular table. Or won't. I've always had a gut feeling that she isn't popular because she doesn't want to be, though I have no idea why she wouldn't. She's perfect for it, with her shiny red hair that hangs down by her butt and her big green eyes that always remind me of clear Caribbean oceans.

My two besties were less than thrilled about my Jake story, which was both disappointing and super irritating.

"So, he just looked at you?" Ariel asked. She loosely gripped her cheese sandwich, giving the thin yellow slices enough room to slip from the wheat bun.

"Right at me," I replied.

The lunch room was wall-to-wall with loud, spoiled teenagers, each sitting at clean, long, white tables. It was actually kind of beautiful with its glass and stone walls, famous food-related paintings, and slightly dimmed lighting. The only bad part about it was the hideous black and green checkerboard floor tiles. The green wasn't a pretty forest green or an interesting emerald green, either. It was gross green. Like some kid had just puked up split pea soup all over it. And the black was ... well ... it was just plain depressing. Whoever the interior designer was really dropped the ball on the floor color scheme.

"Did he say anything?" Jasmine asked. Her cheese sandwich didn't have mayo, mustard or anything else on it. It was just cheese and bread. Seriously, I don't know how she does it. Cheese sandwiches are gross, but dry cheese sandwiches are even worse.

"He said, 'my bad'. Then he kind of, just, looked at me."

"Like, he checked you out?" Ariel asked.

"I think so."

Jasmine's face tightened in disapproval as she eyed my t-shirt and greasy hair.

"In that outfit?"

I nodded, and shoved a green salad leaf in to my mouth. A small piece of it dropped on to the table. I'm not the most graceful of eaters. My table manners lay somewhere between toddler and trained monkey.

"I know. I look homeless," I said, cringing at the thought of my hole-filled sweat pants, "but next time, I'll be ready."

"Do you think there will be a next time?" Jasmine asks.

"Well, my argument with Cole gave me an idea. I am going to ask Jake if he needs an English tutor."

The two girls let out a collective gasp, drawing the stares of a few classmates who sat close by, including the annoyed gaze of the mayor's niece.

"You're serious?" Ariel asked.

I nodded, and took another stab at my salad.

"Super serious. It's time that I stopped being invisible and actually did something for once."

"Maybe you can start by doing your hair," Jasmine said.

I rolled my eyes.

"And wearing non-Goodwill clothes?" Ariel added.

These girls were out of their minds if they thought I would give up my thrifting ways. It was cheap and good for the environment. Two things that were very important to me.

"Maybe." Or maybe not.

"We should go shopping," Ariel said. "Nothing says 'look at me' like new clothes."

I frowned. Jasmine and Ariel were super rich, but I wasn't. My grandparents paid for me to come here. St. Mary's Academy was their alma mater and they wanted it to be mine, too. How they went from wealthier than God to running a horse farm in North Carolina, I had no idea. I made a mental note to ask one day.

"I don't think so," I said, my smile dropping.

One of the reasons that I shopped at Goodwill was because Daddy didn't have a ton of money. Unlike Ariel, Jasmine's parents, and everyone else at this school, Daddy was middle class. He worked at a body shop in Brooklyn. We weren't rich, or even super comfortable. We were making ends meet, with a little left over for ice cream and cookies once in a while. It sucked when Ariel and Jasmine wanted to do stuff that I couldn't afford but mostly, we just hung out at one of our houses and watched movies or listened to music.

"It will be my treat," Jasmine said. "We'll go today after school."

"Can't," Ariel said. "Swim practice."

"And I have to study for my French test next week," I added.

Jasmine looked heartbroken. She loved to spend her father's money on shopping sprees for others. She was the most generous person that I knew.

"Well, at least promise me that you won't wear anything with holes in it," she said.

I pretended to examine a piece of lettuce.

"What if they are ripped on purpose?"

"No holes. Try to look sophisticated. Maybe jeans and a tight t-shirt. And not one of your weird movie quote t-shirts. A girly one with sparkles. Or, if you're feeling daring, maybe a dress. Or," she gasped dramatically, "dare I say it? Heels!"

I laughed out loud, drawing another irritated gaze from the mayor's niece. I could deal with no holes, but not wearing my movie quote t-shirts was crossing the line. I had everything from, 'Say hello to my little friend' to 'Toto, I've a feeling we're not in Kansas anymore' to my favorite, 'Hello, my name is Inigo Montoya. You killed my father. Prepare to die.' What could I say? I was a movie buff. And I won't even get started on my music lyric t-shirts. There were at least twenty of those, most of them handmade by yours truly.

Still, I decided to humor Jasmine because she was one third of our best friend trio.

"I will try my best."

Her eyes narrowed, the way my mother's used to when she knew I was lying. Out of the three of us, Jasmine was closest to the den mother, giving us good advice, checking our clothes for stains and holes, and cheering us when we were down. I was grateful for the mothering, though I didn't tell her that. If I did, she'd become impossible.

"Hm ... I think I should pay you a visit tomorrow morning before school. Just to make sure that you don't wear that *King Kong* shirt that I hate."

I shrugged innocently and took another bite of my salad. So what if it was a boy t-shirt? *King Kong* was the best out of all the monsters. Better than Godzilla or any other lizard out there. But Jasmine didn't care about stuff like that. She was more interested in getting me to wear my hair straightened or making me wear makeup—or worse, the color pink. I loathed the color pink. My official stance was that the color pink set the women's movement back hundreds of years. Hundreds!

"Ladies." Kenny Jennings slid in to the seat next to me. He was a skinny kid with floppy hair who always wore cargo pants and was never without his bookbag. His bony, disobedient limbs were constantly in motion, shaking, bouncing and twisting when they should have been still. For some reason, he smelled like tacos, even though the lunch ladies weren't serving tacos today.

"Looking for a little fun?" he asked.

We collectively rolled our eyes.

"Take your bag of loser, and scat," I said.

He held up his hands in defense.

"Suit yourselves. No need to get testy."

He swore at us under his breath before moving on to the next table to sell his backpack wares. I was glad he was gone. Kenny made my skin crawl.

It was a well-known fact that Kenny dealt drugs in the school. Nothing hard. Mostly weed. And being the son of a senator, any complaints about him were officially wiped off his record. Eventually, everyone stopped complaining all together. Now, he was a staple of St. Mary's Academy. The boy that kids called on Friday nights if they wanted to get high. Most kids didn't buy anything from Kenny and the ones that did were too rich to get in trouble for it.

The bell rang, announcing the end of our lunch period. I was happy about it. It meant that I was one period closer to going home and finding something to wear that would both catch Jake's eye and meet Jasmine's approval. Or, at least Ariel's approval, which was much more relaxed.

We threw our trays in the big, blue bin by the door and parted ways. Ariel and Jasmine went to leadership and I went to the main office.

Due to my good behavior, excellent grades and general lack of anything close to delinquency, I'd been selected to work in the main office as the Student Guidance Counselor.

It was the second best part of my day, after seeing Jake, of course. No grades to worry about, access to the teachers' lounge with all its free soda and snacks and getting to hear all of the popular kids' dirty little secrets was a pretty sweet gig.

Mrs. Bernice, the office aide, greeted me with a smile. The old woman had been at St. Mary's Academy for as long as anyone could remember. She was ancient but also friendly and warm-hearted. She was the type of old person who asked kids if they wanted candy and, if they said yes, she gave them *Halls*. I knew that *Halls* were not candy, but I took them anyway. If anything, they would keep my throat moisturized. Plus, I didn't want to be rude to such a sweet old lady like Mrs. Bernice.

Every day during sixth period, I turned from invisible student to a student who gave other kids advice that they had no intention of listening to. Student Guidance was a program created by Principal Mann last year. The idea was that kids who struggled with personal issues would feel more comfortable talking to someone their own age instead of an actual guidance counselor. And so, with minimal training and a small soap box that I pulled out for special occasions, I listened as my fellow students told me about their parents' divorces, cheating boyfriends, the stresses of popularity and the pressure of trying to figure out who they were and who they wanted to be.

Today, Melanie Pleasant was waiting in my office. It was technically Mr. Mark's office, but I claimed it now. Well, except the motivational cat posters. No one should claim anything that said, *I Have a Case of The Meow-Days*.

Melanie's eyes were already wet with tears when I walked in, her skin turning blotchier by the second. That could only mean one thing. She'd broken up with her boyfriend again.

"He is such a jerk!" she said in to a crumpled facial tissue. I sat down in my chair and tried not to roll my eyes. "I caught him making out with Chrissy Tanner at a party yesterday, so I told him it was over."

She blew in to the tissue, turning her red nose even redder.

To my count, this was Mel's boyfriend's sixth time cheating, and that was just in the last two months. The mystery boy had a habit of sticking his tongue down random girls' throats and getting caught.

Mel sobbed hard, each tear tearing the snot-soaked paper apart. I handed her another tissue, which she took and promptly blew her nose again. I wrinkled my nose and pushed the floral box in her direction.

"Look Mel, this cheating has been going on for a while now. Don't you think it may be wise to consider breaking up with him for good?"

Her tears stopped. She looked at me with shock and violently shook her head. I asked her to break up with her cheating boyfriend and she looked as if I'd just asked her to repair the Sphinx's nose.

"I can't. He's popular and cute. Plus, he..." Her eyes dropped back to my napkin. "There are things that he can do for me that other boys can't. I ... I have to stay with him."

She snatched another tissue from the box and dabbed at her eye. I examined her dark hair with the purple highlights, her black, super short dress with lace details in the arms. Her thigh-high grey boots and fishnet stockings. Mel's look was a cross between goth and glam. Funny, I always thought girls who wore all black were supposed to be tough, but this blubbering mess was quickly proving me wrong. I sighed, breathing in a mixture of potted plants and warmed up left-overs coming from the teachers' lounge.

Eggplant. Eck!

I turned my attention back to Mel and leaned forward a bit.

"Look, Mel. This guy is a sucky boyfriend that makes you unhappy. No matter how popular or cute a guy is, he's not worth your tears."

She narrowed her eyes at me, anger flickering in her dark eyes.

"You don't know anything. You don't know what it's like to be popular. To have everyone watching your every move. If I dumped him, I would have to go to the fall formal alone, like some sort of herpes infested loser. No thanks."

"Mel-"

"You know, I don't know why I come here." She threw her tissues in the trash and grabbed her book bag. "You don't understand the sort of pressure that I'm dealing with."

"What pressure? To dump your cheating boyfriend?"

"No, idiot. One does not just dump their boyfriend. They dump up."

Dump up? That was a new one.

Mel sighed and rolled her eyes as if I was the stupidest person in the world.

"If you break up with someone, do it so that you can hook up with someone even more popular. That's the way the world works, which means that I'll have to wait for the dating pool to open up before I can do anything." She blew out a breath. "I'm trapped. Trapped like a super hot rat with big boobs."

She was right. She did have big boobs.

"You don't have to be trapped." I leaned forward and put my hand over hers. Mel was stuck up and condescending, but deep down, I believed that she was a good person. Just a little misguided. I wanted to help her. If only she would listen to me for once. "You are in control of your own destiny. No one can take that control away from you unless you allow them to. Will you at least try to remember that? You are in control."

She looked out the window, away from me. I could tell that she wasn't listening to a word I said. It made me feel like crap. Just because I wasn't popular didn't mean that I didn't know about life. I knew plenty. And if I had a boyfriend, I would not allow him to cheat on me, no matter how popular he was.

She stood and grabbed her bag, still dabbing at her eyes.

"It must be nice not having anyone see you, Brenda. Freeing. Maybe one day, I'll know what that feels like."

"Bella. My name is Bella."

But it was too late. She'd already walked out of the office, leaving me with my cat pictures and my seething anger.

I knew every mean thing her boyfriend did to her. I knew that her mother snorted cocaine first thing in the morning and that her father ordered hookers over the internet. And yet, she couldn't remember my name.

Now that I thought about it, when she did come to student guidance, which was nearly every day, she never looked me in the eye. Sure, she looked in my general direction, but she never made direct eye contact and she never took my advice.

Just like the rest of them.

A sinking feeling pulled at my throat, making a lump form there. I clenched my jaw and sat back in my chair, hoping that no one else walked through the doors. I wanted to not care about the kids who walked through my doors, but I did. I wanted them to do well. Not just because they were popular, but because we all shared the same basic problems. We were all lost, looking for our voice. Even if that voice was our own conscience. That little person in our hearts who told us the right way to go. The one that told us we were worthy.

Mel was wrong about one thing. I did know the pressure she was dealing with. I was chosen to test out this whole student guidance thing because Mr. Mann thought that I was safe. In adult language, safe equaled boring. He mistook my smarts for blandness, and bland girls didn't get in trouble. I guess he thought that if I could make girls more like me, then the school would be a better place.

I laughed shortly.

He should have let me tutor them, not mentor them. These girls didn't listen to me. I could tell them not to swim with sharks and they'd do the exact opposite, for one very important reason. I was invisible. My advice was just air, easily dismissed though badly needed.

Maybe if I was popular then the other girls would listen to me. Respect me. Imagine the good that I could do if I had a voice. I could convince Mel to break up with her cheating boyfriend. I could convince Marcus Tyson that he didn't have to be a football player just because his NFL father wanted him to. I could tell Lisa Grissel to sit down and talk with her parents about her passion for painting. I would tell Gerald Martin that it was okay to love Tillary Swanson, even if his parents would never accept her because she was black and he was white.

I could do so much good at this school if only someone would listen to me. If only someone would see me. But they didn't. I was barely a blip on their radar. Being here was supposed to help the student body feel better, but it only made me feel worse.

Like I said, invisibility sucks.

I WALKED HOME ALONE, WHICH WASN'T ENTIRELY UNCOMMON. Ariel was on the swim team, and practiced after school four days a week. Jasmine always had family either visiting or leaving. Grandparents, cousins, nieces, nephews, uncles and every other relation from around the world all stopped in at one time or another. They would stay for a few weeks or months then leave, making room for the next relation to step in.

I'd often wondered what having such a big family was like. My family was small but tight-knit. My mom's parents were dead, and my father's parents ran a horse farm in North Carolina. Mom was an only child. Dad had an older brother and sister, Uncle Sam and Aunt Liz, neither of which were married or had children. We saw them every year around Thanksgiving.

Seeing my aunt and uncles every year reminded me of better days.

The days when I wasn't invisible. When I was semi-popular, back in my hometown of Pikes Peak, North Carolina. When things were simple and life went on in unbroken lines.

But that was a long time ago.

Exactly five years, eleven months, twenty-four days, two hours, and fifteen minutes ago, my mother, Leslie French, drew her last breath on this Earth and shattered my entire existence. My mother, who looked at me with love and patience. Who listened to the tales of my life as if they were part of the holy cannon of scripture. Who noticed when my hair was different or my shirt was untucked, as it often was. Whose lap I crawled in to when I got home from school every day, though Daddy told me I was too old for such things. My mother, my life, was unfairly stolen from me. Breast cancer ravaged her body, rendering her unrecognizable. For six months, she warred with it, until one frosty winter morning in December, when she drew her last breath and took me with her in to the oblivion.

I missed my mother. I missed her laughter and her smile. I missed how she always smelled of Sunflower perfume. I missed how Daddy and she used to dance in the kitchen while she cooked dinner. I missed being happy. Missed the time when I was unfettered by sadness and this strange shield of invisibility. Her death was like a jail sentence, damning me to walk with bitterness, confusion and an ever-present sense that I was missing a part of myself.

They say that time changes everything, and they, whomever they are, were right. After six years, I can finally recall my mother without bursting in the tears. I can remember the happy times without falling apart. Like her dancing around the house to eighties music—Mom's favorite. Or us sneaking up on Dad in the winter and pelting him with snowballs as he shoveled the driveway. And the animals. Mom loved animals. It was one of the reasons she'd married Daddy. Not only was he handsome and funny, kind and strong, but he came with his own horse farm, and God, did Mom love horses. Their romance was practically written in the stars. She, a sweet-hearted, sassy, black woman from Charleston, and Daddy, a corn-fed, white farm boy from Connersville. They truly loved each other, and I was a product of that love.

But now Mom was gone, leaving behind Daddy and me, two broken pieces just trying to hold each other up. We didn't always succeed, but we tried. It was what Mom would have wanted. For us to keep trying. For us to not give up.

A shuffling to my left pulled my attention. I looked down. There, in a box marked *Free Puppies,* was a single, small dog.

Just one.

I read the messy scribble on the side of the box again.

Free puppies. Not Free Puppy or Free Dog. Free Puppies, as in more than one.

I looked around, searching for the person that might have left the box. People passed me, their feet stomping the sidewalk, their shoulders bumping into me, their eyes on the ground in the classic way that New Yorkers walked.

But no one stopped. No one paid attention to me or the dog that was now peering up at me with big, black, curious eyes. Its once brown coat was covered in patches of mud, or at least what I hoped was mud. It whimpered a little and backed up in to a corner of the box.

I looked around again, but no one seemed to care about me, or the dog.

How long had it been here? Hours? Days? I didn't remember seeing it before. I would have stopped if I had.

I crouched down and I reached in to the box, intending on patting the shaking creature on a small spot that was clear of the crusted black gunk. The dog wouldn't allow it. It pushed itself even deeper in to the corner of the box and howled.

The poor thing was terrified! I didn't blame it. I'd be terrified, too, if I was left to die in a box in the middle of New York City.

I pulled my hand back and gave the animal a big, reassuring smile.

"You don't have to be afraid. I won't hurt you."

The dog let out a bark, but it was weak. The poor thing was all crusty fur, skin, and bones. When was the last time that it'd eaten? Or had a bath? Or love?

I let out a breath and took another look around.

Still no one noticed me or the dog. If the dog died in that box, no one would care. The creature was invisible. Like me.

"You're not invisible anymore," I whispered to it. "I see you."

I picked up the box, sending the dog rolling out of its corner. The smell was disgusting. Like poop and vomit and dog and dirt and everything else vile. I held my breath, pity crushing my heart. This poor animal had been left in this filthy box with its horrendous smell by some heartless person. How could they do that? How could they live with themselves knowing that this animal might die here?

People sucked sometimes.

"You don't have to worry anymore. You have a home now, and a family."

The dog still looked nervous, but didn't howl again. I walked faster, toward the subway station, anxious to relieve this poor creature from its misery.

He'd have to suffer a little while longer but it would be worth it.

In that moment, I felt closer to Mom than I had in a long time. It was like she'd handed this puppy to me. This small, innocent creature, afraid of the world, jaded by love. Invisible.

Just like me.

The puppy laid in the box, its little paws digging into the bottom for dear life. I crossed the street and walked in to the subway station. Half an hour later, my new, stinky puppy and I emerged in Briar Hills, Brooklyn. Cool air snaked in to my jacket, chilling me. I could only imagine what the dog felt like.

"Don't worry, baby. You're going to be warm soon."

I stopped by the pet store and used my emergency credit card to buy supplies. A crate, a comfortable mat, bowls, food, flea collar, shampoo. Everything ended up costing over two hundred dollars.

My dad was going to go nuclear.

My stomach tightened painfully but I wouldn't let that stop me. I handed the cashier the credit card and held my breath while he ran it through. Daddy would just have to understand that this was an emergency. This poor creature needed a home. Yes, that little doggy jacket may have been a bit of a luxury, but he needed some luxury after what he'd been through.

I discarded the disgusting box in a trash bin and put the dog, who by now was covered in fresh poop, in the crate. It trembled as it walked in, looking through the wires at me. It was a pretty cute dog. It would be cuter when it was clean, but there was something about its eyes, some friskiness that I liked. This dog had spirit. Someone just had to love it, and let it out.

That someone would be me.

I handed it a few kibbles from the food bag, and hoisted everything up on my overburdened arms.

Only two blocks and one elevator ride and I'd be home with what was sure to be my new best friend.

A soft breeze blew, and I imagined that my mom was there, hurrying me home with the new gift that she'd given me.

Thanks, Mom.

By the time Daddy came home an hour later, things had taken a turn for the worse.

"What the- Bella, did you poop in front of the door?"

No, but at this point, I might as well have.

I briskly scrubbed the dog's stubborn coat and waited for my father, Maurice French, to pop his head into the bathroom. I don't know what I dreaded more. Him seeing that I had the dog, or him seeing that the dog had pooped all over the house. Or maybe it was the two-hundred-dollar credit card bill that he'd see in another week. Either way, I was sure that a grounding was coming. But I didn't care. I'd done the right thing. If that earned me a grounding, then so be it.

When Daddy found me a minute later, I was in the bathroom, trying to wrangle a still dirty dog under the detachable shower hose. I could smell his cinnamon gum from across the room. Daddy always chewed cinnamon gum.

"What is going on here?" he cried. "What is this?"

The dog, who had been fighting me for an hour as I tried to wash him, stopped his thrashing and looked at my father. He gave him an innocent expression. So did I. A bit of soap dripped off the tip of my nose. At this point, I was probably just as dirty as the dog.

I gave my father my best smile and hoped he was in a good mood.

"Hi, Daddy."

"Don't 'Hi, Daddy' me. What is going on? Whose dog is this?"

He was not in a good mood, but I would not be deterred. Not when I'd come so far.

I held my hands over the dog, dramatically presenting it.

"This is our new dog."

"New dog?" I didn't know that anger and confusion could co-exist, but Daddy's face showed both emotions perfectly. "Why do we have a new dog?"

"I, uh, found him. When I was walking home."

"So, you brought him here? Why didn't you call the cops?"

"I couldn't call the cops," I said as if it were the silliest thing in the world. The dog stilled, its eyes still on Daddy. I used the opportunity to make a fur mohawk with the soap.

"And why not?"

"They would have called animal control, and then animal control would have put him down. You like dogs, don't you, Daddy?"

"Not dogs that crap right in front of doorways. I nearly stepped right in it!"

I grimaced. Even the dog sat down in the tub and lowered his head as if it knew what he'd done.

"I meant to clean that up."

"I'll bet."

I paused, worrying my lower lip.

"So, I was thinking that we could give him a cool name, like Rex or Tiger or Python."

Daddy held up both of his hands as he often did when he thought I was being crazy.

"We are not keeping the dog. Now, get him out of that tub while I call animal control."

"You can't. They'll put him down if you do."

"That's not our problem."

"You're going to have this poor animal killed because he pooped a little in the living room. Is that the kind of person you are?"

"I'm sure they'll find him a good home." He leaned against the white, tiled bathroom wall, pulled his cell phone out of his pocket and fumbled with the buttons. The light over the sink flickered a bit. Someone must've been vacuuming next door.

"No one is getting put down," Daddy said, wiping at the sweat that pooled on his forehead. The bathroom steamed from the blackening bathwater.

"You don't know that."

"Sure I do, sweetheart."

Sweetheart. He only called me sweetheart when he was losing his patience with me. I had to act fast before he became completely unreasonable.

"Daddy, please. I'll take care of it. I'll walk it and I'll feed it."

"Feed it?" He pushed off the wall, and looked in to the kitchen where I had carelessly dropped all of bags. Oops. "You already bought supplies for this dog?"

My hands shook and I shoved the wet, slippery things in my pockets.

"I got a few things."

His hairline reddened. It wouldn't be long before his temper exploded. Daddy was a bit of a tightwad when it came to money. Sure, we were strapped but to hear him talk, we were one happy meal away from living on the sidewalk.

"You used the emergency credit card, didn't you?" He didn't wait for me to respond. "How much, Bella?"

Well, the jig was up. If I didn't tell him, he'd go online and find out himself. Best to just rip the band-aid off.

"Two hundred and seventeen dollars and fifty-eight cents."

His eyes widened, as if he'd just seen a ghost. I smiled nervously.

The red in his hairline spread to his face. "You did what?"

"It was for a good cause. The dog was dying!"

"You are going to take back everything you purchased. Every scrap of it."

"Daddy, you're being ridiculous." I stood up straight, and squared my shoulders. This dog would have died had it not been for me. I did something good. I helped this dog and I would not be made to feel guilty because of it. My reasons were solid. I knew it. I just had to make Daddy see that.

"I'm keeping him."

"You most certainly are not. You can't save every dog, cat, and roach in the city. We don't have the room nor the money, and I definitely don't have the patience."

"When have you ever helped anything in your entire life? All you do is work and come home. When do you think about anything else?"

"I think about putting food on this table. I think about paying the rent. I think about your education. Your future."

"Mom would have let me."

His hand stilled, his fingers still on the keys of the phone.

I placed my hands behind my back and studied the blue and white tiles on the floor. The blue shower curtain. The soaked blue rug by the tub. Anything to keep from looking at my father's distraught face.

Invoking Mom was a sore spot, but this was an emergency. The dog was on the street. If I didn't save him, chances were that he would have died. I had to do something. Any decent person would have.

"You cannot mention your mother's name every time you want something," he said.

But I could already tell that the fight had gone out of him. His voice roughened, his back bent a bit. My father grieved my mother like the sun grieves the flowers in winter. Completely. Totally. Just the mention of her could send him spiraling in to a sink hole of depression for days. I tried not to speak her name often.

"I'm just stating a fact. Mom would have let me keep the dog."

"Well, your mother isn't here." He paused, and I noticed the small tremor that ran through his voice. He swallowed.

I hated myself for hurting Daddy, but I had to do something. I couldn't let the dog go back out on to the streets. I wouldn't.

I stepped forward, and put one wet hand on Daddy's bare arm. He wore work boots, black jeans and a black t-shirt. His standard work uniform.

"It's just one dog," I said quietly. "Not an army of rats or a giant rabbit."

"We can't have a dog." His voice was softer, yet it still held on to some of its fatherly power. "You're at school all day. I'm at work all day." He turned away from me and put his hands on his hips. "And look at what he's doing to the living room!"

The dog had found its way out of the tub, and was now trailing soap and water all over the house.

So much for being inconspicuous.

"Bella, I'm not doing this. I am not living in an animal house again. I'm not."

I stepped in front of him, narrowed my eyes in righteous accusation.

"You say it like it was a bad thing. Mom loved animals. She always did."

"I know that. But we cannot shelter this animal."

"Why not?"

"For one thing, we don't know anything about him."

"Yet."

"For another, he had no paperwork. He could have rabies or fleas or bubonic plague."

"We could take him to get shots."

"Bella-"

"Daddy, it's just one dog. Just one."

He walked out of the bathroom and put his hands on the breakfast bar. His gray-streaked brown hair fell forward. Daddy was only forty-one, but when he was in a good mood, he looked way younger, with his thick hair, bright brown eyes and smooth skin. He was normally clean shaven, though lately, he'd been sporting a beard.

His resolve was weakening. I saw it in the way his shoulders drooped.

I moved in for the kill.

"Think of what a pet would mean for me. It could teach me responsibility. I'd walk him every day and feed him and change his water bowl."

"I don't want a pet," Daddy said wearily.

"He'll be my pet. You won't have to do anything. I'll take care of him."

He sighed, and ran his hand through his thick hair, pushing it out of his eyes.

"The second I step on another pile of crap, he's gone."

My insides exploded in happiness and I clapped my hands, drawing a small grin from Daddy.

"What's his name?"

"I thought that we could name him together. After all, he is part of the family now."

Daddy and I looked up. The dog had lifted a leg and was peeing on the side of the couch.

"How about Whizz?" he asked.

"I was thinking more like Mojo."

Daddy frowned at me. Mojo had been the name of Mom's horse. A gift from Daddy on their wedding day. Mom loved that horse. I was hoping that this small, scared creature could be a gift, too.

"Mojo, huh?"

I nodded.

Daddy let out a huff and stood up straight. He walked in to the living room, picked Mojo up and put him back in the tub.

"You're on excretion duty," he called. "I want all of it cleaned up by the time I get out of here. And set up his food and water bowls and his crate."

I did a little dance and picked up the paper towels. Yes, Mojo's pee smelled like asparagus, but the point was that he was staying. Our little family just got a bit larger, and it was all because of one destructive, scared little dog.

I couldn't be happier.

3

I started out my day by taking Mojo on a long walk around Briar Park. Or rather, bribing him. The pup had apparently decided that, instead of walking, it would be more entertaining to sit on its little rump and blink up at me with uninterested eyes.

I did not find it entertaining in the least.

I tried gently tugging on the leash, but that only succeeded in moving Mojo an inch. He blinked again and looked away, a doggy eye roll.

He's just a scared puppy, I told myself. He'll come around.

Tamping down my frustration at my unmoving dog, I switched tactics. Dropping the leash, I crouched down to Mojo's level and smiled.

"What's wrong, Mojo?" I asked, my voice honey sweet and imploring. I scratched him behind the ears. "Don't you want to go for a walk? It's a beautiful day."

At this point, most dogs would wag their tails and jump up and down. Maybe let out an excited woof or two. But not Mojo. My little brown pup proceeded to turn his entire body around so that his back was facing me and sat on his butt again. To add insult to injury, he let out a deep whine, as if I were frustrating him.

Me. The girl who brought him in to my home, cleaned up his runny dog poop and now was trying to walk him. I was frustrating him.

If anyone should have been frustrated, it was me. I sat back on my haunches and snorted. Where did this dog get so much attitude?

Shaking my head, I checked the time on my phone. The train would come in a little over an hour, and I still had to get dressed. But I couldn't leave without walking Mojo. So, I did the only thing I could do. I picked Mojo up and carried him around the neighborhood, hoping against hope that he would let me know when he found a suitable tree.

It was a typical lower middle-class neighborhood, with long blocks of uneven sidewalks, tall trees and gated single-family houses. Every other yard seemed to have an angry pit bull or giant mixed breed. The miserable things jumped at the gate the second they saw Mojo. Any other dog would cower, but not Mojo. He barked and growled right back at them.

For a little dog, he did have spirit.

Mojo sat in my arms for three, chilly blocks. When he started to squirm, I put him down, let him do his business, picked up said business plus the dog and continued our walk. By the time we got back to my apartment, my arm was sweating and sore from holding him.

And what thanks did I get? What appreciation did I get from this dog whose poop I held? Who I just taxied around the neighborhood like he was some furry prince?

None. Nothing. Nada.

Mojo walked in to the apartment, had a bite to eat, went to sit on his doggy bed, turned toward the wall and fell asleep.

And just like that, my own dog, the one I'd had for less than twenty-four hours, dismissed me.

Great. Just what I needed. Someone else to ignore my entire existence.

I showered and walked back in to my bedroom to check my phone.

Jasmine had kindly texted me a picture of how she expected my hair to look, as well as suggestions for clothes. Cute tops, fitted jeans, little dresses.

Had she texted the wrong friend? I owned none of these items. I had some clothes, but it was all things an invisible would wear. Jeans that fit me in all the wrong places, tops that all seemed to have a hole in them, oversized sweaters.

I'd never really thought about my wardrobe before, but now, knowing that others would notice it, it looked drab and gross.

A vision of myself setting it all on fire rose sharply in my mind. I smiled. That would be nice. Then, Daddy would have to give me money for new clothes. Minus the two hundred bucks I spent on dog stuff, of course.

It wasn't just the clothes that were drab, though. My room was bare except for a picture of *The Avengers* by my bed. There was no color, no personal touch. Just my twin bed, a desk with my laptop on it, my book shelf—and the stack of books next to it—and an end table with a lamp. The walls were beige. The carpets were beige. Even my sheets were an ugly brown color.

What happened to us?

When Mom was alive, everything was colorful. The living room walls were painted in bright pastels, the floors accented with colorful rugs. We even had red pots and pans. Then she died and everything turned kind of gray. There was no more color. No more life. Just Daddy and me trying to make it through each day without falling apart. Eventually, we sold our house and moved in with Daddy's parents on their farm and after that, we came up here to this apartment that was smaller than my grandparents' bedroom. We'd been here over two years and yet, there were unpacked boxes in the living room. No pictures had been hung. There were no colorful rugs, except for the blue one in the bathroom. The apartment was unloved. Barren. It wasn't home. Just a place to sleep and eat and enjoy a laugh or two. Nothing felt like home since Mom died.

I felt the familiar lump in my throat and swallowed it down. I couldn't break down this morning. I had to find something decent to wear and add some order to my hair before I missed my train. Today was a big day for me. Yesterday, Jake had just glanced at me. Today, he would look just a little bit longer.

I put on the radio. The chorus to "Style" by *Taylor Swift* blasted out of the speakers.

I took it as a sign, and straightened my hair.

4

By the time I got to school, I was already exhausted.

I don't know how girls wake up and glamorize themselves every day. Doing hair, picking out clothes, painting nails, putting on makeup. The entire process was like running a 5K in your bedroom. But, it was worth it. Jasmine and Ariel gave me oohs and aahs of approval as we stood by my locker. I couldn't remember them ever doing that before. I stuffed my army green jacket inside my locker, along with a few books, and soaked in the attention.

"I don't think I've ever seen you with straight hair before," Jasmine said, gently touching my strands. "You look amazing!"

"Thanks!"

"You should bump in to Jake more often. You look stunning!"

I glowed under the light of her compliments. This new look took forever, and I might have given myself a few bald spots. Plus, the roots were already starting to puff back up from the humid air on the train. It was barely fifty degrees out and the subway felt like triple that temperature. Still, it was a nice surprise to see that my hair reached below my boobs. I'd worn it in braids or pony tails for so long that I'd forgotten how long it was.

I'd picked out a faded pair of jeans and, to my pleasant surprise, they actually fit me. I matched them with a sleeveless white camisole and a blue sheer pull over that fluttered when I walked. I reluctantly gave up my red sneakers for brown boots. Every piece I wore was from Goodwill, but I wouldn't tell Jasmine that.

"You totally look like that actress, *Zendaya*," Ariel said. "Doesn't she look like *Zendaya*?"

"Totally."

I smiled. Blushed. Compliments weren't usually thrown my way. I had no idea how to react to them, so I didn't say anything at all.

"Jake is going to trip over himself when he sees you," Jasmine said.

Ariel held up her phone.

"I'm going to record it, so I can tag you in it on your first anniversary."

My stomach clenched. An anniversary? Just the thought of it made me so nervous that I had to pee. I'd spoken to boys before, but never a boy like Jake. What would he say? What would he think of me?

I leaned against my locker.

"I'm nervous," I said, my face squished in a grimace.

Jasmine gave me a reassuring smile.

"You can be nervous, as long as you try. It's the trying that's the important part, right?"

She bumped Ariel, who nodded her head vigorously.

"Right."

The first period bell rang, signaling the start of our school day. In four hours, I would be asking Jake if he needed an English tutor. In four hours, I would speak my first words to him.

My whole body clenched in fear of the unknown.

"Dressing up to get good grades is against school policy."

I turned to see Cole standing next to my locker. Well, his locker. It was only a few feet away from mine.

He slammed the metal closed and leaned against it, holding a bright yellow textbook in one hand.

His hair was smoothed back beneath a black knit cap today, revealing a widow's peak that I hadn't noticed before. He wore a dark t-shirt and one of those black, thick leather bracelets. All the black made his blue eyes stand out. Blue eyes waiting to argue with me, it would seem.

"Did you want something, Cole, or are you just doling out your daily dose of verbal torture?"

He shrugged.

"Just commenting. I've never seen you look so much like a girl before."

My brows pinched. What was that supposed to mean? I know I may have underdressed but my look wasn't boyish, was it? Drab and unkempt maybe, but not boyish.

"And what was I before?" I demanded.

He shrugged again. "A Michelangelo, I think."

I drew in a sharp breath.

"Did you just call me a ninja turtle?"

A third shrug. A scratch to the back of his head.

"Drop dead, Cole. And in the meantime, don't talk to me ever again."

I whirled around and stormed away.

"So, you admit defeat then?" he called after me. "That's not like you."

"You don't know anything about me," I threw over my shoulder.

I did not look like a turtle. Cole could jump in a lake for all I cared.

"I know you're not a quitter!" His loud voice followed me down the hall as I rushed into first period Art.

I slid into my seat, seething. Cole Winsted was the king of all jerks. I imagined him sitting on a tack, leaned back in my chair and smiled.

5

By the time English rolled around, my hands were shaking.

I should have thought this through. I should have had a better plan. I should have run away screaming. But there were only five minutes left in class and if I backed out now, I would never have the strength to do it again. No. It had to happen, and it had to happen today.

My heart banged in my chest, and I took in deep breaths.

I could do this. I could talk to Jake.

The bell rang before I was ready.

No! I needed more time. I hadn't thought through every aspect. Felt every feeling. Evaluated every angle.

God. I had to pee!

Jake slid from his chair, scooped his book bag off the floor and started for the door. He wore a blue t-shirt that showed off his muscled arms and chest. His hair was smoothed back, his body relaxed.

He was gorgeous. Almost too gorgeous.

My breakfast rose in to my throat, and I forced it back down.

You can do this. Fortune favors the brave, remember?

I grabbed my book bag, forced my way through the students who bottlenecked at the door, and found Jake in the hallway, walking to his next class.

My throat closed and my feet felt heavy. I suddenly wanted to break out in tears.

You can do this. You can do this.

By some strength I didn't know I had, I forced air in to my lungs.

"Jake Winsted!"

He stopped.

Oh God. I'd said it too loud. I didn't mean to scream his entire name like that, but if I didn't, it would have gotten stuck in my throat.

He turned, his eyes searching the hallway for who had summoned him. His gaze swept from one side of the hallway to the other before he raised his eyebrow and turned back around.

He looked right through me. I was standing directly in front of him and he didn't even see me.

My breath left me. My heart fell in to my knees. My legs felt weak. I'd never felt such crushing disappointment in my entire life.

I was invisible, after all. It was perfectly clear now.

I, Bella French, was invisible.

My will seeped out of me by the second. I put my hand over my heart, feeling the hard beating in my fingertips. Somehow, I stumbled against the wall and leaned against it.

I am invisible. I'm-

"You're an odd duck, French."

Cole. Why was he always around? He was like a mosquito that I just wanted to slap.

His body, a mirror of his brother's, walked around me and leaned against the egg shell colored walls. I avoided his eyes, looking at his sneakers instead. I noticed that they were basketball sneakers. The kind that people wait in lines all weekend for. Not like my nondescript red ones.

God. I was such a loser!

"You parade around like you're some quasi-genius, then you yell people's names in the hallway like you're an escapee from a mental institution. It's quite confusing."

I closed my eyes and sunk further against the wall.

"Please go away," I groaned.

"Why? So you can go lusting after my brother like every other brain-dead Barbie in this school?"

My eyes opened and I glared so hard that my vision blurred.

"I'm not lusting after anybody."

"So, why were you calling him?"

I looked left then right, assuring myself that no one else was near.

"I was going to offer to tutor him."

One of Cole's black eyebrows raised.

"Like an academic tutor? Or a tutor in the ways of love? Because I think you are underestimating Jake in both departments."

"What does that mean?"

"He doesn't care about school and he's a manwhore. Either way, not on your level. Forget him."

Forget Jake? That was like asking me to forget my own name.

I ran my hand over my face. Why couldn't the floor open and swallow me? That would be so nice.

"Cole, I'm not in the mood for one of your self-righteous lectures."

He held up his hands.

"Not a lecture. Just a word of advice." He scooted closer to me. "Jake is not the greatest of guys. I think you should set your sights a little higher. Someone more academically inclined, maybe more virginal, like yourself."

"If you're talking about you, then I'd rather be eaten by a lion."

He scoffed.

"Hold on there, French. I didn't say God level. I'm just saying aim for above Neanderthal and somewhere in the realm of educated human."

I rolled my eyes and pushed off the wall. Why did I talk to Cole? Why did I give him the time of day? Why did Jake look through me? Why was I so invisible?

"Earth to French." Cole snapped a finger in front of my face, interrupting my swirling thoughts. "You're doing that thing where you check out again. Am I that boring?"

"Boorish is more like it."

He raised an eyebrow.

"If you spell boorish, I will give you a cookie. Not homemade, and it may have fallen on the floor, but I think that you'll enjoy it either way."

I rolled my eyes so hard that I thought they would pop out.

"Leave me alone, Cole."

I pushed past him and made my way down the hall.

"So, you don't want the cookie?"

I ignored him, my mood souring by the second.

One Winsted brother didn't even know that I was alive and the other got his jollies by mocking me.

What was going on with my life?

6

"He didn't even say 'hi?'" Ariel asked, pushing her red hair out of her eyes.

I was presently hunched face down on the table, my arms over my head for extra dramatic effect.

"He didn't even look at me," I said, my voice muffled by the table.

"Was the hallway crowded?" Jasmine asked.

"No."

"Maybe he's blind or something."

"Not helping."

"Aw, Bella baby." She rubbed my back like my mother used to. By some miracle, I didn't break down in to sobs. "He's an idiot if he didn't notice you. You look great today. Way better than you've looked in a long time."

"Not good enough, apparently."

"You know what?" Ariel pulled my hair, jerking my face upward. I squirmed. "Jake Winsted is a butt hole. If he doesn't notice you, then he doesn't deserve you."

"That's right!" Jasmine parroted.

"You deserve someone better than him."

"Who's better than him?" I asked. "Jake is the king of the school."

Ariel and Jasmine looked at each other, then at me. They tried to pretend like they didn't know what I was talking about, but they knew it. Everyone knew it. Jake was the top of the food chain here. No wonder he didn't notice me. I was a fool to think he would.

"You don't need Jake," Ariel said. "He's a jerk. There are much better boys out there."

"Like who?" I asked.

"How about his brother?" Jasmine offered.

I laughed. Though I wanted to fall apart, I literally laughed out loud.

The very thought of Cole and I being anything other than mortal enemies was laughable.

Jasmine frowned at me.

"What? He's cute and smart."

"And he remembers your name," Ariel offered.

"He's worse than his brother. All he does is make fun of me."

"Oh, Bella. That's what boys do."

I raised an eyebrow. As if Ariel knew about boys. None of us had had a boyfriend yet. All we knew was what we saw on TV and read in *Seventeen* magazine.

"It's okay," I said, though it was completely, 100 percent not okay. "I'll just get over it, I guess."

Newsflash. I was not going to get over it. There was no getting over a boy like Jake Winsted. He was the type of guy that women remembered and talked about in nursing homes. I could see me, Ariel and Jasmine now. Wrinkled, bent over, sitting around a table filled with our knitting baskets.

I'd say, "Remember that Jake Winsted. He sure was a catch. I wonder what happened to him."

I prayed again for God to let the earth open up and swallow me.

"I think I know something that will cheer you up."

Ariel pulled out a yellow sheet of paper from her book bag. In big, bold letters surrounded by stars were the words, St. Mary's Annual Talent Show.

It took me a minute to register what she was alluding to. When I figured it out, I pushed the paper back toward her.

"Absolutely not."

"Oh. Come on, Bella! You have an awesome voice."

"Yes. At home. With you two."

Well, more than with them. When Mom was alive, we sang and sang until we were hoarse. Then we sang some more. She had a beautiful voice. Smooth and powerful. She sang lead in our church choir. When she stepped on stage, everyone teared up. When she opened her mouth, they bawled. Me included. I could only wish that I was as good as her.

"At least think about it," Ariel said. "It will be good for you to get up there and show everyone how amazing you are."

"Yeah," Jasmine agreed.

I let out a groan. Mostly miserable, though a little bit of it was curious.

"I don't even know what I would sing."

"Sing that song that we like," Ariel said.

"Which one?" I sang many songs, including a song book of *Disney* classics, anything by *Adele*, and of course, *Beyonce*. I butchered *Beyonce*, but it was still fun to try and hit her high notes.

"Sussudio," Ariel said. "I love when you sing that one."

A sad smile pushed up my lips, before it disappeared again.

"My mom and I used to sing that one," I said softly. I could hear her now, belting it out as if she was filled with yearning and missing and wanting. How she could make such a happy song sound so sad and full, I would never know.

Ariel put her hand over mine. She understood what I was going through. Her mom had died too, leaving her dad and seven daughters behind.

"Promise me that you'll think about it," Ariel said. "Promise me."

I hesitated. Getting in front of the entire school and singing? What if they thought I was terrible? What if I was terrible?

"Your mom would want you to," Ariel added.

And there was the knife in my heart. My mom would want me to. I knew that. In a way, I wanted to, but my fear wrapped around me like a boa constrictor around its dinner. I took a shallow breath.

"I'll think about it," I said, plucking the paper from Ariel's fingers.

She smiled and clapped her hands.

"Whatever you decide, is fine with us," Jasmine said. "As long as I don't have to wear one of those *Madonna* bra cones."

I thought of skinny Jasmine in a cone bra and laughed. Ariel joined in. Pretty soon, we were in tears and, for the first time that day, I felt the weight of the world lift from my shoulders.

❧ 7 ☙

I walked in to my apartment, and immediately stepped in poop.

"Mojo!" I cried out, walking on my heels to the kitchen. If Daddy saw the land mines that this dog left, he'd freak. How could one dog miss ten pee pads? It was almost like he'd strategically placed the poop so that we'd step in it. It was in every doorway, every walk way, right in front of the couch. What was up with this dog and his weird pooping habits?

After spending fifteen minutes cleaning up the gross piles and washing the bottom of my shoes with bleach, I put Mojo on a leash and carried him outside. Yes, carried. I wasn't sure why I insisted on using leashes. The dog obviously preferred for someone else to do the walking.

"There's more poop in there?" I asked as the dog squatted next to a tree. "What have you been eating?"

As if fed up with my questions, Mojo moved to the other side of the tree, away from me.

"I can still see you," I said, crossing my arms over my chest. "You're going to have to learn how to hold it until we get home like every other dog."

Two older ladies in dresses passed by me. They stopped and looked at me with confusion.

"I'm talking to the dog," I said. "He pooped in the house."

They didn't respond. Only nodded, looked at me as if I was insane and kept walking.

I frowned and held up the leash. I didn't need these strangers' approval, but I didn't want them to think that there was a psycho in the neighborhood either.

"Look, I have a leash. The dogs on the other side of the tree. He doesn't like me to watch."

The women grabbed at each other's hand and sped up. I didn't know old ladies could move so fast.

I sighed miserably.

"Don't break a hip," I muttered.

Mojo kicked some dirt over his poop and reemerged.

"Now you show up. Where were you when the old ladies thought I was talking to myself, huh? You couldn't bark or howl or fart or something?"

The dog looked at its pile of poop, then looked at me. An unmistakable sign for, pick up the poop and carry me home.

I'd never seen a more stubborn or sassy dog in all my life. I doubted I ever would.

I did as I was silently told, picked up the poop and carried Mojo home. By the time I arrived, Daddy had already sat down on the couch.

"Is that you, honey?" he asked, cracking open his after-work beer. He allowed himself one per night. Never more. There had been a brief time after Mom died where he allowed himself way more than one. We didn't talk about that dark time. It was too painful.

"Yeah, Dad."

"Where's the dog?"

"Prince Mojo is right here."

I plopped the dog in Dad's lap and sat next to them on the couch.

Daddy scratched the dog behind the ears, picked him up under his armpits, and examined him.

"He is kind of cute, I guess," he said. Mojo squirmed and Daddy lowered him back on to his lap, scratching his ears some more. Warmth filled me. I would have thought that Daddy would still be angry after yesterday. I was glad he wasn't. He was in a strangely good mood, actually. Not that he was always miserable, but today he seemed to have a little extra pep.

"How many piles of poop did you pick up today?" he asked.

I gasped. "Too many."

Daddy nodded. "Well, if Mojo is going to stay, he's going to have to be trained. Crate trained and paper trained."

I groaned. Crate training was one thing, but paper training could take weeks. Especially since Daddy and I were gone for half the day.

"Can't we just get a rumba?" I asked. "It could clean up the poop while we're gone."

"You want to vacuum up dog crap? Are you crazy?"

"I prefer the term creative."

He laughed and shook his head. I laughed, too.

I missed my mom, but I'd always been a Daddy's girl. Some said that I had him wrapped around my little finger, but I thought it was the other way around. From his warm, rich brown eyes to his bear hugs and his rumbling laugh, I loved everything about my father. We fought, of course. I was a teenager, after all, and prone to emotional outbursts, but in the end, I felt safe when I was with him and, since Mom died, he was the last piece of her that I had to hold onto.

"Well, tonight we'll start on the paper training."

"And leash training?" I asked.

"Leash training?"

"He kind of doesn't want to walk on a leash."

Daddy looked incredulous. A dribble of beer fizzled in his beard.

"You're kidding me?"

I shook my head.

"I wish I was."

"Get me the leash. I'll have to see this for myself."

I stood, grabbed the leash from the coat hook by the door, and handed it to Daddy.

He gently attached it to the dog's collar and stood up.

"All right, Mojo," Daddy said, his southern drawl thicker now that he'd had a drink. "Let's go."

And, like the treasonous pup that he was, Mojo walked on that leash like a trained show dog. The two of them walked and jogged around the apartment like they'd been doing it their whole lives.

It was official. My dog was a traitor.

"I swear, he doesn't walk for me!" I cried.

Daddy waved the comment away. "Aw. That's all right. You'll just have to show Mojo who's boss. Here." He handed me the leash, and I jumped up to take it.

"All right. Once around the kitchen and back now."

I let out a breath and looked at the dog, who was now avoiding my eye.

"Okay, Mojo. Let's go."

I wasn't surprised to see the dog sit on his backside, lay down, and close his eyes.

Daddy laughed until he cried. I saw nothing funny about it. Nothing at all.

8

The next morning, I woke up before the sun in the worst way possible. My mind had decided to jolt me awake by making me dream about snakes. I hated snakes. I'd gotten bit by a snake once, back in North Carolina, while walking across a field to retrieve a forgotten bucket. It wasn't a poisonous snake or anything, and it scared me more than hurt me, but that one moment did cement my fears.

So, I laid in bed, the snake dream fading, and my worries and insecurities replacing it.

Yesterday had been a complete bust. Jake didn't even look at me, even though I was standing right in front of him.

Was I that easily ignored?

I planted my feet on the floor, clicked on my bedside lamp and walked over to the mirror that hung behind my door.

I examined myself closely. My wide, almond shaped eyes. The dark brown pupils. My ever-tanned skin, and full lips.

Was I ugly? Was I too plain? Was that why Jake didn't see me?

The girls who Jake normally dated didn't look like me at all. They were all pale and thin with big boobs and designer clothes. I'd inherited some of my mother's melanin, my body was more hour glass than slim, and my boobs were two cups short from being D's.

Still, I wasn't terrible looking. I definitely was not a ninja turtle like Cole said. Maybe all I needed was a little more makeup? A shorter skirt? Some waves to my hair? Maybe if I just tried a little bit harder, I could raise from the realms of invisibility in to the stratosphere of Jake's sexy arms.

I squared my shoulders and marched in to the bathroom. On the way, I turned on *Pandora* on my radio. I needed some get ready music.

Katie Perry's *Roar* came on and I smiled.

Okay, Jake. You didn't see me yesterday. Today, you won't be able to ignore me.

THIS IS A BAD IDEA.

I stood next to Jake's locker, yanking down the uncomfortably tight and whorishly short skirt.

I'd scoured my wardrobe and had come up with an outfit that resembled something like the popular girls wore. A black skirt that showed lots of thigh (because it was too small), a plain, pink blouse that I tied in the back to more perfectly show off my belly button (and because it was too big), and four-inch, black heels. The heels were a size too small and pinched my toes, but, hey, beauty is pain, right?

I'd slathered on some red lipstick and an obscene amount of mascara, and snuck out of my apartment before my dad saw me and freaked out. He still thought of me as the innocent six-year-old girl who clung to her favorite teddy bear and wore pigtails tied with yellow ribbons. If he saw the sixteen-year-old girl in her pinchy heels and exposed midriff, he might have a heart attack.

No. Daddy didn't know this other girl. Heck. I barely knew her. I wasn't the type to go seducing boys. I'd never even kissed a boy. Well, there was Ralph Mooch, but he didn't count. First of all, it was a dare. Plus, his retainer fell out five seconds in to it when he tried to shove his tongue down my throat. I nearly puked at the grossness of it. So, no. Officially, I have never been kissed. I was more the bookworm type. A quiet thinker who lived her life between the pages of *Poe*, *Shakespeare*, and *Whitman*.

Then came along Jake Winsted. He'd always been wrapped around Dana Rich's finger. And what boy wouldn't? Dana was the prettiest girl in the school. One of those model types with long blonde hair and big boobs who always looked like they'd just stepped out of a magazine. It was so annoying! Even when she was sweating in gym class, she looked perfect, like she was posing for an action shot in a magazine. How could life be so unfair!

Or was it? Dana was out of the picture now. She'd dumped poor Jake about a week ago, and had started dating Dustin Rodriguez. Dustin was a downgrade, if you asked me. But that didn't matter now, because her loss was my gain. After two years, Jake would finally notice me. And, if I played my cards right, he would ask me out and we'd have an epic romance to end all epic romances. Better than *The Notebook* or even *Twilight*. They would write books about our love for generations to come, and it would all start with me leaning against his locker, trying on my best come hither glance.

God. Please don't let me embarrass myself.

Jake rounded the corner, just as I knew he would. He was beautiful. A sexy angel with his short blond hair, blue eyes and fantastic physique.

He was a king without a queen. It was a vacancy that I desperately wanted to fill.

Jake threw back his head and laughed at something his friend, Eric Shipman, said. Even his laugh was beautiful. It was loud and deep. One of those laughs that desperately made you want to think of something funny so that you could make him laugh again.

I imagined how our meeting would go. He would see me standing by his locker and our eyes would meet in that intense way that lovers' eyes do. Then I'd tell him how handsome he was and casually repeat the football joke I'd read in *Cosmopolitan* magazine yesterday—you know, so that he could see that I was funny and into sports—and he'd laugh and ask me on a date and kiss me. We would be so happy together, all because I found the courage to lean against his locker.

He was closer now. In a few more seconds, he'd see me. My heartbeat picked up, and I slid my now wavy brown hair behind my ear and readjusted myself on his locker, attempting to casually cross my legs.

And then ... *snap!*

I heard the sound a second before my heel slid beneath me, sending my left hip hurling toward the floor.

Rip.

Cool air whooshed against the top of my thigh. The cheap fabric ripped in half clear up to the waistband as I landed with a dull thud on the hallway floor.

Oh. My. God.

Mortified and half naked, I tried to scramble upward, my hip bone throbbing where it had struck the ground.

Oomph.

The toe of someone's sneaker caught on my semi-upright back. Someone swore. Arms, legs, glasses and wood flew over me, then landed with a crash. I covered my face as splinters of wood flew in all directions.

God, if you're there, please kill me now.

"I'm so sorry. I didn't see you there."

The voice belonged to Phineas Stone. We were in chemistry together. He had the third highest GPA in the school.

I yanked on my skirt, attempting to pull the pieces back together. My plan was ruined. Jake couldn't see me now. Not with a broken shoe, a ripped skirt, and a sneaker print on my back. I had to get out of this hallway. I had to get to my gym locker. Even the threat of wearing gym clothes all day was better than being exposed like this!

A small crowd gathered around Phineas and me. Not to help me up, or offer me their jacket to cover up my naked thigh, or even to pick up Phineas's ruined shop project. They simply pointed and laughed.

High school kids were douche bags.

"Are you all right?" Phineas asked, his shaky hand sliding his glasses back in place.

"I'm fine!" I cried back. I didn't mean to yell at him, but my manners had flown the coop along with the stitches to my skirt. I scrambled to my feet, fully intending on ditching my shoes and sprinting barefoot to my gym locker when the last voice that I wanted to hear came up behind me.

"Hey, Jake!"

Cole stood behind me. Jake turned around from where he stood by his locker. Eric's attention turned to me. My ruined skirt. My out of place hair. My eyes full of tears.

I had never been so embarrassed in my life!

"Have you met Bella?"

My heart stopped.

Jake's eyes fell from his brother's and found mine.

I couldn't breathe.

He looked me up and down, his gaze staying on my barely covered thigh for a few seconds too long. One side of his mouth ticked up in a half smile, making my heart re-animate and start to pound.

"What's up?" he asked.

He saw me. He spoke to me.

My knees felt weak, and, gathering all my will and pride, I stood upright.

"Hi." My voice was so soft and weak that I wasn't sure that he heard me. He gave no indication that he did.

"Bella wants to know if you need an English tutor."

Note to self: Kill Cole. Slowly. Painfully.

My cheeks felt like they were on fire.

Jake's brows furrowed and he laughed a little, though nothing seemed funny.

"No thanks. If I need help, I'll just cheat off my brother." His eyes fell again to my exposed legs.

"Nice skirt."

Eric tapped him on the chest and Jake was gone, walking with Eric down the hall, leaving me alone with his brother.

My plans. My dreams. They all stuttered to a stop. Jake did not want me. He would never want me. I was a nobody.

A nobody with a ripped skirt and a broken shoe.

My hand slid down my face, currently wet, red, and burning.

Slowly, I kicked off my intact heel and turned to Cole, my eyes hard, my spirits low, my eyes filling with embarrassed, angry tears.

"Why would you do that?" I whispered. Cole caught sight of my tears and his smug face softened. "Why would you embarrass me in front of him?"

"I think the falling and ripped clothes did that for you."

"Why are you so mean?"

The edges of his mouth dropped into a frown.

"I'm not mean."

"Then why would you ruin my life like that?"

"Because it's time to get Jake out of your system," he snapped. The fury and anger in his words surprised me, and I stiffened. "You have been pining after him since forever, and I'm sick of it. You've spoken to him, you had your shot, and now you have your answer. Jake doesn't want you."

Each word was like a dagger to my heart. A deep cut dripping with blood, gore and misery.

I shook my head and angrily wiped the tears away.

"I never want to speak to you again, Cole," I growled. "Ever."

He shrugged. "Fine."

I glared at Cole, the boy I hated most in the world, and turned and picked up my shoes. They were gone. Phineas, too. The only evidence that we'd been here at all were a few pieces of broken wood.

"Looking for this?"

My breath left my body. One, long exhausted breath.

I turned back to Cole and, sure enough, he was holding my shoes. His expression was strange. Smug and victorious ... and sad. God. I hated him.

"Why do you care?" I asked. "You're mean to me. We're not friends. Why do you care if I like Jake or not?"

"Because..." His voice trailed off into oblivion. He crossed his arms and looked away from me.

I decided that I didn't care. Cole could jump off a bridge and I wouldn't care. I was completely and utterly done with Cole Winsted. Forever!

I snatched my shoes out of his hand, turned and fled to the gym lockers, leaving a trail of tears behind me.

9

I didn't go back to class.

After changing into my gym clothes, I went to the nurse and told her that I had really bad cramps. After a quick phone call to my dad, I left.

Ariel and Jasmine texted me during lunch, but I didn't feel like telling them about what happened. It was too painful. Too disappointing. Too hard. It was as if someone had sucked all the joy right out of me. What little joy there was, anyway.

The period excuse worked at home as well as it did in school. Dad let me sit on the couch and binge watch *Netflix* for the entire weekend. And so, for two days, I ate pizza, ice cream, and cookies until I wanted to puke. I wallowed in potato chips, self-pity, and regret. I ignored my friends' phone calls, and catnapped every two hours.

I must've looked terrible by Sunday night because Mojo took a break from cuddling up with my dad to actually come over and nuzzle me. It took me hitting rock bottom for my own dog to pay me any attention. I didn't know that I could feel worse, but I did.

I gave him exactly two pats on the head, you know, so I wouldn't look so eager for his attention, and fell back on to the couch. Daddy brought me another bag of my favorite potato chips—baked cheddar cheese and sour cream—and I shoved a handful in my mouth, adding to the pile of crumbs that had accumulated beneath my chin.

"You gonna be all right there, sweetie?" Daddy asked.

He walked in to my view, and placed a cup of hot lemon tea and some *Midol* in front of me. He was one of those fathers who thought periods were contagious, so he kept his distance during those times of the month. All weekend, he'd been placing food in front of me and slowly backing away.

I kind of liked it.

"I'll be-"

I looked up at my father. He was clean shaven and his hair was slicked back. He wore a dark shirt and slacks. No tie. And he smelled like cologne.

Something was up.

"Are you going out?" I asked, not bothering to hide my curiosity.

He nodded slowly, studying the *Midol* bottle like it held the key to eternal youth.

"Yeah. Just to dinner with a few friends. I'll be back in a few hours."

Friends? Daddy had friends? Since we moved to New York, I hadn't seen him hang out with anyone. Not a text or a visit or anything. When did he get friends?

"Um ... okay."

"You need anything before I go?" he asked.

I studied my father, searching for meaning in his eyes that refused to meet mine. In the way his jacket was casually slung across his arm. In the way he shifted his weight on his feet. Something was definitely wrong here.

"Yeah. I'll be fine," I replied slowly. "Are you okay?"

The question seemed to take him by surprise. I could tell by the way he raised his eyebrows. The way he examined me to see what meaning the question held.

"I'm fine."

He wasn't fine. His tone was a little too loud. Too stiff.

What was going on?

He bent and kissed me on the head.

"See you in a bit, sweetheart."

Two seconds later, the door slammed shut. As if he had sprinted out of it.

What was going on? Why did Daddy look so nervous? And, even more importantly, why was he wearing cologne?

10

It was Monday and our English class was bubbling with excitement. Today was the day that we were to be assigned our partners. It was my last hope to have any sort of chance with Jake.

After Friday's disaster, I made an oath. If Jake and I weren't partnered up for this project, then I would accept that it wasn't meant to be. That Jake and I would never become Jake and me. Maybe Cole was right. Maybe it was time to let Jake go and focus on someone else. Someone who actually knew my name. Someone who knew I existed. Someone who saw me.

Of course, I wouldn't go down without a fight.

All morning, I'd been praying. I wasn't a praying person, at least not since Mom died, but this was important. Jake was my everything. Yes, we hadn't actually spoken, and he didn't really know that I was alive, but that didn't dull his amazingness or how perfect we would be together. And so, I prayed to God to give me Jake, a boy that I couldn't let go of, even though I never had him in the first place.

To my surprise and delight, God gave me a sign.

Dad's blueberry pancakes. Dad never made pancakes on a weekday morning. He usually grabbed a cup of coffee and an apple, and ran out the door to his job at *Accelerate Auto Body and Car Repair*.

That was it. That was my sign of magical things to come.

The miracles continued when I found a two-dollar bill on the way to school. Two. As in Jake and me.

I carefully folded the bill and put it in my wallet. It would be something that I would show mine and Jake's children. We'd frame it and put it over the mantel of our mansion. When guests would come over, I would point to it and say, "*When I was sixteen, I asked God for a sign that Jake and I would be together. He gave me this two-dollar bill, and ten years later, here we are.*"

They would ooh and ahh, and I'd graciously accept their applause and admiration.

I sighed.

By the end of today, there would be a Jake and I. I could feel it.

Each time Ms. Mitchell called out a set of names, I held my breath, patiently waiting for her to say mine. My sweaty hands trembled and I nervously wiped them on my jeans, leaving twin palm prints on the dark material. My heart slammed against my ribs, its rhythm somewhere between a heavy metal drum solo and *Flight of the Bumblebee*.

Please, I prayed. Please, oh please, oh please let her pair us together.

"Our next team will be..." Ms. Mitchell paused for dramatic effect. Her sneaky smile was made more humorous by the smudge of red lipstick that streaked her teeth. There was a lot of red on Ms. Mitchell today. The bold color stained her lips, colored her glasses, drenched the flower in her hair and even managed to slip between her thick black strands of hair. Weird.

"...Sorcha Blitz and Ivan Romanov."

To my right, in the center of the front row, Sorcha and Ivan grinned and exchanged glances. I'd seen them at lunch with the semi-popular kids eating little black containers of sushi with chopsticks. They were posers. Cheap imitations. Their clothes were department store discount, their hair home colored, and their sushi was bought at a supermarket. They wanted people to believe that they were part of the elite, but I knew the truth. They were Fakers.

"Ray Dellmen and Susan Carrodine."

Another set of almost cool kids, desperate to be accepted into the popular circle.

Not that I was part of any social circle recognized at this school. Ariel, Jasmine and I were closer to the bottom rung of the popularity ladder. On Friday nights, instead of going to parties, we usually streamed bad horror movies on *Netflix*, ate overly buttered, non-GMO popcorn, and discussed our favorite books. We didn't try to fit in or be 'cool'. In fact, nothing we did could be construed as cool behavior. We preferred it that way.

But, no matter what we said or how hard we tried to deny it, all invisibles secretly yearned to be seen. To be heard. To label ourselves with that dirty, elusive, coveted title of popular. Sometimes, I thought about it. Dreamed about it. Wished for it. But, I didn't tell anyone else that. If my friends knew, they'd call me a Faker and I wasn't. A bit of a dreamer maybe, but I wasn't fake. Besides, being popular would ruin my carefully crafted image of a socially conscious outcast full of teenage angst, and god knew that was all I had going for me right now.

Ms. Mitchell called out the next set of names.

"Cassie Washington and Noah Bronner."

If I didn't know better, I'd say that our teacher was playing some weird version of match maker. This made me even more confident that I would be teamed with Jake.

"Lisa Matthews and Chance Gionatti."

Great. The school sweethearts were grouped together. I called Lisa and Chance The Amazing Lip Locking Duo. They made out everywhere. In the hallway, against lockers, pretty much any solid surface that they could find. It was pretty inappropriate.

I craned my neck, looking past the love-sick Chance and Lisa's googily eyes, and glanced at Jake. He was too busy texting to notice me, but he would.

I hoped.

Butterflies rioted in my belly, and I placed my hand over my stomach to quiet them. It didn't work. In fact, it seemed to irritate them even more and their frail wings flapped even faster.

Ms. Mitchell called out another set of names.

"Poppy Pritchett and Joshua Summers."

My hands shook violently and I placed one under each thigh. I sucked in a deep breath, the scent of cool air and rich perfume filling my lungs. My fellow students didn't walk out of the house unless they smelled like money. Me? I smelled more like soap and *Bath and Body Works* Tropical Flower body spray. Not nearly as expensive as their French perfumes, but I'd never received a complaint about it.

"Nadira Empress and Kiln Slave."

Only four names left. It was happening. It was finally happening!

"Bella French and..." She gave a dramatic pause and my anticipation ramped up so much that I thought I'd die. "Cole Winsted."

What? No!

My eyes widened, my heart dropped in to my sneakers and my back stiffened.

It couldn't be right. I must've misheard her. She couldn't have said my name next to Cole's. It was impossible. I wanted Jake. Not his brother who I hated more than anything. Even snakes!

Ms. Mitchell looked up from her white sheet of paper and smiled at me, as if she'd done something wonderful. But, this was the furthest thing from wonderful. This was a nightmare.

I blinked rapidly and laid my palms flat on my desk. My breathing turned ragged. I slowly turned my head. In the far corner of the room, Cole was bent over his English book. When he heard his name, he looked up. His blue eyes locked on to mine and he winked at me. Winked! I suppressed the urge to bare my teeth and growl. I hated boys who winked. It was rude and pretentious. Come to think of it, winking was perfect for a boy like Cole.

I'd gotten my Winsted brother, all right. The brother that I didn't want! This wasn't fair. I was supposed to be partnered with Jake so that he could see how amazing I was; not with his douche of a brother!

Ms. Mitchell moved on, as if she hadn't just shattered my hopes and dreams. As if she didn't ruin my future.

"Jake Winsted and Dana Rich."

Her words felt like a blow to the gut and I squeezed my eyes together.

Perfect. Not only had Ms. Mitchell saddled me with the wrong brother, but she'd put Jake with his ex-girlfriend.

I looked back at Jake, watching everything that I wanted slip away. He looked uncomfortable, like someone just asked him to stand in front of the entire school in his boxers. And Dana looked downright angry.

My head fell forward and I let out a breath. It was over. My signs had all been lies. I would never be with Jake. Ever. I'd never felt so disappointed in my life. So crushed. I breathed in slowly and let the air out even slower, fighting back the tears that threatened. It was like thinking that I'd won the lottery, then realizing that I was off by one number. My chest constricted. My heart tried to fold in on itself so that it wouldn't feel the pain. I put my hand on my stomach. The butterflies were quiet now. Or maybe they were dead? Maybe that was why I was so nauseous?

It was bad that I wasn't paired with Jake, but having him paired with Dana was even worse. She was beautiful with lots of money. Plus, they had been boyfriend and girlfriend for, like, ever. What if they got back together?

I had to give it one more try. Maybe this was just God throwing me a curveball. Maybe if I talked to Ms. Mitchell after class, she could re-assign the teams?

I had to try.

As Ms. Mitchell neatly folded her white sheet of loose leaf paper into fours and turned back to the blackboard, I rehearsed what I was going to say. When the bell rung, signaling the end of class, I jumped out of my seat and ran to her. Every word that I'd practiced in the last ten minutes was suddenly forgotten, and I resorted to the only thing that made any sense.

Begging.

"Ms. Mitchell, I wanted to be partnered with Jake. Not Cole!"

Red rose in my teacher's cheeks. She adjusted her glasses and cleared her throat, her eyes glancing to the right.

I followed her gaze.

Cole had stopped to look at us.

No. Not us. Me.

Challenge and amusement swirled in his blue eyes. He was so cocky. I hated cocky.

"Relax, French. Maybe with my name on the project, you'll get a passing grade for once."

"I am on track to be valedictorian," I argued, wanting to knock that smug look off his face.

He sucked in a breath through his teeth.

"Oh. I think you have it wrong again. You meant to say salutatorian. Honest mistake, given your grade point average."

My body trembled with rage. God. He was infuriating!

"I'll leave you two to talk about the project." His eyes left mine and went to Ms. Mitchell. "Don't worry. I'll be proofreading her work to make sure it's up to par."

I sputtered. I never sputtered, but my mind couldn't come up with the right words to tell him how angry he made me.

By the time he passed through the classroom door and stepped out of sight, I could only think of swear words, and I couldn't say them in front of Ms. Mitchell.

I turned back to her, but she had already moved back around her desk, sat down, and shuffled a stack of papers as if she were about to deal a hand of poker. After a moment, her eyes looked at me with confusion.

"Did I misread the situation?" she asked, pushing her glasses up her nose and leaning forward.

"Big time. How could you do this to me?"

"I thought you wanted to partner with him. Every time I mentioned the project, you looked back at him."

"I was looking at Jake!"

Ms. Mitchell's brown eyes went from confusion, to understanding, to remorseful.

"Oh, Bella. I'm so sorry. I wish there was something that I could do."

I jumped on the opportunity.

"There is." I leaned on her desk, and gave her a watery frown. These weren't real tears, but I wasn't beneath sinking to theatrics to secure my future as Mrs. Jake Winsted. "You can reassign the groups."

Ms. Mitchell put a pale hand on my shoulder.

"I'm sorry, dear, but no."

"But, Ms. Mitchell-"

"Bella, I know it's not what you wanted but maybe this is a good thing. Maybe it's fate."

"Jake is my fate. Not Cole!" I cried. My faux tears threatened to turn real as I saw my entire future collapsing. No wedding on my grandparents' farm, no vacations to Mexico, no twin baby girls. No dog named Asland. It was all turning to dust.

I wanted to scream but through pure will and pride, held myself together.

Ms. Mitchell laughed soundlessly and shook her head.

"Oh, Bella. It's not that bad. Give it a chance. You might find that you and Cole have a lot in common."

"Like we both want to kill each other?"

"Like you are both human beings."

"Ms. Mitchell, I'm sorry, but I can't do this. I can't be partnered with that chauvinistic jerk!"

Her face turned serious.

"Then you'll fail the project, which, by the way, is two thirds of your grade this semester."

This wasn't my reading buddy now. This was my teacher. An authority figure. The woman who held my grades in her hands. I'd always liked Ms. Mitchell, but today, she'd made herself public enemy number two. Right behind Cole.

I rolled my eyes so hard that they felt like they would pop out. Anger blurred my vision and sent shooting pains through my head.

"Book club is over," I growled. I snatched my book bag off the floor and stomped out the classroom, disappointed tears blurring my vision. I'd seen the signs. I'd hoped for so much. How could this day have gone so wrong?

II

I found Cole at his locker, sorting through a stack of bulky textbooks. If I looked at him quickly enough, he could pass for Jake. Granted, Jake had blond hair while Cole's hair was longer and ink colored. Also, Jake made my heart go pitter patter while Cole made me want to pick up a sharp object and stick it in his eye. Otherwise, they could be twins.

Cole looked at me, a smile pulling at his lips.

I scowled back.

"Ready to come and make nice?" he asked, crossing his arms.

I closed my eyes and let out a deep breath.

Stay calm, I told myself. Just stay calm and don't let him see how much you hate him.

"I have come over here to work out when we are going to work on our English project."

"Well, that depends. You know I have a very busy schedule with schoolwork and football and home stuff. I'm not sure that I can squeeze in tutoring you in English, too."

"You're not tutoring me in English!" I cried.

My hands balled into fists. What was crazy was, the madder I got, the bigger his smile grew. He was enjoying this.

Deep breaths, I told myself. Deep breaths.

"You should relax there, French. That vein in your head looks like it's ready to pop."

I wanted to pop him right in his stupid face.

"I will meet you at your house after school."

"No can do."

"What do you mean no can do?"

"Today's no good. I got stuff going on. Plus, we can't meet at my house."

"Why not?"

He paused just long enough for me to know that he was lying.

"It's being renovated."

The bell was about to ring and I had no time to play Cole's mind games.

"Fine. We will meet at my apartment tomorrow after school to go over the project. If we focus, we can have it finished in no time."

"Are you sure? I mean, you have read *Shakespeare*, right?"

If looks could kill, Cole would be six feet under.

"Of course, I've read *Shakespeare*."

"Like, have you read it or just watched the movie? Because if you've just seen the movie, I can-"

"Shove it, Cole!" I said it louder than I wanted to, but he was like a fly buzzing in my ear. Annoying. My thoughts turned murderous.

"Okay, but I'll need dinner first."

My mind processed what he was saying, and I couldn't help but laugh. If Cole thought he would ever get near me in that way, then he was crazy!

I rolled my eyes at him and turned away, walking to my next class.

"Hey, French," he called.

What could he possibly want now?

I turned around and he winked at me, his smile wide and annoying.

I gave him back a rude gesture before I whipped around and marched to French class.

This was going to be a long two weeks.

12

I thought today was a day of miracles, but as it turned out, miracles were overrated. After French class, my teacher, Mr. Coggs, informed me that he was personally signing me up for tutoring, effective today. My tutor would meet me in seventh period study hall.

I took the yellow slip from his hand and thanked him, while simultaneously hoping that his hair piece got snatched off his head by a near-sighted eagle. I should have felt bad about the evil thought but I was having a rough day. I had an annoying English partner, I was failing French, and I'd come to the depressing realization that Jake would never notice me, no matter how hard I tried.

On a scale of one to ten, this day was a negative eleven.

The only bright spot in my day was fifth period lunch.

Well, it was until I explained my craptastic day to Ariel and Jasmine, who immediately began hugging me as if I just told them that I only had twenty-four hours left to live.

"Don't give up, sweetie," Ariel said. "There's always tomorrow."

"No," I said quietly. "I'm done."

"Maybe if you wore something a little more grown up-" Jasmine began.

I raised a hand to quiet her.

"If you're thinking that I'm going to throw myself at him again, you're both crazy." I chomped on my salad to emphasize how crazy they were for considering it. I may have been love sick, but I still had my pride. I was done talking about Jake, but apparently, my friends weren't.

"Well, here's some news that will cheer you up. I heard this morning that Dana's declared that none of her friends can date any of Jake's friends."

"How is that supposed to cheer me up?"

"Well, now no one else can date Jake, either. That should help you feel a little bit better."

Oddly, it kind of did.

"Where did you hear that?" Ariel asked. "I didn't hear about that."

"I overheard Dana, Stephanie, Mel and Ursula talking about it in the bathroom during third period."

"Dana dictates who they can date now?" Ariel asked. "Those four sound more like a cult every day. By next week, they'll be drinking cyanide-flavored fruit punch and wearing white robes with slide-on shoes."

"It might as well be a cult the way they follow Dana around like she's Gandhi reborn," Jasmine said.

I looked over my shoulder at Jake just in time to see him make the cutest, goofiest face at his friends. Not only were he and Dana over, but she'd personally made sure that no other popular girl went near him. Why was God tormenting me?

Jasmine took another bite of her cheese sandwich, chewed and swallowed.

"The Fall Formal is coming up, and now none of the popular guys can ask any of the popular girls. Someone is going to crack." Jasmine shook her head. "God help them."

Their words swirled around in my brain, dragging my mood even further down in to a depressing pit.

"Are you all right, Bella?" Jasmine asked, raising an eyebrow in my direction. "You look paler than usual."

"I'm just..." I stuttered, trying to make my mind work again. "I'm fine."

Ariel nudged me with a knowing smile. "Still thinking of Jake?"

"No," I lied, chewing on my thumb nail. "There's nothing else that I can do. At least not without ambrosia, nectar and a flock of doves."

Jasmine's brows furrowed. "What?"

I shook my head. "In ancient Greek mythology, ambrosia and nectar transferred immortality to mortals. It made them gods."

"But Jake isn't a god. He's just a boy. Granted, a hot, rich, insanely popular boy, but a boy nonetheless." She placed a hand over mine. "Why don't you go talk to him?"

My cheeks heated. She made it sound so simple but I couldn't just go talk to him. I didn't have the right words. Or the confidence. Or the wardrobe. Or any of the hundreds of things that Jake was, no doubt, looking for.

I chewed more fiercely on my nail and stole another look at Jake holding court at the popular table. The sole girl in his group was his sister, Regina. She was beautiful, with her long black hair, big blue eyes, a long, hour glass figure and perfect fashion sense. She was also notorious for disliking all of Jake's girlfriends and actively showing them how much she hated them with her lies and her fists.

Cole was sitting near the other end of the table. He was laughing so hard that I could see the food in this mouth. Gross.

He caught me looking and opened his mouth even wider, showing me the chewed-up chicken.

Double gross.

I glared at him.

He winked at me.

I turned back around, tamping down my fury.

"Maybe we should head to The Center tonight," Ariel said. She took a bite of her cheese sandwich and wiped a glob of mustard from the corner of her mouth. "We can let off a little steam and scope out the hotties."

"I can't," Jasmine said. She stabbed her salad with a white spork. "Gymnastics practice then volunteering at the animal shelter."

"An animal shelter?" I asked. "Since when did you become *Jane Goodall*? You barely like your cat."

Jasmine shrugged. "For the record, I love Raja. But my dad is freaking out about how my nearly nonexistent extracurricular activities will look on my college resume. He wants me to kick it up a little."

"College," Ariel groaned. She pitched her head forward, causing a mountain of red hair to fall forward like a crimson avalanche. "Don't remind me about college."

They had just begun to converse about how Ariel's father refused to let her go to an out of state school when cat calls erupted from the opposite corner of the lunch room. We turned toward the sound.

"Evil Queen alert," Jasmine announced. She was always the first one to spot them. Like a sixth sense or something.

Dana Rich, daughter of the famous actor, Martin Rich, and Jake's ex-girlfriend.

Melanie 'Mel' Pleasant, heir to Zippy gasoline fortune and the queen of bad choices. Based on her visits to student guidance, I knew her life's story well.

Stephanie Pleasant, Melanie's cousin and granddaughter of the guy who created MTV.

Ursula Meyers, heir to the Meyer's Shrimp and Stuff fortune, and cousin by marriage to Ariel.

We called them the Evil Queens. Everyone else called them the four most popular girls in school, led by Dana. Their Alpha. Their Leader. Their Goddess. If Dana jumped off a mountain, I was sure that Mel, Stephanie and Ursula would follow her like a herd of lemmings.

The four girls in their too short skirts and trendy tops were the furthest thing from invisible in this school. I swore spotlights followed them wherever they went. They walked through the lunch room with confident strides and sat at a table next to Jake's. Just as Jasmine had said, there were now two popular tables. One for the boys and one for the girls. The boys, mostly jocks and Regina, sat with Jake. The girls, mostly cheerleaders, student council members and generally beautiful people, sat with Dana.

"Dana said that even fraternizing with Jake's friends was punishable with banishment from the girls table," Jasmine whispered. "She's already kicked out Julissa Torrington for not breaking up with Chad Jackson."

"But they've been together for, like, ever," Ariel said.

"We're talking about Dana here. The Mistress of all evil."

I looked over at Julissa and Chad. Once part of the royal court, they were now sitting one table over from us, with just each other to keep them company.

They were the sacrificial lambs used to make a powerful point. That Dana was no one to trifle with. She was mean, domineering and sometimes downright cruel. And yet, she fascinated me. I took in everything about her. Her walk. The way she spoke. Her clothes. Her perfect hair. I'd never tell my friends, but I secretly wondered what it was like to be her. To have a perfect life, with perfect looks and a perfect boyfriend. To be seen. To be listened to. To have Jake. If I was her, I would never have let Jake go, no matter what.

I turned back to the boys table, watching as Jake laughed hysterically at something that Eric said.

Ariel sighed next to me. Her obsession with Eric Shipman had started in sixth grade and five years later, it was still going strong.

"You should talk to him," I whispered.

She shrugged. "With you girls, I am a mountain of confidence. Around Eric, not so much."

"I'm sure he'd love you," I replied.

"That's the problem. I know he would." She worried her lower lip before continuing. "I see him online every night. We play the same online RPG game, Ogre Wars. Our characters talk to each other all the time. We like the same music and tv shows. We both like video games and swimming. We have so much in common online, but out here in the real world, I can't even get close to him." Her shoulders slouched, and she pushed her sandwich away.

"You should tell him who you are in the game," I said. "Maybe he'll be into it."

She shook her head. "What if he doesn't like me out here in reality? What if he thinks that I'm ugly or weird or I smell funny? What if his friends don't accept me?"

"You'll never know until you try," Jasmine said.

Ariel smiled sadly. "Maybe one day." She let out a breath and cheered a bit. "I don't see you walking up to boys and making conversation," she said, playfully nudging Jasmine's arm.

"That's because I'm not in to high school boys. Besides, I don't have the time. Between school, family and you two, I'm swamped."

I chuckled. In the years that I'd known her, Jasmine had never publicly admitted to liking a boy at this school.

"So," Ariel turned to me, "Jasmine's out for The Center. I guess it's just me and you?" Ariel asked.

"Yup. Maybe for the last time."

"Why? Are you grounded or something?" Jasmine asked, leaning across the table to hear me better in the loud lunch room.

"Not yet. But Mr. Coggs told me that I'm failing French."

"What do you mean he told you?" Jasmine asked. She relaxed, and put her butt back on the bench. "You already knew you were failing French."

"Yes, but I was hoping that he didn't."

She laughed, flipped her jet-black hair behind her, put down her sandwich and stabbed at her salad.

"Anyway, he signed me up for French tutoring during study hall, starting today. If I don't ace my next test, he'll call my dad, which will mean that I'll be on serious lock down until my grades come back up."

"How do you fail French class?" Ariel asked. "You're French!"

"For the millionth time, I am not French. Just because my last name is French, doesn't mean that I am French."

Jasmine laughed at Ariel and received a scowl in return.

The lunch bell rang, ending our lunch period and sending us to American History with Mrs. Onofrio. After passing notes and barely paying attention for forty-five minutes, I waved goodbye to Jasmine and Ariel and walked in to seventh period study hall, my mind on anything but studying.

In less than two years, I'd be graduating. What legacy would I leave behind? Would it be just footprints in the sand or would they talk about me for years to come? Could I make a significant impact on this school? God knew I wished for it. The thought of being insignificant made me want to run headfirst in to traffic. I feared that my life was just words written in faded pencil on a discarded shred of paper. Something to glance at and never think of again. I feared that I was nothing here. The messed-up part was, I tried my best to be content with my lot in life. But secretly, deep down in my heart, I wanted to sit at the cool table. I wanted to be popular. I wanted to be Dana Rich.

The thought shamed me. Plus, if my friends knew what I was thinking, they would probably never talk to me again and I couldn't have that. I loved Jasmine and Ariel. They were the first ones to talk to me when I moved to New York from North Carolina the beginning of Freshman year. They brought me into their fold without question or thought. They didn't care that I didn't have as much money as them, or that my family wasn't whole, or that my two French braids inspired teases and taunting. They embraced me for who I was. All of me. The three of us were a team. Three pieces of one heart. If anyone messed with one of us, they messed with all of us. It would be treasonous for me to turn my back on them and to pursue a life of popularity that, frankly, I probably wasn't built for anyway.

"Were you thinking about me?"

A deep voice startled me, jerking me from my thoughts. My head whipped around and up, and I gasped. Cole stood over me, book bag tight to his shoulder, blue eyes looking down at me in the smiling sort of way.

I groaned. Literally.

My tutor was Cole Winsted. What did God have against me? What did I ever do to deserve such punishment?

"You know," he slid into the seat next to me, dropping his bookbag on the floor. "When Mr. Cogg told me that I would be tutoring one of his students in French, I never thought it would be you. Especially after that speech earlier. How exactly do you plan on beating me out for valedictorian when you have a sixty-seven average in French?"

I bit the inside of my cheek and stood.

"I'd rather die than have you tutor me in anything," I growled, picking up my bookbag and starting toward the door.

"Suit yourself. Enjoy permanent lockdown when your father finds out about your swiftly falling GPA."

I stopped halfway to the door.

He had me.

I hated him.

I turned around to face him.

"What do you want, Cole?" I asked.

He put his hand over his heart like the question physically pained him.

"Me? I just want to see a fellow student succeed."

This was torture! It was like the entire teacher body had conspired against me. First Ms. Mitchell, now Mr. Cogg.

"Come on, French. Sit down and we'll have you talking like Joan of Arc in no time." He squinted. "Oh, sorry. Joan of Arc was French. I meant that we'd have you speaking French in-"

"I know who Joan of Arc was!" I snapped, stomping back to the table and throwing my bag down.

I glared at Cole, infusing all my hatred toward him in one, single look.

"Ground rules," I said. "No making fun of me while you tutor me. That means no jokes, no weird faces, no nothing."

"Are you sure? Girls like my weird faces."

"I don't like them. At all."

"Suit yourself."

I pulled out my notebook and my French textbook and opened them.

"Let's just get this over with."

He nodded. "Sure. Where should we start? Oh. I have the perfect thing. French fries," he paused dramatically, "are not French."

I closed my book. I couldn't do this. Not with him.

"Neither are French bull dogs or French kissing."

"I'm leaving."

I shoved my books into my book bag to the sound of his laughter bouncing off the walls. So much like his brother's. It must've run in the family.

"No. Come on, French. Don't leave. Lighten up."

He grabbed my hand, stopping me from picking up my pen from the table.

I glared at him and he immediately released me. Both of his hands raised in the air as if he were a criminal and I a police officer.

"Okay, okay. I'm sorry. Look. Just sit down. No more jokes. I promise. We'll get right to work."

I knew I shouldn't have believed him. Cole was not to be trusted. But I needed to pass French and he was my best shot at doing that.

I sat down.

He cleared his throat and opened his book.

"Okay, okay. Chapter one."

I peered at him, waiting for more jokes at my expense. More humiliation. When it didn't come, I pulled my French book back out.

"Okay," he said. "We'll start with the basics. French toast is not French."

Within five seconds, I was out the door with Cole's laugh chasing me down the hallway.

Lesson learned. Never trust a Winsted.

13

Ariel and I walked in to Mr. Reynold's science class, taking our seats in the back of the room.

Only half my brain listened as the thin, youngish teacher showed us a video presentation about electrons. The other half of my brain was concerned with other things. Like random song lyrics, dinner and the new thrift shop that opened on 54th street.

Midway through the video and my musings, Ariel leaned over and tapped me on the shoulder. Her flame red hair was braided to one side now, her freckles dark against her pale skin. She picked up her pencil and ran the rough eraser across her cheek.

"Hey. The Center put in a new pool table over the weekend. We should learn how to play."

Ariel's father donated The Center to St. Mary's Academy a few years ago. It was his way of giving the students a safe environment to hang out in after school.

"Sure," I said. Learning pool in front of the entire school couldn't be any more embarrassing than ripping my skirt in front of Jake, right? God. I hoped not. I couldn't take anymore embarrassment right now.

Ariel put down her pencil and gave me a sly smile.

"I'm sure that Jake and Eric will be there." Her eyebrows wiggled and I suppressed a laugh.

"Probably. But I'm done with Jake. Let's focus on you and Eric for now."

If today had shown me anything, it was that a relationship with Jake was no more than a dream. A farfetched, unattainable dream. It was time to move on. Besides, I didn't need a boyfriend in my life. I could have fun with just my friends. Jasmine and Ariel were ten times more entertaining than a boyfriend could ever be, anyway.

The thought left a bitter taste in my mouth.

I sighed. Why couldn't I have picked a real boy instead of a dream one?

Finally, the bell had rung, announcing the end of the school day. I practically jumped out of my chair, ready to unwind, have some fun, and apparently, learn to play pool. Ariel walked next to me out the door and together, we joined the waves of students that rushed toward the exit.

Out of the corner of my eye, I spotted dark hair and turned toward it. Cole was staring at me. When he saw me looking back at him, he winked, turned and moved deeper in to the crowd.

God. How I hated him.

Someone shoved me from behind, knocking away thoughts of Cole and pushing me outside.

It was the beginning of November, and the unseasonably warm late autumn sunshine warmed my skin. The ground shook as subway cars roared through darkened tunnels beneath our feet. Skyscrapers stood tall around us. Sunlight reflected in their glass windows, making it seem as if they were winking. It smelled like burning gasoline, dirty concrete and the body odor of hundreds of students trying to find their way home.

That's New York for you.

After three years, I still wasn't completely used to it. I missed the country fresh air of North Carolina. The grass, the wide-open spaces, the buildings that had birthed generations of families and that had seen wars come and go. New York air smelled like electricity. North Carolina air smelled like home.

It took Ariel and I a little under fifteen minutes to walk the five blocks to The Center. It looked identical to the dozens of gray apartment buildings on the block.

Ariel rang the bell and a voice answered.

"Name?"

"Ariel Swimworthy and Bella French."

The door buzzed and I followed Ariel inside and up the stairs where a tall, slim man with a large nose and a dress shirt sat behind a half moon desk. He saw us and a smile slid onto his thin lips.

"Ms. Swimworthy. Ms. French," he said. "Good to see you two today."

"Hey, Grim," we replied in unison. "Jinx!" we said together again.

Grim rolled his eyes. This wasn't the first time we'd done this. We pretty much did it every time we came here, which was several times a week.

"Ariel Swimworthy and Bella French," he replied, irritation coloring his voice. Our full names released the jinx and we giggled at each other.

"You know, you are the only girls whose name I have to say twice." He put his hands on his hips. "The next time you jinx each other, I'm going to let you stay silent forever."

"You know you love the banter, Grim," Ariel said with a smile.

Grim shook his head with a fake frown. "No, actually. I really don't."

Ariel signed her name on a clipboard, then she pushed the clipboard to me.

Grim seemed like he'd be better suited working in a fancy hotel or restaurant instead of a teen hang out spot. I often wondered why he worked here instead of some place which probably had a much higher rate of pay.

I slid the clipboard back toward him and smiled politely. "Until next time," I said with a raised brow.

Grim raised his brow, too. "Until next time, Ms. French."

Ariel grabbed my hand and led me through a set of glass doors and in to the heart of The Center.

Two large air hockey tables were in the middle of the room. To my right, a group of guys were split between three big TV screens, playing a football video game. To my left, various girls were sitting at a manicure station, getting their nails and feet done. Weights clanged from the weight room near the bathrooms. One floor up, there was a pool, and one floor down was a basketball court. The tennis courts were on the first floor, and there was a full track, complete with a collapsible dome, on the roof.

Triton Swimworthy spared no expense.

Next to the video game section, several girls were hovering around Dana and Dustin, who were deep in a make-out session.

I closed my eyes and hoped that Jake didn't see. Something like this would really hurt him. I know that if I were Jake, I would be crushed.

"Babe, you're here!"

Jake Winsted's blue eyes hooked onto mine. He looked as if he'd been waiting for me all his life.

My stomach dropped in to my feet.

Was I dreaming? I had to be. Did I fall and hit my head on the stairs? Had a train fallen off the tracks and crushed me on my way here? Was I in my own particular slice of heaven?

Yes. Yes, it had to be heaven. Jake's eyes were so warm and dreamy that this couldn't be anything earthly. It had to be ethereal.

His long, strong legs quickly covered the space between us. His eyes were still glued to mine. I couldn't look away if I wanted to.

I didn't want to.

My heart banged so hard in my ears that I could barely hear what he was saying. It sounded like *I'm so glad to see you,* but I couldn't be sure. Any thoughts of getting over Jake immediately flew from my mind when he stopped inches in front of me. I felt a goofy smile spread across my face. I panted instead of breathed. My palms misted with sweat.

His strong hands slid up my cheeks, warming my face. He leaned forward and the world slowed down. He pressed his lips to mine and my heart stopped. My lungs locked. My knees wobbled. I was excited and nervous and afraid and elated all at once. The raging emotions bolted my feet to the floor and stole the thoughts from my mind. My stomach tied in knots. Every nerve in my body lit up like a Christmas tree. Goosebumps spread from my forehead to my toes.

Then my mouth remembered what it was supposed to do and I kissed him back, my lips clinging to his. My fingers tangled in the golden strands of his hair and I pulled him closer. I stepped closer.

I swore that my feet lifted from the floor in pure ecstasy. Jake Winsted was kissing me and it was glorious.

Or it would have been, had it lasted longer.

All too soon, his soft lips pulled away, leaving me surprised, embarrassed, breathless and tingly all over. My fingertips touched where his lips had been.

What. Just. Happened?

My eyes drunk in his beautiful face as he pulled away. His blue eyes looked surprised, his ruddy skin flushed, as if he couldn't believe he'd just done that.

I didn't believe it either.

"It's cool," he whispered, almost apologetically. "Just be cool."

The magnitude of what just happened slowly sunk in to my brain.

Jake Winsted, my dream boy, had just kissed me and I'd kissed him back. My heart beat so erratically that I thought it would explode. I wanted to jump for joy, clap my hands and fling myself into his arms again but before I could, he grabbed my hand and dragged me in to the hallway.

Behind us, the door slammed shut.

14

The instant the door closed, Jake let go of my hand, leaned against the wall, put his hands on his knees and heaved in a breath.

Two windows showed pale, yellow light in to the hallway, illuminating the white washed walls and revealing red rust on the staircase railing.

My lips hummed. My body prickled. I'd never felt so alive or so confused.

Jake's kiss had played out in my head a million times but I never thought that it would actually happen. Why today? Why now?

He kept his eyes on the floor as he struggled to get his breathing under control. He was dressed like an All-American boy with his pink polo shirt, blue jacket, light gray pants that matched his eyes and loafers. The clothes were simple but he made them look like they were fresh from the runways of Paris.

Finally, his eyes raised to mine and they widened, as if just realizing that I was there.

My confusion grew stronger, making my stomach ache and my chest tighten.

"Hi." I gave him a little wave, feeling foolish and awkward.

"I'm so screwed."

His brows furrowed in what looked like regret.

At this juncture in our relationship, I was not expecting those words. I imagined he'd say, *I've noticed you,* or *I think you're adorable*, but definitely not *I'm so screwed.*

My hands hugged my nervous stomach. I didn't have a lot of experience with boys but I knew that having someone say they were screwed after they kissed you was not good.

"Things just got a little ... out of hand." He stood and raked his hands through his thick, blond hair.

Out of control? What did that mean?

"I don't understand," I said.

"It's just that Dana was making out with that jerk right in front of me and I didn't want to seem pathetic, so..."

His voice trailed off. I didn't need to hear him say the end of that sentence. I already knew what he meant. He'd kissed the first girl he saw so that Dana would be just as jealous as he was.

I was that first girl.

My heart screeched to a stop then cracked into a million pieces. I was a fool. A pawn. Embarrassment washed over me and I felt my cheeks heat. Anger bubbled in my chest and I bit my bottom lip, holding in the threatening tears.

I was just some girl. Some very lucky, very stupid girl.

I sniffed back my tears. One thing was for sure. I would not cry in front of him. Not in a million years! He'd embarrassed me but I had my pride. He would not take that away from me. Ever!

Squaring my shoulders, I reached for the peeling silver door handle. My intent was to grab Ariel, make a quick exit and be swallowed whole by the Earth. Jake foiled my carefully laid plans by running past me and pressing himself against the door. He was a big boy and strong. One tug on the handle let me know that I wouldn't be getting out of this hallway if he didn't want me to.

A new emotion showed up to play. Fear. Fear that wrapped around my arms and slithered over my shoulders. I was trapped in a hallway with Jake. If I ran down the stairs, he would catch me. If I went for the door, he'd block it.

I focused on not appearing afraid, puffing out my chest like the bullfrogs in the lake near my grandparents' house. I took a step back from the door, crossed my arms in front of me and gave him my best withering look. It was the one that my mother used to give me when I misbehaved in public as a child.

"Let go of the door," I commanded.

Was this the boy that I had liked? That I had dreamed about? How could he embarrass me in front of the whole school then trap me in a hallway? What kind of a person does that? What kind of person was he?

"No. You can't go back in there," he said, his eyes wide. Pleading. Less scary. "At least, not alone. Not without a plan. Look, uh, uh..."

He looked around and snapped his fingers.

My stomach dropped. The truth was painfully obvious. He did not know my name. His brother had just introduced us on Friday and by Monday, I was forgotten. My illusions about Jake Winsted melted into a puddle and swirled down the drain of my heart.

He didn't even remember my name.

Infuriated, I rushed to the door and pulled with all my might, determined to escape before I had a complete breakdown in front of him. Before I screamed.

"Get out of my way!"

"No. We need to talk."

"Haven't you done enough?" I cried. "You've just kissed me in front of the entire school and you don't even know my name. What else do you want from me?"

He squeezed his hands together in a praying gesture.

"Please. I need your help."

I shook my head. My chest hurt. My stomach hurt. My head hurt. My heart hurt. I just wanted to find Ariel, go home and hide under my blankets forever.

I backed up, leaning against the wall as he'd done a few moments before.

"There is nothing that you can say to me that I want to hear. I just want to go home."

"Come on. I just kissed you." The thought seemed to impress him because he smiled at me. A big, stupid, cocky grin, just like his brother's. My blood boiled. "That should count for something, right? I mean, what girl doesn't want to be kissed by Jake Winsted?"

He couldn't be that arrogant. No one could be that arrogant.

"You can't be serious," I said.

He shrugged, his chest puffing out in pride.

He was serious. It wasn't a joke. Jake Winsted honestly thought that he was god's gift to women.

It was so crazy that I would have laughed out loud had I not been so furious. I massaged my temples with my pointer fingers. I had to keep my hands busy or else I would punch him.

How could my dreams of him be so different from reality? Had I been that love sick? That naïve? How could I have been so in love with him and not known him at all? My anger with him warred with the anger at myself for my own stupidity. I pushed off the wall, stood up straight and pinned him with a glare.

"If you don't move in the next five seconds, I am going to scream. One, two-"

He held his hands up defensively.

"Look. I just need for you to pretend to be my girlfriend for a week or two."

His words confused me and I shook my head, squinting at him.

"What?"

He couldn't have just said what I thought he said. But he did. I could tell because he looked more pleased with himself with every passing second.

"You and me will go around school for the next two weeks, acting like boyfriend and girlfriend, making out, holding hands, whatever. Then, Dana will get super jealous and beg me to take her back. It's the perfect plan."

Was he serious? That was his plan? I let out a breath.

"Jake, whatever crazy plan you're thinking up, forget it. I have—"

"A boyfriend?"

I shook my head. "No. Pride. Dignity. A life. Morals. I'm not a liar."

"Not a problem. I can overlook that stuff if you can, uh..." He snapped his fingers again. "Uh."

"Bella. My name is Bella French."

"Yes." His words came out a little too loudly. "Bella French. Uh ... you do go to my school, right?"

Now this was just getting insulting. I shook my head and rolled my eyes, my chest tightening. Every second that I was in this hallway made me more and more angry.

"We are in English together," I growled. "We've been in, like, a million classes together since Freshman year. You know what? Never mind. Get out of my way."

I charged forward, pushing at his heavy, unmoving body. Each shove made me more and more angry. I swore that I would never like another boy again.

"No. Wait. This can work out for both of us. A relationship with me will skyrocket you up the popularity food chain. I am offering you an opportunity to change your entire high school existence."

I paused.

"You're a nobody now, right? No one knows your name. But with me, no one will be able to forget it."

I thought about reaching for the door, but for some reason, I hesitated.

"People will kill themselves to talk to you, to sit with you, to dress like you, to talk like you."

I thought about how I had examined every outfit Dana ever wore. The way she walked. The way she talked. I remember how I wished that I was her. That I wished for her life.

"They'll listen to everything you have to say. With me by your side, you could run this school in ways that Dana never could."

I let out a breath. My hands shook. My body felt electric.

It bothered me to think about how tempting this deal was. If I took it, it would make me a terrible person. A liar. A fake. A fraud. I shouldn't have even considered it. And yet, I *was* considering it.

Jake saw the look in my eye. That yearning to be someone better. To be popular. He stood up from the door and stepped forward as if he knew that I was no longer a flight risk.

He was right. I wasn't.

A relationship with him would give me what I wanted. A voice. But did I want it this way? What would my friends say if they knew what I was doing? They'd tell me to run as far and as fast from Jake as I could. But they didn't want the things I did. They didn't care that we were nothing at this school.

I cared that I was nothing in this school.

I did not want to be nothing anymore.

I looked away from Jake, lest he see how much I was considering his offer.

"What about that little red head you came in with? Ayanna, Aretha, Alanna-"

"Ariel." My voice was strained and choked. The air was thick with my wanting. My yearning to rise above the masses. It was so close that I could touch it.

"Yes. Ariel. She's on the swim team, right? Her father owns half of New York."

I didn't respond and he kept talking.

"I have it on good authority that she likes my friend, Eric. I can get him to ask her out. In fact, I can personally guarantee that he will ask her to the Winter Formal. All you have to do is say yes."

I raised an eyebrow. He'd already offered me the pot. Now he was sweetening it to irresistible levels.

"You're selling your friend to us?"

He stood up straight and crossed his arms across his chest.

"No. But I can be very persuasive."

His fingertips ran up my cheek, draining a bit of my anger from me. I had to admit, his touch felt nice.

"I am offering you everything. Popularity. A dream date for your friend. Me. Say yes and you can have it all."

I couldn't believe that I was actually considering this. I didn't want to be Jake's plaything, but now I had to think about Ariel. What would she think of me if I told her that I had said no to the one opportunity she had to date Eric? Would she ever talk to me again? If I were her, would I ever talk to me again?

The answer came immediately.

Absolutely not.

I let out a breath.

"Why are you doing this?" I asked.

Jake's smile faded.

"Dana's already moved on. I just want to show her that I can, too." He shrugged. "She'll see. When it all falls apart, she'll come crawling back on her hands and knees."

"That's a very sad and demented story. But if it's all going to fall apart anyway, why do you need me?"

"Don't you see? You are perfect. You're smart and you wear these hand me down clothes. You will be the catalyst. Once Dana sees that I'm with someone like you, she won't be able to sleep at night. Then, she'll take me back."

I frowned at him.

"Do you know how insulting that is?"

"What? The part about you being smart or the part about the clothes?"

I growled. "All of it. I'm not some weirdo troll that you can manipulate to get your girlfriend back."

"I didn't say that you were. In fact, if you did your hair and wore makeup and clothes that weren't rescued from a dumpster, you could be dateable."

My anger went into orbit.

"I'm leaving."

"No. Please. Just give me a chance. Give this a chance. Think about Ariel. She'd do it for you and you want her to be happy, right? Plus, you can consider this your good deed for life. Please, Brenda."

"Bella."

"Sorry. Bella. Please!"

I was vaguely aware that saying yes to Jake would be equivalent to making a deal with the devil. Jake was a self-centered jerk who didn't know my name and who had insulted me. But he had offered me the thing that I wanted the most. A voice. To leave the realms of invisibility behind and walk among the stars. To have people notice me. The fact that I now had Ariel's happiness to think about took away any choice that I had.

I remembered the first time I'd met Ariel. It was in the first gym class of Freshman year. The teacher, a sadist named Ms. Whittier, had forced us in to a game of dodgeball. Ariel and I were on one team. Dana, Mel, Ursula and Stephanie were on another.

Stephanie had intentionally thrown a ball at my face, making my nose bleed and sending me to the nurse's office. Ten minutes later, Stephanie had joined me with the same injury, screaming about how she was going to get that red-headed witch. I got a swollen nose, a permanent place on Stephanie's crap list and a best friend all in the same day.

Ariel had fought for me that day. I knew that she would always fight for me. And now, here I was, with her happiness in my hand. I had to take this chance. I just had to. She wanted Eric, and if this was the only way for her to get him, then so be it.

I sighed.

I was going to hate myself in the morning.

15

This day had taken so many twists and turns that my head was practically spinning when I walked back into The Center next to Jake, my new so-called boyfriend. Every eye in The Center was now on me, including the dark eyes of Dana Rich. The boy whom she'd previously been making out with, Dustin, tried to go in for another kiss but she pushed him off her, crossed her arms over her chest and glared at me instead.

I glared back. Maybe with a little goading, she could be pursuaded to reconcile with Jake sooner. Well, not too soon. My new relationship might've been fraudulent but I still deserved the promised benefits of it. It was only right.

Jake's lips dropped to my ear, giving me shivers that I didn't need or want.

"Hey, babe. Wanna watch me shoot some pool?"

Twenty minutes ago, I would have watched him sort recyclables. My opinion of him had gone down dramatically since then. I bit back a cutting remark and pasted a sweet smile on my face.

"Sure," I answered my voice tight. "Let me just go to the bathroom and, uh, freshen up."

Ariel approached me on my left and I grabbed her hand before Jake could object. Relief washed over me as she pulled me toward the back of The Center where the bathrooms were.

There was so much to tell her. So much for us to work out. I needed Ariel to help me pick up the pieces of my life that were currently scattered around me like a forgotten jigsaw puzzle. She would know what to do. How to act. How to dress. Her and Jasmine would be my advisors while I bided my time in Jake's royal court.

It wasn't until we stopped in front of the bathroom and I looked in to Ariel's eyes that I realized a terrible, terrible truth.

I could not tell her or Jasmine what was going on. If they knew about my secret arrangement with Jake, they'd tell me to run as far away from him as possible. And worse, if Ariel knew that Jake was nudging Eric in her direction, she'd think that everything Eric said was just one big lie.

I couldn't let that happen. Ariel and Eric deserved a chance. Not just as some weird characters in an even weirder video game, but a real life, honest to god chance. She had done so much for me since I moved to New York. I had to do this for her. I had to let her see if what she had with Eric was real or not. And who was to say that Eric wouldn't like Ariel once he got to know her offline?

This was my chance to give something back to her. To be a real friend.

For the first time in my life, I'd have to keep a secret from Ariel and Jasmine.

I'd never felt so alone.

"Do you mind telling me what that was about?" She hissed as we stood in front of the girls bathroom door.

She looked like she was deciding whether to be angry or happy about the whole me and Jake thing.

"What was what about?" I asked, smoothing my features into a mask of innocence.

"Are you kidding me? Jake Winsted just kissed you in front of everyone!"

My mouth opened and closed like a fish out of water.

"Well, uh, he said he, uh-"

"Hey!"

Suddenly, Regina Winsted, Jake's sister, stepped into my line of vision. She did not look happy.

"So," she said, crossing her arms over her chest. She wore a purple dress that barely reached mid-thigh, and a sweater, belt and low heels all the color of maple wood. Her long, black hair was perfectly layered. I was sure that her hair stylist bill was more than what Dad paid for rent. "*You* are Jake's new girlfriend."

By the way she said *you,* I could tell that she did not approve. She popped her gum while her eyes scanned me.

I nodded my head slowly. "Yes."

Ariel's eyes nearly popped out of her head in shock. She took a step back so that she was fully facing me and mouthed:

"Girlfriend?"

I ignored her, instead focusing on keeping my breathing even and my face relaxed.

"And how long has this been going on?" Regina demanded. She said it as if Jake was doing something wrong by dating me. As if I were tainted. Blemished. Not enough. I tried not to think about how much that hurt me. Maybe slightly less than Jake not even knowing my name.

Jake hadn't gone in to specifics about our dating history and I didn't think to ask. How long were he and Dana broken up for? A few days? A week?

"Just today," I finally said, hoping my anxiety didn't show.

Ariel's eyebrows rose. She was thinking. Seeing my lies in the air and trying to decide why they were there in the first place.

"Interesting," Regina said. She took a step closer, leaving only a foot between us. My nerves grew taunt and my breathing turned shallow. "I am only going to say this once." She held up one manicured finger. Her nails were blood red. "Stay away from Jake. He is not for you."

"And if she doesn't?" Ariel asked, taking a step forward.

I groaned. I appreciated my friend's effort, but this was seriously not the time.

"Then she will regret it. You, too."

"We'll take our chances," Ariel replied, narrowing her eyes at Regina.

Regina looked amused and stepped toward my friend.

I stepped between them. I could not have my best friend leave a fist print on my fake boyfriend's sister's face.

"Thank you for the heads up, Regina, but I'm sure that Jake and I will be fine."

Regina paused. Her eyes slid to me, then Ariel, then back to me. Her lips quirked up at the ends.

"You have twenty-four hours. End it, or I will end you." She gave us one final warning stare before walking back to the video game section where she presided over the boys who were crammed on to the couch.

She didn't look at us again.

"What a jerk!" Ariel said. "Who does she think she is, anyway?"

I let out a breath. "She's Jake's sister."

"Yes. Sister. Not master."

"What do you think she meant by twenty-four hours?"

Ariel waved the comment away. "Who cares? Whatever she has planned, we'll be ready for her. Remember, there are three of us and only one of her. As long as she doesn't bring reinforcements, we'll be fine."

I couldn't help but smile at Ariel's comment. She was the first one to fight for one of us but she was also the first one to laugh. My heart squeezed a little knowing that I was lying to her when she'd done nothing but be a good friend to me.

"And don't think that you're off the hook. I'm still pissed that you didn't tell me you were going out with Jake. Why wouldn't you say anything? I'm your best friend."

I smiled nervously, hating that I was lying to her when our friendship had always been so honest. But I had to. She would thank me later when she and Eric were vacationing in Cabo with their three kids and their dog.

"It just, kind of happened," I replied, my voice going up a few octaves. "I didn't have time to tell you. But now you know, so..."

I cleared my throat.

She took my hand and squeezed, her eyes gazing deep in to mine.

"Why do I feel like you're hiding something from me?" she asked.

I tried to speak, but the words didn't come out. I wasn't a liar, but it seemed that Jake had turned me into one in thirty minutes or less. This had to be some sort of record.

"Friends don't keep secrets from each other," Ariel said.

I closed my eyes, trying to breathe though my chest was tight. I wanted to tell Ariel everything but I couldn't. Not now.

"Jake saw me today and asked me out. I said yes. That's it."

Her eyes narrowed in suspicion.

I let out a guilt-ridden laugh.

She raised an eyebrow, as if she wasn't quite sure that she believed my story.

"Are you sure that's all that happened?" she asked, peering deeper in to my eyes.

I pretended to examine something on the back of my hand. "Positive."

Her eyes went to the ceiling, then back to me.

"Okay then. I'm going to pee, then we can watch your new boyfriend play pool ... I guess."

I nodded and watched her disappear in to the bathroom.

She didn't believe me. Helen Keller could've seen that. Why did I do this? Why did I think that I could pull this off? That I could hide something this huge from my best friend. I wanted to tell her, but I couldn't. But I should have. But I-

As my mind circled the drain of my lies, Cole marched across the floor, heading straight for Jake.

He must've been in the weight room, because his jet-black hair was plastered to his head with sweat. His wide chest bulged beneath his sleeveless shirt. I couldn't keep my eyes from roaming over his amazing body.

When did he get so ... hot?

He walked right past me and cornered his brother by the pool table. The two traded words, then headed out the door. I heard yelling but I couldn't make out what they were yelling about. After a few minutes, Jake reappeared.

Cole did not.

What was that about? Were they fighting over what Jake and I had done?

I was so deep in my conjectures that I didn't notice Ariel coming to stand beside me.

"Do you have to pee?" she asked.

I shook my head, my eyes still glued to the door that Cole had stormed out of.

"Then you'd better get back to your boyfriend."

Boyfriend. Right. I had a boyfriend now. A temporary fake one, but a boyfriend nonetheless.

"Yeah," I whispered. "I'd better get back to my, uh, boyfriend."

She smiled and shook her head. "Shouldn't you be happy about this? This is Jake Winsted we're talking about. Remember? The boy you've dreamed about since I've known you. Why aren't you doing backflips?"

I forced myself to smile, though inside I was having a full-on misery party.

"I don't know. I'm tired, I guess."

"You're tired? What does that even mean? What's up with you? I swear that if Eric ever showed up out the blue and kissed me, I'd sprout wings and fly."

Her face was so happy when she spoke about Eric. So dreamy. Yes, some of that happiness was for me, but some of it was just the thought of Eric. It boosted my resolve. I was doing the right thing.

We walked up to the pool table. Eric leaned on his pool stick while Jake lined up a shot. Kenny Jennings, local drug dealer, quietly leaned one bony hip against the table. His ever present black bookbag was wider than his body, making him appear even skinnier.

"Hey. It took you long enough," Jake said with a teasing grin that I'd seen on his brother before. "I thought you fell in."

It was so weird having him talk to me. Almost as if my *Avengers* poster came to life and Chris Hemsworth showed up in my bedroom, Thor costume and all.

Come to think about it, that would probably be less weird than how I felt right then.

I swallowed and tried to act like everything was cool.

"Your sister came to visit me," I said, quiet enough so that no one else could hear. "She said that we have twenty-four hours to break up or else."

He waved my comment away, his gaze focused on somewhere behind me. I turned to see what could possibly be more interesting than his fake girlfriend's impending murder. A dark-haired kid had approached Kenny. The two walked away, disappearing around the weight room wall.

Really? He was ignoring me to witness yet another Kenny Jenner misdemeanor?

Incensed, I whipped back around to face him.

"Jake," I hissed.

His attention turned back to me, his mood significantly darker than it was a moment ago.

"What?" His voice was harsh, more like a bark. I took a step forward, refusing to be intimidated by him.

"Your sister. She threatened me."

"She's all talk. In a few days, she'll forget about it."

"Didn't her and Dana get into a fist fight outside of the school a few weeks ago?" I asked.

"Yeah, well, that was different." He leaned over, lined up a shot, and pushed his pool stick forward, sending a red ball flying.

"How was that different?"

"Because Dana stood up for herself. You shouldn't have that problem."

My hands fisted and a growl escaped my mouth.

"Jake, either you stop insulting me and rein in your sister or else our deal is off."

He rolled his eyes and grinned at me as if I was the world's biggest fool.

"Is it?"

His chin jerked to Ariel and Eric.

Eric's eyes had latched on to Ariel's, a slow smile spreading on to his face like butter on warm bread.

"Hi," he said, extending a hand. "Eric Shipman."

Ariel looked star struck for a moment. Her arms were limp at her side, a silly grin on her face. Eric didn't seem to mind, though. His warm smile remained, his eyes on her.

After a few, dazed moments, she finally snapped out of her trance. Her cheeks reddened and she put her hand in his.

"Ariel," she replied softly.

Their hands pumped between them, their eyes locked, their smiles full.

"I've seen you around," Eric said. "You're on the swim team, right?"

I could see patches of red on Ariel's neck. I was sure that on the inside, she was melting into a puddle.

"Yeah."

"I went to your last meet. You are the fastest girl I've ever seen."

"Really?"

"Yeah. You should be in the Olympics or something. You're amazing."

Ariel's cheeks turned beet red and she let out a high, nervous laugh.

Eric's smile only widened.

Was this part of Eric and Jake's act or was this something real?

With the way that Eric was grinning at her, I couldn't be sure.

A crack sounded as Jake's stick hit another ball and sent it flying in to a corner hole. He straightened with a self-satisfied smile. His eyes found their way to Eric and Ariel, then he glanced at me with a sly grin.

"Chill out, Brenda. Let's not make this harder than it has to be."

So, this was a trick. A game. Ariel had become a pawn and I had put her on the board. But with the way that her and Eric were whispering and smiling, I couldn't tell her now. That time had come and gone. I had to ride this out and pray that Eric was not planning on hurting my friend.

Before I could ream Jake on all the reasons my name wasn't Brenda, he spoke up again.

"You know how to play pool?" he asked, his eyes moving from me to somewhere over my shoulder. He was obviously looking for Dana, to see if she was watching. From the way his smile turned seductive, I was sure that she was.

How did I get myself into this?

I shook my head, letting him know that I, in fact, did not play pool.

"Here. Let me show you."

My stomach tightened a bit but I did what I was told. Jake briefly explained the game then handed me a pool stick. He ushered me to his side of the table and stood behind me, helping me line up a shot.

His nearness made me feel warm all over.

It's fake, I reminded myself. It is just for show. It's not real.

I repeated my mantra as Jake patiently showed me how to hit the ball just right so that it went in to one of the pockets. He laughed when I hit the ball too soft and it didn't go anywhere at all. He hugged me when I hit the ball too hard and it went flying off the table. When I finally hit the ball and sent it into one of the pockets, he whooped and he gave me a high five before pulling me to him and kissing me on the temple.

Though his hugs felt nice and my treacherous body greedily pulled him closer, my mind and heart told me that it was not me he was hugging. It was Dana. I'd seen him hug her all over school and it was always the same. First a hug. Sometimes a kiss followed. Always one hand on her upper back and one hand on her lower back, right above her butt. He was showing Dana how replaceable she was.

I was his gun and he was using me to wound her, hug by hug, kiss by kiss. For a fleeting moment, I felt bad for her until I remembered that she had just done the exact same thing to him.

It was Eric's turn to take the pool stick but he told Jake that he could go again.

He and Ariel were speaking excitedly about an upcoming concert. He asked her a question that I couldn't hear. Something that made her pause and smile. He held out his hand for a low high five. She slapped it and they both laughed.

Was that real? Was Eric actually interested in her? If not, he was an amazing actor.

16

I walked into my half-unpacked apartment to the smells of spaghetti sauce and garlic bread. I sniffed the air, my mouth watering. Dad must've come home early and started dinner.

"Dad?" I called out, walking toward the kitchen.

My stomach rumbled so loud that I was sure the neighbors heard it. All I'd had to eat today were Daddy's blueberry pancakes, half a salad and a soda.

"Dad, I'm home!"

I stopped by Mojo's bed and gave him a pat on the head. He looked up at me with tired, happy eyes. Then, as if realizing that he wasn't being mean to me, he dropped his head and shifted so that his butt was to me.

What was with this dog? What had I done to him to make him hate me so much?

I let out a breath, picked the dog up—which earned me a frustrated woof—and kissed him on his brown head.

"You are going to love me whether you like it or not," I said. The curious creature squirmed and bucked so hard that I nearly dropped him. I put him down and he immediately retreated to his bed and gave me the butt treatment again.

Great. I had to carry this dog around the neighborhood because he refused to walk and he treated me as if I had leprosy. Just my luck.

I stood, going for the leash to take Mojo out for one of our walk/carry adventures when I noticed something odd. All the pee pads were dry. In fact, there wasn't a spot of poop or pee in the whole place.

Had Mojo learned to use the toilet since yesterday? Come to think about it, the pup looked tired. Exhausted. As if he'd been walking all day. But that wasn't possible since I just got home. Then again, Daddy was home early. Maybe he walked Mojo?

"Dad!"

Something clanged. A dropped pot, maybe?

"In here, honey!" he called back. I could hear the fluster in his voice. Dad was a good cook but the act of cooking stressed him out. Today was the first time ever he'd cooked twice in one day. Typically, I cooked dinner or we ordered take out whenever he got home from work.

I dropped my bookbag by the kitchen entrance and stepped over the threshold just in time to see Daddy twisting off the top of a green can of parmesan cheese and dumping the contents into a pot of red sauce. I smiled. Cheesy red sauce and pasta was one of my favorite dishes. It was almost as good as blueberry pancakes.

My stomach rumbled.

"First breakfast, now dinner?" I stepped deeper in to the kitchen and placed a kiss on Daddy's rough cheek. "What's the occasion?"

"Occasion?" he asked. "I need an occasion to cook for my little girl?"

I raised an eyebrow. He was being evasive again. What was that about? When did Daddy and I start keeping secrets from each other? First the other night with the suit and now tonight with the dinner. My heart anxiously skipped a beat as I looked around the kitchen. The dishes were piled up, the counters spotted with red and brown globs and the garbage can had overgrown to monstrous proportions. All this mess couldn't have been made in just one dinner preparation. Had he been home all day? Why wasn't he at work?

"Did you walk Mojo today?" I asked.

He nodded, his back still to me. "Yup. Mojo and I are getting quite acquainted with each other. He's pretty smart for a puppy. And fast. Boy, can that dog run! Like Grandpa's dog, Wilber. You remember Wilber, don't you?"

I smiled. "The fastest dog in North Carolina."

"That's right!"

I took a wooden spoon from atop the stove, dipped it in to the simmering sauce and casually blew on it.

"No work today?" I asked, trying to sound nonchalant.

"Not today, dear," he said. He searched the counters for the pot holders. Whenever he cooked, he misplaced the pot holders at least once every ten seconds. I spied them on the kitchen table but continued my prodding.

"Did you take a vacation day?" I asked. I sipped the cooling sauce. It was seasoned to perfection.

"Nope," he said. "I got fired."

I gasped, choking on the sauce. Taking a step back, I hacked in to my elbow until I could breathe again. I was choking, drowning in red sauce and worry. I took in a deep breath, trying to keep calm.

"You were fired?" The question came out rougher than I wanted it to.

He nodded, not looking at me, still searching for the pot holders as if they were more important than our future.

A million scenarios raced through my head at once. Us begging for discarded bagels on the streets. Sleeping out in the cold. Living in an abandoned freight car with all our belongings tied in a handkerchief at the end of a stick.

"Why?" I asked, already knowing the answer.

"A customer complained, apparently."

My blood boiled. "You've been doing your experiments again."

He finally found the pot holders and rushed back to pull the garlic bread from the stove.

"I thought that the compound would be right this time." His voice was frantic. Like my heartbeat. Like my anger. Like my confusion.

He said he would stop. Why didn't he stop?

Grabbing a knife from the side board, he viciously sliced the garlic bread into even chunks as if he didn't hear our entire world crumbling to dust.

But I heard it. I heard it loud and clear, and it made me sick to my stomach.

My father, Maurice French, was raised on a horse farm in North Carolina. At night, when other boys dreamed of the big city and beautiful girls, my father studied chemistry. His life's dream was to become a chemist so that he could create alternative fuels. Especially car fuels. Daddy tried to follow his dream by going to community college and studying chemistry but the dream was deferred by a beautiful brown-skinned woman who hoped for a family. And so, Daddy married my mom and fell in to a comfortable life as a mechanic. Then Mom died and Daddy's experiments began.

I didn't know at first. After all, I was only ten and it was beyond my young comprehension to understand why my father kept losing his job. It wasn't until I was fifteen that I finally figured out that my backyard chemist father was testing his mixture in other people's gas tanks. Sometimes, the clients didn't notice. Sometimes, the engines exploded. Either way, it always ended the same. In a firing. He'd conducted his experiments state wide until no one would hire him. Now, we were in New York and he was doing it again. Again!

I closed my eyes to keep my cool. To keep from screaming at him.

"Daddy, you promised no more experiments."

"I know. I know."

My mind went a mile a minute, fueled by worry. Where would we get money for rent, or food, or train fare? How could he stand there slicing bread when we were about to be out on the streets? What were we going to do?

My eyes pinned to his back that moved erratically around the kitchen, draining pasta, mixing it with the sauce, adding the meatballs. I wished he would turn around and talk to me instead of doing this *too busy to care* act. It was annoying. Especially when I was freaking out.

"Daddy, you promised you'd stop."

His hands paused mid-air, still filled with lettuce leaves. His chin dropped to his chest.

"I thought I got it right this time."

The lettuce fell like thick, green rain on the counter. On the floor. They stuck to his shirt and pants like little green scarlet letters, screaming that he'd sinned.

"You promised me that you would stop," I repeated through clenched teeth.

He dropped the remaining lettuce and turned to me, his face contrite. That was no surprise. He was always contrite.

"I'm sorry, honey." He tried to pull me in to a hug but I broke out of his hold and stepped away from him. Anger shook my hands, my cheeks. My whole body felt consumed by it. How could he do this to us? How could he do this to me?

"I really thought I got it right this time," he whispered again.

His pleading hands were extended to me but I was all done being the supportive daughter. I wanted to scream. I wanted to wail. I wanted to open my mouth and yell at him so badly that I closed my eyes against it. Parents were supposed to be responsible. He should have been doing his job and being a father instead of chasing this crazy dream in the absolute worst possible way. Now, we were stuck and I blamed him.

"You have to fix this," I said, my voice shaking. "How are you going to fix this?"

His eyes dropped from mine, searching the floor for something I couldn't see.

"I called your grandmother. She said that I can go back and work on grandpa's farm if I needed to."

My heart froze.

"Back to North Carolina?"

No. He couldn't do this to me. I had a life here. It wasn't fair. It just wasn't fair!

My chest tightened and I squeezed my lips together. My anger begged for release. I tried so hard to keep it in but it wouldn't be contained. Not anymore.

I exploded.

"You always do this!" I screamed. "You always ruin everything!"

His head dropped on to his chest and he bit his lower lip.

I didn't stop. I couldn't. I had to make him understand how foolish this was. How dangerous. He had to know that he was single handedly ruining my life.

"Why can't you just be normal for once? Why can't you be a father instead of chasing this crazy, stupid dream?"

His head picked up then, his eyes hard.

"It's not a dream. It's a reality. Or at least, it can be. I just need more equipment. More tests. I need more time."

"There is no more time, Dad! You have been wasting time for years. And now, you've lost yet another job. Where does that leave me, huh? What about me? How can you decide to just run back to North Carolina without even asking me?"

A single tear fell down my cheek. Then another.

"I'm doing what I have to do to make sure you're taken care of," he said.

"No, Dad. What you had to do was not blow up other people's cars."

He frowned at me, and I didn't care. It was time he heard the truth.

"You screwed up, and now my life is over because of it. God. I can't believe how selfish you are! How could you do this to me?"

"Sweetheart, I'll make it right. I'll do what I have to do this time."

"Oh, really? All of a sudden?"

His hard gaze turned lethal.

"I am still your father."

"You are my father? Then grow up and act like it! Stop blowing up cars and start thinking about your family for once. You promised Mom that you would take care of me, and once again, you're breaking that promise with your stupid, selfish dreams! God. I hate you so much!"

I wanted to take the words back as soon as they came out. As soon as I saw the pain that dropped his face when he heard them. But there was no going back now. The words were out there, and although I regretted hurting him, I wasn't one hundred percent sure that I didn't mean what I said.

He ran his hand over his face, exasperated.

"Let's give it a few weeks. If I can't find anything by the end of the month, then..."

"I'm not moving back."

"You will."

"I'm not moving back!"

"Bella, it's over. Done. Period. If I can't find anything by the end of the month, we're moving back, and that's final."

The air between us turned heavy, like a choking cloud of angry fire. Our words turned quiet, like tiny missiles aimed right at each other's heart.

"If we leave New York, my life will be over."

"You're young. You'll survive."

"Survival is not living."

"You're being dramatic."

"I'm not being dramatic! I'm concerned about our future. One of us has to be."

"I am concerned. That's why I made a plan for us."

"A plan that you didn't think to ask me about!"

"I don't have to ask you anything. You're sixteen."

"So, my opinion about my life doesn't matter?"

"Not when it comes to adult decisions, no."

"And was it an adult decision to put experimental fuel in every car on the east coast? To ruin our family's future? To get fired a million times? Was that an adult decision?"

My father looked taken aback. His mouth opened slightly, then closed.

"Your dreams are ruining my life and you don't even see it," I said. "This would never have happened if Mom were here!"

I snatched my backpack off the floor, stomped in to my bedroom and slammed the door, shaking the apartment. I threw myself on to my bed and angrily wiped away my tears.

My head felt hot with all the emotions that ran through me. I groaned and put my hands over my face. What was going to happen to us? To me? If he said that we were going back to North Carolina, there was really nothing I could do about it. North Carolina was nice and I had some friends there but Pointe Peak was a small town with small minded people. If you farted in the morning, it would be on the news at night. I didn't want that anymore. I wanted to live in a big city with big possibilities. I didn't want to leave my friends, my school, my home.

I wanted to stay here.

Still in my school clothes, I pulled the blankets up over my head and closed my eyes. My body wanted to sleep, but my brain wouldn't let it.

It was childish to yell at my dad. Mean, even. But I didn't care. I was tired of being the adult around here. I wanted to be a normal teenager. Not my father's guidance counselor.

I sighed and turned over on my stomach.

What would tomorrow bring?

What would happen to us?

How could I stay in New York?

17

After tossing and turning until three in the morning, I finally sat up, threw off the sheets, and put my feet on the floor.

My mind refused to shut down, though my body was exhausted. I pressed my palms to my temples and squeezed my eyes tight.

"Shut up, shut up, shut up!" I begged my brain, but it didn't stop the terrible thoughts. Thoughts about me moving back to my grandparents' horse farm. Of small towns. Of starting over.

If Dad couldn't find another job, I would have to say goodbye to people here that I loved. Ariel. Jasmine. Ms. Mitchell before she paired me with the wrong brother. If I left New York, my heart would be broken and I doubted that anything would ever be okay again.

Something shifted at the end of my bed and I turned my head. It was Mojo.

I had to look three times. One, because how did the dog get in to my room? Two, how did he get in to my bed? Three, why was he associating with me in the first place?

The answer to my question came with one look at the door. It was open slightly. Just enough for a small dog like Mojo to get through. He must've walked in, jumped on the bed and fell asleep. But why?

"Are you lost?" I asked.

The dog shuffled again, then lifted his head to look at me. I was shocked to notice less malice in his eyes since yesterday. Had Mojo seen me in my desperate condition and had a change of heart?

As if he had all the time in the world, the pup rose, stretched and walked over to me. It looked at me with a serious expression—well, as serious as a dog could look. Then, to my surprise, it licked my arm once, sneezed, walked back over to the end of the bed and promptly fell back to sleep.

I was stunned. What had just happened? Was that supposed to be a friendly gesture? A show of empathy? Pity?

I had no idea why Mojo licked me or why he was laying on my bed snoring softly, but I did know one thing. It felt good, like it was the start of a beautiful friendship. I sniffed back a happy tear because I'm a sap and laid back down.

For hours, I stared in to the blackness above my bed, anxiety wrapping twisted lines around my heart. Before I knew it, the sun was peeking through the curtains, my alarm was going off and my phone was beeping. Even Mojo had arisen and scratched at the door, begging to be taken out.

My bed sucked me in to its clutches, hugging me, beckoning me to stay and sleep forever. I wanted to. I was exhausted. Even the thought of going through this day with zero food and no sleep was enough to make me fake another menstrual cycle.

I prayed for a blizzard but seeing how the sun was shining, I was sure that God had ignored my request.

Before long, I heard my father moving around the apartment. I felt terrible that we had fought. I felt even worse that I said I'd hated him. I had never told him that before. Then again, he'd never made me so mad before.

Please God, let Daddy find a job, I prayed. I don't want to leave New York. My friends are here. My life is here. I want to stay. Please.

My answer came in the form of Mojo barking and pawing the door, as if to tell me to hurry up.

Some answer, God.

I quickly dressed in ripped jeans, an oversized shirt and a messy bun and took Mojo outside. To my surprise, he actually walked today. Down the stairs, out the door, down the street. His little legs blurred as he raced to the same tree that he'd peed on yesterday.

He must've really had to go.

"Sorry, boy," I said, crossing my arms while Mojo did his business. "It's been a long night." I sighed. "We'll probably have to move again. To someplace bigger. Greener. With less pit bulls. Less..."

My voice trailed off. The same two old ladies had stopped and stared at me.

Didn't they ever do anything else but walk around this neighborhood?

"I was, uh, talking to my dog," I said, shifting my feet.

"You do that a lot?" the one on the right said. She wore a little pink pill hat with lace and flowers at the top, along with a floral blue dress and kitten heel shoes. There was a leather magazine holder in her hands. Colored papers peeked from the top and sides.

"I've only had the dog for two days," I said.

They nodded uncertainly, looked at each other and walked on.

Something splashed against the tree. Gross. A moment later, Mojo walked from behind the tree and sat on his butt.

It was my cue, I guess.

I picked him up in my arms and carried him back home.

I ALMOST WENT TO SCHOOL WITH WHAT I HAD ON, BUT THEN I remembered a very important point.

I was Jake Winsted's girlfriend now. There was no way that I could be seen in what was akin to rags, and bags the size of Rhode Island under my eyes. And so, I glammed it up a little.

Being the opposite of a girly girl, only two make up items graced my nightstand. Mascara and lip gloss. I slathered on a healthy coating of each and pinched my pale cheeks to give them some color. I added hair gel to my curls to give them some semblance of control and picked out a long sleeved, dark blue dress that came right above my knee and a pair of tall boots. A quick coating of nail polish completed my look.

I examined myself in the mirror and smiled. It was amazing that a little makeup and hair gel could make me feel like a completely different person. Someone confident. Someone in control. Did that make me shallow? Maybe, but honestly, I was too tired to care. I transferred my books from my bookbag to an oversized bag that went nicely with my outfit and headed out the door.

The house smelled like last night's spaghetti. I glanced in to the kitchen. It was a complete disaster. Red sauce splattered the dishes, the counters, the cabinets. The salad was turning brown after being left out all night and the garlic bread looked like it could be used as a blunt weapon.

I shook my head. I was not cleaning it up. As of right now, Bella French was officially off kitchen duty.

Daddy was the one who was unemployed. He could clean up behind himself.

Where was he, anyway?

I looked in to the living room, then at his open door. He didn't appear to be here. Hadn't I heard him moving around this morning? Where could he have gone? Job hunting? It was only seven in the morning and he didn't say goodbye. Daddy always said goodbye, whether we were fighting or not. Was he that mad at me? Did he really think that I hated him? Had I caused irreparable damage to our relationship with my harsh words?

Words of truth, I reminded myself. Everything I said was the truth. Except the hate part. But everything else I meant. He'd realize that ... eventually.

Sighing, I grabbed a green apple out of the fruit bowl and took a big bite. Daddy and I fought, but we still loved each other. He couldn't be mad at me forever, could he?

The sweet pulp got stuck in the lump that formed in my throat.

I was right about everything I said, I reminded myself. I was right.

I took another bite of my apple and walked out of the apartment after locking the door behind me.

18

I met Ariel and Jasmine outside of my apartment. Every morning, we took the subway to school together. Taking the subway alone sucked. It was only two stops, but they lasted forever and I always got stuck sitting next to the person who smelled like dirty socks or who fell asleep on my shoulder.

Gotta love New York, right?

When I approached them, Ariel and Jasmine were already hovering over Ariel's phone, deep in conversation.

Ariel threw her arms around me from the front.

"Oh my god, Bella. You look great!"

Jasmine hung back and smiled.

"New boyfriend, new look, huh?" she asked.

I groaned. "You know?"

"Are you kidding?" Jasmine asked. "Everyone knows! You are the new queen of St. Mary's Academy right now. Boy, is Dana going to be jealous."

I rolled my eyes and started walking toward the subway.

"I don't think so." No matter what I wore, I was no Dana Rich. Still, the comparison was nice.

"I'm serious! Dana and Jake were like Romeo and Juliet, sans the death. And now you have risen from the unwashed masses to take Jake out from under her nose. Bold move, girl."

She gave me a high-five. I half-heartedly returned it.

"I didn't actually take him," I corrected her. "They were broken up. He kissed me and asked me to be his girlfriend. I'd be stupid to say no." It wasn't a complete lie. More of a three-quarter truth, really.

"Just be careful," Ariel said. "I mean, we'll be watching your back, but still. Keep an eye out for Dana and for Regina."

"Maybe we should start carrying around switch blades and walkie-talkies," Jasmine said. "Just in case they corner you or something."

I chuckled. "I'm not going to carry around a weapon! I'll be fine."

Jasmine put one hand on my shoulder. "Would you consider a whistle?"

"Definitely not!"

"Just a thought."

"Honestly, you two are being a tad dramatic, don't you think?"

Jasmine frowned. "I like to think of myself as a planner."

"Speaking of me," Ariel chimed in. "Did you see my text this morning?"

I shook my head.

"What text?"

"Eric has been texting me all night."

My heart flipped in my chest.

"That's ... that's great, right?"

"Um ... yeah it is! I mean, I knew that we had stuff in common, but talking to him as me, and not as Gelda the Witch, is amazing. We're talking about meeting up this weekend. Maybe by the Sea Port or something."

Ariel's face turned euphoric. She was happy. Really and truly happy. And just like that, my worries about being Jake's fake girlfriend faded away. To see the look of pure joy on Ariel's face was all the validation I needed. I could do this.

"Sounds like you two are a match made in heaven," Jasmine said. She sighed. "My best friends are in love and climbing the social ladder and here I am, alone and lonely."

"What happened to Michael, the boy that went to St. John's

University?" I asked. Jasmine had a thing for older college guys. I still wasn't sure if her parents knew or not.

She waved her hand. "He was a smoker. Ugh. I dropped him like a bad habit." She sighed. "I'm sure that my boy toy is somewhere out there. I just have to find him."

I placed my hand on Jasmine's sagging shoulder. I knew what it was like to feel left out. I never wanted Jasmine to feel that way. Maybe Jake had another older friend that Jasmine would be interested in. I'd have to remember to ask him.

"Come on," she said. "Let's hurry up before we miss our train."

The three of us set off to the train station in the November sunshine. It was cooler than yesterday and my thin coat did nothing for the chill.

The streets were nearly empty. Sidewalks twinkled in the sunrise. Light reflected off the skyscraper windows. Blue sky stretched between gigantic buildings. The smell of coffee and bacon drifted from the bodegas that we passed. The city was beautiful. Not country beautiful like my grandfather's farm was, but beautiful in a cramped, corporate, raw sort of way. I loved it. I'd miss it if I had to leave.

Please God, don't let me leave.

"So," Jasmine said. Her voice had a lyrical accent that made me jealous. It gave her an exoticness that I could never possess. "You and Jake going out tonight?"

I inwardly groaned. Was Jake expecting me to go out with him after school hours, other than on the dinner date he mentioned? Hopefully not. It amazed me how fast my opinion of him changed. Ten minutes with him and I was irreparably turned off.

"Maybe. We haven't made any solid plans."

Those green specked, chocolate eyes gazed at me as if they knew secrets I didn't know I had. Her mouth pulled down into a frown and she shrugged.

I crossed my arms. "What?"

She shrugged. "I would have thought that you'd be more excited. I mean, you've been talking about this guy for nearly three years and now you have him. Why aren't you happy?"

My arms dropped. Was it that obvious?

"I'm happy," I lied.

"You don't look happy," Jasmine said.

"That's because I'm tired. Besides, people in relationships aren't happy all of the time."

"Yes, but I don't think the honeymoon phase has a twenty-four hour expiration date."

I waved her away, trying to inject some faux happiness in to my face.

Ariel turned back to Jasmine, a warm smile on her face.

"Leave her alone. She's probably just nervous."

"Shouldn't she be glowing? She's not glowing."

Ariel laughed. "She's not pregnant!"

"Not that kind of glow. The glow of a woman who's found love."

"You read too many romance novels," Ariel said with a snort.

Jasmine clasped her hands together, a serene smile on her face. "I call them instructional manuals," Jasmine said, her voice dreamy.

"Instructions on what?" I asked. "How to throw yourself dramatically on a bed and sob?"

"If necessary," Jasmine replied with a smile.

"You two are crazy," Ariel said. "You should be more like me."

"Hoarders?" Jasmine asked.

Ariel shook her head. "No. Practical. And I told you that my things are collector's items."

Jasmine caught my eye, giving me a *yeah right* look. Ariel's room was filled with old cork screws, smoking pipes and intricately designed forks. She was one candlestick away from a televised intervention.

"Beanie babies are collector's items," Jasmine argued. "You are more like an unpaid recycling center."

"As opposed to the animal rescue center that you live in?" Ariel said. "With your millions of birds and your crazy giant, biting cat that hates me."

"I only have twenty-three birds," Jasmine corrected. "And my cat does not bite. She nibbles."

"My tetanus shot says different," Ariel said.

We walked down the stairs to the subway. The smell of urine and steam immediately assaulted my senses.

"That settles it," I said, trying not to gag on the strong smell. Ariel and Jasmine didn't seem to notice it. "We are going to meet at my house tonight to study. No recyclables-"

"Collectors' items." Ariel said.

"And no petting zoos."

"A Savannah F-1 cat and enough birds to feed said cat."

"So, that's why you keep so many birds!" Ariel cried.

Jasmine shrugged. "He's huge! What else are we supposed to feed him? Kibbles and bits?"

"You two," I laughed, "are impossible."

"So says the new Queen of St. Mary's Academy," Jasmine said as we stood on the train platform. She gave me a fake bow. "All hail the queen."

We all giggled, nearly falling over as we stepped on to the train.

I wondered what school would be like today. Jake didn't text me to tell me what the plan was and I didn't text him either. Now that I thought about it, we didn't have each other's phone numbers, so texting was impossible. This wasn't a well thought out plan. It was a web of lies that we were going to get caught in.

Jasmine had already sensed that something was off. Would she question Jake? If he thought I wasn't playing the role, would he tell Ariel what I'd had done? Why did I agree to play this game of his?

Jasmine gave a conspirator's grin to Ariel. She gave it back.

"Since no one else has the guts to, I'm just going to ask it," she said. "Are the rumors true? Is he an amazing kisser?"

I wasn't exactly a kissing connoisseur. I'd only kissed two boys in my life.

I looked down at my shoes. "It was okay. Kind of short, but okay."

"Just okay?" Ariel pressed.

I made a face. "It was only our first kiss and I was nervous."

"That bad, huh?" Jasmine asked, taking my hand. "You know, I hear it takes a while for a couple to get used to each other. To see what each other likes and to work on it. Maybe that's what's going on with you and Jake?"

I raised an eyebrow. "Did you read that in one of your romance novels?"

She shrugged. "Romance. *Dr. Phil.* Does it matter?" She put her hand on my shoulder and pinned me with a serious expression, like she was a wise old grandmother or something. "The point is that it's good advice. Keep working on it and it will get better."

I chuckled and rolled my eyes, my cheeks growing hot. I had no plans to work on kissing Jake.

The train roared in to the station, blessedly halting our conversation. The truth was, Jake was handsome and a decent kisser, but he was also rude and condescending. Plus, our relationship wasn't real. There was nothing to work on. Nothing to perfect. I doubt he'd even kiss me again, and I was one hundred percent okay with that.

The three of us stepped on to the train and squeezed in to a seat that was only big enough for two people. We giggled as we tried and failed to maneuver our way into a position that was close to comfort.

To my left, a dark head wrapped in an even darker zip up hoodie caught my eye.

Cole.

What was he doing on this train? I always assumed he drove to school with his brother and sister.

"Don't stare," Jasmine whispered in to my ear. I turned to her grinning face, my cheeks heating up again.

"I'm not staring," I argued.

"You were," she said with a knowing look.

I rolled my eyes. Cole was my nemesis. I would only stare at him if I had laser beams instead of eyeballs and could set him on fire.

The train came to a stop and we maneuvered out of the too tight seat in the most hilarious way possible. Finally free, we stood, smoothed down our clothes, and walked out of the subway car.

"We're going to get bagels," Jasmine said. "You want one?"

I shook my head. I had a half-eaten apple in my bag already. Besides, with my father losing his job, I'd have to watch every penny.

"No thanks. You go ahead."

They nodded, moving against the crowd to a breakfast stand toward the end of the platform.

I stood a little away from the wall, waiting for them.

Across the tracks, a heap of darkly colored clothes moved. At first,

I thought it was a trash bag, but on further inspection, it was a person. I couldn't tell if it was a man or a woman, but I did notice the white of its eyes, and the two fingers that it held up.

The peace sign.

The person was as still as a statue, fingers in the air, not moving.

What was that person's life like? I wondered. What path had they taken to end up living in a subway? Was this where mine and my father's lives were heading?

I shook the thought from my head. I would not think about Daddy and his lost jobs today.

A flash of black rushed past me.

"Cole?"

He stopped his march toward the outside and turned to look at me.

"What?!"

The look he gave me made my heart speed up and my stomach clench. It was hostile and furious.

I took a step back.

"Nothing."

He glared at me for a moment more before he took off again, jogging up the stairs in to the sunshine.

What happened to Cole since yesterday? Why did he look at me as if he wanted me to burst into flames? The teasing was one thing, but this was something else. Something darker. We'd been frustrated and irritated with each other, but never openly hostile. What was his problem?

I put my hand over my heart to stop its reckless beating.

"That looked intense," Ariel said, chewing on a small piece of bagel. "What did he want?"

I shrugged, hoping the movement would seem nonchalant.

"Just saying hi. Or not saying hi, I guess."

I shook my head. If anyone was furious, it should have been me. Cole had been the one who teased and prodded me all day. What did I ever do to him?

"Are you guys still studying at your place tonight?" Ariel asked.

"Yeah. I think so."

If he didn't kill me with an axe first.

Ariel nodded thoughtfully. "Okay. Call me if you need me to come over if, you know, whatever."

"Whatever?" I asked. "So, you're going to fight him off if he attacks me or something?"

"I'll hit him with a right and a left, New York style." She smiled at me.

I smiled back.

Jasmine jogged up to me, one tea and one coffee in her hands. She handed me the coffee. I hadn't asked for it, but it was exactly what I needed. Jasmine was awesome like that.

"Hurry up. We're going to be late!" she called, her backpack bouncing against her back as she fled toward the stairs.

Ariel and I looked at each other and ran to catch up.

19

The second we made it back to street level, my phone buzzed. I pulled the *Daisy Duck* case from my pocket and looked at the screen. It was a *Facebook* message. Someone wanted to be friends. Curious, I typed in my passcode and looked at my friend request screen. Jake's profile picture looked back at me.

A friend request? What did that mean? Dana wouldn't see our conversations. She and I weren't friends on *Facebook*. What could he want?

I accepted his request and noticed that I had a new message. I clicked that, too. It was also from Jake.

Jake: Why don't I have your phone number? Meet me in front of Ms. Davis's class before first period. Don't be late.

I bit my inner cheek, feeling used. I turned to Ariel, but her face was in her phone, her smile bright.

Jasmine caught my eye.

"Ariel and Eric sitting in a tree. K I S-"

Ariel shushed her and looked around.

"What are you shushing me for? If it was me, I would be sitting on the roof of his car right now."

"We're trying to keep it light," Ariel hissed. "We don't want any gossip like-"

She looked at me and her mouth clicked shut.

"Like me," I said, hurt spearing through me. "You don't want to become a spectacle like me?"

She sighed.

"Me and Eric are just friends right now, and I don't want to ruin that," she said. "That's all."

I wanted to tell her that my spectacle was the reason why her and Eric were friends. I wanted to tell her that this was her chance to see if it was real or not and that in two weeks, she may discover that Eric wasn't the dream boat she'd thought he was, just as I'd discovered with Jake.

But I didn't say any of those things. Instead, I hugged my heavy bag to my chest.

"I have to meet Jake," I said. "I'll see you guys later."

"Bella, wait-"

I didn't turn around. Instead, I walked in to school and down the hallway to Ms. Davis's class.

"Hey, Bella." I looked up at the mention of my name. Claire Thomas made eye contact with me, smiled and waved. I awkwardly waved back. Claire Thomas was a cheerleader, which meant that she would never demean herself to speak to me.

"Hey, Bella." Jeffrey Wolowitz, or Wally as he was known around school, nodded and waved at me, too.

"Hey, B. What's up?"

"Bella French!"

"Oh my god. I love your dress!"

"Your hair looks awesome today, Bella!"

Students who'd never looked at me before now knew my name. Kids on student council, cheerleaders, jocks. Suddenly, I existed to them. Suddenly, I was no longer invisible.

My heart sped up in excitement and joy. I adjusted my walk, swinging my hips like I'd seen Dana do. Casually flipping my curls over one shoulder, I waved to my very new, very adoring public. By the time Mrs. Davis's class came in to view, I was on cloud nine, my confidence through the roof.

Being popular was already turning out to be pretty amazing!

Out of the corner of my eye, I saw another student approach Kenny with something in his hand. It looked like a wad of money. Kenny took the money from him, pushed off a locker, and the two of them walked further down the hall.

An odd sense of doom washed over me, but when I saw Jake leaning confidently against the wall, waiting for me, that all went out the window. He was absolutely gorgeous this morning in his football jersey, jeans and high-topped sneakers. His blond hair was purposefully messy and his skin without a blemish. He gave me an easy smile and held out his hand. I took it. His gaze caressed mine and for a moment, I forgot that this was fake. I forgot that we were making Dana jealous. I even forgot that I was supposed to hate him after the way he'd treated me yesterday. In this moment, it was just him and me, those beautiful eyes, and the memories of fantasies, wishes and dreams.

"Hi," Jake said, pulling me close and placing my hand on his shoulder.

I gave him my best smile. He leaned in for a kiss, but at the last second, I turned my cheek. His shoulders tightened beneath my fingers.

"What was that about?" he asked, his tone low enough for only me to hear. He pretended to nuzzle my neck, but I could sense the tension in his large body.

"No kissing on the lips."

"Why not?"

Because I don't kiss fake boyfriends, I wanted to say. But I didn't.

"I just don't want to," I replied.

"You wanted to yesterday."

"You caught me off guard yesterday."

"So?"

"So, this isn't real." *And I don't want to get any more confused than I already am*, I silently added. "Let's keep it on the cheek, okay?"

"That's ridiculous. I'm not kissing my girlfriend on the cheek like some loser."

"I reserve my lips for real boyfriends. You know, ones who remember my name and that I go to this school?"

He let out a hot breath against my neck. I cringed.

"Fine," he said. "I'll let it slide for now."

That statement was like cold water dumped on my head. For now? What did that mean? What was Jake planning? I got the feeling that, whatever it was, I was not going to like it.

"Anyway," he said. "we have to exchange numbers. I am not going to be *Facebook* messaging you all the time."

He placed one hand on my hip and maneuvered me so my back was pressed against the locker.

I kept my smile in place and peeked over his tall shoulder.

Sure enough, Dana was glaring at us. No. Not us. At me.

But why would her anger be directed at me? Where was her new boyfriend?

"Is she looking?" Jake pressed.

"Yes," I replied.

"Is she pissed?" he asked.

"Super."

"Excellent."

The first period bell rang and he gave me a peck on the cheek. His lips moved from my cheek to my ear.

"For now," he said. There was an undertone there that made my blood run cold.

Was that a threat? I wondered. No. It couldn't be. Jake was a jerk, but he wouldn't threaten me.

"I'll see you at lunch," he said, stepping back and walking in to his classroom.

A shiver raced from my ear down to my toes.

He didn't just threaten me, did he? Jake would never do something like that, would he?

I pulled on my book bag straps and started to walk back down the hallway to my first period class.

Out of the corner of my eye, I saw Cole's blue eyes examining me, his mouth in a hard line.

Just as the second chime of the bell rang, he was gone.

"Hey!" Ariel rounded a corner, sans bookbag. She waved at me, phone in hand. "I was just coming to find you. You have to see this text."

"What text?" I danced in my shoes. If I was late for Art, Mr. Weathers was going to be pissed.

"From, well, you know."

By the way her eyes widened, I knew immediately. It was a text from Eric. My curiosity got the best of me, and I stopped my power walk.

She squealed, her cheeks reddening in excitement as she handed me the phone.

I took it and read the message on the screen.

Eric: Guys wait their entire lives for girls like you.

Wow. Was he for real?

"Aw. He's so sweet," I said, handing the phone back to her. "He seems to really like you." I smiled to hide my confusion.

"I know, right! I really hope that I don't mess this up."

Impossible.

I placed my hand on her shoulder.

"If he really likes you and you really like him, there is no way that you could mess this up."

Her smile brightened.

"Really?"

I nodded. "Really."

She threw her arms around me, almost knocking me backward.

"This is like some sort of weird, beautiful dream. I don't know how it happened, but I definitely do not want to wake up." She pulled away, her cheeks reddening in happiness. "Now go to class before you get a tardy."

It was too late for that, but maybe I could get Mr. Weathers to let me slide this once.

"I'll see you in second period," I said.

"See you."

I jogged to my first period art class. Half of my mind was trying to figure out how I was going to get out of this tardy. The other half of me was happy that my friend was happy.

I slid in to my seat in art class just as Mr. Weathers walked in and placed his bag on his desk.

He looked at me for a moment, then looked down at his bag.

"Well, Ms. French, since we both were late this morning, I'll let it slide. Just, don't let it happen again, okay?"

"Yes, sir."

I opened my book and took out my pen as Mr. Weathers began to write on the black board.

20

Being in the spotlight was exhausting, but in a good way. Like a day at *Disney World*. For the past three years, I'd only spoken to Ariel and Jasmine. Today alone, I'd had a gazillion conversations. People wanted to know where I got my dress, who my hair stylist was, where I got my shoes. They wanted to make plans with me and advice on life. They asked me to put in a good word for them at the popular table and asked how things were going with Jake. I'd spoken to more people today than I'd spoken to in my entire life.

It was amazing. I pinched myself three times today and hadn't woken up yet. Yes, this was my reality now. I was officially popular.

"Hey, Bella." Pamela Meyers walked next to me and smiled. My stomach tightened. Pamela was the biggest, cattiest bully in this school. Her victims of choice were defenseless freshman, but she did find the time to make fun of anyone else she felt was different. Just last week, she pulled one of my braids and called me a dog face.

Needless to say, I hated her, and didn't want to hear whatever she had to say to me.

"I'm having some people over this weekend if you and Jake wanted to come. Just some wine coolers and a movie. My mom's totally cool with it. You in?"

Pamela Meyers dunked my head in a toilet on my second day at this school. I still tasted the disgusting blue water. Now here she was, blonde, busty and acting like we were friends.

Newsflash. We weren't.

I pretended to think about her invitation, but what I was really thinking about was my impending pettiness.

I sucked in a breath through my teeth and made a face that oozed of regret.

"Oh. I'm sorry. We have plans this weekend but if anyone cancels, we'll let you know."

Her smile drooped like a dying planet. It felt like my own little slice of revenge.

"Great. Hope you can make it."

Pamela, and her droopy smile, moved deeper in to the crowd and out of sight.

Boy, did that feel good. Not only did her party sound lame, but I didn't want to be around someone who was a cruel jerk to people who weren't like her. I already had to deal with Jake the jerk. I did not want to deal with Pamela, too.

Ariel and Jasmine met me at the door. We grabbed our trays and picked our sandwiches from the lunch line. When I turned to follow them to our regular seats, a wave caught my eye.

Jake was waving me over to his table. A table full of every jock who had fifth period lunch, plus Regina.

Did she always hang out with guys? Where were her girl friends?

"Guess you better go sit with your new boyfriend," Jasmine said, sending me a giddy smile.

I frowned. I didn't want to sit at a table full of strangers. Especially one who threatened my life yesterday. I wanted to sit with my friends.

I bit my lower lip.

"Come with me?" I asked. "Please?"

They both shook their head at me.

"You have to be invited to sit at the royal table and our invites haven't arrived yet," Ariel said. I sensed the disappointment in her voice. "Go on. We'll be here waiting for you when you get back."

Jasmine's nod was enthusiastic. "You look great. They'll love you."

Or see right through me.

I took in a deep breath, turned from my friends and walked over to Jake's table. It was the first time that I had sat with anyone but Ariel and Jasmine at lunch since I came to this school. My heart squeezed painfully, wanting to be where it felt safe instead of on high alert.

Eric and Jake made a space for me, and I sat between them with twelve guys looking back at me. Everyone except for Cole, who refused to look my way.

I recognized the guys from around school and at sporting events. It was a hodgepodge of the football team, the lacrosse team and one baseball player.

"Guys," Jake said, a big grin lighting up his face. "This is Bella French, my girlfriend. Bella, this is the guys."

He didn't introduce them by name, which I thought was odd. Was he reinforcing the fact that I was a placeholder girlfriend, or did he just not care to tell me who everyone was? Was everyone in on our little charade?

"Jeff Hobbs," said the boy sitting across from me. He had dark blond hair and a slim build. He was on the lacrosse team. "Matt Hobbs, my brother." His brother had the same dark blond hair, but his eyes were a black, instead of brown like his brother's, and his nose was slightly crooked. A hunk of sandwich hung from his mouth and he looked surprised that his brother had made an introduction at all. He gave me a little wave, then went back to devouring his food.

"Eric Shipman," Eric said, holding his hand out to shake mine. "We met yesterday."

Up close, Eric Shipman was breathtakingly beautiful. Steel blue eyes that tilted up at the ends. Jet black hair, a full mouth, high cheekbones. He was a full head taller than me and always had a little smile on his face, as if the world was so full of life and joy that he couldn't help but be happy in it. A spicy mix of expensive cologne and aftershave drifted in to my nose. It reminded me of warm sand, salty water and fresh air.

I could see why Ariel drooled over him. He was gorgeous.

"I remember," I replied, a little breathless.

He dipped his head to my ear. "You're Ariel's friend, right?" he asked.

I nodded.

How I managed to sit between two of the hottest guys in school, I'll never know.

"You want me to put in a good word for you?" I asked, surprised that I hadn't melted into a puddle by now.

He gave me a sly smile.

"Make it two."

Le pant. Le sigh. Even though I didn't like him like that, I swooned a bit at having Eric so near. I wish I knew what Jake had said to him. Was Eric fully on board with the plan or had Jake just nudged him in Ariel's direction? The questions killed me.

On Jake's other side was Kenny. Kenny gave me a bad feeling. Like I was at the top of a roller coaster about to drop. Only, there was no bottom. Just water, sharp rocks and sharks. Big sharks.

With his thin body, beady eyes, and nearly non-existent chin, he looked like a weasel. A drug dealing weasel. His sandwich shook a bit as he raised it to his mouth. He hadn't gotten through two chews when another guy came up behind him and tapped him on the shoulder. A moment later, they were gone. I knew Kenny sold marijuana, but I never remembered so many kids buying it off him. Especially not on a Tuesday. Why was he so busy all of a sudden?

The conversation rose like a tide when one of the kids toward the end of the table—I recognized him as a wide receiver named Mo—started talking about the new car his parents had promised him for Christmas. I wasn't sure why anyone would want a car in New York City, but the rich kids used them as status symbols. They roared down the streets with their *BMW*s, *Ferrari*s and *Bentley*s, and crammed them in the tiny parking lot behind the school. The kids who weren't super rich, like me, rode the subway.

"It's a *Volkswagen Golf*," he pouted. "I asked for an *Audi*."

"That sucks," Flynn, a kid sitting next to Mo said.

"Why does that suck?" I asked.

The whole table looked at me as if to say, dumb girl.

I shifted uncomfortably in my seat.

"Because who wants a Golf?" Mo asked.

"It's the same car," I replied.

The table looked at me as if I had two heads.

"Yeah," Mo said. "Okay. Why don't you stick to clothes and mani-pedis? The big boys are talking now."

A few of the other guys laughed, infuriating me. Just because I was a girl didn't mean that I was ignorant about cars. My dad was a mechanic, after all. I wasn't a show off, but this guy needed to be taught a lesson, big time.

Lucky for him, I was in a teaching mood.

"Under the hood, the *Audi S3* and the *Volkswagen Golf R* are just about the same car. Only the Golf is better. They both have a 2.0 liter turbo 292 horsepower engine, but with the Golf, you can get a manual, giving you more control. The *Audi* only comes with a duel clutch automatic. You should count yourself fortunate that your parents know cars, because you obviously don't."

The mouths of the boys around me fell open and I smirked. Even Jake looked impressed.

Check and mate.

"How do you know all that?" Jake asked.

I shrugged. "My dad fixes, uh, works with cars for a living," I said. "I kind of picked up a few things."

There was a brief silence of disbelief, followed by a deluge of questions about cars and parts and the best engines. I was in my glory. That was one thing that my dad did right. He taught me about cars. If I had my own car, which I didn't, I could change my own oil, fix my own flat tires, swap out brake pads and rotors and I knew the difference between coolant and power steering fluid.

I silently thanked my dad for the knowledge, and answered questions the best that I could.

"Wow, Jake. Where did you pick this one up?" John Hobbs asked. "She's no cheerleader."

"Not yet," Jake replied. He looked at me with a proud smile and threw his arm over my shoulder. "But we're working on it."

The table broke out into laughter and, for once in this school, the popular kids were laughing with me and not at me. For once, things were going right. For once, I was not invisible.

And then it happened.

Ice cold milk sloshed over my head, running in to my eyes, down my dress and in to my shoes. Even my toes were milky.

The lunchroom went silent.

My lungs tightened. I was so shocked by the cold milk, and the fact that I was covered in it that I didn't know what to say. What to think.

"Oops."

I knew that voice. Regina.

Enraged, I banged my fist on the table and stood up.

"You did that on purpose!"

"I told you that you had twenty-four hours to walk away from my brother. Time's up."

"So you dumped milk on me?"

Not only was she crazy, she couldn't count. I had four hours left until my time was up.

She crossed her arms over her chest and glared at me.

"Maybe next time you'll listen when I tell you something."

I shoved her.

I'd never shoved another living person in my life, but in that moment, I was pissed off! More pissed off than I had ever been.

Regina stumbled back, flailing her arms to find something to keep her upright.

I turned around, grabbed whatever was in reach and started pelting her. Sandwiches, milk cartons, bowls of salad, cookies, someone's lunch box. Every item was a dart, aimed at Regina's hair, her face, her clothes.

She landed on the table behind her and put her arms up to cover herself from the food assault.

"Bella, that's enough."

Jake's voice stroked my anger. I whipped around to face him.

"She poured milk on me!"

"She's my sister."

"I don't care!"

I grabbed the last sandwich from the table when, like lightning,

Jake stood and grabbed my hand, forcing me to drop the bread and meat.

"I said, that's enough," he growled.

I hated him. I hated him and his stupid sister.

Her hands lowered and she stood, pushing food and milk from her ruined clothes, her eyes wide in shock.

I took a step toward her.

"Don't you ever come near me again," I said, my voice lethal. "Do you understand me?"

Ariel and Jasmine had come up behind me. Ariel took one of my hands, and Jasmine took the other and together, they pulled me toward the doors.

"Time to go, Bella," Ariel said.

"Don't ever come near me again!" I screamed again.

Regina looked taken aback, like she couldn't believe that I had stood up to her.

She had it coming.

Who knew that it would take Regina dumping milk over my head to make me realize that I could fight back?

Ariel yanked me and I followed her through the lunch room doors. Behind me, the entire student body applauded.

21

Mrs. Grace, the assistant principal, had kindly waived Saturday detention for the lunchroom debacle. Apparently, Regina's assault record proceeded her. By the way Mrs. Grace smiled, I could tell that she was glad that Regina finally got a taste of her own medicine. I did have to apologize though, which I did through clenched teeth. Regina didn't respond. Oddly enough, she didn't look entirely upset either.

Maybe this was some sort of test that her and Jake cooked up? Maybe she gained some respect for me since I'd fought back against her? Either way, the Winsteds were officially on my list of weird families.

I walked in to seventh period study hall dressed in my gym clothes. I was a mess. No. Not just a mess. A hot mess. My hair was far from its earlier cuteness after I washed it with Jasmine's shampoo and conditioner. Products that were not meant for curly hair, by the way. I braided it into two braids, but even those were frizzing without the requisite gel or mousse that I normally added. And now I had to go sit in front of a boy who looked as sour as the milk I'd left rotting on the floor of the lunch room.

Why was this my life?

Cole sat at our usual table, books in front of him, pencil ready.

I slid in to my seat and put down my bags.

Would he be angry at me for pelting his sister with meat and fixings? Jake surely was. He'd told me how inappropriate my behavior was via text. I'd responded with two emojis. One was a cow. One was a pile of poop. I hoped that he was smart enough to get the point.

"Let's start on chapter two," Cole said, not looking at me.

What had I done to him? Why was he treating me this way?

I never thought I'd say it, but I kind of missed our banter. Yes, he was a cocky jerk, but this boy sitting in front of me was b-o-r-i-n-g.

For forty-five agonizing minutes, he quizzed me on French without even glancing at me. When I got an answer wrong, he simply said wrong, told me the correct answer, and asked me the question again. If I got the answer right, which I of course, did, he moved on to the next question.

It was tedious and not at all what I was used to. I mean, it was nice that Cole wasn't teasing me for once, but it was as if all the life had drained from him, leaving this angry, sullen husk of my arch nemesis.

I didn't know whether to be happy about it or sad.

When the bell rang, he didn't say anything. No goodbye. No see you tomorrow. No great job, kid.

He just stood up and walked away.

What was his problem?

☙ 22 ❧

When I got home, I thoroughly scrubbed my hair and skin in the shower. After maneuvering through a fresh pile of poop in the hallway, I walked in to my room and attacked my curls, brushing, combing, gelling and smoothing them back into their two braids.

I missed my straight hair, even though I'd only had it for two days, but my curls were a part of me. A little piece of my mother she'd left behind. I smiled at the thought of her wild curls and ever-present smile. I missed her so much.

Mojo ambled in to the room and sat beneath my window. He had gone from completely ignoring me in the living room to completely ignoring me in my bedroom. It was as if he wanted me to know that he was not speaking to me and so he made dramatic gestures to make his point clear.

"I get it, Mojo," I said. "You're ignoring me. Point taken."

His little black nose went in to the air and he laid down on the floor, still staring at the wall below the window.

I bent down in front of him, well his back, and fake frowned.

"You look like you could use some cheering up," I said, stroking his brown head. He let me, though his body was stiff. After a moment, I came up with the perfect plan.

My phone was still in my gym shorts pocket. I pulled it out and clicked on the cute pink Music icon. I selected the perfect song and grabbed a hairbrush.

It was time to get Mojo out of this funky mood the way my mother would.

Through song.

The opening chords of *Sussudio* by *Phil Collins* came on, and I put a hair clip over the tie of my towel so that it wouldn't slip off. I whipped my braids back and forth, my body bouncing and danced to the song that I'd heard and sung so many times before. I'd even thrown in a little spin. Not that Mojo cared. He continued looking bitterly at the wall, in his best attempt at disinterest.

When the first verse came on, I belted it out like never before, pointing at Mojo's back with my free hand.

When the pup didn't budge, I turned the music up and sang louder; danced harder.

Still nothing.

Finally, with no other way to make Mojo understand, I picked him up in my arms and danced with him around the room.

"It feels so good if I just say the words ... Su-su-sudio!"

The trumpet section came on, signaling the song was almost at its end. I put Mojo down on the bed and did a little shimmy in front of him.

At the end of the song, I bowed, then knelt in front of him. He was panting. Almost smiling.

"Did you like that, boy?" I asked.

He must've forgotten our stand-off, because he licked my cheek, barked once and panted some more.

"I'll take that as a yes." I threw my arms around him, hugging his little neck. "Let's not fight anymore, okay? We're family now. That means you love me and I love you. Deal?"

Mojo barked again. I know that this wasn't human conversation, but boy, did it feel good to get along for once. Maybe he'd even start to walk on a leash without me carrying him. My arms would be grateful for that.

He barked again. Only, this time, it wasn't directed at me. It was directed over my shoulder.

I turned around.

Cole was standing in the doorway, his eyes wide, mouth open, his body tense.

I screamed and immediately covered myself with my hands, which was ridiculous because I was still wearing the towel that covered me down to my knees. My cheeks turned beet red, my face on fire.

How long had he been standing there? Why didn't he say something?

"Get out of here you ... you ... peeping Tom!"

His head shook slightly, as if awakening himself from a trance. He closed his mouth with a click, muttered sorry and moved out of my doorway, presumably in to the living room. I threw myself at the door, closing it tight.

My heart raced, as if trying to escape from my chest. I imagined it jumping out the window and, for a moment, wished that I could, too.

Cole had just seen me singing to my dog in a bath towel. My stomach hurt so bad I thought I would puke. I couldn't face him now. It would be too embarrassing. I slid down the door, the wood rough against my skin. My head fell back and I let out a breath.

God. Why did these things happen to me? Why didn't he say something?

The thought made my lungs tight. Anger mixed with my embarrassment then overpowered it.

If Cole thought he could just walk in to people's houses and stare at them, he had another think coming.

I threw on a pair of shorts and a capped sleeve *Wonder Woman* t-shirt and stomped out of the bedroom.

Cole was sitting on the couch. His eyes were glued to the floor. His body was still.

"I don't know how you operate in your neighborhood, but here in Brooklyn, you knock before you walk in to a stranger's house!"

"I did knock," he said, not looking at me. "The door was cracked and I heard music so I let myself in."

"You can't just let yourself in. This is Brooklyn. People get shot for that sort of thing."

"Shouldn't you be glad that it was me and not some creep." His shaky fingers slid through his hair. "Jeez. If it had been someone else, do you know what could have happened? They could have ... I mean ... Jeez, Bella!" His voice raised to a roar and he jumped to his feet, his eyes full of fire. "Lock your freaking door!"

His outburst momentarily halted my anger. His eyes pinned to mine and there was something there. Concern. Fury. That sadness that hung over him like a shadow. There was so much emotion there that my lungs tightened. I swallowed to loosen them.

He broke eye contact, his gaze dancing around the room. Looking at anything but me.

I didn't want to admit it, but he was right. If the door had been open then it was lucky that Cole had found it first. Who knows what could have happened otherwise?

I cleared my still tight throat and clasped my hands behind me.

"We both have raised valid points," I said, my voice even and sure. "I should have made sure that the door was locked and you should have announced yourself when you saw me ... uh ... whenever."

He turned his back to me, dropped his head and placed his hands on his hips.

"I think that my point is a little more valid than yours," he said, not turning around.

"Then we agree to disagree. Let's get the project over with and never speak of this again. Deal?"

"Whatever."

He threw up one hand and dropped to the couch, sliding as far away from me as he could.

I rolled my eyes. Why was Cole so concerned about me anyway? He didn't get to treat me like a mutant then pretend to be concerned about my safety. He didn't get to do that. It wasn't allowed.

I pulled my notebook from the table and muttered, "You should have said something when you saw me in my towel."

"Learn to lock your doors," he replied quickly.

I frowned at the side of his head and opened my notebook. He was right about one thing. This project needed to be done as soon as possible so that Cole and I never had to speak again. Ever. The sooner he left, the better.

"So, we're working on a *Midsummer's Night's Dream*?" I asked.

He frowned. We hadn't talked about what Shakespearian work we were going to do, but *A Midsummer's Night's Dream* was my favorite. If he said no, I planned to fight for it, using idle threats if necessary. But it wasn't necessary. Cole's jaw clenched and his eyelids fluttered, like he was holding back a comment.

"Yeah. Whatever."

My mouth dropped open. I had made a group decision and Cole didn't fight me on it. It was the first thing that we didn't fight over since, well, ever. My embarrassment and irritation dimmed at my small victory.

"Okay then."

I pretended to write something on my paper, just so that my hands could look busy. I wasn't exactly sure what we were supposed to be doing and Cole wasn't saying much of anything. Were we working on the essay first or the dramatic piece? I had no idea, but judging by the way his pen flew across the pages in his notebook, apparently Cole did.

What was he writing? I raised an eyebrow, and leaned a little closer to see. It looked like the essay, but he couldn't be writing the essay because we hadn't discussed anything yet.

"What are you writing?" I asked.

"The assignment," he replied shortly.

I restrained myself from gritting my teeth.

"What part of the assignment?"

"All of it."

"All of it?"

"Yes. All of it."

"You can't do the entire assignment by yourself. Ms. Mitchell said that we have to work together."

He dropped his pen in to the middle of his notebook, looked at me and glared.

"I don't want to do anything with you. Especially not this assignment. Why don't you go sing to your dog some more and let me finish working in peace?"

I swore that Cole Winsted was the most irritating, pretentious, jerkiest boy that I had ever met in my life! I saw red, picked up a pillow and threw it at his head. He ducked at the last minute, his glare harsher now.

"What was that for?"

"For being a jerk."

"I am doing the assignment!"

"Yes. Alone. It is a group assignment. We are supposed to be doing the assignment as a team. That means that you have to come down off your precious pedestal and actually speak with me! You know, collaborate?"

He raised an eyebrow.

"Spell collaborate and I will let you see what I'm writing."

"How about I spell something else and then sic my dog on you?"

"When did you become so violent?"

"I can't help it. You inspire violence."

A small smile came back to his mouth.

"You still haven't spelled collaborate."

I threw another pillow at his head. He ducked and it went over his head, landing on the other side of the pea green couch.

"Drop dead, Cole!"

"And fail this assignment? No way. If I don't pass this class, my average will be as sucky as yours."

"You are one tenth of a point ahead of me."

"One tenth. One hundredth. Does it really matter?"

My hands balled into fists. My heart beat hard. One more word out of Cole and I knew that I would punch him. I wanted to punch him.

"Resorting to violence again, French? You'd better watch that. One might question your upbringing."

I lost it, flinging myself at him, fist flying. He caught me mid jump, gripping my flailing fist in his hands. Somehow, in the span of an instant, he tucked me against him and fell on to the floor with me on top of him. There was just enough room between us and the coffee table for him to roll on top of me and pin me to the ground.

"Get off me!"

His too wide grin fanned the flames of my anger.

"You are the one who attacked me. Maybe you should apologize before I tell Mommy and Daddy what you're really like."

A hot breath left my nose.

"My mother's dead, you jerk. Now get off me before I scream."

All the blood drained from his face and he immediately sat back on haunches. Furious, I scrambled up and walked across the room, catching my breath. My anger burned so hot that I closed my eyes against it.

"I ... uh ... I'm sorry. I didn't know."

"Well, now you know. Happy?"

"No." He paused. I heard a hitch in his voice. "I ... I didn't mean ... I mean."

"I know what you meant, Cole."

I marched back across the living room and sat down on the couch. I was tired. Tired of arguing with Cole. Tired of him saying terrible things to me. I wanted to get this project over with and for him to get out of my apartment.

I pulled out my notebook and readied my pen.

"What are we writing about?"

Cole was still on the floor, staring at me, regret in his eyes.

"Bella, I'm sorry. I didn't mean-"

"Look. I don't want to talk about it. Let's just get this over with."

His eyes dropped from mine, and he sat back on the couch.

"Fine." His voice turned softer. "I thought we could start with an overview of the play, followed by character breakdown and overall themes. Then the conclusion. Simple."

"Fine. You do the intro, since you seemed to have already started it. I'll do the character break down, you do the overall themes, and I will do the conclusion."

"Okay."

"Fine."

I sat back on the couch and began writing.

Character breakdowns were simple. I would start off with the lovers and their families. Out of all the characters, my favorite was Helena. Poor, sweet Helena. Helena and I had two things in common. We were both in love with an unattainable boy and we'd gotten that boy through extraordinary circumstances. I wondered if Demetrius lived up to everything that Helena imagined after they got married. God knew that Jake didn't.

The tapping of nails pulled my attention from my paper. Mojo had reappeared, making a bee line for Cole. The traitorous pup—a pup that I had just sang my heart out to by the way—put both paws on the couch and whined a little, begging Cole to pat his head.

"Hey, buddy," Cole said. "Enjoy your peep show?"

His voice held less of the tease that it once held. I could see that he was slipping back into the sad, dark, silent Cole that he'd been since yesterday. I didn't care. A quiet Cole equaled a happy Bella.

I tried not to glare as Cole scratched Mojo behind his ear. Mojo panted happily, before walking right past me, sitting on his bed and watching us.

I expected Cole to say something like, cute dog, or some other small talk that a normal person would say. But he didn't. He continued to work on his paper, his expression darkening by the second. What was with him? Why was he so moody like a girl?

I told myself that I didn't care what Cole felt. He was a jerk who'd basically just insulted my family and who insinuated that I was stupid every chance that he got. If he was in a bad mood, that was not my problem.

My pen flew across the paper, discussing Titania and Oberon's torrid love affair, but it was hard to focus. With Cole's mood slipping further and further over the edge, it was hard to concentrate. My curiosity got the best of me. Cole and I weren't friends, but my inquiring mind had to know why he was so miserable.

"Long night?" I asked.

"You can say that."

"Studying?"

"No. Minding my own business. You?" His eyes rose to meet mine and I was shocked by the anger in them. He wasn't tired. He was pissed. He was pissed at me? If anything, I should be the one pissed with him. Especially after the stunt he pulled with Jake when I fell, the unwarranted room entry and insulting my entire family lineage.

"Why are you so angry at me? What did I do?"

The anger deepened and he slammed his book shut.

"I'll finish my part tonight. Tomorrow, we'll start working on the dramatic scene." His bag rustled as he shoved books back inside of it.

"Is this because I got in a fight with your sister?"

"No." He paused for a moment. "Regina deserved that." A sigh escaped his mouth and his stuffing intensified.

"Well, what is it then? Is it something at home? Is it something with football?"

"You don't like me," he said, his eyes blazing. For some reason, my breath caught in my throat. Goosebumps skittered across my shoulders. My emotion's whipped and whirled within me. Cole's eyes were so full of sadness that it made my heart hurt. "And I don't like you. You said it yourself. We are nemeses. You're the Joker and I'm Batman. We're complete polar opposites."

I frowned, trying to ignore this new, strange feeling that Cole caused to rise within me.

"Why do you get to be Batman?" I didn't know why I said it, but it seemed like the right thing to say at the time.

"It doesn't matter. The point is that you don't get to butt in to my life or ask me what's wrong or how I'm doing."

I shook my head. How heartless did he think I was?

"Uh, not sure if you're aware, but I'm not actually some sort of crazy supervillain whose only goal in life is to screw you over. I'm still a human being. I mean, if you were on fire, I would pee on you to put you out."

He stilled, his face tightening.

"That's very kind of you."

"You can tell me, you know."

"Tell you what?" he asked, his voice barely a whisper.

"You don't have to act surprised. I already know."

I leaned toward him. His eyes were as wide as dinner plates. I could see his Adam's Apple bob beneath his skin. I leaned a little closer, smelling the mix of vanilla and spice that wafted off him. I wasn't sure why my chest was so tight. I swallowed and pulled a mask of sympathy over my face.

"You're on your period, aren't you?"

The smallest hint of a relieved smile ghosted across his lips before it was gone again, lost in his deep frown.

"I'm not in the mood for games," he replied, though some of the edge had left his voice.

"How about one last one? I'll play you for it."

"Play me for what?"

"I'll play you one hand of poker. If I win, you drop this piss poor attitude and go back to the Cole that I want to throat punch on sight."

One of his brows raised high on his forehead.

"And if I win?"

"That depends," I raised an eyebrow, matching his expression. "What do you want?"

I watched his Adam's Apple dance again. He did that a lot when he was nervous. Uncomfortable.

"If I win, nothing changes. I get to be as moody and miserable as I want, whenever I want, however I want and you have to promise not to give me crap for it."

The gauntlet had been thrown. I had to win this game.

This miserable version of Cole sucked big time. There was no way that I was getting stuck with him for two weeks.

I held out my hand.

"Deal."

He shook it. I tried to ignore the way my arm heated in his gentle grip.

"Deal."

Twenty minutes later, we found ourselves at the dining room table, cards shuffled and dealt, eyes watching each other's for any semblance of a tell.

He bounced his leg under the table. Did that mean that he was excited about a good hand, or anxious about a bad one? I couldn't be sure.

"All right, Cole," I said. "Time to put up or shut up."

"You're using idioms now?"

"If they're appropriate."

"I'm surprised that you didn't pull out your cowboy boots and put on *Kenny Rogers*."

"I would have, but I thought that you might be embarrassed, what with you not having cowboy boots and all."

"I don't own any cowboy boots."

"Bummer. It's been said that a man isn't a man until he owns a pair of cowboy boots."

"Is that what they say in the weird, old western town you're from?"

"I'm from North Carolina. That's in the south east. I know that geography isn't your strong suit."

"So, you're a Redneck. Even worse."

I shrugged. "That I may be, but I sure do play a mean hand of poker. Now, show me your cards."

"You first."

"Guests first. House rules."

"This isn't even a house."

"Apartment rules, then."

"Fine."

He put down his cards on the table.

A five, six, seven, eight, and nine of clubs.

"A straight flush," he said, a victorious smile on his face. "Guess you'll have to deal with my piss poor attitude a little longer."

My face fell.

"Yeah," I said. "A little longer."

I placed my cards on the table.

Ace, Queen, King, Jack, and ten of spades. A royal flush.

I won! I stood up, my smile widening as his fell through the floor.

"Now," I said. "Go home, change your tampon, write your paper and come back tomorrow with a better disposition. Can you do that?"

He bit his lower lip and crossed his arms over his chest.

"Rules are rules," I said, leaning across the table. "Maybe you should practice smiling. Go ahead, give me a smile."

He did. He gave me the most gruesome smile that I'd ever seen. All big teeth and crossed eyes and shaking head. He looked like a weirdo monster. I laughed.

"Perfect." I grinned. "Just like that."

He realized that his plan to gross me out failed and he rolled his eyes.

"Whatever. I'm sure that the deck was rigged."

"Probably. I always rig the deck in my favor."

One of his eyebrows quirked, before settling again. It was so fast that I wasn't even sure that he noticed it.

His phone beeped, and he pulled it out of his pocket. The relaxed expression that had settled on his face was replaced with an irritated one.

"I have to go," he said, rising and picking up his bookbag. "Practice your conjugations and how to say what's in a house for French tomorrow."

I saluted him. "Yes, *capitaine*."

He pulled open the front door.

"That's the first French word you've said right all week."

Before I had a chance to reply, he shut the door behind him.

23

Alas, life continued to poke me.

It was already seven thirty and Daddy still wasn't home, nor was he answering his text messages. Where was he? Was he still job hunting? Why wasn't he looking for jobs online like a normal person?

My worry got the best of me, and so to allay my fears, I called Ariel and Jasmine and told them all about Cole, his bad attitude and our poker game.

"I heard that Cole and Jake got in to a big fight in the locker room yesterday after football practice," Jasmine said. "They say that Cole punched him in the face and got suspended from the team."

"He punched Jake?" Ariel asked, her voice high in shock. Ariel had six sisters and to the best of my knowledge, they argued and screamed at each other constantly. Why was hitting so far-fetched to her? Especially since she was so willing to get into brawls for her friends.

"That's what I heard," Jasmine said.

"Does anyone know why he's so mad?" I asked.

"Nope," Jasmine said.

"He ran out of my house after the poker game like his pants were on fire," I said. "Maybe that has something to do with it."

"I don't know," Jasmine said. "Hey. I hear there is a party at Stephanie Pleasant's house on Friday. They said that all of the cool kids are going to be there."

I had no idea how Jasmine always got all the hot gossip. She must've had connections outside of Ariel and I, though I'd never seen her with anyone else.

"They must've lost our invitation in the mail," Ariel said.

"Stephanie Pleasant is a skank," I replied. "I wouldn't want to go to her stupid party anyway."

"Not even if Jake asked you to?" Jasmine said.

I paused. That's right. I was Jake's girlfriend now. If he went to a party, it would look suspicious that I wasn't there.

Crap.

"I guess I'd have to," I said with a sigh.

My phone vibrated and Jake's number flashed across my screen.

I frowned. What did he want?

"Speaking of Jake, girls, I have to go."

I didn't really want to talk to Jake, but I didn't really feel like talking to Ariel and Jasmine any more either. It was late, my dad wasn't home and I was hungry and tired.

I bid goodbye to my friends and picked up Jake's call on the third ring.

"Hello?"

"Bella! What's up?"

His good mood grated on my deteriorating one.

"Hey."

"Happy to hear your voice, too."

I frowned. Was this some sort of game? Was Dana around and that was why he was calling me and being nice? I couldn't be sure.

"Is everything okay?" I asked.

"Yeah, yeah. Everything is fine. I just thought that you would be a little more excited to hear from me."

"Would I? Did you forget that you yelled at me via text earlier? That doesn't exactly inspire anxious anticipation."

He smoothly ignored my comment.

"Most girls in school would be excited to hear from me and seeing as how no one really knew your name before yesterday, I thought that it would be, I don't know, thrilling for you."

I was so not in the mood for his condescending conversation. Was that how he talked to Dana, too? No wonder she'd dumped him. I rolled my eyes so hard that I thought they would pop out of my head.

"What do you want, Jake?"

"Just cementing our plans for this week."

"Plans?"

"Yup. You have the distinct honor of having plans with the one and only Jake Winsted. Prepare for a heavy dose of awesome."

A week ago, I would have killed for this phone call. Now, this phone call just made me want to kill Jake in particular. Was he always so arrogant?

"I'll get my date book," I said. I did not have a date book but I didn't want him to know that. Instead, I grabbed a pen and wrote in the back page of my chemistry notebook.

"Okay. I'm ready."

"I will meet you at my first period class every morning before school starts for a crazy make-out session. There will be tongue, so make sure you floss and gargle. A clean tongue is a happy tongue."

I wanted to break my pencil in half.

"How about I meet you at your first period class every morning and give you a hug instead?"

"Peck on the lips?"

"Kiss on the cheek."

He didn't respond at first. I could feel his frustration through the phone.

"I suppose that I could tell everyone you're a virgin and that we're moving slow because you grew up a prude. But that's only a short-term solution. You can't hold out forever, Bella. Especially not against me."

My skin crawled.

"I'll keep that in mind."

"I guess it's not all bad." His voice sounded farther away, making me think that he was talking more to himself than to me. "It will make me look cooler if we're making out by week two. People will think that I am the king of de-virginizing."

"That's degrading," I stated loudly.

"More degrading than my girlfriend not wanting to kiss me? Definitely not."

"I'm not your girlfriend."

"According to the student body of St. Mary's Academy, you are."

"Did you get dropped on your head as a child?"

"Yes; right in to a pool of rich, young and hot. Moving on to item two."

"Is there really a list?" I asked.

He laughed. "There is always a list, babe."

Great. Perfect. Wonderful.

"Item two. You will dress appropriately for all occasions. Appropriate clothing includes mini-skirts, mini dresses, hair down and blown straight or wavy and heels. Make-up is not optional."

"You're joking."

"Not at all."

"You do realize that I'm doing you a favor, right? You know that I am doing this because you asked me to."

"You are doing this for Arianna."

"Ariel."

"Whatever. Now, what is the price of her happiness worth to you? A shaved leg and a little lipstick? Come on."

"You can't give me a dress code. Especially not in Autumn. I'll freeze to death."

"It's not a dress code. More like guidelines on how to be a girl."

"I don't have to dress up in heels and hooker skirts to be a girl. I could dress in jeans and sweatshirts and still be a girl."

"Biologically."

"Do you know how sexist that sounds? You do realize that it's no longer 1950, right? Women are no longer confined to the kitchen, just waiting to be impregnated while we cook your dinner and mop your floor."

"Dear God. Please press the mute button. I'm not having a conversation about feminism. I am letting you know in the nicest way possible that your clothes are not up to par with your new popularity and that I am going to buy you new ones."

"New ones?" I stuttered.

"Tomorrow, we are ditching school after first period and I will personally take you shopping."

"You're going to take me shopping?"

"Yes."

"Can't I be trusted to pick out my own clothes?"

"You've been picking out your own clothes since Freshman year. The answer to that question is no."

My stomach twisted in knots.

"Item three. Friday night. We will meet up at Stephanie Pleasant's pre-party, then head over to the Stamford Club for an under twenty-one party. You are required to attend."

Exhaustion pulled at me. I hadn't slept the night before and this conversation wore me down to the bone. I just wanted to get off the phone and never speak to Jake again. Unfortunately, that was not possible either. I sighed.

"What time?"

"Stephanie's party starts at seven."

"As long as we're back by ten o'clock."

"Why?"

"I have a curfew."

"Then you will be breaking it."

I snorted. "I can't break my curfew. My dad will freak."

He ignored me again. He did that a lot.

"Moving on. You will spend every lunch period at my table and you will talk about any cool things that you do or know. The car thing was spot on. Talk about more of that, but don't talk too much because girls who talk too much think too much and girls who think too much are not for me."

I imagined grabbing his neck and wringing it.

"Are we done?"

"Last item on the list for this week is that I will address you as Baby and you will not give me a dirty look about it. I just figured that you were one of those types."

My body shook in anger and I hung up the phone and hurled it across the room.

He was just as infuriating as his brother! Worse! How could I stand to be around him for two weeks? Was it worth the humiliation to be popular? To give my best friend her dream boyfriend, who may or may not even like her back? I had half a mind to call Ariel and tell her exactly what I was up to. I wanted to walk away from this stupid plan and this even stupider dream of popularity and leave it all in the past.

But I couldn't. It wasn't possible. I had to see this through for myself and even more importantly, for Ariel.

I blew out a harsh breath and walked to the window. I didn't think again until my heartbeat slowed down and my hands unclenched.

I couldn't tell Ariel, just like Jake couldn't tell Dana. We had to keep quiet and play our roles until the time was right. When Jake was back with Dana, Eric and Ariel were cozy, and I was ... well, I didn't know where I would be then. My life had taken so many twists and turns in the last two days that even thinking about tomorrow seemed overwhelming. Like it was a grand mystery that I wasn't ready to solve.

I sighed.

Where was Dad? It was almost eight o'clock and he still wasn't around. Why didn't he text me? Was he out looking for a job? Was he at a bar?

I crossed my bedroom, picked up my phone from where it had landed in my hamper and checked it.

To my relief, Daddy had texted back while Jake and I were on the phone.

Dad: Be home soon. I love you.

I texted back telling him that I loved him, too, before I laid back down on my bed.

This had been the longest day ever. God only knew what tomorrow would bring.

24

It was only Wednesday and I felt like my entire life had turned upside down.

I took the longest shower of my life and put on my standard jeans and t-shirt. What did it matter? I was going shopping with Jake for new clothes anyway. That meant that today would be the last time that anyone would see me looking like me for the foreseeable future. I pulled my *I Heart Inigo Montoya* T-shirt over my head. It always cheered me up before but today, no such luck. If it were possible, I was in an even worse mood.

Joylessly, I flat ironed my hair and put on make-up.

You're doing this for Ariel, I told myself as I applied my third coating of mascara. *You are doing this for Ariel.*

When I was ready, I pulled my door open to find my father sitting at the breakfast bar, eating some eggs, toast and coffee. When he heard me come out, he put down the paper he'd been reading and turned to me.

"Hey."

He wore a small, hesitant smile. One that matched mine.

"Hey."

I pulled my backpack closer to me, waiting for him to speak again.

"Look, kid. I'm sorry. I lost my job and I turned our life upside down again. I just ... I..." He held his hands out in front of him, first in fists then opening them, as if letting something go that he'd held on to for far too long.

"I'm just sorry. You shouldn't have to think about money or stuff like that. You're a kid. You should be thinking about *Barney* and dolls and playing dress-up."

I stopped myself from rolling my eyes at what Daddy thought I should be concerned with. It wasn't the right time. Instead, I took a small step forward.

"I'm sorry, too. Some of the things that I said on Monday were hurtful."

He ran his hand over the graying stubble that covered his cheeks and chin. "That didn't make them any less true."

"It does. I don't hate you. I love you, Dad."

His smile grew, and he pulled me in to a warm hug.

"I love you too, sweetie."

The world seemed to fall in place again as he kissed the top of my head and held me tight. My insides turned gooey with love. I hugged him so hard that my arms hurt.

"We're going to be all right," he whispered. "I found a job yesterday."

I pulled away, surprised and delighted.

"You did?"

He nodded.

"It doesn't pay as much as the old job, but we don't need much. I put down first and last month's deposit on a new apartment across town near Central Park. It's closer to where I'll be working."

I gasped.

"Seventy six?" I asked.

He nodded, a smile growing on his face.

"That's where Ariel and Jasmine live!" I screamed and threw myself back in to his arms.

76 Central Park West was closer to my school, too. Maybe this wouldn't be so bad after all.

"I know."

"How did you get in there? It's way more expensive than this place."

"Well, I went back to the car shop to collect my tools when I saw this guy outside. I'd fixed his car once and we'd talked a little. Anyway, he asked what was going on and I told him that I was fired and that I might have to move and everything that was happening. So, he tells me that his aunt, this woman named Fleckenstein, has two apartments over at 76 and one of them is rent controlled. She held on to the second apartment for years, paying both rents."

"Why?"

"One is for her and the other is for Lad, the kid I met. It turns out, he goes to school across town and his parents have this huge house and he's never going to use the apartment. The lady is cooked in the head or something, I think. Anyway, he told me that he can get us in the apartment and we'll just have to pay the rent to his aunt under the condition that he can stay there if he ever needed a place to crash."

"Oh my god. That's fantastic!"

"We move in next Saturday!"

I hugged my father again, relief washing over me. We were going to be okay. Everything was going to work out.

"So, what's the new job?"

He frowned. "Well, it's not as glamorous as my old job, but..."

"But?"

"You know those horse carriage rides that they give around Central Park?"

"Yeah."

Was he going to be giving horse carriage rides for fifty bucks a pop? That was a long way from fixing cars.

"Well, I'll be working in the stables."

"Just like you did back on Grandpa's farm?"

He nodded, his smile waning.

"I guess I can't get away from the farm life, huh kid?"

I sighed. This was not where Dad saw himself when he left North Carolina. I could see the disappointment on his face and it made my heart ache.

"I'm sorry, Daddy. I know you had dreams."

He let out a breath.

"Sometimes, we have to put our dreams on hold for our children," he said. "One day, I'll find that perfect formula. But in the meantime, we have to eat, right?"

I smiled, feeling proud of my father and his decisions.

"Yeah."

"Good."

"And I have to go to school, so..."

He stood and grabbed his jacket from the back of his chair. "I'll walk you downstairs."

We smiled at each other. Daddy and I were going to be okay. Everything was going to work out. Joy took over as we walked down the four flights of stairs, discussing details for the move and what our new place would be like. I couldn't wait to tell Ariel and Jasmine.

We reached the door and I turned to him.

"See you later, Dad," I said.

"I'll see you, kid."

I kissed him on the cheek and nearly skipped to my friends.

Ariel and Jasmine waved. "Bye, Mr. French."

Dad waved at them before he headed in the opposite direction.

"He's walking you to the door now?" Ariel asked. "What are you; eight?"

"He was telling me the good news."

"What news?" Jasmine asked.

"We are moving."

Both Ariel and Jasmine stopped walking to look at me, wide eyed.

"Moving?" Ariel's voice sounded on the edge of hyperventilation. "Where?"

"To 76 Central Park West!"

We all screamed and jumped and danced around in a circle.

"This is going to be awesome!" Jasmine cried.

"Super awesome!" Ariel yelled.

"Mega awesome!" I joined in.

The thought of all three of us in the same building filled us all with happiness.

Ariel lived in the penthouse suite with her super rich father and her two sisters. There were seven sisters in total. Four of them were already out of the house and off to expensive in-state colleges. Two of them, Adella and Alana, were freshmen at St. Mary's. Her apartment was cluttered but swanky, with big windows, a huge pool and a beautiful patio. Each room even had its very own themed aquarium.

Jasmine's apartment was no less swanky with colorful walls, intricately beaded pillows and throws and thick braided rugs. Plus, her father, Sultan Patel, made the best tea I'd ever tasted. Jasmine lived with her father and four brothers, all college aged and super cute. Though I didn't tell them that.

The news that I was going to be in the same building with my two besties was almost as good as the news that my father had found a job. This day was shaping up to be the best day ever.

Our good mood continued through our train ride and on our walk from the subway to the school. It improved further when Jeff Schwartz met us at the school doors.

"Ladies."

"Jeffy."

Jasmine hugged him around the shoulders, while the rest of us waved. Jasmine had recently joined the chemistry club to up her extracurricular activities for college. Jeff was the president of the chemistry club, though not for long I'd bet. Jasmine had a thing about being in charge, and I had a feeling that she was planning a possibly hostile takeover in the near future.

"You all look well rested and lovely as usual."

"Aw, Jeff. You're such a charmer."

"I try." Jeff grinned. "Anyway, I am having some friends from school over on Friday. I thought that you ladies may want to stop by."

"That sounds fantastic," Jasmine said.

I raised my hand. "I can't. Plans. Sorry."

"Plans?" Jasmine asked. "What plans?"

"I got invited to a party on Friday."

Ariel and Jasmine frowned at me.

"Stephanie Pleasant's party?" Ariel asked.

I nodded, feeling embarrassed and stupid for going to the same party that I had condemned only a few hours ago.

"It's a pre-party. Some of the kids are heading to the Stamford Club afterward. I just found out last night," I said apologetically. "Jake invited me after I hung up with you."

My friends looked at me with expressions that said, 'what else haven't you told us'.

I cringed.

"Next time, Jeff," I said.

Jeff shrugged, though I could tell that he was disappointed. After all, I was now the coolest girl in school. Having me at his party would have given him a few extra popularity points for sure.

"Yeah," Jeff said. "Next time."

Ariel and Jasmine's judgy frowns made me shift my weight. I decided to use my out instead of explaining myself further.

"I have to meet Jake. I'll see you guys later."

I could tell that my friends weren't happy, but I had no choice. I was doing this for them, after all. Well, mostly for them.

I walked down the hallway, my name echoing off the walls as my fellow classmates called for my attention.

"Nice shirt, Bella!"

"Hey, Bella. Want to hang out after school?"

"Awesome sneakers, Bella."

I nodded, smiled and called my hellos back to them, even as the flags in my mind stirred. I wanted people to know that I existed, but the fact that it took me dating Jake to make it happen made me feel dirty. If Jake never asked me out, no one would care what I was wearing. They wouldn't even know that I was alive.

Was this what I wanted? To have my voice depend on who I was dating? What would they think if they knew I got the shirt and the sneakers from a half-off sale at *Walmart*? Would they still think they were cool? Would they still think I was cool?

As I gazed at the girls around me, I noticed something odd. Whereas before the look was straight hair, aka Dana, today there were way more curls and French braids. For once, other girls' hair looked like mine.

Not only was I not invisible anymore, I was being copied. But were they copying me, or were they copying Jake's girlfriend?

I sighed. Suddenly everything in my life ended with a question mark, and I had no idea how to find the answers. It sucked.

Jake spotted me and smiled.

I forced a smile on to my face and walked in to his arms.

"Hey, baby."

He smelled like expensive cologne. Like some well-crafted mix of spicy, sweet and lavender. He didn't dab it on, either. It smelled like he'd dumped the entire bottle over his head. I struggled to breathe.

"I'll meet you by the lunch room after this period," he whispered.

"Fine. But I have to be back by the end of school. I have an English project with your brother to work on."

"Cole?" He raised an eyebrow. "You two are working on an English project together?"

I nodded. How did Jake not know this? He was there when Ms. Mitchell teamed me with Cole. How Jake passed without doing any of the school work was beyond me. I would have given him a dirty look if I hadn't been so lightheaded over his cologne. What was in that stuff? Meth?

The first period bell rang.

"We'll talk about it later. I'll see you." He kissed my cheek and walked in to his classroom. With his mind-numbing cologne dissipating, I could finally think clearly. From across the hall, Dana scowled at me.

I scowled back.

Then, to my surprise, she walked over to me. Her long blonde hair was perfect as usual, cut into long layers that fell gently around her perfectly heart shaped face. Her makeup was perfect, her seafoam green mini dress fit her perfect body like a glove and her kitten heels were the height of style. Dana Rich was perfect. Next to her, I felt like a cheap imitation.

She looked at me with bright green eyes that matched her dress and smirked.

"I hope you know what you're getting into," she said. "Being with a Winsted is all fun and games, until it's not."

I straightened my shoulders, wishing that I had dressed up today.

"I know exactly what I'm getting into," I replied.

She smirked, and took a step back.

"You want a free piece of advice?" she asked.

I nodded, because it felt awkward not to.

"Run."

Then she turned, flipped her hair over one perfectly pale shoulder and walked away, her body swaying down the hallway.

Run? From who? Jake?

I frowned. I expected her to say something catty like, "stay away from my man", or "Jake is still in love with me". But, run? Why would she say that?

Pursing my lips, I walked to my first period class.

Maybe she was just trying to scare me? Maybe she was still in love with Jake and this was her way of showing it?

If she was, I hoped that she would hurry up and beg for him to come back. God knew I wanted him out of my life.

I put Jake and Dana out of my mind and slid in to my seat in Art.

25

I pushed the curtain open with a whoosh and stepped out on to the red, carpeted floor of *The Boutique*, a small shop on Fifth Avenue. Thank god that I shaved my legs that morning, because every dress Jake picked out only came down to mid-thigh and had some form of pink. I normally hated pink, but in these expensive clothes, I didn't mind it so much.

My current outfit was a white, sleeveless shirt, a mini, pink, pleated skirt and a fitted pink sweater. The pink heels were already at the register. I'd seen this outfit before. On Dana.

Had he chosen her clothes too, or just memorized her outfits?

"Wow," he said, a big grin on his face as I stepped in front of him. He looked at me as if I were a bowl of cream and he were a cat. It made me feel dirty. Did he see me in this outfit or was he picturing Dana's head on my body?

"You are going to blow everyone away tomorrow."

"Isn't this a little much?" I asked, stepping forward. "The clothes, I mean." I looked at the price tag hanging off the skirt. It had three figures and was more than our electric bill. "This stuff is expensive."

He chuckled. "Expensive? What does that mean?"

He held out his hands and I stepped forward, taking them. He looked me up and down, his grin turning wolfish.

"Very nice."

I snatched my hand back.

This wasn't me. I wasn't some plaything to dress up and show off. I had a mind. I had pride. I probably would have protested more but the clothes were cute, and I'd never be able to afford them on my own. I was positive that this made me a hypocrite and the worst kind of person but I had to admit that it felt nice to wear clothes that hadn't been rotting in the back of somebody's closet.

"So, I hear that Eric is taking Ariel to the Stamford Club on Friday night. It's their official coming out."

"Coming out? As in they are going to be an official couple?"

My heart did happy flips. I forgot about my broken moral compass and mentally patted myself on the back.

Jake nodded.

"He's going to be making it *Facebook* official soon. Funny. He didn't need much nudging, either. I said her name and he practically did a backflip."

Happiness fluttered within me. So it was real. Eric liked Ariel for real.

"That's fantastic."

"It is, as long as you continue to play along. I mean, you know Ariel, right? How would she react if she knew about our little arrangement? It might be hard to stay in a relationship based on a lie."

My good mood dissipated.

He released my hand and sat back.

God. I wanted to kick him.

"Why don't you try on another outfit? The black one, maybe? With the heels this time." He leaned back on the couch, stretched his legs out in front of him and put his hands behind his head. "This day is turning out to be way more fun than I thought. Where have you been hiding that tight little body of yours? It's amazing."

"Beneath books, homework and extracurricular activities."

He looked me over again.

"Shame."

I closed my eyes to keep from strangling him. When I opened them, he was standing, a navy blue, velvet box in his hands.

"I was going to wait to give this to you but after seeing how amazing you look, I just couldn't wait."

He held out the box to me, a half smile lighting his beautiful face.

How could one boy be so gorgeous and so manipulative at the same time? It should have been illegal.

"What is it?"

He shrugged.

"Just a little present to say thank you."

I eyed him wearily, then opened the box. Inside, amidst soft white lining was a gold necklace with a diamond heart. My breath caught in my throat as the sparkles from the diamond caught the light. It was easily the most beautiful thing that I had ever seen.

I gasped and put my free hand up to my mouth.

"Jake, this, this is..."

"This is yours."

He gently pulled the box from my hands, took out the necklace, stepped around and clasped it around my neck. The diamond was surprisingly lightweight. I ran my fingers along its rough edges.

"It's just a little present to say how grateful I am."

I went on high alert. Jake was being ... nice? For what? What was this new angle? What did he want?

"And to keep away any other dudes sniffing around. Once guys see that necklace, they'll know exactly who you belong to. I don't want you wandering off before I'm done with you."

And there it was. The reality of the situation. He was branding me with the necklace and I had fallen for it. Stupid me.

He moved in front of me and placed my face between his hands.

"What do we say?"

His lips were a breath from mine. I considered kneeing him between the legs.

"If you don't take a step back, I am going to personally ensure that you never have any children. Ever."

He heeded me and retreated.

At least he had sense enough to do that.

"You're weird."

"Am I?"

"I buy you thousands of dollars worth of clothes, expensive jewelry, compliment you. And yet, you still resist me. Why?"

I scowled. "Because this isn't real. We are doing this so that you can get back with Dana, remember?"

He shrugged. "Can't we have a little fun, too?"

"You might be used to skanky girls but I'm not one of them. Keep your hands to yourself and everyone will be happier for it."

"What if I was someone else?" he asked, his eyes narrowing. "Maybe you'd rather be here with a different brother."

My heart sped up. I smoothed the shock from my features.

"I'd rather be here with your credit card while you are far, far away in the jungles of India, getting trampled by an elephant with dysentery," I said. "It looks like neither of us are going to get what we want today."

He kept his eyes on me for the longest time before he turned and walked to the register.

"Get your stuff," he growled.

The workers had already started to pick up the clothes and shoes that I'd left in the changing room and bring them to the register. Jake pulled out a black credit card and paid.

He didn't look over his shoulder as he called to me.

"You'd better put on your shoes or else we're going to be late to the stylist."

I frowned. Stylist?

"I can feel you frowning," he called, still not looking at me. "Do it while we walk. You're getting a haircut."

26

By the time I arrived at Mr. Reynolds's science class, I was a new person. My clothes were trendy, my hair was blown straight and cut into layers and my makeup was flawless. My favorite piece though, was the necklace. It was gorgeous.

Like a blood diamond, I reminded myself. A symbol of everything that Jake's holding over my head.

The entire classroom stared at me as I walked in and took my seat.

Ariel looked as if she was about to faint.

"Who are you, and what have you done with my best friend?"

I shrugged. "Just a little shopping spree, courtesy of Jake."

"Jake took you shopping?"

I nodded.

"That's incredible. He must really like you."

I didn't reply. Jake didn't like me. I was a toy to him. Something to use for his own means and toss away. I smiled at my friend, reminding myself why I was allowing Jake to use me in the first place.

Science class passed quickly and Ariel and I parted. She went to swim practice and I went home to await Cole.

I'd missed our seventh period French tutoring session, thanks to Jake's shopping spree. I wondered what he'd say about it.

Would he be back to the old, smart mouthed Cole or would his mood be as miserable as it was the day before? I hoped it was the former. I kind of missed our banter.

I unlocked the front door and walked in to my apartment.

I froze. My dad was there. Along with another man in a suit that I'd never seen before.

They both turned to look at me.

"Bella," Daddy said, covering the space between us and wrapping me in his arms. He looked like he was about to fall apart.

My stomach clenched. What was going on?

"Bella, what have you done?" He hissed in my ear.

"Miss French." The man in the suit stood, and put one hand in his pocket. "My name is Detective Bruce Harding from the NYPD Drug Enforcement Task Force, and I'd like to ask you a few questions about your boyfriend."

27

This had to be a dream.

What this man, Detective Harding, was saying had to be made up.

It couldn't be real.

"Honey, if you don't want to do this, you don't have to," Dad said. "It's completely voluntary, and frankly, I don't know if you should be involved with this kind of stuff."

Detective Harding had told me the impossible.

Jake Winsted, my fake boyfriend, was the leader of an organized drug ring in my school. The Drug Task Force were initially tipped off when several parents anonymously reported that some students, presumably their own kids, were in possession of marijuana, cocaine and ecstasy. After doing some digging, the officers came up with a name. Kenny Jennings. But Kenny was a little fish in an ocean of sharks. Putting away one junior at a high school would not solve the problem. They had to find out who was supplying Kenny with the drugs. And, according to Detective Harding, all signs pointed to Jake.

Detective Harding gazed at me with brown eyes that looked like they'd been kind once. Now, they were hard. His mouth was permanently turned down at the corners and he wore an ill-fitting gray suit and a striped blue and black tie. He seemed young to be on a Task Force. No more than thirty, if I were to guess. His skin was still smooth and he still had a full head of slicked back, dark brown hair.

"We are not asking you to arm yourself, or to go snooping, or to do anything that would put you in danger." His voice was like sandpaper. Rough. A gun peeked out from beneath his suit jacket. Had he killed anyone with that gun? Was he planning on killing Jake if he ever came across him?

"Of course, she'll be in danger!" Daddy cried out, jumping up from the couch and running his hand through his hair. "Just being around this guy, this Jake, is dangerous!" Worry flowed beneath his skin, mixing with his blood. He turned to me again, his eyes pleading and full of fear. "I want you to break up with this guy. I want you to stay as far away from him as possible."

My mouth opened and closed like a fish out of water and I momentarily lost the power of speech.

"Sir, I can't tell you how to parent your child, but we have been trying to put away Ivan Sokolov for years. And right now, our best shot at getting to him, is your daughter."

"Ivan Sokolov?" I gasped. "The drug lord?"

The detective nodded.

"What does he have to do with this?" I asked.

"Ivan Sokolov is Jake's father," Detective Harding said.

My blood ran cold. My lungs locked. It couldn't be. Jake's father couldn't be a drug kingpin? That was insane. This was real life. Not a movie.

"No. It's not possible," I stuttered. "They don't even have the same name."

Detective Harding reached in his bag and pulled out a manila folder. He placed three pictures on the table. One of Jake. One of Cole. One of Regina.

"Yakov, Kolenka, and Regina Sokolov. Children of Ivan Sokolov and Sabine Petit, a French national. Ivan immigrated to this country sixteen years ago, when his wife was pregnant. He's been running New York's Russian drug cartel ever since. Six years ago, Ivan went underground. No one has seen or heard from him, and yet according to our informants, his business is still booming. We think that he may have passed the business down to his son, Jake."

I couldn't believe it. Russian drug cartels. Yakov Sokolov. This had to be some sort of mistake.

"This is nuts," Daddy whispered. "St. Mary's Academy is a good school with good kids. Plus, it costs a fortune. How could this happen? The mayor's niece goes there. Senator's kids. Children of actors and musicians. These kids have their own private yachts. How could they be involved in a drug ring?"

"Sir, this school's drug problem is a very small part of a very large picture."

I stared at the pictures of three people who I thought I knew.

How could they hide something like this? How could no one else know?

"I know that it's a shock," Detective Harding continued. "But I need you to tell me if you've seen anything suspicious with your boyfriend. Any car rides to strange areas? Picking up large packages? Multiple cell phones? Unexplained behavior? Anything?"

I looked at my wringing hands. On the way back from the boutique, Jake made a detour to a small warehouse near the docks. He backed his red *Ferrari* in, and someone came and loaded some boxes in the trunk. The men wore ski masks. When I asked about it, Jake said that it would just take a minute and then we'd leave. When I asked again, he told me to just relax.

My eyes opened wide. Had I witnessed a drug pickup? Was this the sort of things that Detective Harding was talking about?

"Have you seen anything at all?" the detective prodded.

I needed time to think. To weigh out the consequences. After all, it wasn't just Jake I had to think about. It was Cole and Regina, too. Would the information that I passed along to Detective Harding affect them in some way? What about Eric? After all, he was Jake's best friend. And if it affected Eric, then it affected Ariel and I couldn't have that.

I had to think this through. There was too much at stake.

"Nothing comes to mind," I finally said.

The detective and my father frowned at each other.

"You know that if you withhold any information from this investigation, you may be liable as an accomplice."

An image of me in an orange jump suit came to my mind. I pushed the image away. I wasn't really withholding information. Just verifying that it was valid. That wasn't a crime, was it? Besides, I wanted to see what Cole knew about his brother. Regina was a lost cause but Cole may be able to tell me something useful. Plus, it would give me a chance to make sure that he wasn't in on it. We were enemies but right now, Cole was the only Winsted that I didn't want to see in jail.

"I understand," I said.

Detective Harding didn't look convinced. Neither did my father. But what could they do? I wasn't talking.

The detective handed me a card and I took it.

"Take your time and when you are ready, call me. I'll be in touch."

The man stood and walked out of the door, leaving Dad and I alone.

The door had only just shut when Daddy put both hands on my shoulders, squeezing them hard.

"Bella, what have you gotten yourself in to?"

"Dad, he asked me out and I said yes. I didn't know he was part of a drug cartel."

"Didn't know or didn't want to know?"

He walked over to my room and flung open the door. Bags and boxes filled with clothes that Jake had gotten me from the boutique covered the floor. They must've delivered them when I was at school.

I bit my lower lip.

"How do you explain all of these purchases? Did they just appear out of thin air?"

The sheer amount of stuff that I now owned overwhelmed me. I took a step into my room, not believing that I'd gotten an entirely new wardrobe in only a few hours.

"Jake took me shopping," I said softly.

"That's more than a shopping trip. That's the whole store."

"I told him it was too much but he wouldn't listen."

"And when did this happen?"

I sucked in a sharp breath. "Today."

"Today? You mean you cut school?"

Oops.

"Unbelievable. What has gotten in to you? Dating the son of a drug lord, cutting school, expensive gifts, new hair, new jewelry, new clothes."

"Dad, it's not like I asked for any of this."

"Good. That will make it easier to take it all back."

"Take it back? What do you mean take it back?"

He waved his hand at the bags. "All of it. I want all these gifts out of my house and I want your word that you are officially breaking up with this Jake boy and staying away from him."

"Dad, I can't do that."

"You can and you will. What if you get hurt? Or get mixed up in his life? You could get addicted to drugs. Or worse, you could get yourself killed."

He let out a harsh breath and ran his hands through his hair.

"I sent you to a good school so that you wouldn't get in any trouble and now look at you. My god! If I wanted this, I would have sent you to public school!"

"Dad, would you just-"

"No buts. The clothes, the jewelry, the boy. They all go. Understand?"

He looked at his watch.

"Oh God. I'm late!" He powerwalked to the door. "I told my boss that I had a family emergency and that I'd be back in an hour."

"When are you going to be home?"

"Around six or so. Stay out of trouble. And remember, it all goes."

The door slammed shut behind Daddy, leaving me in a room where my breathing echoed against the walls.

My heart raced. My stomach flipped. Jake's father was a drug lord. I was Jake's girlfriend. The cops wanted me to gather information about Jake.

What would they do if I said no? Would they put me in prison? What if Jake found out what I was doing? Would he turn me over to his father? Would he shoot me himself?

A knock on the door made me jump a foot in the air like a cat who'd just seen a cucumber. My heart ended up somewhere in my throat, my stomach somewhere in my shoes.

Another knock.

Who could it be?

Daddy was gone. Had he forgotten his keys? Was it Detective Harding, coming back to ask me some more questions? Or worse, take me to jail as an accomplice?

A third knock.

"Who's there?" I called out.

"Who else would come by this dump after school unless they absolutely had to?"

Cole.

I ran to the door and opened it.

His eyes raked over mine, his teasing smile turning to a frown of concern.

"What happened?" he asked. He looked around the apartment. "Is someone in here?"

I shook my head and waved him in. "No."

"What's the matter? You look like you just had to castrate your cat."

"I don't have a cat."

"I know that. It was a joke."

I shook my head. "Sorry. I'm not in a joking mood right now."

I walked away from him and sat on the couch.

"That's not fair. If I have to be in a good mood then you have to be in a good mood, too. That was the agreement." He walked behind me, and sat on the middle cushion.

"Whatever."

I grabbed the leash and went on the hunt for Mojo. I found him laying on top of a pink sweater inside of a bag. I put the leash on him and pulled it a little. He didn't budge. I sighed and picked him up, rushing from the room.

"Where are you going?" Cole asked.

"We are taking Mojo for a walk."

"We?"

I turned to him, dog in one hand, my other hand on my hip.

“Let’s go, Winsted. We have a dog to walk.”

Cole let out a breath and stood, following me out of the door.

After what I’d just heard, there was no way that I was leaving Cole —No. Kolenka—alone in my house. Who knew what he’d do? We didn’t have anything to steal but I still felt better with one eye on him.

We walked down the humid staircase in silence, then broke out in to the cool November sunshine. I walked as quickly as I could to Mojo’s favorite tree. My heels made my arches hurt. I longed for my sneakers.

“Why are you carrying the dog?” Cole asked, slowing down his walk to a stroll. I matched his pace.

“He doesn’t walk for me.”

“What do you mean he doesn’t walk for you?”

“He doesn’t walk on the leash for me.”

“Why not?”

“I don’t know. He just likes me carrying him, I guess.”

Cole laughed shortly. “No man wants a woman to carry him.”

“Apparently, it’s different with dogs.”

Cole reached out his hand to Mojo.

“May I?”

I shrugged and put Mojo in Cole’s arms. He bent down and placed Mojo on the cement. And of course, the dog walked in front of him like he’d been doing it all his life.

“I’m beginning to think that the dog is sexist,” I said. “He only walks for men. Not for me.”

Cole shrugged. “Nah. It’s all about confidence. If your body language tells the dog that you’re the boss, he’ll do what you want him to do.”

“How do you do that?” I asked.

“Easy.” He pulled in a breath, dramatically pressing back his shoulders.

“Shoulders back. Relax. Easy strides. Confidence. When you’re walking, there shouldn’t be any doubt in your mind that the dog is going to follow what you say.”

“Uh, what do you think I’ve been doing?”

“You’ve been hesitating. Like you do with everything.”

I snorted. "What is that supposed to mean?"

"You're not sure of yourself."

What? That was totally off base.

"I'm sure of myself."

"No. You're not. You run every major decision past your friends first, don't you?"

"Not all. Some."

"Most."

I frowned.

"Maybe with the important ones, because that's what people do. They discuss important decisions with people they care about to make sure that it's the right one." Then just because he'd aggravated me, I added, "We can't all be lone geniuses like you."

"Who said that I'm alone?"

"Uh, because you are. You're never with anyone else."

He looked at me as if I were telling a very funny joke.

"So, you don't know any of my friends?"

"No one does because you don't have any."

His smile widened and he shook his head.

"Poor French. Can't you see anything passed my brother's very large head?"

"Oh believe me, I see plenty past him."

He raised an eyebrow.

"Trouble in paradise already?"

"No," I said, a little too quickly. I cleared my throat. "It's just..." It's just what? I had no idea what I was about to say. I didn't even like his brother. I crossed my arms and examined the tree that Mojo was presently pooping behind. "Whatever."

But Cole was insistent.

"What do you see in him?" he asked. The tease in his voice was less now. "Besides the looks, the money and the popularity, I mean. What do you really see in him?"

The edges of my mouth pulled into a frown. The truth was that I didn't have an answer to his question. At first, I liked Jake because he was good looking. But now that I was getting to know what a manipulative jerk he was, I didn't like him at all. Not that I could tell Cole any of that because I was supposed to be his brother's girlfriend.

I cleared my throat, and bounced nervously on one hip.

"Lots of things," I finally replied.

Cole took a step forward.

"Name one."

I scowled and uncrossed my arms.

It was then that Mojo blessedly reappeared, giving me something else to look at besides Cole or the sidewalk.

"I don't have to explain anything to you," I said, yanking the dog's leash from Cole's hand and storming away.

God, Cole got under my skin like no one else. After years of being invisible, I wasn't used to people seeing beyond what I wanted them to see. Sure, Ariel and Jasmine knew me pretty well, but Cole seemed determined to pull back each of my carefully crafted layers until he exposed me. The real me. The thought of anyone seeing that part of myself was terrifying.

I increased my pace.

Cole must've gotten the hint that I no longer wanted to talk about Jake, because he silently followed me all the way back to the apartment. I let us in and took a moment to refill Mojo's food and water dishes before I sat down again. The minute my butt hit the couch, his inquisition continued.

"Where did you go this afternoon?" he asked.

"Go?"

"Yes. Go. You weren't in English, you weren't in the hallway or at lunch and you definitely weren't there for French tutoring, which was a bummer because I had some real zingers about your new look that I wanted to tell you."

"Like what?" I asked.

He looked at me from top to bottom. My cheeks turned hot beneath his gaze.

"You look good, French," he said softly. "Nice, even."

My throat tightened. I could only croak back.

"Was that a compliment?"

His eyes never left mine. He didn't respond. Only nodded a bit. Such a small nod. A whisper of movement.

Then, something strange happened. Goosebumps broke out all over my body. A weird, unfocused feeling took over me, like I couldn't think straight. My gut twisted. It was like a bright, consuming spotlight had just turned on. I bit my lip, trying to refocus on... On what? On Cole? It had to be because my eyes refused to leave his.

"French." He placed his thumb and forefinger on my chin.

Vaguely, in my peripheral self, I was aware how close Cole was. How his fingertips felt on my skin. How his blue eyes were still locked on my brown ones. On how alone we were.

I breathed him in, an intoxicating mixture of vanilla, spice and soap. It wasn't an overpowering smell. It was light. Airy. Nice.

My breath caught in my throat as I examined the face of my nemesis. For the first time, I noticed how handsome he was. His strong nose. His full, very kissable lips. His smooth skin. How could I not have realized it before? He was beautiful, dark and, suddenly, so very tempting.

My goosebumps got goosebumps. Heat sprouted from where his fingers touched my chin.

To my surprise, my body leaned toward him. His grip on my chin strengthened, pulling me closer.

My chest heaved.

I closed my eyes.

I pursed my lips.

Then, his phone rang.

We froze. We were so close to each other. It would only take another inch and our lips would have pressed together.

The ferocity with which I craved that inch stole my breath away.

The phone rang again.

His hand dropped from my chin.

It took all I had not to pull it back. Not to pull him toward me.

A third ring.

I hated that phone.

His eyes stayed on me as he sat up. There was sadness in them.

Sadness and anxiousness, and something else. Something that made my heart thump hard and my mouth go dry.

He grabbed his phone from his pocket and glanced at it. His expression turned angry.

"I have to go," he whispered.

"Why?" I asked. "What is it?"

"Not what. Who. It's Jake."

My heart sped up. Had Jake seen us? Did he know what we were about to do?

I felt the loss of his heat as Cole backed away, reaching for his bookbag. I'd never been so cold. A gaping hole seemed to open in my chest wide enough for wind to howl through. I sat dumbly on the couch with my curious new feelings while Cole stood and walked to the door.

"French," he said. His hand was on the knob, his back was to me. "You're my brother's girlfriend," he said, his voice choked. "I can't-"

He couldn't kiss me. It was against the rules. We were against the rules.

When had we become a we? Just this morning he was my nemesis and now we had almost kissed. What had happened between us? What had changed?

I closed my eyes and put one hand over my racing heart.

"I know."

It was all I could say.

28

It was settled.

I'd signed up to enter the talent show. I had no idea what I was going to sing yet but I would do it. I would sing in front of an audience for the first time since Mom died.

The thought was both exciting and terrifying. After all, this was not a church. The people in this crowd wouldn't cheer for me regardless of whether I was terrible or not. The kids at my school were brutal. I imagined them pelting me with tomatoes, the red pulpy insides soaking through my clothes.

I could not suck.

I clicked through my music collection, searching for a song to sing. I dragged each one that I liked into a folder labeled Talent Show. So far, I'd added *Sussudio*, *Walking on Sunshine* and, just because I was feeling super brave in that moment, *Bohemian Rhapsody*.

My mom always said that I sang with soul, so I started to look for more soulful music. *Alicia Keyes. Amy Winehouse*. I could probably struggle through *Beyonce*'s, *If I Was a Boy*, but it was too slow. I wanted something more upbeat and fun.

It'd never sang for a contest before. For the most part, it was just for fun. A way to say the words that I couldn't say in my day to day life.

When I was mad, I screamed the lyrics to old rock songs. I loved the feeling of the artist's anger in my mouth. I'd bellowed those songs until my face turned a shade of red as furious as my mood and when I was done, I'd lay sprawled and breathless on my floor, my demons purged. Old bands like *Linkin Park* and *Metallica* were great for angry days.

When I was sad, I sang the blues while lying in my bed, hugging an old pillow and wishing that I was old enough to drink whiskey just because it seemed appropriate to do so in that moment.

Pop songs were great for expressing my happiness and I sang old hymns when I especially wanted to feel closer to God.

Music was my voice. An outlet in which my soul spoke words that my mind could not form. It was a shame that I didn't sing that much anymore. Maybe that was why I felt so sad sometimes. Because my soul had no outlet in which to speak. Perhaps with a little more song, I could be the person that I wanted to be. Strong. Confident. Happy.

I'd just *Google* searched Soul Singers when my phone exploded in a flurry of text and social media messages.

Ariel: Eric just invited me to spend the day with him at South Street Seaport. Sooo excited. What should I wear?

Jasmine: Where are you? Have you checked *Facebook* lately?

Jasmine: Oh My God. Go on *Facebook* right now.

Ariel: We are going to kill Dana.

Ariel: This is bullying. We should call the cops.

What were they talking about?

I opened *Facebook*. One hundred and fifty-two friend requests.

What?

I clicked through the list. Who were these people? Not one face looked familiar. Why would they all choose to friend me?

I clicked out of the screen and looked at my wall.

Ugly words looked back at me.

Slut.

Whore.

Are you pregnant?

I had to speed scroll for a good ten seconds to get to the bottom of all of it, anger filling me with each swipe. My hands shook with rage. The comments were all about me or Jake or both of us. Some people even tagged him, though he hadn't responded to anything yet.

Did he see the awful words? Did he care?

The friend request jumped to one hundred and sixty. Who were all these people? How had they heard of me? Was someone making fake profiles to stalk me? Who would do something like that?

My blood boiled. There was only one person that it could possibly be. Dana. She was behind it. She had to be. She'd enlisted her cronies to create fake *Facebook* profiles just to call me names and harass me.

I called her a very unchristian name. She could have just said that she wanted Jake back. Why did girls always make the next girlfriend the enemy instead of the guy? It wasn't as if I'd stolen Jake from her. Did she forget that she'd dumped him?

I tried not to let the comments hurt me, but they did. They talked about my frizzy hair, my breasts, my clothes, my face. The attacks were personal, like tiny missiles, each aimed at a different piece of my heart. I sniffed back the tears. I would not cry.

Taking a deep breath, I allowed the logical side of me to take over. I changed my privacy settings so that only friends could post on my wall, then one by one, I deleted the ugly words.

Hot tears threatened but I kept them at bay. I would not give Dana and her dumb friends my tears. They didn't deserve them.

Each word deleted and profile blocked fueled the angry fire that built within me. I was friends with family from back home on this profile. I'd even friended my father, though he rarely used *Facebook*. How could they do something like this? I'd never done anything to anyone and now they were calling me names like slut and whore? I was a virgin. I'd only kissed two boys, including Jake. They had gotten me totally and completely wrong.

I growled.

This was all because of Jake. Jake and his stupid plan. The worst part was, he wasn't even man enough to defend me in the posts, even though he was tagged in them. Just like he hadn't defended me at lunch during the food fight with his sister.

The urge to find out every sordid detail of his life and turn it over to the cops rose strong. I couldn't wait to get this deal over with and go back to my regularly scheduled life.

My profile now cleaned, I laid in bed, put on my headphones, and blasted "Mean" by *Taylor Swift*. At the end of the song, I allowed a single tear to fall, closed my eyes and fell in to a restless sleep.

29

After the insanity of the week, I just wanted a normal day. I didn't know how impossible that was until I put on a black leather skirt, a pink jacket and a black T-shirt that spelled out A Little Bit Dramatic in rhinestones. I paired it with a pair of low black heels and a pink purse that couldn't fit any of my books.

It amazed me how much I'd changed since Jake kissed me. Pink was my least favorite color. Worse than crap brown. And now, I was wearing a pink jacket and a pink purse. I looked in the mirror at my outfit. How much more would I have to change before Jake was through with me?

I glanced at the clock. My train would be here soon.

By the time I finished doing my make-up and flat ironing my hair, I was exhausted. I didn't know how the popular girls did this every day. I walked out of my bedroom, fanning my shirt against myself.

"Hey, pumpkin," Dad called from the kitchen. He was eating his standard toast and eggs. The newspaper was folded up in front of him.

"Hey, Daddy."

I kissed him on the cheek then reached over and grabbed an apple.

"Heading to school?"

"Yup."

"Then back home?"

"Yup."

"Nowhere else?"

Three questions in a row? He was digging for information.

"No, Daddy. Nowhere else."

He nodded slowly.

"Just text me when you get home, okay?"

"Yeah. Sure." My brows furrowed. "Are you worrying? Because there really isn't anything to worry about. I'm not in any trouble."

He squeezed his lips together, let out air through his nose and pushed the newspaper in front of me.

The headline read: Two dead in drug related shootings.

I put my hands over my lips.

"Please tell me that you broke up with that boy," Dad said. "I don't want to read your name in the paper."

I felt Daddy's anguish in his words and put my arms around him, holding him tight. Was Jake involved in this? Was his father? I shook my head, trying to clear it from millions of questions that ran through it.

"It's fine, Daddy. I broke up with him."

His shoulders sagged in relief.

Mine tensed with the ease of my lies.

His hug around me tightened.

"Good girl," he said. "Very, very good."

He pulled away, brushing the hair out of my face.

"Just be careful, okay? Keep an eye out. You see anyone running or screaming, get to a safe place and stay there. And if you ever feel unsafe, call the police then call me, okay?"

I nodded. "Okay."

My steps were heavy with guilt; my mind full. I felt almost zombie like as I walked to the door. I'd lied to my father about Jake. Every lie I had to tell over the last few days had been about Jake. But they came from my mouth, I reminded myself. No one told me to lie. I did it on my own. That was who I was now. Popular, well dressed and a liar.

I gulped in a breath of air. Was this really the life that I wanted? Did I want to be a liar? A fraud?

"Hey, kid!"

I turned back to my father, my breathing still uneven.

"I love you."

I nodded, putting my hand on the door handle.

"Love you too, Daddy."

The words came out quietly. Or at least, I thought they did. I couldn't hear them. I could only hear the voices in my head.

You. Are. A. Liar.

My guilt grew heavier on my back. I felt so bad that I barely heard Ariel and Jasmine as we walked to the train station.

"Bella, are you okay?" Jasmine asked, her eyes filling with concern. "You're all pale and splotchy."

I cleared my throat, as if that would help my complexion.

"Nothing," I said. "I'm fine. Just tired."

"Well, don't be tired," Ariel said. Her happiness was usually infectious. Now, with my mood in the toilet, I found it annoying. "Eric invited me to the Stamford Club on Friday, so take your B-12 because we are going to rock the dance floor."

I halfheartedly nodded. I didn't want to rock anyone's dance floor. I wanted this Jake business to be over. I wanted him out of my life. I wanted to tell Ariel the truth. I wanted ... something. Someone. Someone that I shouldn't have wanted at all.

Cole's face came in to my mind, and I crushed it. I couldn't like Cole. Not only was he my nemesis, but he was my fake boyfriend's brother. It was dangerous. Too dangerous. Especially with what Detective Harding had told me about his family. I pasted a smile on my face and pretended not to care, but it was all another lie.

The train ride to school was a blur and before I knew it, we were passing through the front doors. I turned to my friends.

"I have to meet Jake at first period," I said. "I'll catch up with you guys later."

Ariel and Jasmine said their goodbyes and I went to put my heavy books in my locker.

I froze.

Someone had taken a picture of me from my *Facebook* page, printed it out and written WHORE in big, red letters across it.

I read the word again. Slower this time. It was like it was written in Mandarin. My mind couldn't process what was happening. I looked at the surrounding lockers, verifying that this was mine. Slowly, reality caught up with me. Overtook me.

It was my locker. And someone had written whore on it. Someone had just called me a whore.

I was angry. So angry that I saw red.

Several students stopped, whispered and laughed at the picture. The same students who had called my name and complimented me on my clothes when I walked in this morning.

Vultures. The second they smelled blood in the water, they turned on me.

My body felt hot with rage. My eyes scanned the crowd, looking for the culprit.

"Who did this?" I whispered.

I wanted to punch something. I wanted to punch someone.

"Who did this?" I demanded again.

More students approached, laughed and pointed at me, sending my rage into orbit.

"Who?!"

Cole appeared by my side, ripping the pictures down, tearing them to shreds and scowling at the laughing kids.

They quickly moved along.

My heart was racing, my breathing quick, my hands formed into claws.

I wanted to scream at something. I wanted to yell and cry out. I wanted justice.

Cole put his hand on the small of my back and bent down to whisper in my ear.

"It's okay. Just breathe."

A small bit of my anger seeped out of me, but not enough. I felt like it would never be enough.

"Oh my God, Bella. Are you okay?"

Regina approached me, her hand over her heart, her pink lips turned down into a worried frown.

She resembled Cole, with her jet-black hair and blue eyes, but her personality held the meanness and domineering that I'd recently seen in Jake.

I was immediately on high alert.

"I can't believe that someone would deface your locker like that. I'm so sorry."

"What do you want, Regina?"

"Just to show solidarity to my brother's girlfriend." She pulled me in to a tight hug and held it for a moment before letting go and taking my hands. "I know that we've had our differences in the past, but I want you to know I'm here for you. I've realized the error of my ways. You are a good girl. Not like that tramp, Dana. I can't believe she would do this to you."

I narrowed my eyes in suspicion.

"How do you know that Dana did this?" I asked.

Regina nodded. "Don't forget, Dana and I tend to run in the same circles. She's practically on a one-woman crusade against you and Jake. Yesterday at The Center, she was going on and on about organizing something big on social media. I guess this was her plan." Regina looked at the papers scattered around my feet. "If there is anything that you need, anything at all, please let me know."

I shouldn't have believed her, but she sounded so genuine. Maybe she had turned over a new leaf.

"Why are you being nice to me?" I asked.

"Yeah, Regina," Cole interjected. "Why are you being nice to her?"

Regina looked hurt at our accusation. "Can't a girl change for the better? Bella is a good girl, and no matter what happened in our past, she doesn't deserve this." She squeezed my hands. "I suggest that you march over to that brother of mine and let him know that he needs to get Dana in check, pronto."

Though I didn't completely trust Regina—after all, she had threatened me twice this week—I couldn't fault her logic. Dana was responsible for this. She had to be. And with Dana being Jake's ex-girlfriend, he should be the one to tell her to lay off me.

I was going to put a stop to it, once and for all.

I threw my bag in my locker and marched down the hall to where Jake waited for me. I somehow knew that Regina and Cole were hot on my heels but I didn't stop or turn around.

When Jake saw me, he gave me a big smile.

"Hey, babe," he said.

"Don't babe me!" I cried out.

I knew that he wasn't the one who put the mean things on my *Facebook* wall or who put the picture on my locker but somehow, it still felt like he was responsible.

He frowned at me and stepped forward.

"What's the matter?"

"You know what's the matter. Someone put horrible things on my *Facebook* wall and on my locker this morning, and I want you to put a stop to it."

"Me?"

"Yes. You."

He looked incensed that I would even ask him to step in and defend me. Well, if he wanted my help, he was going to have to work for it.

"What am I supposed to do?"

"What are you supposed to do? Stop her."

"Her who?"

"Dana. She's behind this. She's behind all of it."

"Dana? Why would she-"

"Don't be stupid. You know why!"

He frowned, and I could tell that he was warring within himself.

"Look," he said, shoving his hands in to his pockets. "I-"

"Just fix it or I'm gone." I whipped around, and stomped away.

"Don't forget why you're here," he shot back.

And just like that, any confidence I had that Jake was going to do the right thing was gone. I stared at him, good and hard. In that moment, I hated him. I hated him for putting me in this situation. I hated him for manipulating me at every turn. I hated everything about him. And I hated myself for letting him do this to me.

I was so angry and frustrated that my throat choked up. God, I hated that. Why did I cry when I got too emotional? It made me feel weak and stupid. I wiped my nose and walked away, forgetting about our good morning kiss on the cheek and hug. I didn't have to look behind me to know that Dana was somewhere listening, with a smile on her face.

30

I was angry.

I was so angry that I wasn't sure who I hated more. Jake for putting me in the situation or myself for agreeing to this stupid plan.

I told Ms. Mitchell that I didn't feel well and she gave me a pass to the nurse. Instead of going, I took a detour and went to my one place of solace in this entire school. The library.

Mrs. Smalls, the librarian, smiled at me when I walked in. She didn't speak much unless she was talking about books. I appreciated her for that, seeing as how I wasn't feeling particularly chatty today. Murderous was more like it.

I staked out the very back table and put my head in my hands, dreading the next bell. All my anger was draining. My eyes drifted shut as I tried to wrangle my crazed thoughts.

The fifth period bell rang and I didn't move. I couldn't. I just sat there in the library with my head in my hands and my world spinning around me until a familiar voice called my name.

"Bella?"

I looked up from my one-woman pity party to see Ms. Mitchell pulling out a chair. She wore a navy, sleeveless top and a matching skirt today. Her red glasses swung from around her neck. She was still wearing her T-strapped heels.

"Honey, what's wrong?"

Hot tears formed behind my eyes. Suddenly, all the stresses I felt that week hit me all at once. I threw myself in to her arms and sobbed. Jake's plan, Ariel, my strange feelings for Cole, Detective Harding. All of it etched itself in wet, dark lines on Ms. Mitchell's shoulders. I cried until there were no more tears left in me. And through it all, Ms. Mitchell silently rubbed my back like my mother used to. She didn't say anything. She had no questions. She was just there. A warm body with loving arms, catching me as I fell apart. It was what I needed. A place where I felt safe enough to fall, knowing that there would be someone to catch me.

After what felt like an hour of crying and boy did it feel good, I sat up and wiped my eyes with the back of my hands. I was sure that all my makeup was absolutely ruined but I didn't care. I had to let my worries and my fears free. If I didn't, they would have crushed me.

Ms. Mitchell gave me a small reassuring smile and handed me a few tissues. They turned blacker with every swipe across my eyes and cheeks.

God. I must've looked like a raccoon.

I cleaned up as best as I could, all while Ms. Mitchell ran her fingers through my hair in that comforting way that parents do to their children. I only had one parent left but I was glad that Ms. Mitchell filled in today. I needed it.

"My mom always said that people only cry when they've been strong for too long." She brushed a long string of brown hair behind my ear. "Have you been strong, Bella?"

Strong? No. I've been weak. I'd let Jake manipulate my life until it wasn't recognizable anymore. The problem was, I didn't know how to make him stop. How was I supposed to get off this runaway train? I needed advice but I couldn't let Ms. Mitchell know who I was referring to.

"Have you ever told a lie that grew and grew until you didn't know where the truth ended and the lie began?" I asked, still dabbing at my raccoon eyes.

Ms. Mitchell nodded. “Everyone lies, Bella. Even old matrons like me.”

I didn’t believe that Ms. Mitchell had ever told a lie in her life. At least not like the lies that I’d told. I didn’t mention it, though.

“But, do you know what’s more important than a lie?” she asked.

I shook my head.

“Telling the truth when it counts.”

“What if it’s not enough?” I asked.

She smiled and brushed another hair from my face.

“Oh, sweetie. It will always be enough.”

She pulled me in to a tight hug, then set me away from her.

“Now, go wash your face and reapply your make-up. You can’t face the world looking like a drowning raccoon.”

She stood and smoothed her skirt. I wished she’d stay. I needed some more mothering, if just for a little while.

“What if I’m not ready to face the world?” I asked.

She chuckled and started toward the door, her heels clicking their slow Morse Code with each step.

“Bella, dear, if there is one thing that I know about you, it’s that your heart is bigger than you realize. Don’t worry about if you’re ready to face the world. The world should be worried about facing you.”

31

They say that dictators empower themselves while leaders empower those around them.

I walked into the lunch room, determined to become a leader.

Dana Rich had messed with the wrong person this morning. I was no longer invisible. I had power now. People knew my name. It was time to exercise that power and start to overturn Dana's stupid rules, and I knew just which one to start with.

I stopped in the invisible section. My sights were set on two people.

Jelissa Turrington and Chad Jackson.

"Hey," I said, standing in front of them.

The ousted lovers looked up at me with frowns. None of the popular kids had talked to them since Jake and Dana had broken up. I was proud to be the first.

Dana and her crew stood a few feet behind me, their high-pitched gossiping going silent.

"I'm Bella French," I said. "Jake Winsted's girlfriend."

"We know who you are," Jelissa replied. "Everyone does."

I cleared my throat, gathering my courage and control.

"Okay. Well then, I would like to personally invite you to eat lunch with me today."

They looked at each other in shock. Then they looked back at me.

"At Jake's table?" Chad asked.

"Yes."

"With the popular kids?" Jelissa asked. "Dana said that we're not allowed over there."

"Yes. I know that Dana tried to oust you but she's not important anymore. I am. Will you sit with us? Please?"

Chad and Jelissa looked at each other again, unsaid words passing between them. Finally, Jelissa stood.

"Sure."

Chad stood, too.

I was vaguely aware that the lunch room had gone completely silent. The gauntlet had been thrown. I, Bella French, had defied Dana's command. I had given my first pardon to someone that she'd condemned to social death. A sizzle of power and pride rushed through me. I wasn't just sitting by the sidelines watching the game. I had thrown a ball. I had done something good. Worthy. Gallant. All eyes turned to us as I led Jelissa and Chad to Jake's table.

Eric saw me coming first, along with my two guests. He caught my eye and winked.

A moment later, I knew exactly what that wink meant when he stood up and held out his hand to Chad for a high five.

"Chadwick!"

Chad looked shocked for a moment before he slapped his hand against Eric's with a confused smile.

Eric's show of support touched my heart. I sent him a grateful smile.

He smiled back.

I then turned my attention to Jake, awaiting his sign off on my little stunt.

Jake's gaze swept over me, a mixture of confusion and irritation. I could read exactly what he was thinking. He wanted to know why I was defying Dana.

I wanted to tell him that I defied her to bring peace and unity to the student body again. I wanted to say that I defied her because no one should have the power to banish students to the realms of invisibility, like she'd done with Chad and Jelissa. What I wouldn't tell him was the biggest reason of all. A reason that I didn't want to admit. I defied her out of plain old revenge. I'm sure that made me a selfish person but after what I'd been through, a little selfishness didn't seem so bad. Besides, she'd thrown the first stone. I was returning with cannons. Now, the ball was in her court. Whatever she threw at me, I'd be ready.

I was a leader now and all Dana was ever going to be was mean.

Chad, Jelissa and the rest of the lunchroom watched us, wondering if Jake would agree to this treasonous act.

After a moment, he let out a breath through his nose and stood. With unhurried strides, he walked around the lunch table. Expensive sneakers, jeans and a football jersey made him look like he was about to take the field at an NFL game as the hot shot quarterback. There was no doubt about it. Jake Winsted was hot. Maniacal, but hot.

He stood in front of Chad, who stayed seated.

"Chad Jackson," he said, holding out his hand.

Chad looked at Jelissa with something akin to euphoria, stood and held out his hand to complete the handshake.

And just like that, Chad and Jelissa were popular once again by order of King Jake, and with a little nudging from Queen Bella.

I raised a victorious eyebrow at Dana. She practically had smoke coming out of her ears.

Good. I hoped her hair lit on fire.

The lunchroom returned to whispers and discussions of what this all meant. I was the Queen of the school as Jake's girlfriend, but I was a new Queen. Dana had held the title for years and had developed many faithful followers. Followers who were torn. Who was in charge now? Did Dana still rule, or was my word law?

I half listened to the passionate debate that carried on around me while the rest of my brain focused on what was going on at my table. Chad and Jelissa had been absorbed back into the folds of popularity.

Pride rose within me. I did this. I'd given two students a second chance.

The small accomplishment made me wonder what else I could do? Who else's life could I change?

Jake's eyes wandered over to mine. He looked surprised. No one had ever defied Dana before. Did that put me in the doghouse with him? After all, wasn't this whole charade so that he could get back with her?

I nibbled at my sandwich and tried to put it out of my mind. Out of the corner of my eye, I saw Regina staring at me, a small smile on her face. I ignored her. She may have turned into an angel overnight but I still didn't trust her. There was something in her eyes that screamed fake. Like the Devil offering Eve the fruit. I would not be so naïve.

"Wow." Dana talked obnoxiously loud from her table next to ours. "Three dogs at one table. We should totally call the dog catcher and tell him that we have a mutt problem."

Her friends laughed and gave her high fives.

I didn't find it funny at all. It was time to do my second good deed for the day.

"Save your jokes, Dana, because believe it or not, your reign of terror is over," I said. "From now on, the girls in this school can date whomever they want, whenever they want. The ban is lifted."

The popular girls at Dana's table sat up straight, their eyes glued to their leader. But Dana was not one to give in. She feigned innocence, but I could smell the lies on her.

"Ban? I didn't ban you girls from dating anyone, did I?"

Some of the girls looked down, while the others nodded their heads in agreement.

"See. My friends are free to do whatever they want. Why don't you go find more homeless puppies to stink up the cool table with? Oh and when you do, remember that you and your new animal friends are not invited to Stephanie's party on Friday."

Jake looked directly at Dana.

"Cole and Jelissa are coming to the party Friday."

Dana leveled him with a hard gaze of her own. "No. They're not."

"They are." Jake said. "Stephanie already said they could. Didn't you, Steph?"

Stephanie's mouth opened and closed like a fish as she looked between Jake and Dana. She loved her queen, but Jake was Jake. There was no stopping the storm that would come upon her if she went against him. Everyone knew that.

"Um, sure. They're welcomed, I guess."

Jake gave her one of his sweet smiles.

"Thanks, Steph."

"You're welcome, Jake."

Stephanie was instantly turned into a giggly, gooey mess. I felt sorry for her. She was a power leech. The kind of girl that wanted the biggest, baddest guy in the room as her boyfriend so that she could feel safe from the world and at the same time, feel free to talk as much crap as she wanted without fear of reparation. She'd had her eye on Jake for as long as I'd known her but recently, she'd been secretly flirting with the other boys around the table too, including Cole.

Dana scowled at her.

"Well, I guess I've been overruled," she said. Her eyes turned dark. Conniving. She raised one eyebrow in Jake's direction. "It doesn't matter who is at the party as long as Dustin is there."

Up until then, the guy who'd been sitting next to her was buried in his phone. I'd seen him around. Dustin Rodriguez. The same boy that she'd made out with at The Center a few days ago. He was on the low end of the popularity totem pole, but his awesome clothes and his laid-back personality had him climbing fast. I wasn't sure why he would make enemies with the popular guys in school just to side with Dana.

He looked like he'd been playing a game or something on his phone. At the mention of his name, he perked up.

"What's up?"

Dana grabbed his collar, pulled her to him and kissed him slowly, seductively.

I watched Jake's hand grip the edge of the table. I was sure that it would snap off. I had to do something before he murdered Dustin. Not that I cared about Dustin, but judging by his surprised look when Dana pulled away, it was clear that he was a little more than an innocent bystander in this relationship.

Were Dana and Jake playing the same game against each other?

Either way, I had to get Jake out of there before he did some serious damage.

"Uh, Jake, can you help me with something in the hallway?"

He didn't hear me at first, his murderous eyes locked on Dustin.

I hit him with the back of my hand, pulling his attention to me.

"Jake, can you help me with something in the hallway?"

I stood and walked through the lunchroom. I didn't stop until I had walked through the double doors and entered the hallway. Right past the doors, Kenny and another kid were huddled in the corner. Another drug deal, no doubt. I remembered what Detective Harding had said about Jake's new pastime. Was the drug problem really that bad at our school? How long until Jake went down with this drug fueled ship? Would I be the one to take him down or would I sink with him?

Jake arrived a second after me. His eyes met Kenny's and both of the guilty parties power-walked down the hallway and disappeared.

I could see that Jake wanted to punch something but there was only walls and lockers out here.

"That Dustin kid is a joke! When we get back on the field, I'm going to hit him so hard that his fillings come out!"

"She's just trying to get under your skin."

"She's trying to get me to murder Dustin Rodriguez."

He swore and kicked a locker, leaving a huge dent in the bottom of it.

"God. I hate that kid!" he cried.

"Jake, you have to calm down!"

"She's playing me." He kicked the locker again, his large body still stalking the hallway.

"Look. Maybe this is a sign. Maybe we should end this game that you and Dana are playing. You obviously still like each other or else you wouldn't be trying to make each other jealous."

He kept up his rant, not hearing a word that I was saying.

"Why don't you tell Dana how you feel?" I asked. "We can end this right now. March in there, pull her off Dustin and carry her away in to the sunset."

He shook his head. "I can't."

"Why not?"

"She knows how I feel about her. If she wanted to come back, she would have been back already."

"But-"

"Just stay out of it!" he bellowed.

I bit off the flurry of curses that I wanted to say and used this opportunity to move the conversation in a new direction.

"Did you see Kenny out here?"

"Yeah. So what?"

"He seems to be around a lot more than I remember. Weird, huh?"

"What's weird about it?"

I shrugged. "I just don't know much about him, except that he's the pot hook up around here." I smoothed my features, trying to keep my voice even and casual. "How well do you know Kenny?"

He shrugged. "All my life. Why?"

"Don't you think it's weird that he's always lurking in a corner somewhere? I mean, before he was-"

"Leave it alone."

"But I'm just saying-"

"I said..." He turned to face me and my blood ran cold. There was so much threat in his eyes. "Leave it alone."

I wanted to run, but I wouldn't run from Jake's threats. I had too much pride for that.

"You can't bully me, Jake. You can't force me to say what you want me to say and to think what you want me to think and not question anything."

He narrowed his eyes at me.

"You will stay away from Kenny. You will not ask any questions about Kenny. You will continue to do what I tell you to do or I will march in to the lunch room, pop your little popular bubble, and break up Ariel and Eric permanently." His hand clamped on to my upper arm. He was close. His nostrils flared. He was glaring down at me.

"Do you understand me?"

"You can't intimidate me, Jake." The strength in my voice surprised me, considering that I was freaking out. We were in an empty hallway and he was twice my size. I'd never thought that Jake would hurt me but as I stood alone in this hallway, with him glaring down on me and knowing who he really was, I began to reconsider that thought.

"Don't presume to tell me what I can and cannot do, Bella. You'd be surprised."

"Get off her, Jake."

The commanding tone came from by the door. I looked. It was Cole.

"Mind your business, brother," Jake said.

"I said, get off her."

"And I told you to leave."

Cole was by my side in an instant, his face turning a crazy shade of red.

"I am going to count to three, and then I'm going to break your arm."

The two brothers glared at each other, with me standing awkwardly in the middle. I felt the heat coming off them. The rage.

"One," Cole said.

Jake didn't release me. In fact, his grip tightened.

"Two."

Suddenly, blood flowed in to my arm as Jake's grip loosened. I stumbled back, rubbing the soreness away. Without me between them, Jake and Cole were chest to chest. With their identical height and build, it was difficult to see who would win if they started fighting. I prayed that it would be Cole.

"Stay out of my business," Jake said. "We all have our secrets. I'd hate to share yours."

"You touch her again and I will rip your head off."

"I'd like to see you try it."

They stared at each other for a long minute. One side of Cole's mouth ticked.

"Consider this your only warning. If I catch you beating up on her, me and you will have a problem. If you even breathe in a way that she doesn't like, I will be there to make you regret it."

"Oohh. I'm shaking." Jake held out one hand and jokingly shook it.

Cole was not amused.

I'd never seen anyone stand up to Jake before. The fact that it was

Cole, and that it was over me, stole my breath away. I was both fearful and grateful.

"You will. You know what I'm capable of."

"And you know what I'm capable of."

"I guess we'll see then."

The bell rang and the brothers stepped back from each other. Jake walked down the hallway and turned the same corner that Kenny had while Cole came to me.

"Did he hurt you?" he asked, eyeing my arm.

I shook my head.

"No."

He looked like he didn't believe me and frowned.

"If he does anything that makes you uncomfortable, anything at all, tell me immediately. You understand?"

I nodded. "Yes."

"Text, phone, social media, smoke signals, however you need to contact me. Got it?"

"Yes."

"Good."

We stood our ground, gazing at each other while the rest of the student body flowed around us.

"Why did you stand up for me?" I asked.

Cole's eyes turned sad. Like he wanted to tell me something. I stood, waiting for him to speak. To reveal what was going on in his head.

"I, uh..." He scratched his head. "If something happens to you, then I fail English and French. I gotta keep my grades up, so..."

He jammed his hands in his pockets.

I knew two things in that moment.

First, Cole was lying.

Second, I hated that he felt like he needed to lie to me. Why couldn't he just talk to me? I wanted him to talk to me.

"Just, uh, keep me posted, okay?" he said.

"Yeah. Okay."

He nodded and walked backward.

"I'll see you in study hall."

"Yeah."

He took a few more steps backward before finally turning and walking away, leaving me confused and shaking in the hallway. In that moment, I knew that I had to stop Jake and Kenny and their drugs. I had to get the information to Detective Harding before any real damage was done. Before they killed someone.

But how?

32

Something weird was going on inside of me.

At first, I hated Cole. Now, I didn't hate him so much. What did it all mean? I was so confused and oddly enough, lonely. I couldn't talk about my problems to Jasmine or Ariel, lest I give away the fact that Jake and I were not real. So, the only person that I had to talk to was myself and I had no answers.

Cole sat on a scratched, wooden chair in study hall, waiting for me. I remembered yesterday at my house. How close we were. How his lips had nearly touched mine. Little shivers of anticipation ran through me.

Whoa. Where did that come from?

I cleared my throat and walked forward. I couldn't think about Cole like that. He'd said it himself. I was his brother's girlfriend. Cole and I were off limits. Wrong. Dangerous. A fuse that, if ignited, could change everything forever.

I had to keep my heart far, far away from Cole Winsted or else.

He looked at me as I sat down, his eyes hooded, his mouth in a tight line. Had he gotten into another fight with his brother?

"What's wrong?"

He shook his head. "Nothing. Jake's just being a douche."

"You too, huh?"

"Yeah. No one misses being hit by the Jake train. That's what we say at home, anyway."

"Appropriate."

I let out a breath. I could do this. I could be friends with Cole. Friends and nothing else.

We began reviewing parts of the house in French.

Living Room. *Salon.*

Door. *Porte.*

Kitchen. *Cuisine.*

Window. Fenêtre.

All this talk about French houses had me thinking about what Cole's house was like. His father was some sort of drug lord, right? Did they live in a mansion somewhere? A penthouse? A normal-sized house?

What was his father like? I imagined him to be some big, muscly, bald guy with a scar running down his cheek. At least, that's how Russian drug lords were portrayed in movies. Was he like that? Was he a mean dad? Was he around at all? What about his mom? She was the reason why Cole spoke French. Were they close?

"French!"

I looked up in horror, realizing that I had spaced out again.

"Sorry," I said, refocusing on my book.

"What?" he asked.

I looked up at him again.

"What?"

"Why are you zoning out on me?" He dropped his pencil on the scarred table and bridged his fingers. One teasing eyebrow raised high on his forehead. "Am I that boring?"

"Truthfully?"

"Yes."

I let out a breath.

"I might have fallen into a slight coma," I replied. "I can't help it. Your voice is like *Benadryl*."

"It cures allergies?"

"No. It puts me to sleep."

He snorted.

"I guess you like me better when I'm not speaking."

His eyes tipped up at the ends.

Was he teasing me about our almost kiss yesterday? My cheeks turned hot.

"Right now, I'd prefer you non-existent."

He laughed out loud then. I bit the inside of the cheek to keep my laughter inside.

How could he be so cavalier about our almost kiss? It'd been fluttering around in the back of my brain ever since. Maybe it didn't mean anything to him. Maybe he went around almost kissing girls all the time.

I tried to remember if Cole was a player. Had I seen him with other girls?

"Stop thinking, French. You're killing me."

"What? I'm not thinking."

"You are. I get it. Lots of girls dream about me."

I threw my pencil at him. It bounced off his shoulder. The same shoulder that now shook up and down with laughter.

This time, I laughed out loud, too.

"You're an odd duck, French, I gotta tell you. You get all red in the face when somebody even mentions kissing." He leaned forward. "Are you a kissing virgin?"

My cheeks were hot before. Now they were on fire.

"No. I'm not a," I lowered my voice, "kissing virgin. I've kissed lots of boys."

"Oh yeah? Name one. Besides my brother, I mean, which, by the way, I still think was not consensual."

"What makes you think that?"

"I have my reasons. Now spill. One guy."

I rolled my eyes.

"Okay. Fine. Ralph Mooch."

His gaze fuzzed as he tried to place the name.

"No one here," I said.

His shoulders visibly relaxed.

"He was back in North Carolina, and his retainer fell out when he tried to stick his tongue down my throat."

He grimaced.

"That is, quite possibly, the grossest thing I've ever heard."

"Tell me about it."

"Everyone knows that you're supposed to take your retainer out before you kiss a girl."

I made a face. "So, you're an expert then?"

I wanted to take the question back as soon as I said it. I didn't want to know the girls that Cole had kissed. The very thought of it sent my stomach into knots.

"Well, I'm not a novice, if that's what you want to know."

"And how many girls has Mr. Not a Novice kissed?"

"Two."

Two? Somehow, I thought the number would be higher. Not that I knew Cole so well. Still, he seemed like the kind of boy that girls would want to kiss.

"Okay. I gave you a name. You give me one."

"Trudy McClentoch."

My eyes bulged "The Calculator?"

Cole nodded. We called Trudy 'The Calculator' because she was a math genius. I was sure that she did square roots in her sleep. This year alone, she'd gotten her picture on the MATH WHIZ board every month. That board was reserved for kids who got a 100% on every math test. If Trudy did half as well in her other classes as she did in math, she would be valedictorian for sure.

"Does that surprise you?" he asked.

I shrugged. A little.

I pictured Trudy. Tall and skinny. She wore the school uniform every day, though it wasn't required once you became a Junior. Navy skirt, white shirt, school jacket, high socks and black shoes. Every. Single. Day. She was okay looking. Not beautiful. Not ugly. Just okay.

"I guess I imagined you with someone more like-"

"Like Dana?" he asked. "Blonde, busty and brick headed? No thanks. Jake looks at what's on the outside. I prefer to sink a little bit deeper."

His eyes held mine and I shivered. Although we were in a library full of kids, somehow, us, at this scratched up table with gum beneath it, felt intimate. Like it was just me and him.

I leaned back and crossed my arms, trying to shake Cole from my head.

"And did Trudy get to see the great Winsted mansion?"

He ran a hand through his hair.

"No girl gets to see Winsted mansion. Not now, anyway. My mom is, kind of-"

"Particular? Judgy?"

"Dying," he blurted out. "My mom is dying."

My spirts dropped, empathy for Cole pulsing within me. Sadness radiated from Cole's eyes, infusing into mine. I placed a hand over his and squeezed.

"I'm so sorry."

He gave me a small smile.

"Thanks."

"If you don't mind me asking, what is she-"

"Cancer."

My mouth formed an O and I shuffled in my seat.

"I know how hard it is."

"I know."

"If you need someone to talk to, you can talk to me." I squeezed his hand again. "Remember. Text. Call. Smoke signals. Whatever."

He smiled. A genuine, bright smile.

"Yeah. I remember."

We sat at the table, our hands clasped, our eyes glowing with emotions that neither one of us understood.

Something changed between us. There was some spark there. A sense of our lives racing, out of control, down an uncertain course. I hoped that the course ended someplace good but I feared that it didn't.

He cleared his throat, breaking the moment. His hand slid back from mine, leaving me cold. Lonely.

"We should probably finish up."

"Yeah. Sure."

I placed my hands in my lap. They hummed, remembering the feel of his skin against mine. Tiny butterflies burst to life within my belly, eating me from the inside out. I moved my hand to my stomach, trying to quiet them.

It didn't work.

I glanced at Cole and saw him staring at me, an odd look on his face. It was less sad than before. Less angry. More ... I don't know.

He gave me a smile.

I gave him one, too.

"All right, French. Conjugate the following verbs..."

33

Mojo was freshly walked and I was freshly showered, moisturized and perfumed when Cole showed up at my doorstep after school. The day had been a nightmare but somehow, with Cole here, there was a little bright spot in it, too.

"How long have you guys lived here?" he asked, plopping down on the couch. He looked more comfortable today than he did the last time he was here. For some reason, that made me happy. I wanted Cole to be comfortable here.

"Going on three years," I replied. "We moved my Freshman year."

"So, in the three years that you've been here, you've yet to unpack a single box?"

I spied the stacks of boxes around the room. Some of them were half unpacked, some of them weren't even opened yet. To our credit, we did have five boxes flattened and stuffed behind the sofa. Five out of a bazillion was something, right?

"We're kinda not settled in yet," I said. "But I guess it worked out because we're moving on Sunday."

"Moving? Where?"

My phone buzzed in my pocket, interrupting my answer. I pulled it out and examined the number while *Play That Funky Music White Boy*, my father's favorite song, played.

"Hey, Daddy. What's up?"

I heard the whinny of horses in the background. If I closed my eyes, I could smell the manure.

"Hey, honey. Forget something?"

I frowned, mine and Daddy's agreement rushing back to mind.

"Oh, yeah. Sorry. I forgot to call you when I got home."

"So I noticed." There was a slight edge of irritation in Daddy's voice. I'd be hearing about my misstep later. "What are you up to?"

"Just studying. Cole and I have an English project due next week."

"Cole? You have a boy in the house?"

Oops. I guess I forgot to mention that, too.

"It's okay, Daddy. He's vile. And Mojo's here, too."

I stuck out my tongue at Cole and smiled, letting him know that it was just something I said to soothe my father's worried nerves. He stuck out his, too.

"Let me speak to him."

Uh oh. I handed him the phone with an apologetic expression.

"He wants to talk to you," I said.

Cole took the phone as if I just told him that *Beyonce* was at the other end.

"Hello, Mr. French."

My stomach tied in knots. What would Daddy say to him? Would he tell him to leave and never come back or would he be normal? I glanced at my bedroom doorway. Mojo was sitting in it, with only his upper body visible. He stared at the conversation, as if supremely interested in what was going on.

Nosey pup.

Cole continued to speak a little too loudly into the phone.

"We met at the science fair last year ... Yes, that's me ... Yes, I did win. Bella's project was okay, too ... Yes, I understand how worrying it can be but I'd like to assure you that I am only here to study ... I understand. Believe me, if it was up to me, I would have let you know that I was coming by ... I think that would be a great idea. Let me give you my phone number. That way, we'll both be on the same page..."

Cole rattled off his phone number to my father, while I sat wide-eyed with my stomach doing full-on somersaults. "Yes, I am scheduled to come by every day after school for an hour or so. Maybe one day I can stay for dinner and we can get to know each other a little better ... That would be fantastic ... Yes, definitely ... I'll see you soon ... Okay. Bye."

He handed the phone back to me, a big grin on his face.

"Your father's a cool dude," he said. "He invited me to dinner next week."

My mouth dropped open.

"He didn't."

"He did." Cole leaned back on the couch and put his hands behind his head. "Parents do love me. Of course, who wouldn't love me?"

I made a barfing expression and stuffed my phone back in my pocket.

"So, your ringtone is a bit on the old side for you, isn't it?"

"What's wrong with my ringtone?"

"*Wild Cherry*, 1976. I wouldn't peg you for a funk sort of girl."

"Oh yeah. What would you peg me as?"

He shrugged. "At first, more angry chick music. But now, I'm not so sure."

"I'll have you know that I am a music connoisseur. I have music that goes back to the nineteen twenties."

He sat up straight, his eyes locked on mine. "Oh really. Name one song from the twenties."

"*Brown Eyes, Why Are You Blue*, by *Nick Lucas*." One of my favorites. My grandfather sang it to me sometimes when I was sad as a kid.

One of Cole's eyebrows raised.

"Not many people know this but I, too, enjoy a musical tune every now and again."

"You like music?"

"Does that surprise you?"

"Well, you are a nerd jock. I guess nothing should surprise me about you."

"Now you're learning, French."

He pulled out his phone, typed in something and placed it on the table.

"What are you doing?"

The teasing, challenging glint in his eyes made me want to smile. I bit my cheek instead.

"You should know better than anyone what this is."

"Some sort of test?"

He grinned wide. "Everything is a test. Now, in a minute, you'll hear some music come on. You will have thirty seconds to answer the questions. Because of my superior math skills, I will be keeping score. The person who wins gets bragging rights."

Bragging rights over Cole? I was in!

He walked to the other side of the table and knelt so that we were face to face with the table between us.

"I should warn you. I'm very, very good at this."

The music began and, for the next hour, we shouted out names of artists, song titles and music trivia.

"Madonna!"

"Prince!"

"The Monkees!"

"Al Jolson!"

"The Hudson Brothers!"

"Michael Jackson!"

By the time the battery on his phone had whittled down to a measly one percent, he was leading me seventy-two to seventy. But I didn't care. I was breathless, my throat hurt, my heart was racing and my adrenaline was pumping. I was surprised to discover that I had actually had fun with Cole.

Go figure.

"You weren't kidding when you said you knew music," he said. "Not as well as I do, of course, but you're not half bad."

"You only got those two points because you know the name of all the Hanson brothers. I wouldn't brag about that."

"Whatever."

I smoothed my hair back from my face as Cole stood and came back to sit on the couch.

"So, do you have a favorite band?" I asked.

He smiled. He did that a lot, it seemed. More than I remembered. Was Cole having as good a time as I was?

"I am tempted to make you guess," he said. "More than tempted." His eyes swept over my face, stopping on my lips for a moment before raising back up to my eyes. My cheeks flushed hot. "I'll tell you what. I will give you three clues. We'll see if you can guess the band from there. And no Googling."

I shrugged. I didn't need to *Google* music facts. They were all in my head.

"Fine," I said, trying to pretend like I didn't care. But I did care. Games with Cole were fun, even if he was super competitive.

"Their logo is inspired by a Hindu Goddess, Martin Scorsese directed a live concert film for them, and the lead singer is a ballet dancer."

I frowned, trying to think of who the band would be.

"No thinking now, French. We will discuss it after school tomorrow. Then maybe, if you're nice, I'll let you quiz me."

I rolled my eyes, even though I was having a great time.

"Whatever." I sat back on the couch and picked up my copy of *A Midsummer Night's Dream*, but I wasn't ready to go back to our project just yet. "76 Central Park West."

"What?"

"You asked where we were moving to. It's 76 Central Park West."

"Ooh. That's ritzy for a mechanic."

"How did you know that my dad was a mechanic?"

He shrugged. "You mentioned it when you first came to sit at our table, remember?"

I half smiled. "Well. That's different."

He half smiled, too. "What's different?"

"I'm not used to guys actually listening to what I say."

"Listen, just because my brother's a jerk, doesn't mean you have to paint the rest of mankind with the same brush. We are not all Jake Winsted. Some of us are good guys."

"Good guys, huh? Is that what you think you are? A good guy?"

"I don't think, French. I know. Multitudes of women approach me every day. They fall to my feet, their faces streaked with tears, all to say how good of a guy I am."

Cole had a flair for the dramatic. It was amusing but I wouldn't tell him that.

"And of these hordes of girls, have you picked one? Is there someone special for Cole Winsted?"

I waited for his answer like a drowning man waited for a lifeline, though I wasn't sure why. Why would I care if Cole had a girlfriend or not? We were sorta friends, but nothing more. His dating history should have meant nothing to me. And yet, I salivated for his answer.

When did I become so pathetic?

"I'm going to let you figure that one out."

I laughed and threw a pillow at him.

"So much for being Mr. Nice Guy."

"What can I say? I like a little mystery."

I laughed so much my stomach hurt.

"I guess that you can take the animal out of the gentleman but you can't take the gentlemen out of the animal," I said. "Or something like that. What I meant to say was that men are animals but it came out wrong. Okay. Start over."

"That was the worst metaphor that I've ever heard in my life. It was so bad that it literally made me want to cut my ears off."

We burst into a fit of giggles until tears ran down our cheeks. We laughed and laughed, and when we were done with laughing, we laughed some more.

"I have to tell you, French, you are not the Girl-Zilla that I thought you were."

"Is that what they called me? Girl-Zilla?"

"Well, not they, really. Just me."

"Nice. I guess that my nickname for you was just as appropriate."

"And what was that?"

"Jerky McJerkface."

He howled in laughter. "That's the worst name ever! Oh my god. You are banned from talking ever again."

"It's better than what I call Kenny Jennings."

"What do you call him?"

"Mc-Coke-Head."

He threw his head back and let out another laugh.

"That name is definitely worse."

"You're right. Your name is better. But your IQ is pretty low so you may not understand the awesomeness of it."

"My IQ?" He was on me like a shot, his thick fingers pressing in to my side, tickling me in my most ticklish spot ever. My sides.

"My IQ is genius level, I'll have you know," he cried, while I wailed with laughter on the couch. "Say that I'm a genius. Say it!"

"Never!"

I could barely get the word out, I was laughing so hard.

"Say it or be ready for death by laughter."

"No, no." My stomach ached, my throat ached and I'd never been so thoroughly amused in my entire life.

"All right, all right!" I screamed.

His fingers stilled on my side.

I laid on the couch below him, panting, my cheeks red, my body electric. He hovered above me, ready to move in for another tickle at the earliest sign of my hesitation.

Our eyes dueled. Cole's expression was a fluid sea of happiness and joy, then sadness and sorrow. Then something else. Something that darkened his blue eyes to nearly navy. His gaze dropped to my lips and I could barely breathe.

He was so close. So close, and yet, not close enough.

His familiarized himself with my mouth, inspecting it. Committing it to memory. Goosebumps flew up my spine. Heat pooled in my gut. My cheeks caught on fire.

What would his lips feel like against mine?

Without warning, he cleared his throat, looking at anything else in the room but me.

He climbed off me and sat back on the couch.

I wrapped my arms around myself, trying to stop the shivers that raced through me. I wasn't sure if it was from the loss of his heat or something else.

"Maybe we should, um..."

His gaze wandered over to me. One side of his mouth tilted into a half smile before stretching into a laugh filled with awkwardness and the unsaid words that hung between us.

"Well, that was weird. And it was like the second time it happened, so it was, like, double weird."

My stomach hurt from all the butterflies that beat within it. Something sparked to life when he looked at me. Some crazy mix of joy, hope and fear. I bit my lower lip against the warring emotions. It felt like I could sit here all day, staring at him while he stared at me. But apparently, Cole had more control than I did. I guess it was all those honed social graces that came with being popular all one's life.

He picked up his copy of *A Midsummer Night's Dream*. I pulled out my copy too, feeling very much like Hermia. Or was it Helena? Titania, perhaps? Why was my brain so foggy all of a sudden?

"Maybe we should focus on our dramatic play," he said. "I do have one condition, though."

"And what's that?"

He raised a teasing eyebrow at me. "That you let me pick the title."

I threw a pillow at him and we laughed some more. Somehow, my rotten day had just gotten a little bit brighter.

34

Jasmine and Ariel walked in a half hour after Cole left.

It had been at least a week since we'd had a girls night and I needed one bad. Not that I could tell them much about what was going on in my life, but it felt good to just have them there, eating ice cream, throwing popcorn at each other and watching *The Notebook* on permanent repeat. We may have not had much experience with boys but we were still true romantics at heart.

"So, did Eric propose yet?" I teased.

Ariel's cheeks reddened and her eyes lit. Her silver spoon dipped in to her bowl, before reappearing with a glob of chocolate ice cream. She put it in her mouth and sucked on it thoughtfully, a slow smile spreading across her face.

"Spill," Jasmine said, placing her bowl down on the bed and leaning toward Ariel. "What's new with lover boy?"

Ariel sucked on her spoon for a few more seconds before placing the bowl on the floor and crossing her legs beneath her.

"Ladies, I think I'm in love," she screeched.

Me and Jasmine screamed while we threw pillows at Ariel's smiling face.

"That's not news!" I said. "You've been in love with Eric for forever."

"No. I've been in love with the idea of Eric forever. With his popular persona and his online persona. Now, I'm in love with him."

"What's the difference?" Jasmine asked.

"Because," Ariel tipped her chin in the way she always did when she was going to lecture us, "I didn't really know him before. Now, it's different. There is just so much about him that's sweet, and kind, and strong. God. I just want to eat him up!"

We screamed again and put our hands over our hearts, pretending to be scandalized.

"Why, Ariel Swimworthy, what would your father say?" Jasmine asked.

"Daddy loves him."

Jasmine and I gawked at our red headed friend, our mouths hanging open.

"He's met your father?" I asked.

Ariel nodded.

"When?"

"Yesterday. When he showed up at my door with flowers and chocolates and asked Daddy's permission to sit with me on the front steps of our building and talk."

"No way," Jasmine gasped.

"Yes way. Daddy called him respectful."

For Triton Swimworthy, calling someone respectful was like calling them a saint. Respect and manners were huge in Ariel's house. Eric had scored some major points.

"So, what did you two do? Just sit on the steps and talk?"

"Until ten o'clock. Then he walked me back upstairs, thanked my father for the opportunity to talk to me-"

"He said that?" Jasmine asked.

Ariel nodded. "He walked in and said, 'Mr. Swimworthy, thank you for allowing me the opportunity to get to know your beautiful daughter. Here is my phone number in case you ever need to get in touch with me'." Ariel's eyes rounded. "I've never seen Daddy's mouth hang open like that. Ever."

"That's incredible. And so romantic!" My heart was racing just from hearing Ariel's amazing story.

"You should have seen it. My sisters were lined up in the hallway and he introduced himself to each one of them on the way out. Then, when he told me good night, he kissed my hand. Girls, I thought that I was Juliet and he was Romeo."

"Does he have a brother?" Jasmine asked.

Ariel fell back on to the bed, arms splayed open as if she was trying to make snow angels in my sheets.

"Then, when he got home, we texted each other all night."

"Who knew that he was such a gentleman?" Jasmine said.

"His grandfather is an oilman from Alabama. His father is an interpreter for the French embassy. Charm is practically running in his veins."

"And respect," Jasmine added.

"Yes. Respect, too. He asks a lot."

"What does that mean?" I asked.

"He asks me a lot of questions. How are you feeling? How was your day? Do you like to do this? Is it okay if I kiss you? What are you thinking?"

"Wait, wait, wait," Jasmine said. "Back up. He's kissed you?"

Ariel shrugged and moved her feet around excitedly. "Well, only on the hand. But he always asks, 'May I kiss you? Can I kiss you? Is it okay if I kiss you?' God. I just want to write him a permission slip that says, kiss me anytime you want."

"So, this was more than a one-time thing?" I asked.

"Whenever he sees me, he kisses my knuckles, then puts his hands over it, like the kiss is going to fly away or something. Then, when he says goodbye, he kisses my palm and closes my hand over it. I just want to drag him behind the bleachers!"

"Ariel, you have struck gold!" Jasmine said. "Respectful, nice boys with hot bodies and cute faces are very hard to find. You better marry him before he flies back to heaven with the other angels."

I laughed out loud.

"Amen to that," I said.

"So, when are you going to announce to the world that he's yours?" I asked.

Ariel shrugged. "Soon, I hope. I've seen Ursula sniffing around him and I'm too young to go to jail for murder."

Jasmine chuckled.

"It's true. They'll put your hair in corn rows and make you wear orange jumpsuits. I'm not sure that goes with your complexion." She poked at Ariel's chin and the three of us exploded in laughter.

Laughter so loud that we almost didn't hear my dad knock on the door.

"Girls," he said. He'd just gotten home from work and he looked tired. There was dirt beneath his fingernails and he smelled like hay and horses.

"You have some more visitors."

More visitors? Who would visit us? I wasn't expecting anyone.

He disappeared from the door and Stephanie, Mel, and Ursula stepped over the threshold, taking in my unpacked house and my barely decorated room. Mojo followed after them, growling.

What were they doing here?

"Are you lost?" Jasmine asked.

"Nope," Mel said. "We just came to pay a visit to Bella. We figured that now that you're popular that you'd need some friends worthy of your new status."

"Aren't you Dana's friends?" Ariel asked. "Isn't this some sort of conflict of interest?"

"Not at all." The three girls stepped deeper in to the room. They looked around in disgust. Like they would catch a disease from the carpets or something. "With Dana on the outs socially, we thought that we'd start exploring other options and Bella's name was the first to pop into our collective minds."

"Well, you know what they say," Jasmine said. "Small minds think alike."

Stephanie narrowed her eyes at Jasmine.

"Anyway, Bella. We thought we'd come by and let you know that anytime you need anything at all, you can let us know. Consider yourself arrived."

"Great," Ariel said. "Now you can arrive yourself back to the strip club that you crawled out of."

Stephanie took a step toward Ariel.

"Maybe if you had better manners, people who mattered would actually remember that you exist."

Ariel stood and stormed forward, standing nose to nose with Stephanie.

"The people who matter to me are in this room. Minus the three of you, of course. Why don't you run along before I decide to throw Nair in your hair?"

Stephanie gasped, then looked at me.

"Aren't you going to reign your friend in?"

"No one reigns me in," Ariel growled.

"That's funny," Ursula said. "I've been hearing that Eric has been reigning you in just fine. Though I'm not surprised. He's always liked to slum it."

The second the words left Ursula's mouth, Jasmine and I jumped up, holding Ariel's outstretched hands back from Ursula's throat.

"Don't you dare say his name!" Ariel cried.

Ursula gave her a sly smile. "Why wouldn't I? He's already said mine. Over and over and over again."

"Eric would never touch a fat whore like you!"

Ursula's eyebrows rose. "Wouldn't he?"

In a sudden burst of strength, Ariel ripped herself out of mine and Jasmine's hold and charged at Ursula. In record time, we grabbed her again.

Mel, Stephanie and Ursula stood back, smiling at us.

"You know, Bella, I would rethink my associates. We came here to extend our support and your red-headed beastly friend just attacks us out of nowhere. Is this what you want us to tell everyone at school tomorrow? That you associate with wild animals?"

"I'll show you an animal!" Ariel continued to buck and shove us away, desperate to get to the girls.

I couldn't let that happen. If Mel, Ursula and Stephanie were extending an olive branch to me, I had to take it. One, it would give me unmatched insight into Jake's life. Maybe they could tell me if he was, indeed, involved in dealing drugs like Detective Harding thought he was. Plus, they would be able to give me valuable tips on being popular. Tips that Ariel and Jasmine didn't have. And, if they started spreading rumors about Ariel, those rumors might reach Eric. What would he say? What would he think?

"Ariel, stop."

Ariel's wide eyes zeroed in on me as if I had just cursed her father.

"What?"

"Stop. Just be cool."

"I will not be cool," she said. "Not around them."

"They're just being friendly," I said. "Can't you just be normal about it?"

"Have you forgotten that Stephanie dunked your head in a toilet?"

I sighed.

"That was Freshman year."

"Or that she spread that rumor that there were crabs in your hair?"

"That was sophomore year."

"Or that they're probably working with Dana to cover your locker with crap every morning?"

"For the record," Stephanie said, "we had nothing to do with that."

"Yeah. I'll bet," Jasmine said.

"I just want us all to get along," I pleaded with them. "Can't we all just be friends?"

"I can't be friends with someone who attacks me and my friends," Stephanie said.

"And I can't be friends with a bulimic spaz."

Stephanie's face stretched in outrage and she glared at Ariel.

"Them or us, Bella," she said, her voice dropping to lethal tones.

"Can't we-"

She glared at me. "Them or us."

I took in a deep breath, my eyes darting between my best friends and the girls who'd tortured me since Freshman year. I had to make a decision. A decision that would affect everyone in our school. With Kenny being Mel's on again, off again boyfriend, I was sure that she could tell me exactly what I needed to know about Jake and his drugs.

Maybe the four of us could convince Jake and Kenny to stop dealing in our school.

I, Bella French, could clean up St. Mary's Academy once and for all.

I let out the breath and kept my eyes on the carpet, my stomach tied in knots.

"Maybe you should go," I said.

"Ha!" Ariel cried out. "Get back out on the streets before your pimp comes back."

"I meant you."

I looked up, watching Ariel and Jasmine's face squeeze in confusion.

"Us?"

"Just for tonight. Just until you cool down."

"You are kicking us out. Your best friends? The two people that you can actually trust, for these skanks?"

I felt terrible, but if Stephanie, Ursula and Mel were offering an olive branch, I had to take it. It was the only way I could think of to get information about Jake. I couldn't just let them walk out.

"I-"

"Don't answer. We're leaving. Come on, Jasmine. We shouldn't stay where we're not wanted."

My heart sank to my feet as I watched Ariel and Jasmine put their ice cream bowls on the table and walk out of my room. They didn't even turn around.

I'm a terrible person, I thought. I am a terrible, awful person.

But I had no choice.

Stephanie, Mel and Ursula turned to me with smiles. Smiles that, deep down in my heart, I knew were mocking me.

"Now," Stephanie said, "let's talk all about your new boyfriend."

35

After Ariel and Jasmine left, Stephanie, Mel and Ursula sat on my bed and divulged all the latest gossip. It was mostly fluff and meanness. Nothing like the conversations that Ariel, Jasmine and I had, but there were some useful parts. Like how Kenny had moved on from marijuana to cocaine and mollies, and the entire school was getting onboard. After that, Mel disappeared in to the bathroom, only to reappear five minutes later, sniffing and shaking. I had a sneaking suspicion that she wasn't peeing in there.

She sat on the floor next to me, letting out a heavy sigh.

"I wish I was dating a supplier. You're so lucky. You'll never have to pay for anything."

My breath caught in my chest. My heart sped up.

Supplier? Did she mean Jake?

I wanted to ask more questions. To grill her for all she knew. But Stephanie started talking about my change in clothing choice and all the best ways to wear my hair, steering us back in to safer waters. The moment had passed.

After that, they got up and left, leaving behind promises of forever friendship and more questions than I had answers to. Questions that circled and spun in my mind until nearly nine o'clock when Dad called me in to the kitchen for dinner.

He'd insisted on grilling up two steaks. Steaks normally meant good news. That made me happy. I needed some good news today.

My mind turned to quicksand, sinking in to a hole of theories and conjectures as I sat down at the table, a steaming hunk of sirloin with a side of mashed potatoes and corn in front of me. Dad had whipped it all up in thirty minutes. Yes, the kitchen was a mess, but he didn't complain and swear like he normally did. In fact, he seemed like he was in a pretty good mood.

I sniffed the air, catching a whiff of steak, butter, and ... cologne?

For the first time since I sat down, I took a good, hard look at my father. His face was shaved, he wore a clean, black button up shirt and a red tie. He'd even gelled his hair. He looked like he was going out again. Where was he going so late at night?

"So," I said, cutting in to my beef. "Steak?"

"Yup." He popped a piece of steak in to his mouth with a grin. "Steak. There will be lots and lots of steak around here from now on."

"Did you win the lottery or something?"

"I wish. Today, I was made manager!"

I gasped and sputtered, nearly choking on my steak.

"Manager? It's only been two days."

"The other guy quit, and with my experience, Mr. Carson made me the new stable manager. I guess the lack of choices worked out in my favor this time." He lifted his knife up in victory. It was silly but I did the same.

"The best part is that I'll be making more than what I made at the mechanics shop. Things are looking up. Thank God."

I closed my eyes and said my own prayer of thanks. More money meant a happier daddy. Maybe if he had some more joy in his life, he would start to relax a little.

We ate our steaks with gusto—I even slipped Mojo a small bite—and after dinner, I baked a batch of cookies and we sat down to watch a documentary of lions in the wild.

As I cuddled next to my dad, smelling of steak and cookies, I felt safe. Grounded. Loved. We'd gotten through this trying time together with our unbreakable bond intact.

I sighed and, for a moment, wished that I could tell my father everything. I wanted to spill my guts about Jake and our stupid arrangement. I wanted to tell him about Cole and how he made me feel happy and sad all at once. But it wasn't possible. He was already freaking out about the cop showing up here. Plus, I was still wearing Jake's clothes. It was only a matter of time before Daddy brought that up again.

My mind went back to Jake, his drugs, and surprisingly, Mel. If there was someone who was going to tell me everything, it was Mel. But how could I get her to talk to me? We spoke in Student Guidance Counseling or at least we did until Jake made it mandatory that I hang out with him and his friends by his car instead. I wondered how long it would be until Mr. Mann discovered that the student guidance counselor program was missing its only counselor.

"Well, pumpkin, I have some plans tonight."

Daddy kissed me on the head, pulling me from my thoughts.

"Plans?"

He stood, grabbing his jacket from one of the dining room chairs.

"Yes. I'm going out with a few friends."

I frowned. "A few friends, or one friend?"

"Sweetie." He walked back over to me. "I'll be back soon."

The words tumbled out of my mouth before I could stop them.

"You're not dating anyone, are you, Daddy?" As soon as the words left my mouth, my stomach soured. My mother had been dead for six years, but she was still my mother and Daddy's wife. He couldn't date anyone else. He still fell apart when I mentioned her name. We weren't done grieving her yet.

He frowned down at me. "Honey, I am just going out with some friends. I'm allowed to do that." His gaze turned hard. Parental. "I'm still the adult around here, aren't I?"

His defensiveness said it all. There weren't a few friends. There was one friend. A woman friend.

"Do your friends know that you were married?"

"Yes; they do."

"Do they know that you have a daughter?"

"Yes; they do."

"Do they know that your daughter doesn't approve of you dating anyone?"

One eyebrow rose. "Doesn't she?"

"No," I replied. And I meant it. It was too soon for Daddy to date. Mom's memory was too fresh. Her life still a whisper in our ears.

He nodded. "Well, when and if I start dating, I will be sure that we sit down and have a long talk about it. After all, I want you to be comfortable with whomever I bring home."

"But not anytime soon?" I pushed.

He nodded. "We'll talk about it."

"Who is she?" I blurted out. "I want to know who she is!" My voice was raising to hysterical levels. I'd never thought that Daddy would date again. Ever. But, now that it was a possibility, it turned my stomach. He couldn't just replace Mom like this. Like she never existed.

"Honey, you're tired." He went to kiss my forehead and I jerked away. I didn't want his kisses. I wanted his truths. I wanted to know who he had chosen to replace my mother. "Get some rest. When the time comes, we'll talk about it."

"Daddy!"

"Get some rest, honey. I'll be back soon."

Exactly three seconds later, the door shut behind him. He was gone. Off to see some woman who would smile at him and dance with him and cast her spell over him the way my mother used to. I was so angry that I couldn't sit still.

He couldn't go out with anyone. I wasn't ready for it. He wasn't ready for it.

It was time for me to make sure that he knew it.

36

The train ride to school the next day was awkward. After the stunt that I pulled yesterday, Ariel, Jasmine and I weren't exactly on speaking terms. If I were them, I wouldn't speak to me, either. Especially since I couldn't tell them the whole story about Jake and the drugs and our arrangement.

In silence, we walked in to school and I broke off to find my fake boyfriend and do our first period dance. But, to my surprise, Ariel came with me.

"Don't worry," she said, the anger in her voice clear. "I won't get too close, lest your precious new friends see me."

"Ariel, it wasn't like that."

"All I'm saying is that Jasmine and I have been by your side since the beginning. We protected you from those girls and now, the second you sniff popularity, you go running off to them like a little lost puppy."

"It's not like you were exactly friendly to them."

"I don't have to be friendly to them. They dunked your head in a toilet."

"In Freshman year!"

"That's not the point. The point is that it happened."

"And I'm over it."

"Yeah. Now you are. Two days ago, you called them skanks. Evil Queens, remember? Now you're best buddies with them? I'm sorry but it all seems a little flip floppy to me. And not even the good flip flips. The cheap ones you get at the dollar store."

"Are you calling me a cheap flip flop?"

"If the shoe fits."

I let out a breath as she stomped away.

How could Ariel say that to me? I thought we were friends and now here she was calling me names? Whatever happened to forgiveness? Whatever happened to sticking together through good times and bad? How could she treat me like this, all over one night with three girls? Three girls that she threatened, no less.

My blood was boiling by the time I reached Jake by his locker.

He kissed me on the cheek and I accepted it begrudgingly. Next to him, Eric gazed over my shoulder, as if he were waiting for someone.

Tough luck, pal. She wasn't coming anywhere near me today.

37

The first period bell rang again but I didn't hear it. My eyes couldn't unlatch themselves from my locker.

WHORE.

A thousand pieces of loose-leaf covered my locker, each white page marked with the ugly word. As I pulled the papers down, dozens of students stopped to point, laugh or whisper at me.

Who was this mystery person who kept defacing my locker? It had to be Dana. It just had to be. The question was, what was I going to do about it?

Ariel and Jasmine walked up just as I pulled the last piece of paper off my locker. The pages laid at my feet in small heaps like crinkly snow.

Hot tears pooled behind my eyes but I didn't shed them. I didn't want to cry. I wanted to punch something. I stomped my foot instead and instantly felt like a child.

"Are you okay?" Ariel asked.

If you call wanting to bash Dana's face in okay, then yes, I was perfectly okay.

"Yeah. I'm fine."

"Maybe if you weren't acting so different," Jasmine said. "Maybe if you just, I don't know, acted normal for a change, she would leave you alone."

My frown deepened. How did this become my fault? Newsflash. I was the one with the defaced locker. Not Dana.

I carefully kept my temper in check. I had already pissed off my friends last night. I didn't want this crazy stunt and my unsteady temper to force me to say more things that I'd regret.

"Look, I'm just trying to figure out where I fit in. I know things are crazy right now but they'll be normal again."

"I hope so," Jasmine said. "And soon."

She walked away, leaving Ariel and me standing in the piles of paper that drifted across the floor like wayward snowflakes.

Ariel stepped forward.

"It's so many changes so fast. We're just trying to keep up."

"I'm the same person that I've always been."

"Really? You're clothes. Your hair. It's all so different, I guess."

"Clothes and hair don't make a person. My heart is the same."

"And you hanging out with Stephanie, Ursula and Mel? How is that the same?"

I sighed. "They're nice girls, for the most part."

Ariel smiled at me but I could tell that she was frowning on the inside. Without another word, she turned and walked away, leaving me cold and lonely.

I closed my eyes. I needed to think. I needed to stop Dana in her tracks. I needed to-

"She's really something, isn't she?" Regina pushed the balls of paper around with her boot. "That Dana. Man. She's nuts. I should know. I've been dealing with her since Freshman year."

"I'm going to say something to her," I said. "I can't let her get away with this."

Regina crossed her arms and stood next to me, looking at the newly cleaned locker.

"I completely agree. Though, it may be better coming from Jake. That's his ex. He needs to be a man and stand up for you. I mean, who is his girlfriend? You or Dana?"

Her words made sense. I had to admit, they made sense.

"I already asked him to do something about it. He doesn't want to get involved."

"You should make him get involved. It's what a real man would do. And Jake's a man, isn't he? As a matter of fact, he's *your* man." She kicked a ball of paper out of her way. "If I were you, I wouldn't stand for it."

And then she was gone and I was off, marching my way to Jake's classroom. He was just coming out of the door when he spotted me. I saw his vision go up and down the hall, obviously looking for Dana. I had discovered that if Dana was around, Jake was an absolute sweetheart. If she wasn't, then he was an absolute douche hole.

This time, Dana wasn't around, which meant that the smiles, kisses and babys were not on his agenda.

"I need to talk to you," I said.

He rolled his eyes. "Make it quick. I don't want to be late."

"Did you see what Dana did to my locker?"

"No. What?"

"She covered it with papers. She called me a whore."

"And that is my problem because?"

"Um ... because she's your ex. Fix it."

"No time."

His eyes laid on something further down the hall. I followed his line of sight. It was Kenny.

"I got to go."

"You just said that you were going to be late."

"I am."

"But what about Dana?"

"I don't know. Handle it."

And then, like his sister, he was off down the hall, to whatever very important business that he had with Kenny. Drug business, no doubt.

Meanwhile, I was alone in the hallway, late for Art and wondering how I had come to find myself in the crosshairs of Dana Rich in the first place.

Oh, that's right. It was all because of a little lie.

38

I sat at lunch with Ursula, Mel and Stephanie. Dana's table sat empty now. I wondered where she was. Hiding in the library? In the parking lot?

Coward.

"Your hair is amazing and it smells so good. You have to tell me your secret."

Stephanie flipped her blonde, nearly white hair over her shoulder. She reminded me of an angel, all pale skin, light freckles, blonde hair and rail thin. It wouldn't surprise me if she had wings under her belly bearing tops.

"Just shampoo and conditioner, I guess."

"Strawberry?" She smiled at me with perfectly shaped white teeth. I wondered how high her orthodontist bill was.

I nodded. "Strawberry."

"I have to try it. I love fruity conditioners." She grabbed my hand and pulled me a little closer. "I can tell that we are going to be best friends. You and me. We're practically twins."

I wanted to ask how me and her were practically twins but Jake and Cole sat down and I was no longer the center of attention.

Stephanie turned her entire body to look at Cole. She leaned forward a bit, giving him what must've been an excellent view down her shirt.

Why did that make me grit my teeth?

"Hey," she said, giving him the smile she'd given me just a minute ago.

His eyes widened in surprise before he smoothed his expression.

"Hey, Steph."

"So, are you going to my pre- party tonight?" she asked, leaning forward on her hands.

God. I wanted to pull her hair.

"Yeah. I guess." There was a weird expression on his face. Somewhere between a smile and a grimace.

"And the Stamford Club afterward?"

"Sure."

"Great. We can meet up at my party and go to the club together." She flipped her hair over her shoulder and turned back to me.

"You're going too, right, B?"

B? I was B now?

"Yeah. I guess so."

"Fabulous. Our first party together. It's going to be awesome!"

One side of Cole's mouth ticked up in a smile. My hands gripped my salad tray until my knuckles turned bloodless.

Stephanie smiled so big that I thought her face would break.

"It will be like a double date."

Double date?

The words ran through my mind. A double date would imply that Stephanie was dating Cole. But Cole would never go out with her. She wasn't his type. He needed someone smart and funny and down to earth. Stephanie was none of those things. She was too much. Too pretty. Too smiley. Too skinny. Too blonde for Cole to consider.

I sucked in a deep breath.

No, I told myself. He would never go for her.

Still, it just felt like another lie.

Cole didn't look at me, which was weird because I was staring holes in to his face.

I swallowed and reassured myself that Cole wouldn't go for a girl like that. But, just to be sure, I made a mental note to tell him how wrong she was for him as soon as possible.

39

Cole had asked me the same question in French three times but I hadn't heard any of it. Every time I looked at him, I saw Stephanie practically throwing herself at him during lunch.

It was absolutely insane, of course. Cole wasn't mine to be jealous over. Not by a long shot. Plus, I was with his brother. I had no rights to Cole. Still, I couldn't shake the feeling that I wanted to scratch Stephanie's face off.

"Earth to Bella French," Cole said, waving his hand in front of my face.

I sat up straight and cleared my throat.

Just be calm, I told myself. You can be calm.

"I'm sorry," I said, placing both of my hands on the scratched table. If they were flat on a strong surface, he couldn't see them shake. "It's just been a long day."

He closed his book and bridged his fingers in front of him. I'd come to know this as Cole's listening position.

"Okay. The doctor is in. Tell me all about it."

I smirked. I couldn't tell Cole about it. If I told him that I was jealous that he was with another girl, he would freak. I searched my mind for other, safer topics.

"So, how's your mom?" I asked.

A little bit of the joy seeped from Cole's eyes.

"Not too well," he said. "She's fading, little by little, every day." He sat back, his bridged hands moving to his lap.

"I'm sorry."

He nodded. The movement was slow. Sad.

"Do you want to talk about it?" I asked. I moved a seat closer, placing a hand over his.

He shook his head but didn't move his hand away.

"No. Us Winsteds don't really talk about feelings. It's just not our way."

"I didn't ask if your family wanted to talk about it. I asked if you wanted to talk about it." I leaned forward. "Do you want to talk about it, Cole?"

He considered me for a moment, examining my eyes, my face. He inclined his head, as if a light bulb had just gone off.

"There is something that I want to talk about," he said. He leaned forward now, his head closer to mine, our foreheads nearly touching. "Someone sent my mom a bouquet of bright, yellow sunflowers. You wouldn't happen to know anything about that, would you?"

I dropped my eyes to the table. I did know about that. I'd ordered the flowers and sent them to Cole's mother. I didn't send a card or sign my name or anything. Did he think I was imposing? That my gesture, as innocent as it was, was out of place?

I nodded, my throat tight, my stomach aching with anticipation of his reply.

"Yes. I sent them. When my mom was sick, she said that sunflowers made her feel better. I picked fresh ones for her every day and put them in her room. They helped her. I hope they helped your mother, too."

Cole looked at me for a long while.

Finally, he said, "That was the sweetest thing that anyone has ever done for my mother. I consider it a personal gift to me. Thank you." He kissed the back of my hand then quickly ran his thumb over the now overly sensitive spot.

"Don't mention it," I replied, softly. Breathlessly.

"My father said to give you a message."

I raised an eyebrow.

"Did he?"

Cole leaned even further forward and said something in a harsh, guttural language. The force and tones of it gave me goosebumps.

"What does that mean?" I asked.

He smiled. "It's Russian for, 'Tell her thank you, and I hope she's just as pretty as the flowers'."

I smiled now at the warm message.

"I see that he's quite the charmer."

"Well, I had to get it from somewhere."

I bit the inside of my cheek. I knew what Cole and his family were. I knew who his father was. But I wanted to know more. Not just the things that Detective Harding had told me but things that would help me to understand why Cole was the way he was. What made him so driven to succeed in every aspect of his life?

It suddenly occurred to me that I wanted to get to know the boy who sat in front of me. Who really was Cole Winsted?

"Are you and your father close?" I asked.

He shook his head. "Not very. My father is very old school Russian. I joined the football team, hoping that it would impress him but I couldn't compete with Jake. He was always the favorite. He was the warrior. The golden son. Regina had a mind for business. But me, I was more, I don't know, inward, I guess. More like my mom." His gaze turned far away. "No. We're not close."

"Have you talked to him about it?"

Cole shrugged. "Winsteds don't talk about stuff like that." His voice dropped to that guttural Russian language again. Then he translated. "True men talk with fists." His face took on that sad look, like the weight of the world was on his shoulders. I slid my other hand into his and he squeezed it tight.

"I'm sorry, Cole. I'm sure there is a way to get him to understand you. You just have to figure it out."

He dropped his head to his chest. "Maybe." I saw him inhale a deep breath. It must've been agonizing to feel like the odd one out among people who were supposed to love you and care for you. It must've been even worse to have the one person who you felt closest with be on their deathbed.

I sniffed back tears that weren't mine to shed. I'd felt these feelings before. I felt them now. The loneliness. The isolation. The pain. The fear of rejection. These were emotions that I carried with me since my mom died, and now, I saw those same emotions in Cole's face.

My heart broke into a thousand pieces. I wished that I could pick them up and restore the cracks in Cole's heart but it was impossible. All I could do was be here for him right now, when he needed me.

I squeezed his hands tighter.

He let out a breath and laughed shortly.

"Well," he said, his joking manner coming back. He was closing up again. Hiding behind his walls of laughter and teasing. Hiding all the pain that he went through behind jokes.

I wish he wouldn't hide. Not from me.

"That got intense," he said, looking at me with eyes that had turned red with unshed tears. "We should take a walk or something. Shake off all of this tension, huh?"

"Cole, you don't have to do that."

"Do what?"

"You don't have to hide behind this façade with me. Phone, text and smoke signals, remember? I am here for you whenever you need me. If you want to be hurt, or sad, or angry, or even throw yourself a full-on pity party, I want you to know that I'm here for you. Okay?"

"Come on, French." His joking smile was in place now. He leaned back in his chair and crossed his arms.

I needed him to understand. I needed my words to get under his mask so that he could hear him. I stared at him hard, willing him to see the truth in my eyes.

"I mean it, Cole. If you need to talk, I'm here. Okay?"

His eyes locked with mine and after a long moment, he nodded.

"Okay, French," he replied. "Okay."

The room turned heavy. A tension hung over us that I didn't understand. It made me feel light and grounded, all at once. Like I was standing in the middle of a giant compass and its needle was pointing North. To Cole.

Our eyes didn't leave each other until the bell rung and when it did, we stayed in our seats. Something had shifted between us. Some unspoken rule had been broken. Somewhere between us getting stuck with these assignments and sitting in this room, we had become friends.

Maybe more.

The bell rang again and I gathered my things.

"I, uh, better get to class," I said.

Cole didn't move. His eyes were on the table in front of him.

I stood and put my hand on his shoulder.

"Are you going to be okay?" I asked.

One of his hands engulfed mine, warming me through.

"I'm going to be okay," he whispered.

I nodded and left. All the while, something inside of me had cracked open, letting Cole's light shine in.

I texted Jake to meet me at The Center after school so that we could talk. I wanted to break the news to him in person.

I was not going to the Stamford Club. Just as I had suspected, Dad had put the kibosh on it after hearing what time it ended. I'd argued that he had gone out at ten o'clock last night and received a 'we'll talk about that later' response. That was Daddy's way of saying that we weren't going to talk about anything.

Shaking my head, I walked up to Jake. He'd been standing outside of The Center, head buried in his phone, looking as if he were at a fashion photo shoot with his blue sweater over a pink button up that he'd left open at the neck, khaki pants and dress shoes. Meanwhile, I was half frozen in a long sleeve top, a mini skirt, and boots.

He didn't look at me when I walked up. Just scrolled through his phone as if he was barely tolerating my presence.

"What's up?"

I took a deep breath.

"I can't go to the party tonight," I said.

His looked at me then, his expression a mixture of frowning and amusement.

"You're joking, right?"

I shook my head. "No. My dad said that it started too late."

"So, tell him you're at a friend's house studying or something." His demeanor changed and he took my hand and gave me a sexy half grin. I was immediately suspicious. I'd come to see that Jake could turn on the charm when it benefited him. When it didn't benefit him, he was a Grade-A jerk. Worse than his brother ever was.

"Please," he said.

"I'm sorry. I can't."

"I have to say Bella, you're predictable. I expected this. Planned for it even." He put his hand into his pocket. "I brought something for you."

I raised an eyebrow.

"What?"

He shrugged. "I don't know. Something expensive and sparkly. Maybe even something to match the necklace that I got you."

I touched the chain around my throat. It was gorgeous and hadn't left my neck since he'd given it to me. I told myself that I wouldn't accept more gifts from him but the necklace was the most beautiful piece of jewelry that I'd ever owned. I didn't want to give it up but I didn't want to add to it, either.

"Jake, please, no more gifts."

He looked completely taken aback.

"No more gifts? Jeez. That's not something that I thought I'd ever hear a girl say." He pulled out a small box and handed it to me. "Here. I was going to wait until tonight but it looks like I'm going to need a little something extra to change your mind."

I took the box from his palm and opened it.

Inside was a beautiful tennis bracelet set with the same stones as the necklace. It sparkled, even in the low light outside.

I ran my fingers over the smooth silver and encrusted diamonds.

His smile was proud. Self-satisfied.

"It's beautiful. But..." I closed the box before I changed my mind, and handed it to him. He didn't take it. "But I can't accept it."

His face turned a bright shade of red.

"What do you mean you can't accept it?"

I dropped my outstretched arm and sighed.

"I ... I just can't."

He looked like he'd just been slapped. Fury rose in his face. I took a step back and clasped my hands behind my back, lest he try to grab me again.

"So, if you don't want gifts, then what do you want?"

All the things I wanted flashed through my mind. For Jake to stop supplying drugs to my school, for Ariel to be happy, to maintain my popularity without the weight of Jake's lies. I picked one that he would understand.

"I just want Ariel to be happy."

"Who is this girl? Did she give you a kidney or something?"

"She's my friend. Friends want each other to be happy. I'm not doing anything for her that she wouldn't have done for me."

"Friends come and friends go. You're sticking your neck out for a girl that you won't even remember after you graduate. It's pathetic."

I narrowed my eyes at him.

"Maybe to an evil, heartless, manipulative robot like you."

He raised a threatening finger.

"Watch it."

"Don't threaten me, Jake. Ever again."

He laughed shortly. "Do you think that my brother is going to jump from behind the bushes and save you? You think he's some super hero?" He leaned in closer, an evil smile on his face. "I wouldn't count on that, sweetheart. Cole and Stephanie Pleasant are probably wrapped up in each other right about now."

My stomach dropped in to my shoes.

"What?"

Jake leaned back, briefly looked at his nails and put his hands on his hips.

"You heard me." He shrugged. "Not surprising. That chick is so desperate for my attention that I'm not surprised that she's trying to shake some other branches of the family tree. If it wasn't him, she might've moved on to Regina."

My anger exploded.

"You're lying! He would never date a girl like that."

"Am I?" He lifted his chin. "Why do you care?" He tilted his head to the left. "Got a secret that you want to tell me?"

My hands shook and I stuffed them in my pocket. Cole couldn't have been with Stephanie. She chased popularity like a mosquito chased blood. Cole would never get tied up with a girl like that. Ever. Especially not since...

I didn't allow myself to think about the rest. I blinked back my feelings and struggled to get a grip on my crazed emotions.

"Face it. It's just us, French. Us against the world. Well, until I get Dana back."

My breath came out in huffs.

Jake's face turned sour.

"Fine. No more gifts. But you have to be at this party tonight. Non-negotiable. If you're not there, I'm spilling everything that I know and I know a lot."

I turned from him. I couldn't look at Jake. Not for another second. I walked away from him, my head spinning.

"Tonight, right?" Jake asked as I walked away.

What choice did I have? I had lied one too many times and now it was catching up with me. Hard.

"Yeah. Tonight."

☙ 40 ❧

I walked in to my bedroom and slammed the door closed. The mirror vibrated in protest and I slapped my hand against it, halting its shivering. I studied myself. Every freckle. Every curl.

Cole had been on my frenzied mind since fifth period. His face, his words, his warmth.

Did he think I was attractive? Did he think I was more attractive than Stephanie Pleasant?

I knew that I shouldn't care. That my confidence should be within myself and not based on what a boy thought of me. But I did care what Cole thought of me. I cared if he thought I was prettier than Stephanie Pleasant.

Why would he hook up with that skanky girl? Where was she when I held his hand after he told me about his mother? Where was she when he defended me against Jake's attack? When did this happen? How long had they been together?

I sat on the couch, arms crossed over my chest, foot shaking, knee bouncing. Nervous energy pulsed through my body.

By the time Cole knocked on the door, I was already thinking of where I would hide his body.

I stomped across the floor and snatched open the door.

"Hey." Cole's smiling face dropped into a frown. "You okay?"

"Why were you smiling?" I demanded.

He put his hands up in a defensive pose.

"Um, because I was told to leave my piss poor attitude at the door. Remember?"

"Who told you that?"

"You did. What is this, an interrogation?"

He slipped past me and walked over to the couch.

I followed behind him, my anger blazing.

"Where were you?" I asked, leaning on one hip.

"Robbing old people with a potato gun." He flopped down on the couch and put his feet up on the coffee table. He was comfortable. Too comfortable. It grated on my already taut nerves.

"This isn't a joke, Cole."

"Oh, really? Because I find your little attitude quite funny." One dark eyebrow raised high. It would have been cute if I wasn't so angry. "Did anyone tell you how amazing you look when you're mad? All flushed skin and flaring nostrils and quivering cheeks."

"That's not funny!" I cried.

My anger seemed to be feeding his humor and he wiggled his eyebrows at me.

"Who says that I'm being funny?"

"Not me. Though I know one girl who might."

"Oh yeah?"

"Yeah."

"Who's that, pray tell?"

"Stephanie Pleasant."

His smile faded a bit and his head tilted to the side as he examined me.

"Why would you mention her?"

"Your brother told me that you two were hanging out. What are you? A thing?"

"What do you care?"

I shrugged, trying to sound like I didn't care. I definitely did.

"I don't care." Another lie. "I just wanted to tell you to shower after you see her. I don't want any of her crabs crawling on my couch."

His hand went over his heart.

"Ouch."

"I'm serious."

"French, come on. Stephanie is a nice girl and she only had good things to say about you."

"I'm sure. What do you see in that girl, anyway? Or is it what you don't see in her?"

He stood and walked to where I stood, shaking with anger. I could tell that his patience with me was running thin by the way the smile faded from his lips. The tease in his eyes was gone, leaving behind only frowning brows and a turned down mouth.

"What is it, French?" he asked, his eyes hooking into mine. His jaw tightened and his eyes turned sharp. "What is the real problem?"

My heart beat so fast that I felt like I was having a heart attack. I took a step back, then turned to the kitchen, avoiding his eyes for fear that he would see my secret. The secret that I wasn't ready to admit, even to myself.

"I just don't want you to get hurt," I said. "Stephanie isn't right for you."

"Oh yeah? Then, tell me who is."

I opened my mouth and shut it again. That was a dangerous question.

"French, what is going on in that mind of yours? I can practically see the thought bubbles over your head. They're filled with spelling errors and grammatical faux paus."

"I'm really not in the mood, Cole."

"Fine. Then we'll get it all out. You don't want me with Stephanie. Why? Who would you rather me be with?"

My brain refused to think it. My mouth refused to say it. It was forbidden. Not allowed. There was no way that it would work.

"French."

I could feel his heat getting closer. Drawing me to him like a moth to a flame. My body trembled and my hand went over my heart.

I couldn't say it. Couldn't even imagine it.

"Please."

Gathering the last of my strength, I pulled myself together and whirled around.

"Maybe you should leave, Cole. Go back to Stephanie. I hope that you two live happily ever after."

Before I could take another breath, he descended upon me. Two large hands cradled my face, his mouth so close. So inviting. He breathed out. I breathed him in. Then, I stopped breathing all together, as if my lungs wanted to hold a piece of him within me forever.

It took all that I had not to close the last inch that laid between us. That wretched inch.

I couldn't. It was impossible.

"You're not breathing," he whispered. "Do you know what that means?"

I shook my head, trying not to give into the dizziness that overwhelmed me from the lack of oxygen.

His chin tipped forward, his lips barely brushing mine.

My feet danced beneath me. They wanted to lift my body just the tiniest of inches but I wouldn't allow it. I couldn't allow it.

"It means that you're with Jake."

He took a step back, releasing his hold on me.

I have never wanted to throw myself in to someone's arms before. The feeling was powerful. Hypnotizing. I let out a breath and choked one back in.

"You're with Jake," he repeated, taking another step back. "And I'm with Stephanie. That's what it means."

"Unless." The tiny word slipped out, unchecked. Cole's eyes widened and he took a step forward.

"Unless what?" His tone turned frantic.

My bottom lip trembled. My chin trembled. I was shaking all over.

This moment felt so big. So overwhelming. If I said the wrong words, I could ruin not only my life, but Ariel and Eric's as well.

"Unless what?"

Cole stepped in front of me, his hands on my shoulders. His touch was so gentle. So warm. It made me want to loosen my tongue. To reveal my greatest secret to him.

"Tell me." His voice was soft. Pleading.

A single tear dripped down my cheek.

I stepped out of his hold and away from him.

"*Rolling Stones*," I said. "The answer to yesterday's question. The *Rolling Stones*."

He looked confused and angry as I stepped around him and backed toward my room.

"Goodbye, Cole."

I hadn't yet closed the door when my hands flew over my face to keep in the sobs that rocked me to my core.

A moment later, the front door closed and Cole was gone.

41

My lies were racking up by the minute. I'd just lied to my father and told him that I was going to study at Ariel's house. Then, I changed in the hallway and ran down the stairs in my hot pink mini dress and a pair of black heels that were guaranteed to make my feet hurt.

I was sure that my father was right behind me but it was only my imagination. I sprinted through the lobby, ran out of the door and jumped in to Jake's awaiting car.

"You made it," Jake said, giving me a smile. "I was sure that you would."

"Did I have a choice?" I muttered.

His jaw clenched.

"Say hi to Ariel and Eric," he said, throwing the car into drive and speeding off.

I slowly turned my head. Ariel gave me a little wave.

"Hey Bella," she said. I could tell by the tightness in her voice that she was still pissed at me.

"Hey," I replied. My eyes slid to a smiling Eric, then back to her. "I guess I should say congratulations on finally making it official. You deserve it."

Ariel's face relaxed a bit.

"Thanks. I have you and Jake to thank for it."

My breath caught in my throat. Me? Had Jake told her what we'd done?

She took Eric's hand and laced it with her own. "If you guys hadn't started going out, I probably never would have spoken to Eric."

My lungs relaxed. She didn't know.

"Don't mention it. I'm just glad that you two are happy."

"Very happy," Eric said, taking Ariel's hand and kissing her knuckles. His eyes stayed on mine. "Very, very happy."

I couldn't read his expression in the darkness but something in his message said that he was telling me something. Something important. I made a mental note to have a conversation with Eric later.

"Did Jake tell you that my cousin runs the bar?" Eric asked. "He said that we can get some drinks if we're cool about it."

I caught Ariel's eye. We would not be drinking tonight, I told her with a look.

She ignored me and looked out of the window.

"Whiskey for everyone!" Jake hooted, lurching the car forward, the engine purring beneath my seat. The cherry red convertible smelled like new leather interior, expensive cologne and freshly purchased clothes. If wealth had a scent, this was it.

I turned around in my seat, put on my seat belt, pulled my lip gloss from my purse and slathered on another layer.

Just be cool, I told myself. Just be cool.

"The DJ at this place is killer," Jake said. "I met him at Sharon Anderson's party this summer. I'm trying to convince him to do the Winter Formal."

"Dude, isn't your brother's band trying to get that gig?"

Jake nodded. "Yeah, but who wants to listen to that crap all night. I want some real music. Not a lame cover band."

I frowned. Cole was in a cover band? When did this happen? Why didn't I know that?

"Dude, did you hear *Jay-Z*'s new album?" Jake asked Eric. "It's amazing. I downloaded it this morning."

Eric leaned forward. His head nearly touched my left shoulder.

"Put on track three. I love that song."

The car shook as Jake pumped the music and him and Eric proceeded to rap the lyrics to four *Jay-Z* songs in a row. The songs were cool but I wasn't in a rapping mood. I was much more interested in Cole's band. What was their name? What did they play?

I tried to imagine Cole as a drummer but I couldn't. He didn't have the raw aggression that drummers needed. He was probably a guitarist. A singer, maybe? Was that why he was so shocked when he caught me singing in my room? Maybe he didn't think I was musically inclined.

I wanted to pull out my phone and text him my questions but then I remembered who he was probably spending his time with. Stephanie. No. I couldn't text Cole. I couldn't do anything with Cole. We were friends and that was all we'd ever be.

My heart sank as the car raced around corners and down busy streets, zooming its way toward the docks.

Didn't Stephanie live on the other side of the city?

I looked back at Ariel but she was gazing in to Eric's eyes as he slowly kissed the inside of her wrist. He'd left off rapping with Jake several minutes ago. Now I knew why.

"Aren't we going to Stephanie's party?" I asked.

"What?" Jake shouted over the booming music.

I spun the volume dial, turning the music back to manageable levels.

"Aren't we going to Stephanie's party?"

Jake shook his head. "Nah. We're not going to make it in time. We'll make this stop and go straight to the Stamford Club."

"After the fuss you made about Jelissa and Chad going to the party, you are not even going to show up?"

He shrugged. "I was only doing it to remind certain people that they don't have a say in what goes on in this school anymore." He winked at me. "It really pissed her off, didn't it?"

I frowned and turned back to the front of the car, watching the city fade away into rows of warehouses.

Detective Harding's words came back to me. He mentioned to keep my eye out for any suspicious stops, and warehouses at night was definitely suspicious. This place appeared to be the same warehouse that Jake had stopped at when he took me clothes shopping. It was dark now so I wasn't a hundred percent sure, but it looked pretty similar.

My eyes looked for any identifying marks but there was nothing. No signs. No weird shaped windows. Just water and a dark warehouse in a row of a dozen dark warehouses. I couldn't lead anyone back here if they paid me.

Crap!

Jake backed in to a dark entranceway and the trunk popped open, obscuring my vision of whatever was going on behind me. Out of my side view mirror, I made out several men walking toward us. They all wore ski masks and carried black garbage bags.

Probably bags full of drugs that Jake and Kenny were going to sell at the party.

I looked back at Ariel in the rearview mirror. Our gazes touched for a long moment. I saw her questions. Her suspicions. I mentally sent to her that everything was going to be okay. She nodded, getting my message.

The car rocked and the trunk shut. Someone banged twice on the back of the car and we pulled away from the warehouse. My stomach was in knots. What was in the trunk? What if we got stopped? We'd all get arrested!

None of these questions seemed to phase Jake, though. He flew across town at what seemed like double the speed limit until finally, we pulled in to an underground parking garage. I stepped out first, anxious to get inside and collect my thoughts. I had to keep my eyes and ears open for any suspicious activity. Anything that I could pass on to Detective Harding.

Eric and Ariel detached themselves long enough to climb out of the car and head to the door. We showed our IDs and walked into the club.

Being a country girl from a small town, I had never been in a club before. Sure, we had parties in barns and churches and people's houses from time to time but never in a place like this.

Loud music shook the floor. I felt it rumble through my shoes and all the way in to my heart.

There were bodies everywhere. I smelled their perfume. Their sweat. Something sweet and sharp, like liquor. How many people were cool enough with Eric's cousin to get him to break the law? What would happen if the cops came in here and busted everyone?

You shouldn't be here, my mind screamed at me. *You should go home.*

My heart, however, was singing a different song. It raced with exhilaration. This place was dangerous. I was in a club, with liquor and dancing all around me. It made me feel very grown up. Like I'd matured just a little more since I left my house. It felt ... good.

I bounced a little to the beat and turned around to find Ariel and Eric sliding in to a booth, laughing and holding their heads close together like they'd been in love all of their lives.

I couldn't leave now. There was too much evidence floating around. I had to stay and observe. Plus, it was Ariel and Eric's official first date. Even though she hated me, I wanted to celebrate with them.

I put leaving out of my mind and looked around some more. It was darker than I imagined a club would be. The dance floor was nearly pitch black with strobe lights. Some of the kids wore glow in the dark necklaces or rings. One girl had a glow in the dark dress on. It was all so new and different. I wish I had someone to experience everything with, but with Jake's sudden disappearance and Ariel and Eric being so cozy, I realized that I would have to fly solo tonight.

I sighed and decided to use my alone time to gather my thoughts.

Jake was obviously planning to distribute the drugs at this party. I needed pictures of him in the act. Some hard evidence of the crimes that were surely going on around me.

I looked around again, saw no signs of Jake or Kenny, walked to the bar and ordered myself a water. Loneliness hollowed my chest. This was not how I imagined my first time in a club to be. I wanted my friends around me. I wanted to laugh and be catty with them. Instead, I was the chick alone at the bar, sipping on a water and looking miserable.

Life sucked.

My phone buzzed and I pulled it from my purse to answer it.

Cole: I was guaranteed three questions today. You're slipping, French.

I smiled, remembering how nice our time together was before it got ... well ... intense.

I thought a minute and wrote back.

Me: Stewart Copeland, Certifiable, There's a blind man looking for a shadow of doubt.

That last line always gave me goosebumps. I loved *The Police*. My mom sang Police songs to me when I was a baby. I swear that I still remember her singing *King of Pain* as she rocked me in our rocking chair. Her melodic voice rang in my mind and I smiled at the memory.

"Wow. Those clues were too easy and you're a bit young to be drinking."

Cole appeared next to me, phone in hand, looking carefree and teasing like always. He wore a white shirt, purple tie and black pants. His hair was smoothed back from his face. I took a moment to admire how handsome he was. Then I reminded myself that he wasn't mine to look at and scowled instead.

"It's just water," I replied, examining the fingerprints on my glass.

Hadn't he thought at all about what happened between us this afternoon? I know I hadn't stopped thinking about it. Even now I remembered how close he was. The minty scent of his breath. The strength of his hands. How was he so unaffected?

"You sure it's not vodka? If it is, I'll have to call the cops."

His eyes warmed to me, the teasing in them back in full effect. My mouth went dry and I took another sip of water.

"So, your boyfriend abandon you?" he asked.

I shrugged. "It seems so. And your girlfriend?"

"I wouldn't call her that but she's not here as far as I can tell. Probably still cleaning up from her party. Where were you, by the way?"

The music changed to one of the rap songs that Jake had played earlier in his car.

"We had to make a pit stop."

One of Cole's eyebrows raised. "Where?"

"A warehouse or something."

I watched his eyes for any sign that he knew what the warehouse was but his expression didn't change. I took another swig of my water.

"What a pair we make," he said. "Two lost souls, standing at a bar, drinking water out of dirty glasses, alone and lonely."

"Sad."

"Pathetic, really."

"Unbearable."

"Pitiful."

"Wretched."

"Trite."

"Miserable."

He laughed out loud. "Okay, French. You win." He sighed. "Do you want to dance with me?"

Cole danced? Yet another thing I didn't know about him.

"What? No."

"Come on. You don't want to sit by the bar all night, do you? Besides, I love this song."

Before I knew it, he'd plucked the water from my hand and pulled me on to the dance floor.

"Cole, I don't want to dance."

"Come on!" He held up one of my arms and spun me around. "You're too young to act so old. Have some fun for once."

Fun? This wasn't fun. I was on a mission.

I searched the floor for Jake and Kenny but there was still no sign of them.

The rap song boomed over the floor. I felt it shimmy through my heels and up my calves. I liked the feeling.

I guess dancing to one song wouldn't be the end of the world.

Cole pulled my hands on to his shoulders and did a two-step from side to side. Surprisingly, it was on beat.

"You're actually good," I said, moving my hips from left to right.

He grinned. "You say that like you're surprised."

"I am."

"Well, the feeling is mutual. I thought that you danced like you spelled."

"And how's that?"

"Not great."

I went to slap his arm but he turned me around, bringing my back to his chest. We swayed together, his arm slung across my belly, holding me to him. I placed my hand over his and for a moment, imagined that this was okay. That it wasn't a punishable offense.

The music changed again, playing *One Direction*'s *Best Song Ever*.

To a girl born in the 2000s, it was pure nostalgia.

The dance floor exploded, everyone who had sat down now packing on to the dance floor to jump in time to the music. I turned and ruffled Cole's hair, smiling. He took my hands and placed them on his tall shoulders.

Together, we lip synced the lyrics, made funny faces and jumped every time the chorus came on.

It was the most fun I'd had in a long time!

After the Georgia Rose verse, he turned me around for the slower part of the song. Somehow, through the noise and the shaking floor, I heard his voice. So sad. So sweet. So ... good.

"I hope you remember how we danced..."

My eyes widened in shock. Cole could sing? I tried to turn around and call him on it but he pulled my back to his chest and we jumped in time to the chorus again.

Shivers broke out all over my body. My heart floated, slipping through the music, through the screams of the crowd. I imagined that it would land right on to Cole's shirt and sink in to his chest, nuzzling in tight to his heart.

For a single moment, I wished that it would stay there forever.

But then the song ended. The jumping stopped. The floor cleared. The moment passed.

Weak, a slow, soulful ballad by 90's band SWV, floated through the speaker. Our bodies slowed down with it. He turned me around and held me close, wrapping me in his arms while we rocked together to the melody. It felt right to be in Cole's arms. So right, yet terribly wrong.

"I'm not finished with our conversation," he whispered in my ear. "One day, you'll have to tell me."

"There's nothing to say," I said, not hiding the sadness in my voice.

"I don't believe you," he whispered back. "I think there's plenty to say."

He pulled back a little, forcing me to look in to his eyes. The teasing had disappeared, replaced by a serious expression. His eyes were darker now. The color of the ocean at sunset. I could almost see the waves crashing within them.

"Who would you rather me be with?"

My treacherous tongue wanted to reply. I squeezed my mouth shut instead. His face moved in to mine and I felt myself falling. Falling into him. Into arms that I craved. Into a body that I fit so perfectly against. Into a heart that was quickly wrapping around mine.

And then...

"You came!"

Stephanie's shrill scream cut through our moment, slicing through the connection that Cole and I had created. My heart ached but I refused to allow myself to dwell on it.

It was too painful. To dangerous.

Cole's face fell in irritation for a moment before he slid his mask back in place.

"Hey, Steph."

I stepped back, allowing her to hug him like she obviously wanted to do. The thought of her touching him made my skin crawl and I looked away.

"There you are," Jake said, coming up behind me. "I've been looking for you."

His eyes narrowed at me and I saw what he meant.

Dana had arrived and he wanted to parade me around like some new trophy he'd just won.

"I've just been here dancing with Cole," I said.

For some reason, I wanted to say it. I needed him to know what I was doing and who I was doing it with. I wanted him to say something. To react.

Instead, he shrugged.

"Not too close, I hope."

I opened my mouth to speak but he grabbed my hand and led me back to the bar.

"You left me here alone. Where did you go?" I demanded.

What I really wanted to ask was, why did you bother coming back?

"I was taking care of business," he said, casually placing my hand on his shoulder as we leaned against the bar.

I then remembered why it was so important that I be here in the first place. I was looking for information about Jake and the drugs he so obviously was distributing. Solid evidence that I could take back to Detective Harding.

"What kind of business?"

"Important business."

"With Kenny?"

He raised an eyebrow.

"I told you not to ask me those kinds of questions. They are none of your concern."

"Aren't they? What if I wanted something from you? Something that you're selling."

He laughed shortly. "You couldn't handle what I have to sell."

"And all these other kids can?"

"The cool ones can, yes."

"Doesn't being with you make me cool by association?"

"No. Just keep your head in your books and out of my business and we'll be fine. What I have, you don't need. It's not for you."

"Funny. Your sister said the same thing to me about you."

"She was right." Jake's mask of charm fell. Dana must've disappeared. "Watch yourself, Bella. Don't get too comfortable. You're written in pencil. A place holder. Don't get any ideas."

He turned and walked away, again leaving me alone at the bar to slink back in to the shadows. Shadows that I knew that Kenny lurked in, too.

I didn't like Jake but his words still stung. I leaned against the bar, trying to shake them off. This party, and Jake, sucked.

"You look like someone just peed in your favorite purse."

Mel Pleasant sat on a bar stool next to me, her eyes roaming over the crowd.

"It feels like it," I said, climbing on to a chair, too. I wondered if Cole was in the crowd with Stephanie. Was he dancing with her like he'd danced with me? Did he hold her like he held me? Did he sing to her like he'd sung to me?

"Life's not turning out how you thought?" she asked.

I shook my head and clasped my hands in front of me.

"You thought that you were going to waltz in on Jake's arm and be swept in to the sea of popularity and that doors would open and everyone would fall at your feet and all would be right with the world. It must suck to know that the more popular you are, the worse things are for you. You feel them staring at you in your sleep. Their judgements seep in to your skin. And when you fall apart, they all smile and applaud."

She turned her head to look at me.

"I miss you at student guidance," she said.

My eyes bugged out of my head. Mel missed me? She didn't even look at me and she definitely didn't listen to anything I had to say.

"I've, uh, been busy," I replied. I raised my hand and signaled to the bartender for another water.

"Busy with Jake, huh?"

"Yeah."

She shook her head. "That's a shame. You were the only one who ever really listened to me. The only one who tried to give me good advice." She shook her head and closed her eyes. "Does that make me pathetic?"

"You called me Brenda," I replied. "Every day when you left, you called me Brenda."

Her eyes opened and she smiled as if I'd said something very funny.

"I knew your name, Bella," she said. "It was just hard, you know. Everyone thought I had this perfect life and here I was taking advice from a girl who nobody even knew existed. You had your life together while mine was falling apart. It was hard to swallow." She shook her head again. "I called you Brenda because I didn't want to believe that I was taking advice from Bella French, school weirdo. I pretended that you were someone else. Brenda Keegan."

"The senior?"

She shrugged. "I know. Lame, right?"

She laughed and took a sip from whatever was in her cup. It was brown and smelled strong.

"But why would you do that? You never took my advice."

"That didn't mean that it wasn't good. At least you tried. None of my other friends knew what was going on in my life but you knew it all. And now, here you are with your clothes and your boys." She downed the rest of her drink and grimaced. "Here is some good advice. Probably the only good advice that I've ever given anyone." She put one hand on my shoulder. "Go back to being invisible. These people will kill your spirit and they won't think twice."

We looked at each other, Mel and I. After two years, we finally looked in to each other's eyes and I was surprised to see so much pain in hers. She looked so worn out. Like a piece of old leather. Her appearance shocked me. What happened to her? Was this what popularity did to people? Would this happen to me, too?

Kenny Jennings came bounding up, looking like he'd drunk one too many cappuccinos. His body unnaturally bounced and shook, refusing to be still. It was like electric currents ran through him at odd intervals, jolting and stinging his bones.

He put his arm around Mel's shoulder and took a deep sniff of her hair.

She looked sad. Defeated.

"Ready for some fun?" he asked.

The way he said it made my skin crawl. Why was Mel even talking to him? He was nothing but a drug dealing loser, and an unpopular one at that.

She worried her lower lip between her teeth and climbed down from her chair. I could tell that she didn't want to go with him but she leaned into him anyway.

Something was wrong. Very wrong. I wanted to tell her that she didn't have to go. That she could stay with me and we could go somewhere and talk.

But I didn't.

I stood there, watching as Mel was led away by Kenny.

Halfway across the floor, she turned her head to me and mouthed words that made goosebumps break out across my back.

Don't trust anyone.

42

I watched the door that Mel and Kenny went through like a hawk. I told myself that, at any minute, she'd walk back out. That she'd run through the door and far, far away from him. But I didn't see her and I wasn't sure if I should go after her.

What if I was reading the situation wrong? What if she wanted to go with Kenny?

Something told me that she didn't want to do anything. A voice whispered that she had to go with him. But why? What could Kenny have that Mel needed that badly that she would follow him in to some, no doubt, creepy room?

I walked back to the booth that Ariel and Eric were sitting at and plopped down in a seat. Something didn't feel right and I wasn't sure what it was. I crossed my arms over my chest and tried to convince myself that Mel was okay. That she was doing what she wanted to do.

"You okay?" Ariel asked, her eyebrows pressed into a frown. It was the first thing she'd said to me all night and my heart did a little leap of happiness. Eric's arm was slung around Ariel's shoulder. The two of them seemed pretty cozy.

"I'm fine," I said. I sent her a look that said I was not fine. I could tell that she saw it because her frown deepened.

She opened her mouth to speak but Jake showed up, carrying a tray of four glasses.

"Ho ho! When did you become a waiter?" Eric asked.

"Just helping out," he said. He slid a glass in front of me and sat in the chair next to me, cradling his own glass.

The glass smelled like beer and I wrinkled my nose.

"Relax," he said, leaning in close. "It's the crap non-alcoholic beer that they serve at these parties."

"Yeah," Eric said, shaking his head. "Super lame."

I remembered Mel's comment. Don't trust anyone. Was she referring to Jake? I frowned into my drink. She hadn't been drinking nonalcoholic beer. I was certain that she was half drunk when she spoke to me.

"Come on. Drink it," he scoffed. "No girlfriend of mine would refuse a beer. Especially a nonalcoholic one."

I wanted to tell him that I wasn't his girlfriend but Ariel and Eric, who had already drank their supposedly nonalcoholic shots, were staring at me. I sniffed my drink.

I'd never liked the smell or taste of beer. I was sure that I wasn't going to like the nonalcoholic kind, either. But with the three sets of eyes on me, I had no choice.

I gulped mine down, the sickening taste sliding over my tongue. It tasted like bitterness and lemon. I suppressed a gag. How could people drink this stuff?

"Another round!" Eric cried, banging his hand on the table.

"None for me, thanks," I said, waving my hand like I was shooing away a fly.

"Ah. Come on, babe," Jake said. "Live a little!"

"No. I think I'm okay."

Jake leaned in close, his lips touching my ear, one hand on my knee. I suppressed the urge to shake it off.

"I'll tell you what. If you can out drink me, I'll let you out of our little deal."

My stomach clenched and my heart raced. I was only one drink away from being done with Jake Winsted forever. One drink away from getting my life back.

The words were out of my mouth in an instant.

"Deal," I said.

Jake's hand left my knee and he was gone, leaving a grinning Eric, a confused Ariel and me.

"What did he say to you?" Ariel asked.

What would it take to keep Ariel happy? Some bitter lemon beer? I'd drink a vat of it.

"He said that he was going to get some more drinks."

Eric knocked on the table again, while Ariel threw her hands in the air with a hoot. I smiled, basking in the relief that was sure to come out of Jake's new clause to our deal. I could outdrink Jake. I knew I could. I had more to lose than he did. More to gain, too.

Jake returned a minute later. He turned our chairs to face each other, a sly smile on his face. His top button was undone and he'd untucked his shirt. I saw the competitive edge in his eye. I knew that I would probably barf up the foul-tasting drink before the night was over. But I had to do this. I couldn't fail.

He picked up the first glass.

"Ready," he said.

I rolled my eyes. "Set."

"Go."

I slung the first drink back and it burned down my throat.

Then the second. And a third.

I didn't know what number Jake was at, but by the fourth, I was starting to feel dizzy.

Light headed. Swoony.

I was half way through my fifth glass before my empty stomach lurched and threatened.

"You call it?" Jake asked, his eyes still sharp.

I didn't know if I nodded or not before I raced to the bathroom. I barely made it to the stall before all five glasses of my beer came up at once.

It tasted worse the second time.

Ariel came in to the stall after me, pulling my hair back from my face.

"Jeez, Bella. What was that about?"

My response was another round of vomiting.

When I had emptied my stomach, Ariel helped me to the sink and I rinsed out my mouth and washed my face. My makeup was ruined but I didn't care. This night was a bust. I didn't get anything concrete on Jake, Cole was still dancing somewhere with Stephanie and I had just thrown up.

Time to throw in the towel and beg Jake to take me home.

"Well, that was exciting," Ariel said.

That wasn't the word that I would use but my head was swimming too much to argue.

"Why did you do it?" she asked. "It's not like you to take sucker bets."

I shrugged. Apparently, I wasn't yet sick enough to not lie.

"Jake asked me to do it and I did," I said. "You can't say no to Jake, right?"

She frowned.

"He likes you a lot, you know." She pulled off another paper towel and dabbed at the wet spots of my face. "Eric told me."

"I'm sure he doesn't like me all that much."

She leveled me with a look.

"Bella, listen to yourself. Your boyfriend likes you. It's time to stop trying to fight him off and start to embrace it. Jake Winsted was your dream and now that you have him, you won't even let him kiss you."

"Is that what Eric told you?"

She shrugged. "Amongst other things. Look, just give him a chance, okay? He's a nice guy."

She balled up the paper towel, threw it in the trash and put her hands on her hips.

"Promise me."

"Promise you what?"

Why were there two of her all of a sudden?

"Promise me that you won't dump him because you don't think you're good enough."

"Good enough for Jake?"

"Yes, Bella; good enough for Jake. He likes you. You should be confident in that and not think that it's all going to blow up in your face. He's not like that. He's a good guy. Everyone says so."

My head was throbbing, my vision was blurring and my mouth tasted like vomit. I was in no mood for lectures. Especially on subjects that Ariel didn't understand.

"I just want to go home."

I pushed past her and stumbled through the door.

The music seemed ten times louder, shaking my heels. I moved forward and walked right in to a hard chest. Cole. His blue eyes were wide, his face full of concern.

"Bella, we have to talk."

I didn't want to talk to him. Especially with Stephanie lurking nearby.

"Leave me alone. Go back to your girlfriend," I growled.

"Bella-"

"I said leave me alone, Cole!"

I stumbled away from him and directly in to the path of Stephanie, Ursula, Mel, and Dana.

Great.

"Well, look what the cat dragged in."

Stephanie's voice lit a hatred in me that I hadn't known I'd possessed. I felt like I was about to die and my vision was doubling but I managed to glare at both images of her. She'd never done anything mean to me but just the fact that she was Cole's girlfriend made me want to punch her.

"Just leave me alone, Stephanie."

"I am going to say this once. Stay away from Cole. He's mine. Do you hear me? Mine!"

"I don't want Cole. You can have him!"

"Good."

I narrowed my eyes, trying to focus on her. For a split second, I saw her clearly. All traces of our brief friendship were gone. She was back to being what I had always known her to be. Evil.

I shuddered and my stomach lurched again.

"Oh," she said. "And by the way..."

Someone shoved me from behind and I stumbled forward. Before I could regain my balance, I was shoved backward. The circle around me tightened. Ursula shoved me to Dana, who shoved me back to Stephanie. I felt like a hot potato, constantly caught and released.

My stomach churned in anger and my head hurt so much that I could barely see. I landed on Stephanie but before she could shove me forward again, I swung, my fist connecting with Ursula's chin. There wasn't much power in the punch but it was insulting enough.

All four girls descended on me, punching and kicking and scratching until I could only curl up into a ball while they pulled my hair and slammed their fists in to my back. I screamed but was sure that no one heard it over the loud music.

Then, the beating stopped.

I looked up.

The three girls had surrounded Ariel, backing her in to a corner. Then Eric was there, standing in front of Ariel and pointing at the door.

Stephanie reached up and slapped Eric hard across the face.

Ariel ran around Eric and hurled herself at Stephanie. The two girls fell to the floor, punching and scratching each other as they rolled on the ground.

Jake and Eric managed to part Ariel and Stephanie and pull them up.

I pressed my back to the bar, trying to hold down my churning stomach bile.

That was when the bouncer showed up.

43

Three hours later, I sat in the back of my father's sedan as he drove me home.

I wished that he would yell at me. That he'd tell me what a terrible daughter I was. That he would ground me for life. Instead, there was only crushing silence.

It was the worst punishment of all.

By the time we arrived at our apartment, I was so on edge that it felt like my chest was going to explode. Between the tension, the headache and the nausea, I was sure that I was going to die soon. I hoped that it happened before my father grounded me forever.

Dad walked in, threw his keys on the counter and massaged his temples.

"Daddy, I'm sorry," I said. "I didn't mean for any of this to happen."

He walked over to the couch and sat down, his fingers still on his temple.

I took off my shoes and sat next to him.

"Daddy, I-"

"Who are you?" he asked.

I frowned.

"Who are you?" he repeated.

I wasn't sure that I understood the question so I said the simplest thing that I could think of,

"I'm Bella. Your daughter."

"No." Daddy sat back, and waved his hand in front of his face. "No. You can't be, because I told my daughter that she couldn't go to this party. And yet, here I am, picking up this girl who dresses different than my daughter, who has these different rich friends, who sneaks out of the house to get drunk, gets into a bar brawl, who lies and nearly gets arrested. If that jerk kid—Jake, is it—if his father didn't call in a favor, I would have had to bail you out of jail. So no, you are not my daughter, because my daughter wouldn't do such things."

I'd never seen Daddy so angry. Then again, I'd never done anything like this before.

"I'm sorry, Daddy."

"Don't Daddy me. Go to your room and get some sleep. Starting on Monday, you will be volunteering at the horse stables after school so that I can keep an eye on you."

"What?"

"That's right. Apparently, you like to sneak off. Let's see if we can redirect that energy somewhere else."

"But that's not fair!"

"Let's not talk about fair, Bella! Not when you still reek of beer. Now go to your room and try to stay there this time!"

I stood and walked barefoot to my room. I felt terrible. Worse than terrible. I had lied to my father and almost gotten arrested. Who was I? When had I become this person?

I showered and brushed away the taste of alcohol from my mouth. I still felt kind of dizzy, but apparently, three hours in a holding cell was great for sobering me up.

I changed into my pajamas, climbed in bed and pulled the blanket up to my chin.

Before I fell asleep, I wished that time would turn back. That I could be what I was before I knew what Jake was doing. Before I knew who Cole really was. Before I had lied to everyone that I had ever cared about.

I wished that I was invisible.

44

I awoke the next morning with a pounding headache and a slew of text messages.

Jake: Meet me at eight tonight in front of your apartment. Wear something nice.

Ariel: Are you okay? I am in major trouble. At least I got to punch Stephanie in the face. I would do it again just for one more go at her.

***Jasmine**:* I heard about what happened. Are you okay? I told Ariel that that party was bad news. Call me when you can.

***Cole**:* Are you okay?

I texted Ariel first.

I'm okay. I am grounded and have to volunteer at the horse stables after school. It is totally going to suck.

Then Jasmine.

I'm okay. I'll call you later.

And finally, the one person that I did not want to talk to. Jake.

Thanks for trying to give me alcohol poisoning. I'm grounded so no party tonight.

I got an immediate text back from Jake.

Can't you sneak out like last night?

Me: I know that you don't know what grounded means so let me spell it out for you. I cannot go anywhere again ever.

Jake: You have to go.

Me: I.AM.GROUNDED.

Jake: I am not asking you.

Jake: Give me your word that you are coming tonight or else I will personally call Ariel and tell her what you did. One hour. That's all you have.

Me: I'll see what I can do.

Jake: See. All you needed was a little persuasion. See you tonight.

I threw my phone across the room. Just when I thought that Jake was a human being, he pulled this crap. I had to find a way to get away from him. If not, he would hang this secret over my head forever. Maybe I should just call Detective Harding and tell him what little I knew and get it over with. Maybe I should just tell Ariel the truth. Maybe I should have done that from the beginning.

I got up, got dressed and called Jasmine. I begged her to come over tonight for a sleep over and she agreed.

I hated myself for that, too.

45

Jasmine watched in awe as Ariel and I recounted our crazy night filled with drinking, fighting and jail time. Well, technically we were in holding but it was close enough.

By the time we got to the train, our fight from before was forgotten in favor of our new legal troubles.

"So, how long are you grounded for?" Jasmine asked.

"'Til I'm dead," I replied.

"When my children become grandparents," Ariel said.

Jasmine's eyes went wide and she shook her head.

"That sounds absolutely insane! If I ever got arrested, my Dad would have a stroke."

"My Dad did last night," Ariel said. "Two of them, I think."

"My Dad has officially banned me from all things Jake Winsted," I said.

"Banned?" Jasmine asked. "As in, you can't go out with him anymore?"

"Yes. I mean technically, he'd already banned me from going out with him but now he's being super strict about it."

I should have felt relief at such a ruling but I didn't. Jake would never let me go over something so small as a parental decision. Sometimes, I feared that he'd never let me go at all. That I'd be dead and buried and still tied to him. It terrified me. Jake was a stone around my neck. Yes, a stone that came with pretty jewels, nice clothes and popularity but something inside of me still knew that it was all smoke and glass. That someone would hurl that millstone in to the sea and I'd go down with it.

The sound of crying greeted us as we walked up to the school doors. A crowd had gathered in the doorway, blocking anyone else from entering.

My stomach dropped to my shoes. Was this another locker incident? Or worse, some sort of terrorist attack? In the city of New York, one could never be too careful.

"It's crazy, isn't it?"

Margie Macintyre's pale skin looked almost translucent today, as if the life had been drained out of her.

"What's crazy?"

"Mel Pleasant's in the hospital. They found her passed out at some party. I heard it was a drug overdose or something. Anyway, Dana, Stephanie and Ursula are inside losing it in front of Mel's locker."

Her words echoed in my mind. Mel overdosed last night?

My lungs clenched and I felt nauseous.

She'd left with Kenny last night. I should have stopped her. I should have said something to make her stay with me. Now she was in the hospital and deep down, I knew that it was all my fault.

"Are you okay?" Margie asked. "I mean, no one is okay today but you look like you're going to throw up."

My hand flew over my mouth. I did feel like I was going to throw up. This was all my fault. I should have done something. I should have-

"Hey." Jake jogged up to me, looking completely unfazed by the sadness saturating the air around us.

"Mel's in the hospital," I choked out. "She overdosed last night."

He shrugged, as if I had just told him that taxi cabs were yellow.

"Yeah. I heard." He itched a spot beneath his football jersey. "It sucks."

"That's all you have to say? That it sucks? She might die!"

"Look, Mel did more than she could handle. It happens all the time."

"How could you be so casual about this? I thought Mel was your friend."

"I don't make friends with clients," he said. "So, party tonight?"

"That's all you can think about? Partying?"

"Why not?"

"Because Mel is in the hospital."

"Why should you care? You spoke to her, like what, once?"

"We went to school together. Just because we weren't super close doesn't mean that I wanted her dead."

"Would you relax about it? Mel doesn't matter. I heard she's practically a vegetable, anyway. What matters is that you are going to that party with me tonight, like it or not."

I shook my head, shell shocked. Jake didn't care about Mel. He didn't care about anything but himself and getting Dana back.

I wrapped my arms around myself.

What had I gotten myself into? What monster had I gotten tangled up with?

Kenny appeared and Jake followed him through the crowd, toward the school doors. Kenny's backpack bounced behind him.

A backpack filled with drugs.

Drugs that Jake supplied and Kenny distributed.

The same drugs that caused Mel to be lying in a hospital bed right now.

It suddenly became clear what I needed to do. This was bigger than Jake or my need to be noticed, even Ariel. This was about stopping an epidemic in my school before it was too late. This was about doing the right thing.

I squared my shoulders and made up my mind.

Jake's reign over this school was over and I was going to be the one to end it. Tonight.

46

"It's such a tragedy."

Ms. Mitchell stood in front of my English class, hands folded in front of her, expression somber. It seemed as if the loss of Mel's presence placed a gray cloud over my entire school. Even Ariel and Jasmine's enthusiasm had dampened. "If anyone would like to talk about what happened, we have an excellent guidance program that includes our own Bella French, Student Guidance Counselor." All eyes turned to me and I placed a weak smile on my face.

"I encourage all of you to take a moment and talk to someone that you trust about the devastating effects that drugs are having on our student body."

My eyes rolled to Jake. A normal person would have cowered or shown some form of regret. Not Jake. His back was strong, his hands folded in front of him as if he was a model student. As if the drugs didn't come from his car.

How could he be so unaffected by all of this? He may not have thought of Mel as a friend, but she was a human being who he'd hurt. How could he not feel anything when the crushing weight of my inaction weighed on me?

I looked forward. I had to. If I looked at Jake for one more second, I'd scream, then our secret would be out.

That couldn't happen.

The weight on me increased later on while I sat in Student Guidance Counseling. The line stretched in to the hallway with students, all clamoring for fifteen minutes to talk about how much they missed Mel. Or so they claimed.

Little by little, I came to understand that these kids weren't coming in to mourn Mel's overdose. They were coming in to either be seen or to get information.

"Have you seen her? Is she okay?"

"What did she overdose on?"

"Who sold her the drugs?'

"What was she wearing when they found her?"

I grew sicker and sicker the more they spoke. These kids didn't care about Mel at all. They were leeches who just wanted something to gossip about later.

When the bell rang, I sprinted out of the room, past the line of bodies still waiting to speak to a guidance counselor. In the last forty-five minutes, I'd realized a very important truth.

Popularity didn't make people love you. It made people jealous of you. It made you a target. Mel was right. She had a bullseye on her back and when she fell, the vultures came to pick at her remains.

Popularity was a lie.

The chorus of *Black Balloon* by the *Goo Goo Dolls*, one of my favorite 90s bands, played in my head as I walked to my next period. I closed my eyes and said a little prayer for Mel, though I knew that she never would have done the same for me.

I SLID INTO MY CHAIR, WAITING FOR COLE TO TEACH ME ALL THE French he knew.

I felt him before I saw him slide in to the seat across from me.

"You're chipper. Is Mr. Cogg getting deported?"

I rolled my eyes, pulled a piece of paper from my book bag and slapped it on the table.

"No, though that would be nice. Read it and weep."

Cole picked up my French quiz and whistled.

"A one hundred. Nice."

"My first hundred in French ever."

"What can I say? I'm an excellent teacher."

I raised an eyebrow.

"You may have helped ... a little." I smiled. "So, what are we going to go over today?"

Cole gazed at me, making my face hot. Being with Cole made me feel so light. Like my heart had sprouted wings. It was refreshing to be with a guy who actually listened when I spoke and who was interested in what I had to say. It made me feel cared about and secure.

His eyes dropped to the earbuds sitting on the table.

"Another quiz?" I asked.

"No. Today, we are going to improve our French pronunciation by listening to some French music."

"What? Here in the library?"

"Sure. Why not?"

He stood, grabbed his bookbag and the headphones off the table and headed back to the digital library. It was a small, dark room in the back with big touchscreen TVs. Most people used it to download books from class.

Today, the TVs were dimmed and the room empty.

"Me and Mrs. Smalls had a little talk. She agreed to give us the room, as long as we were quiet and promised not to make out. I told her I could only speak for myself."

I hit him with the back of my hand and smiled.

A vision of Cole kissing me sent the butterflies in my stomach into a panic. I was glad that the room was dark. I was sure that my face was red by now.

Cole led me to the back of the room, where he'd laid down a blanket.

"Where did you get the blanket?" I asked. It was blue and white checkerboard and looked threadbare.

"From the emergency kit in the storage room. I promised the custodian that I would return it later."

"Is there anyone you didn't make a promise to today?" I asked.

"Besides you?"

I stuck out my tongue at him.

We laid down on the itchy blanket, his phone between us.

"Just one pair of headphones?" I asked.

"Don't be so hoity-toity. It will be more than enough."

"Did you just call me hoity-toity? What is this, 1932?"

"Shut up and put in the headphones."

I complied, and put one earbud in to my right ear while he put one in to his left.

"Any particular song?" I asked.

"That's part of your homework. You will give me the name of the songs you hear as well as a translation of the chorus. What's the rule?"

I rolled my eyes in the darkness, though he couldn't see me.

"No Googling."

"That's right."

He pressed play and for forty-five minutes, the most beautiful music floated through my ears. I didn't understand all the words but I did recognize a few things. Talk of love, hope and happiness. A tear ran down my cheek at the beauty of it all.

I thanked God again for the dark.

I closed my eyes and let the music overtake me. Somewhere along the way, Cole's hand entwined with mine. I gave it a squeeze. He squeezed it back.

And somewhere deep within my heart, I fell for him a little more.

The warmth in my heart from French tutoring carried me right through to my English project. Cole knocked on the door and stood there, waiting for me to take Mojo's leash and walk him.

I had already walked Mojo but there was something about walking with Cole that felt so nice. So natural. I gave Mojo a treat and we started on our way.

I was proud of Mojo's accomplishments. He had stopped pooping in the house and only occasionally did he pee on one of the pee pads.

He walked on his own and had stopped scowling at me. I'd say that I was becoming a pretty good dog mother.

"So," Cole said, walking next to me at a relaxed pace. "I happened to come across two tickets to a certain Broadway play and I was wondering if you might be free in two weeks."

A Broadway play? I'd cut my arm off to see a Broadway play.

I didn't hide my enthusiasm for his offer.

"I'd love to see a play. Which one is it?"

He shrugged. "A good one. But, I only have two tickets. Do you think your boyfriend will have an issue with us going out together alone?"

"I don't know. Technically, you are kind of my brother-in-law so I think it's okay."

He put up his hands. "Whoa, whoa, whoa! No one is getting married. Especially not to Jake."

"Would you have a problem with that?"

"Yes. A huge one. My brother is a pig. If you even thought about marrying him, I'd have to kidnap you and lock you away in a cottage somewhere. For your own good, of course."

I scoffed. "I'll keep that in mind."

"Ugh. You can't marry Jake."

I laughed out loud. "No one is marrying anybody. Now, let's do a music quiz before you barf."

He shook his head. "We should change it up a bit. How are you with movies?"

I shrugged.

"I can hold my own." It was a massive understatement. I loved movies almost as much as I loved music.

"Favorite movie?" he asked.

"The Princess Bride."

He looked at me for a long time. That Cole gaze that warmed my cheeks and made my heart pound.

"What?"

He smiled and shook his head.

"Nothing."

"Are you making fun of my movie choices?"

"No. Never."

"Fine. What's your favorite movie?"

"How about you guess?"

"Fine."

He cleared his throat and took a deep breath. His legs spread apart and he put his hand up in front of him, like he was about to stab someone with a sword.

"My name is Inigo Montoya, you killed my father, prepare to die!"

My eyes went wide.

"No."

"Yes."

"No way!"

"I have the shirt to prove it. I believe that you do, too."

My heart exploded with a joy that I knew I couldn't keep. I turned toward Cole, ignoring Mojo as he pulled me forward.

"Why?" I asked.

"What?"

"Why tell me all of the things we have in common now? Why didn't you tell me years ago?"

He shrugged.

"You hated me then."

"I didn't hate you."

"Didn't you?" He raised an eyebrow and I started walking again.

"I may have but that was because you teased me all the time."

"Just banter. You took it too seriously."

"You could have stopped."

"And miss speaking to you every day?" He stopped walking and turned to me. Every time Cole looked at me, my whole body seemed to come alive. As if he plugged himself directly into my soul, electrifying me from the inside out.

Captivated, I stood and allowed him to run his thumb down my cheek. I felt it all the way down in to my toes. My entire body blushed and he grinned at me, dropping his hand.

"You're an odd duck, French. A real odd duck."

I gave him my best fake glare.

"Shut up, Cole."

I took another step but my dog sat tight. He'd apparently found a new place to poop. A patch of dirt with a wooden tub full of flowers. Even the sharp smell of the small pine bushes couldn't hide the gross scent that emitted from Mojo's butt.

I handed Cole the blue bag that I carried for just such an occasion.

"You're on poop duty," I said.

He wrinkled his nose.

"Why me? It's your dog."

Mojo emerged from his bathroom, ready to head home again.

"I don't have hands, remember. I'm a duck." I smiled, did a quack quack and walked back toward the apartment. Cole followed closely behind, a new, warm package in his hands.

"Are you serious?" Jasmine hissed.

I threw a pair of heels in to my bag. They would make too much noise when I snuck out.

I convinced Jake to pick me up at eleven instead of nine. Daddy is always in bed by ten, so that gave me plenty of time to get dressed.

I had to go to this party. Up until this point, I'd only seen Jake and Kenny talk to each other, but there was no evidence that Jake was actually the one supplying the drugs. The only lead I had in that regard was Stephanie's comment about Jake being a supplier but at this point, that was just hearsay. I'd seen Kenny actually handing drugs to people and getting money in return but Kenny was the small fish. I had bigger fish to fry.

Unfortunately, I couldn't tell Jasmine all the sordid details of my secret spy mission so I just asked her to sleep over and cover for me while I was at the party. Needless to say, she was less than enthused.

"Bella, this is insane. I don't feel comfortable doing this."

I combed on more mascara, my heart pounding with nerves.

There was a second, more selfish reason that I wanted to go to this party. Once Jake was caught, my short time in Popularville would be over. I felt like I hadn't experienced as much as I should have. The kids at school knew my name now, I was invited to parties and they said hello to me in the hallway. But there had to be something else. I was happy with the attention but it still felt hollow. Empty. There had to be more to it than just greetings, lies and pretty clothes. Some spark, some flash of light that satisfies their hunger for life. There had to be something more than waves and social media friend requests. I hoped that I would discover what that something was tonight.

"Bella, are you listening to me?" Jasmine's dark, unapproving eyes followed me around the room, her arms crossed over her chest. "This is crazy. You are lying to your father. That's not the Bella that I know. Jake has changed you into something that you're not. Into one of them!"

"Would you keep your voice down before my dad hears you," I hissed, dabbing at my lip gloss. Yes, what I was doing was wrong but Jasmine was being a little melodramatic about it. I wondered if she was jealous that she wasn't going to the party, too. The thought shocked me. I had never thought about my best friend that way. Maybe Jasmine was right. Maybe I had changed.

"I hope he does hear me. I hope that he comes in here and talks some sense into you."

I went to sit next to her on the bed and slid on a smile. The same charming smile that Jake used when he wanted me to do something. I watched my friend's face soften and a little piece of my heart froze and broke off.

"Jasmine, please. I am asking you as a friend."

"I just don't understand why you are doing this. It's not because you like Jake because I can tell that you don't. I see the way you two look at each other. There is nothing there. So why?"

I stood and pretended to fix my dress, avoiding the eyes that saw my truth clearer than I ever did.

"He's my boyfriend," I said. "I'm trying to make him happy."

"You're lying."

I sighed.

"Look. The why is not important."

"It's important to me."

I threw my head back. My shoulders sagged with the heavy secrets that they carried. Ariel. Drugs. Popularity. Mel. Jake. Cole. I wanted to tell Jasmine everything. Every sordid detail. But I couldn't risk the secrets getting out. And more importantly, once Jasmine found out what I did, there was a huge possibility that she would never talk to me again. It was selfish of me but I wanted to hold on to our friendship for as long as I could before everything was exposed and my life turned to crap.

So I stood, grabbed my purse and opened my room door.

"I'll be back before sunrise."

Somehow, I knew that she wouldn't be here when I got back.

I had to risk that, too.

47

Breathless, I climbed in to Jake's car and strapped myself in.

"Where's the fire?" he asked, pulling the car out on to the busy New York City streets.

"Oh. You mean that fire that is sure to rain down upon me if my dad ever finds out that I'm sneaking out?" I mumbled.

"Relax, babe. Tonight, all your geeky dreams come true. You wanted to see how the other half lived, well here is your chance. No one throws parties like Bree."

"Bree?"

His phone rang, stopping our conversation. It suddenly occurred to me that Jake and I didn't really have conversations. He gave me orders and I followed them. Like I was one of his foot soldiers or something. I sat back and crossed my arms.

I wouldn't be a foot soldier for long. Once I got some hard evidence, Jake Winsted or whoever he was, was going down.

Jake reached into his pocket and pulled out a phone that I'd never seen before. Jake's regular phone case had a picture of him and Dana at a candlelight dinner. They were gazing in to each other's eyes, looking really happy and full of hope. When I saw that case, it reminded me that Jake did have a heart. Dana.

I examined this new and different phone case. It was black and scratched up. Why had I never seen it before?

Jake glanced at me, then put his eyes firmly back on the road.

"I can't talk. What is it?"

I frowned and looked down, pretending to smooth my skirt. My heartbeat picked up. Was this one of Jake's drug deals? Was this the evidence that I'd been looking for?

I strained to hear what the person on the other line was saying but the loudness of Jake's sports car—a red *Dodge Charger* with a hemi engine—drowned out any other sounds. I'd never known someone who changed cars like they changed clothes. It really put my dad's gold sedan to shame. Then again, my dad wasn't a drug dealer like Jake was. Or Jake's father, for that matter.

"Whatever. Just don't take too long."

Jake pressed the end button on the phone and stuffed it in to his pants pocket.

"Is everything okay?" I asked.

A smile passed across his lips. I'd come to know this as the *shut up and mind your business* smile that Jake gave me when I asked too many questions.

"Everything's fine. We're making a stop."

"At the warehouse again?" I asked.

Jake blinked, then looked at me, his brows furrowing.

"We seem to stop there a lot," I said, my nerves taunt. I wanted information. I needed information. "What do they put in your trunk?"

He bit the inside of his cheek and let out a breath.

"I am going to tell you this one time. You never saw a warehouse. If I find out that you ever told anyone about anything you saw while in one of my cars, you are going to be sorry."

My stomach clenched.

"Are you threatening me, Jake?"

"I am promising you." His voice was low, lethal, like a razor's edge. "What we do in this car is private. Anything you see or hear never happened, you got it?"

I nodded, not wanting to push Jake too far.

"Yeah, Jake. I got it."

He peered at me, trying to determine my truthfulness but it was dark and I kept my face smooth enough to not arouse suspicion. Frustrated, he pulled in to a spot in front of Kenny's building.

Kenny hopped in, all jittering arms and legs. He sniffed, like he was fighting a cold or something.

"Hey, Kenny," I said.

"Hey."

I swallowed.

"So, you and Mel, huh?"

It surprised me how strong my voice was. How easily I prodded for information without breaking down.

"What?"

"You and Mel. I saw you two at the Stamford Club the other night. You left together."

"I don't know what you're talking about." I looked in to the rearview mirror. Kenny was wiping his nose with the back of his hands, his eyes darting around the car.

"You were with Mel when she overdosed, weren't you?"

"What are you? A cop?"

"No. Just a friend."

"Mel didn't have friends."

"Besides you?"

Kenny glared at me in the mirror.

"I didn't do nothing to her that she didn't want me to do."

"I'll bet you didn't."

"Enough with the cross examination," Jake said. "Everyone just relax."

"Whatever you say, boss." I heard Kenny's back slam in to his seat. The car fell into silence, except for Kenny's nervous twitches.

We cut across town, back to the docks and the warehouse that Jake frequented. The warehouse that I wasn't supposed to see, though he'd brought me to it three times already. I guess he thought that his threats were enough to keep me quiet. Little did he know that I was going to be singing like a bird soon.

Jake cut the engine and the roaring car quieted.

Unlike the other two times, this time the trunk didn't open and close right away, giving me a chance to look around. Most of the lights were either out or turned off, bathing the dock behind me in a tangerine colored darkness. The moon was high, spilling its light over the water. I heard its soft waves lapping against the wooden dock.

Desperate for something, anything that could identify this place, I carefully examined my surroundings. It all looked the same as the other times. Dark, rusted walls. Water behind me.

Water.

I looked through the rearview mirror, scanning the water. That was when I saw it.

A blue octagon with white letters that read Pier 19. Or was it twenty-nine? It was dark and the moon was playing games with my vision. Was that a one or a two? I was almost positive it was a one. But if I squinted, the one looked like a two and the nine looked like a zero. Was it pier twenty?

Kenny caught my eye in the rearview mirror and I quickly dropped my gaze to my shoes.

Pier nineteen, twenty-nine or twenty. I am near pier nineteen, twenty-nine or twenty.

Two burly shadows passed my window and I looked up again.

One of them was carrying a glittering silver box, gift wrapped with a bow.

"Here we go," Jake said.

He pushed his push button starter and the engine roared back to life. The trunk popped open and the car rocked as the men dropped their package inside. The trunk slammed shut and they banged twice on it. Then, we took off at a desperate pace away from the docks.

48

Jake told me to wait by the steps while he and Kenny met by the taxi's trunk. I obeyed, standing in front of the biggest house that I had ever seen. No. Not house. A mansion. A castle on the water, complete with columns, a doorman in a black suit and stained-glass windows. We had to take a water taxi to get here then a cab the rest of the way. I'd never taken a water taxi before but the way that it sliced through the water made my heart race with excitement.

I'd have to take Ariel up on one of her boat trips one day.

I took in a shallow breath and closed my eyes. For a few minutes, I was *Cinderella* climbing the steps to the ball. Would my prince be inside, waiting for me? Would I escape, shoeless and filled with wonder at the visions that I'd seen?

The yellow cab's trunk closed, shattering my illusions.

Jake was zipping up Kenny's too full bag. Once the book bag was secured, he picked up the silver present box and joined me on the steps. I watched the cab pull away, leaving us stranded here.

"Let's go."

We walked through the gold-plated doors and stepped inside. White and gold marble floors greeted me. Loud music played from somewhere. A large, pearl-colored staircase led up to a lit second floor.

It was like a fairy tale. I'd never seen a house so beautiful. Maybe in movies, but not in real life. I half expected everyone to be dressed in ball gowns instead of slinky, sequined dresses that weren't at all appropriate for the cold fall weather.

Kenny, still with his book bag, walked ahead of us, looking anxious to get somewhere. Kenny always looked anxious, though. He was in such a rush that he tripped and his ever-present bookbag came off his shoulders and burst open when it hit the ground. Little, clear bags of white powder and colorful pills scattered across the floor, turning yellow beneath the lights.

Drugs. I had seen it with my own eyes. Kenny was carrying drugs. I reached into my purse and snapped a quick picture of the book bag with my phone.

"Kenny, you idiot!" Jake roared. "Pick it up and meet me at John's. And don't lose anything."

He put his hand to my back and led me forward, deeper in to the house.

"Was that-"

"Keep your mouth shut. Keep walking."

I had gotten my first piece of evidence. Up until this point, I'd only seen Jake go to the warehouse and men in dark clothes loading things in to his trunk. I had nothing on him. But he filled Kenny's bag. He knew what was inside. There was no doubt about it now. Jake was supplying Kenny with the drugs that he distributed to the school.

Fear and excitement shot through me. If Jake knew what I had just done, my body would be in the river. I was sure of it. I had to tell Detective Harding as soon as possible.

We walked beneath an archway and past a super-long food table that smelled like heaven. I wanted to stop but Jake was a man on a mission. I hoped that I could find the food again later. We passed under another arch, walked down a hallway and then through a huge set of double doors.

This was where the real party was.

The Olympic-sized swimming pool was filled with bodies of what looked to be bikini clad super models even in the chilly, mid-November temperatures. I looked closer and saw steam rising from the water. Was it heated? I didn't know that you could heat a swimming pool this big. I wanted to dip my toe in but Jake continued on his march.

Ahead, a DJ booth was built onto a platform above the pool. Leaning against the platform stood a girl that I'd seen in the newspapers before. She was Breena 'Bree' Labado, one of the twin daughters of the mayor of New York. She was what they called a socialite. A fancy way of saying a party girl. Her long black hair was pulled up, her body clad in a red bikini top and a see through, floor length skirt. She looked up at the booth impatiently.

"Bree!" Jake called.

The girl looked around for a moment before her eyes landed on us. She smiled and opened her arms, waiting for Jake to fall into them. He did so without the slightest hesitation.

"Jake, it's so good to see you!"

"You, too." Jake took both her hands in his and took a step back to admire her body. "You look great."

Bree cheeks pinkened with the flattery.

"So I'm told."

Jake stepped aside, revealing me.

"This is Bella French, my new girlfriend."

Bree held out her hand to shake mine.

"It's nice to meet you, Bella," she said.

We shook hands. Hers were impossibly soft, like she'd never washed a dish a day in her life. I'm sure that mine felt leather tough to her.

"You, too."

"We should go on vacation sometime," she said. "Daddy just bought an island off the coast of Jamaica. It's small but it's private. Maybe the beginning of next year?"

I nodded dumbly. I'd never been to an island, a coast or Jamaica. Whatever she was planning, I was sure that I could never afford it. But to save face, I lied.

"Sure. I'll talk to my dad."

"Awesome. What does your Dad do?"

I cleared my throat.

"He's a stable manager."

For the first time in my life, I was embarrassed by my lack of money. I thought that was a thing that only shallow people did until about five seconds ago.

"Is that like a hedge fund manager?" she asked.

There was no use explaining my real-life story to her. Especially since I was not planning on seeing her ever again. I nodded.

"Sure."

"Awesome. We definitely should get together."

Jake looked over Bree's shoulder.

"Would you ladies excuse me?" he asked. He jogged up the steps with his silver box to the DJ booth before we could reply.

"So," Bree said. An awkwardness hung between us. The awkwardness of being stuck with someone that you didn't know and you were sure you had nothing in common with.

"You and Jake?"

"Yup. Me and Jake."

"I'm just surprised, I guess. I mean, with Dana being here and all, I don't want any unpleasant disagreements."

"Oh. I didn't realize Dana would be here." Of course, I realized Dana would be here. If she weren't, Jake wouldn't have bothered bringing me.

"Yeah. I'm guessing that the boy on her arm is her rebound guy." She shrugged. "So it goes, right?"

I smoothed the impending frown from my face.

"I'm sorry. It's just that it's been Dana and Jake for such a long time and you're just so different."

"Is that a good thing?"

She looked me up and down for a full five seconds before she put a plastic smile on her face.

"Sure."

I rolled my eyes and crossed my arms over my chest. Where was Jake? I was ready to be done with the dark-haired Kardashian wannabe.

"Sorry. I'm making this weird," she said, shaking her head.

I looked up at the DJ booth. The DJ handed Jake a wad of cash, which he promptly shoved in his pocket. Then, the DJ shook Jake's hand and pulled out his phone. After a couple of seconds, a girl in a silver sequin dress walked up the stairs. She took the box and walked back down the stairs, moving among the crowd like one of those cigarette girls in the old movies.

The teens flocked to her, pulling out bags and waving them in the air like they'd just won a prize.

I gasped, feeling a nervous lump in my throat.

"Looks like the goodies have arrived," Bree said with a smile. The girl in the sequin dress passed us and Bree reached in, pulling out two bags of white powder. She handed one to me.

"Here. It will help loosen you up."

I took it from her, examining the contents. The powder was fine, each grain smaller than salt. Bree looked from the pouch to me and smiled, her eyes beckoning me to take it.

Even if I wanted to and I didn't, I had no idea how I was supposed to ingest it. Instead, I opened my purse and put the white packet inside.

Exhibit B.

"Maybe in a little bit," I said, trying to sound casual, even though I wanted to run away screaming. "I should eat first."

Bree nodded. "Good idea. It's better not to get high on an empty stomach."

It was then that Jake chose to walk down the stairs, his trademark smile on his face.

"Getting to know each other, ladies?" he asked.

Bree smiled and nodded. I didn't.

"We're becoming best friends," Bree said. She looked at me oddly, as if wondering why I didn't parrot her words.

Earth to Bree. I was not a parrot.

Jake took my hand and pulled me to his side. He must've spotted Dana.

"I'm going to go show Bella off some more. We'll catch up soon."

"Nice meeting you, Bella," Bree called after us. "Don't get in too much trouble."

She laughed too loudly to be genuine as Jake and I walked away.

"So, you've met Bree," Jake said. "She's amazing, isn't she?"

I swallowed my fear before answering.

"Sure."

"Me and her met after I got back from boarding school. I've known her my whole life. She's like my sister."

"Great," I said. My eyes went to the pool.

"What's wrong with you? You look like you've seen a ghost or something."

I was in the middle of a high school version of *Scarface*. I was terrified.

"Me? No. Just a little overwhelmed. It's an amazing party."

He shrugged. "You'll get used to it."

"Is, uh, is that drugs they are passing around?"

"You say it like this is a lame after school special."

I shook my head, ignoring his comment. "Bree gave me some."

"Oh yeah? What?"

I shrugged. "Some powder or something."

Jake raised his eyebrows at me. "Are you going to take it?"

I shook my head, my hands shaking.

"No. It's just weird. They're passing it out like candy."

"To be fair, it's really good candy."

"That you brought here?"

His eyes hooded.

"Why do I have the sneaking suspicion that you're going to narc on us?"

"I'm not narcing on anyone. I'm just curious. That's all."

Jake examined me for a moment.

"How about I give you a dollar and show you how to satisfy that curiosity?" he asked.

A shiver ran down my spine.

"I'm not going to use it, Jake."

"You sure?"

"Yes."

He held out his hand, silently asking for the powder in my purse.

I pulled it out and dropped my second piece of evidence in to his awaiting palm.

"If I find out that you told anyone about this, they will find your father's body at the bottom of the school swimming pool. Understood?"

I swallowed down the horror that raised within me and quickly nodded.

"I won't say anything. I promise."

Jake's eyes looked at me a moment more before his face relaxed. "Good. Keep it that way."

Just then, Cole and Stephanie walked in. When she saw the box of drugs, she clapped and jogged over to it, leaving Cole to stand awkwardly by.

Our eyes met. I wanted to run to him but I couldn't. He was with Stephanie and I was stuck with the knock off version of El Mayo Zambada.

I bit my lip and turned away.

"I have to go to the bathroom," I said.

Jake looked at his phone again. The black scratched one.

"Hurry back," he said, not looking at me. "We have girls to make jealous."

I nodded and walked back into the house.

The majority of the people were outside, leaving the hallways mostly deserted, except for the line that stretched down the stairs.

The girls bathroom.

Why did the girls bathroom always have a line?

"I know about a secret bathroom. Of course, if I tell you, I'll have to kill you."

I turned to see Cole ambling toward me. Relief touched me from the top of my head to the bottom of my toes.

"You've been here before?" I asked, suppressing the urge to run to him.

"Only a million other times. Our families are kind of tight."

I nodded. "I guess what they say is true. Millionaires stick together."

"Yeah. I guess. So are we going to stand around and leave a mess for the help to clean up or do you want to see that bathroom?"

"Lead the way."

Cole led me into another hallway. The floors were made of rust colored marble, the doors heavy wood, the side tables gold. I could probably sell one table and pay my rent for a year.

"So, what is it like to party with the rich and famous all the time?" I asked.

"Not as fun as you would think. The people are phony and the conversations are hollow."

"And the drugs?" I asked.

He shrugged. "I stay away from that stuff. It rots your brain. You?"

"Same. That girl, Bree, offered me something. Cocaine, I think. She said that it would loosen me up."

"That it would. You will be as loose as Kenny Jennings."

I laughed shortly. "That's not loose. That's just weird."

"Yeah."

A comfortable silence fell over us. We turned down another empty hallway.

"You don't look like you're having fun, French," he said.

"What makes you say that?"

"You lied about having to go to the bathroom and now you're in an empty hallway with me. Not exactly a barrel of laughs."

I stared out of the windows that we passed, my eyes fixed on the water lapping against the beach that surrounded the house.

"Is it my brother?" he asked. "Did he drag you here against your will?"

"I wouldn't say against my will."

"What would you say?"

I frowned. What could I say? That I was investigating his brother for running a drug cartel?

"Did he threaten you? Did he hurt you?"

Yes. Not yet.

Still, I stayed silent, drawing a frustrated breath from his lips.

"You're being weirdly quiet about it," he said, stuffing his hands in to his dress pants pockets.

I shrugged.

"There's nothing to say, really."

"Is that right?"

We stopped walking and leaned on a window ledge. The moonlight poured in to the hallway, giving Cole a pale glow that made my heart stutter. He was so beautiful. So genuine. I turned away from his knowing eyes.

"What do you see in him?" he asked.

I shook my head.

"He's popular."

"He's popular? That's it? That's the one quality that drew you to him?"

I bit my inner cheek, still not looking at him.

"Funny. I thought you had more substance than that."

"Are you trying to bait me, Cole?"

"No. I'm trying to get you to talk to me. I'm trying to understand what this weird relationship is that you have with my brother. And don't tell me that you love him. You barely like him. You can barely look at each other half the time."

"You sound like you've taken notice."

"What if I have?"

My heart thudded hard. I finally looked up at him. His hard eyes, his stubborn chin, the red that rose in his cheeks. His gaze was focused on me so intently that I squirmed.

"I can't do this."

"Do what?" he demanded.

"I can't have this conversation with you." I pushed off from the window and walked back the way we came.

"So not only are you a popularity chaser, you're a coward, too."

My feet stopped, my body whipping around.

"What did you call me?"

"I called you a coward. A chicken. Full of fear. Do you need more synonyms?"

"You are the biggest hypocrite that I have ever met!"

"You don't want him! You can't stand him. I know it." His long legs slowly covered the distance between us.

"You don't know anything."

"I know that you're afraid of what would happen if you admitted it."

"Admitted what?"

"That you don't want to be with him."

"And what good would that do for anyone, Cole? How would that help anyone?"

"Tell me what you want, Bella." His eyes bore into mine, piercing my soul, my spirit. My feet rooted to the floor, my lungs sucking in the smell of him until my head felt light and my heart felt full. "Tell me who you want."

"I can't."

"Why?" His hands encircled my face, his mouth so close to mine. My eyes closed. My lips puckered.

"Because..." My brain fogged. All reason fled from me. There was something that I should have said but I couldn't remember. Cole had taken up residence in every part of my mind. My soul.

"Tell me and I swear to you that I'll say yes."

Electric currents raced through me. He was closer now. I only had to lean forward for our lips to touch. I wanted to. I had never wanted to do anything else in my life. But I couldn't. To kiss Cole would be disastrous, but by god, I wanted to watch the world burn with him.

"Tell me."

My lips parted, forming the words that would ignite both of our worlds.

"I want..."

A sliver of my mind was still in control, but it grew smaller and smaller by the second.

"I want..."

"Bella." His voice was rough. Tight. It awoke something in me that I didn't understand. Drew me toward him. Beckoned. Called me like a deadly siren. "Tell me."

I couldn't hide it anymore. I couldn't fight it. Couldn't fight him. I had to say it. I had to tell him or else I would explode.

"Y-"

"Are we interrupting?"

Our heads whipped to the right, staring down the hallway.

Stephanie and Jake stood at the end of the hallway, watching us.

"Did you forget who you came here with, Cole?" Stephanie asked, her screeching voice echoing off the walls, breaking the bubble of desire that Cole and I had erected around us.

He didn't step back. Didn't move his hands from my face.

Jake's cheeks grew redder by the second. One more shade and he was going to explode.

I stepped back and smoothed my hair behind my ears.

"We were just talking," I said. It was a stupid thing to say but with Stephanie and Jake's hate filled eyes on me, I couldn't think of anything else.

"What they put on your locker is right." Stephanie's heeled feet ate up the space between us until we were nose to nose. "You are a whore."

Like a flash, Cole was between us.

"Leave her alone," he said.

"And you. You, I can't even stand to look at. From now on, stay away from me."

"I told you that we were just friends."

She reached up and slapped him hard across the face, her eyes narrow slits.

"Now, we'll be ex-just friends."

With one final glare at me, she was gone, the echoes of her heels bouncing off the walls.

I looked at Jake.

"I'll take my girlfriend back now," he said, reaching out a hand to me.

"She doesn't want you," Cole spat.

A slow, devilish smile spread across his lips.

"Guess what, little brother? It doesn't matter. Bella and I have an agreement. She's mine for as long as I'll have her. Isn't that right, Bella?"

I hesitated. My hands wrapped around my mid-section, my body going cold.

"Isn't that right, Bella?" Jake repeated.

Cole turned to me. His fingers stroked my chin. I felt the warmth in those fingers. The affection. The gentleness. Things that I craved but couldn't have.

"You don't have to go with him," he whispered. "You can stay here. With me."

Those pleading eyes crushed my heart into powder. I looked away, taking hateful steps toward Jake. Each step made me want to sprint back to Cole but I couldn't.

It was impossible.

Jake threw an arm around my shoulder and sneered at Cole.

Cole's face fell. He looked defeated, that sad look returning to his eyes. I had put that sadness there. This was my fault. It was all my fault.

"Tough luck, bro. Maybe next time."

Jake's arm dropped to slide around my waist and I allowed him to guide me back to the party.

It will all be over tomorrow, I thought. I'll call Detective Harding tomorrow.

Dread filled my gut.

The second I made the call, everything about my life would change.

Ariel, Jasmine and Cole would probably never speak to me again. I would be alone.

Before I was invisible.

After tomorrow, I wouldn't be anywhere at all.

I felt like I was walking through a fog. Like a piece of myself was left in that hallway with Cole. I smiled a little. At least that piece of me was happy. The rest of me was an inch above misery and falling fast.

Jake paraded me around in front of Dana but I barely registered it. He kissed my cheek and somehow managed a feel on my butt, but I barely felt it. My life was going to change in the worst way possible. I would be alone and it was all because of one, little lie.

"Jeez. Lighten up," Jake said, leading me to a chair next to the pool. "You're like the mummy out there."

I didn't respond, my mind sinking deeper and deeper in to dark thoughts.

He handed me a drink and I swallowed it down, not thinking about what it was or what was in it. It burned a little, but the burning felt good. It was a small reminder that a little piece of me was still alive.

He handed me another and I drank that too, relishing in the sweet taste and my stinging throat.

I was surrounded by the children of movie stars, rock stars, politician and wealthy businessmen. Teens who had no idea what it was like to struggle. To want. To need. To pull together an entire family's life savings just so that you could go to a good school.

Jake handed me another glass and I quickly swallowed it.

My head felt dizzy. My body felt light.

His lips touched my ear. "Ready to make some new friends?"

I nodded, not knowing why. My mind slowed, drifting like a boat on the sea.

The lies came quickly now. Naturally. My father became a rich hedge fund manager. I had no idea what a hedge fund manager was but fortunately, no one else did either.

I spoke non-existent truths and spun tales of money that I'd never seen or possessed.

"Isn't it great to be rich? My family's fortune stretches back generations."

"Yes. I own a diamond tiara. Don't you?"

"We summer in Australia because Mom has a thing for koalas."

"Do you boat? I own a yacht on every continent."

Lies. Lies. More lies. Every dream of travel, wealth and power all came alive within me. I laughed at the right times. I sipped Jake's magic drinks until my head spun. I flirted with Jake and let him kiss me on my forehead and hold me tight to his chest.

I was my own fantasy all under the lights and marble and gold of this castle.

It was glorious.

I hated myself for it.

Jake pulled me close and we danced near the warmth of the pool.

"I have to say, I like you better like this."

"Like what?" I asked.

I didn't recognize my own voice. It was deep. Strange.

"Loose. Without the weight of the world on your shoulders. You're almost tolerable. If I had known that, I would have gotten you drunk earlier."

"You say such pretty things."

He laughed out loud and we continued to slow dance to the house music that pumped around us.

Someone lit a fire on the lawn and everyone cheered. Marshmallows appeared at the buffet table and we roasted them on wooden stakes stolen from the chocolate fountain.

After my third marshmallow, I pulled off my shoes and walked to the pool, hiking up my skirt and dipping my toes in.

"That's not how you go into a pool," Jake said, opening his cufflinks. "This is how you go into a pool."

He pulled off his shoes and socks, ran forward and did a cannon ball in to warm water. Everyone cheered as a Jake sized wave rose up, splashing the girls who stood too close to the edge.

Jake hooted and suddenly, the rest of the boys were taking off their shoes and socks and jumping into the pool. It didn't matter that their suits costed thousands of dollars. It didn't matter that they would have to drive home soaking wet. What mattered was that they were having fun.

I smiled at Jake.

He smiled back at me and for the first time, I wondered if I could live this way. With him. Sure, he wasn't as smart as Cole, or as kind or gentle. He didn't make my heart quake and my breath catch. He didn't make my skin hum and my world fill with music. Jake was hollow. A shell.

Maybe that was what I was, too. A walking, talking, lying shell.

"Don't you want to join your boyfriend in the pool?" a voice slithered into my ear before I was airborne, slipping off the edge of the pool and sinking to the bottom.

Water went up my nose. In my mouth. I flailed, trying to relax my body and float back to the top. It didn't work. Panic set in. I kicked but the pool was deep and I wasn't a strong swimmer. I reached for something, anything to hold onto, but there was only black water that stung my eyes and nose. The sound of bubbles. The feel of deathly liquid surrounding me. Invading me.

One horrific thought flashed through my mind over and over again.

I am going to drown.

I opened my mouth to scream and water rushed in, filling my lungs. Something gripped me around my waist, pulling me upward. I fought against it but only for a moment. Suddenly, I was out of the water and lying on the side of the pool.

Someone pressed their lips to mine, breathing air in to me. Hands pumped on my chest, pushing air out of me. Into me. Out of me again. I sputtered, coughed then vomited up the water that was in my lungs.

I'm alive. How am I alive?

I raised my head. Though my vision was blurry, I could see that the party had stopped and everyone was staring at me.

For a second, I wished that I had drowned.

Cole's face hung over me, his eyes wide with worry.

"Bella. Bella, are you all right? Can you talk?"

My cheeks heated with embarrassment. I slid to the left, moving away from the vomit that I'd just ejected.

I was freezing, barefoot and soaking wet.

I was a fraud. A disgrace. An embarrassment.

There was no room for anger in my still shocked mind. No room for fury. Just sadness. Sadness that I thought I could belong with these people. I didn't belong here.

I picked up my shoes and silently walked to the door, fat, hot tears running down my cheeks.

"Bella," Cole chased after me. "Bella, wait. Let me take you home."

"Leave me alone," I said, my voice cracking, my feet moving faster.

"What do you plan on doing? Walking home?"

"Leave me alone!" I screamed. "I don't want your help. Ever!"

He stopped. Stunned. "You don't mean that."

"You Winsted boys are all the same. You only think about what you can get from people. What you can get from me."

He took my hand in his.

"Bella, you know that's not true."

"It is. It is, and I'm done. I wish I'd never met your family. I wish I had never met you!"

I shoved him off me and took off down the stairs.

With no idea where I was, no ride home and too much pride, I asked the valet to call me a cab and a water taxi to get me back to the mainland. He did and informed me that it would be a thirty-minute wait.

Great. I had just made a scene in front of god knew how many people and followed it with the most epic, dramatic exit. Now, I was standing on the front lawn, waiting for a cab.

I was such a fool.

Stuck in the darkness, alone, wet, freezing and nearly drowned, I searched for a place to hide until I could escape. Some place where my dramatic exit would stay intact.

There wasn't much. Bree's house was the only building on this island of darkness, grass, water and expensive cars. A few sheds dotted the property. I tried two of them but when the locks didn't give, I abandoned searching the rest. I considered sitting in someone's car but I was sure that the valets would have locked up the keys somewhere and going back to the party was not an option.

I sighed. There was only one choice left.

Shoes still dangling from my hand, I walked down to the beach and let the cold waves lap at my even colder toes.

Tears filled my eyes.

What would Mom think of me now? Lying to people that I don't know or care about to make them accept me? And for what? So Jake would look good enough to get back with his ex-girlfriend? So Ariel could have her happily ever after? So I could sample what it was like to be rich and popular? So I could save a school that didn't even bother to learn my name?

If Mom were here, she'd tell me all my reasons were utter crap. She'd tell me I should be true to myself and that I shouldn't try to change so others would accept me. She'd tell me it was shameful to lie about my father's job to get in good with these people—the same people who tried to drown me ten minutes ago. But most of all, more than anything, she'd tell me I shouldn't have lied in the first place.

'Lies are easy to get into, but they sure are hard getting out of', she'd say.

My mother had never been more right.

Cold droplets of water sprayed me, wetting my already soaked face, arms and legs. I could smell the long island sound, a gross mix of fish and dirty water. The waves roared with each assault and retreat on the shore. Moonlight lit the beach, making the sand glow an odd bluish gold.

I wrapped my shivering arms around my middle and closed my eyes.

Just breathe, Bella. Just breathe.

"Did I ever tell you that I hated the beach?"

Cole's deep voice sent gooseflesh across my cold back.

"I told you to leave me alone," I said, my voice strong.

He didn't reply. Just then, my back was warm. My arms and shoulders and chest were warm, and I was surrounded by Cole's spicy vanilla scent.

"I figured that you could use my jacket."

I frowned.

"I don't want your jacket," I said, though I pulled it closer, the warmth of his body sinking into mine.

"God, French. You are the most stubborn girl I've ever met."

"I'm sorry that I'm not one of those girls who silently bend to your magnanimous will."

"Well, I am magnanimous." There was no mistaking the grin in his voice.

Two hands briskly ran up and down my arms, warming me even further. My eyes closed. I had never felt so warm. So safe.

Something strange tightened in my chest. A strong desire to sink in to Cole's touch. To forget the world and grab a boat and sail away to our own private adventure, letting the wind take us where it pleased.

I shook my head.

Get your head out of the clouds. It can never happen. He said it himself. You are with his brother. He can never be with you.

And my head was right. I couldn't be with Cole. I shouldn't be with Cole. But, why did his touch make me feel so centered? Like my feet were steady on the ground and I was certain about who I was. Why did Cole feel so very right, even though he was so very wrong?

"Let me take you home, French. You don't belong here."

I whipped around, glaring at him.

"What is that supposed to mean?"

"You are telling me that you like hanging out with these self-serving, hollow, drug-fueled people? These are your friends and comrades?"

"Those people are nice to me." They kind of weren't but I didn't want to give Cole any ground. Besides, I was upset at how my night had gone to crap and he was the only one here to take it out on.

"Those people don't care about you."

"Oh yeah? Well, if they are so terrible, then why are you here, Cole? Why would you hang out with a bunch of hollow losers?"

"I came here because I knew that you were coming with Jake and I wanted to make sure that you were okay."

"Oh. I see. Poor little Bella French needs her tutor and English partner to babysit her because she is entirely too low-class to be trusted around such high-brows."

"I didn't say that."

"What is it then, Cole? You think that I'm not good enough for them?"

"No. I think that you're better than them and I didn't want you to come here and be made to feel like you're not. You are above them, Bella. Those girls in there can't hold a candle to you. They are not fit for you and I am here to make sure that you know that." He touched my cheek. "Don't make them think that you are not worthy when you are worth everything."

One tear fell. One tear for Cole. The only boy in my life that deserved it.

I heard the grind of wheels behind me.

My cab.

"I don't need your protection." I hated my words. "I don't need your sympathy or your pity." I hated my lies. "And I most definitely don't need you to babysit me." I hated myself, but there was no stopping it. No other way to keep him away. To keep myself from hurting when I knew that I couldn't have him.

I hurled his jacket at him, hoping that it hit him in the face.

Instead, he caught it and folded it over his arm.

He would.

His blue eyes looked at me, long-suffering and pleading. It was the look of a man who was talking to an unreasonable, stubborn girl. Well, I was both of those things. But I was also vulnerable and raw and confused and frustrated. Those last few things had nothing to do with the party and everything to do with the beautiful boy standing in front of me.

"Bella-"

"Just leave me alone, Cole."

Chilled without his jacket, I ran to the cab that would take me to the water taxi, which in turn, would take me to another cab. I slid into the car, asked the middle eastern driver to pump up the heat and looked down at my lap. I had my purse but somewhere along the way, I had dropped a shoe and here I was, in an orange cab, going back to reality.

Maybe I was *Cinderella*. But this was no fairy tale. There would be no happy ending. Deep down, I knew that my prince was somewhere standing on a beach, though he hated getting sand in his shoes.

I closed my eyes and silently fell apart.

⁂ 49 ⁂

I crept back in to the apartment somewhere between two and three a.m. Jasmine was lying in my bed, one hand behind her head, the other beneath the pillow.

I tip-toed around the room, taking off my dripping wet dress and removing my single heel. I didn't bother to wash my face. I was too tired.

I slipped in to the bed next to Jasmine, a zombie about to rest in her grave, when Jasmine spoke up.

"You're back," she said. Her voice was steady and strong. She hadn't been sleeping at all.

"Thank you for covering for me," I said.

"It's the last time."

"What? Why?"

"You've changed, Bella. I can't be a part of your lies anymore."

Lies? What did she know?

"The clothes, the hair, the parties, they aren't you. They're Jake. Can't you see what he's trying to do? He's making you into her. His own personal Dana. I can't stand by and watch that happen to you."

"What are you going to do about it?" I asked.

She sighed.

"I'm leaving. You know how to reach me when you remember who you are."

She stood up, walked out of my room and out of my life.

When the door closed, I knew that she was not coming back.

50

The next morning, Daddy and I packed all our belongings in to the moving truck and moved across town to Ariel and Jasmine's apartment building. 76 Central Park West. Ariel was there to help us unpack, as well as Ariel's sisters, Adella and Alana, twins about to graduate 8th grade. They didn't look like Ariel at all. They had dark hair and eyes, and were gangly. But what they were good at was putting together a home.

The apartment has been professionally cleaned before we moved in and the girls went right to work, hanging photos that hadn't been unboxed since Mom died, adding fresh flowers in vases long forgotten, hanging drapes, putting down rugs. By the time six o'clock rolled around, we had every last box unpacked.

It'd been a long time since we'd been unpacked. Since pictures hung from the walls. I hadn't looked at Mom's picture since we left North Carolina. Now, her and Daddy's wedding picture sat in a nice white frame on the side table. I picked it up and examined it. Mom was beautiful that day. Her caramel skin glowed, her dark eyes were full of happiness, her smile was bright.

I ran my fingers over the picture and sighed.

"Welcome back, Mom," I whispered to it.

I put the picture down and picked up the one next to it. I didn't know we owned a picture of my old horse Sweet Lips but Adella and Alana had fished it out from the boxes of our past. I stared at the girl I used to be. Curls flying. Eyes wide and full of life. Beneath me, the Overo Paint Horse was magnificent. The brown in its coat looked unfinished, like a child had begun to color the horse in but got distracted and walked away, leaving large areas of white behind. I closed my eyes, recalling the feel of her beneath me. The pump of her lungs, the smell of her sweat, the rhythm of her runs.

I let out a shaky breath. So many memories all at once. So many things forgotten.

I opened my eyes and examined our new apartment. A large window, complete with a window seat, let the filtered fall sunlight fill the living room. Our old brown couch was the same, but the girls had discovered a red and white Indian blanket—a gift from my grandfather—and draped it over the top of the couch, giving it new life. A giant rust colored rug sat beneath the coffee table. They'd found a red chair—or had they brought it down from their apartment? —and placed it next to the couch, forming a circle with the television, couch and chair.

One more couch beneath the window would make the room perfect, I thought.

Crown molding gave the living room and dining room a proper separation. Our small table for four seemed too small in the open area. The girls had tried to make it work, adding tall plants to the corners and lots of family pictures on the walls. My baby pictures, Mom standing in a sunflower field, Dad petting a horse, Grandma and Grandpa on their wedding day. The table was set with fancy dishes and plates the color of tangerine peels.

The kitchen had no windows but the large, super bright, overhead lights made up for it. There was plenty of counter space and a big refrigerator. The girls had decided on a country theme with this room, pulling out an old watering can for the small corner breakfast nook, adding decorative dishes to the walls, a mat with a rooster on it next to the sink. They promised that they would come back and paint the walls yellow.

"You two are life savers. Are you majoring in interior design?" I asked.

"How'd you guess?" they replied in unison.

I made a mental note to send over thank you cards and flowers as soon as I could.

After a full day of moving, unpacking and decorating, we finally sat down and dug in to our pizza. I got two bites in when there was a knock on the front door.

I picked a piece of pepperoni off my slice, popped it in to my mouth and jogged to open it. When I pulled the door open, Cole was looking at me with those big blue eyes. His dark hair was a mess of curls that hung in his eyes. No gel today. His tall, strong frame was wrapped in a dark jacket, white t-shirt, dark jeans and sneakers.

God. He was handsome.

"Hey," he said.

"Hey."

We stared at each other for a moment, taking each other in. He ran his hands through his dark hair and gave me a half smile that made my heart speed up. His shoulders were slightly hunched, his face paler than I remembered. Like he'd lost a little of his joy between yesterday and today.

"I just came by to see if you were okay."

I stepped out in to the hallway and closed the door.

"I'm fine."

When I woke up that morning, my mouth felt like cotton and my head verged on splitting open. After nearly a gallon of water and about ten ibuprofen, I was finally able to get out of bed.

"Last night didn't go as I expected," he said.

I crossed my arms, remembering his jacket so warm and delicious smelling around me. I wished that I had taken it with me. I wanted to wrap it around me whenever I thought of him, which by the way, was much too often.

"What did you expect?" I asked.

He laughed shortly. "Not World War III."

"Did you think that I would just fall into your arms while my boyfriend danced in the other room?"

I wanted to hurt Cole. I wanted to hurt him because he hurt me by being with Stephanie.

"I'd hoped," he said.

"What a thing to say to your brother's girlfriend."

I had to hurt Cole. It was the only way to keep him away. To keep my heart safe.

"You don't want him."

"Does it matter?"

"It does to me."

"Did it matter when you were making out with Stephanie?"

I had to keep my heart away from him. If he took it, I'd never get it back.

"I never made out with Stephanie."

"That's not what Jake said."

"Jake is a liar and an idiot."

I shrugged, though knowing that Stephanie had never touched his lips made me feel a little bit better.

"Stephanie seemed to think that you two were pretty cozy."

"I told Stephanie that we were friends. She knew that."

"I'll bet."

"Why are you doing this? Why are you pushing me away?"

I put my hands on my hips and shifted my weight on my feet.

"Cole, we are English partners and you tutor me in French. I really think that you are taking our relationship to a place where it wasn't meant to go."

Where it couldn't go.

He shook his head. "That's not true."

"It is true."

Please go away. I don't want to hurt you.

"I don't believe you," he said.

"You have to believe me."

Just walk away. I don't want to hurt you.

"Cole, I am Jake's girlfriend."

"For reasons still unknown. Reasons I'm beginning to care less and less about."

"You have to care about them. He's your brother."

"Why are you with him, huh? Did he pay you? Do you need money?"

"So now you think that I'm a whore, too?"

Please don't make me hurt you. Please don't make me hurt you.

"No. I think that you're a fake. A fraud. You're with him but you don't want to be. You want to be with me."

My heart beat hard. My chest ached.

"How do you know that?"

"Because I'm not an idiot, Bella. I open my eyes. I observe things. You laugh at my dumb jokes, you argue with me, whenever I touch you, you stop breathing. Just admit that you like me already."

"Is that why you came here? To gloat? To add me to another notch in your belt."

He scowled darkly at me. "You know that's not true."

"That's pretty much what it sounds like."

He growled.

"You are the most stubborn girl I have ever met in my life."

"Great. Thank you for sharing. Maybe you should go, Cole."

"No. No. I'm not going. Not until you admit that you want to be with me."

I shook my head.

"Leave, Cole. I don't have time for this."

I turned my back, intending to grab the door handle but he grabbed my shoulder, swung me around, pressed my back to the wall and moved in close.

Too close.

His arms encircled me, pressing our trembling bodies together.

His lips descended upon me like a hawk diving for its dinner.

Relentless. Demanding. Breaking down my every wall. Stripping away every excuse.

Cole's kisses were like dynamite. His lips set the charges that exploded through me. Goosebumps broke out over my skin. My hands were everywhere, touching every piece of him that I could. I felt wild, frantic, desperate for more. My mouth opened and his tongue brushed against mine, sending delicious shivers through my entire body. My heart beat out of my chest, my racing pulse our own, personal melody.

His fingers played at my back while his learned lips gave me exactly what I needed, pressing to me when I wanted more, pulling back when it was too much, changing the angle when my heart beat slowed, smiling against my lips when it beat too fast.

Gradually, he slowed down the pace, his lips softening, his kisses turning gentle.

"I have wanted to do that since Freshman year," he said between teasing nibbles on my bottom lip.

My hands had somehow gotten tangled in the black curls at the nape of his neck. I kept them there, playing with the dark strands, trying to catch my breath.

"I like you, Bella. A lot. You're too stubborn to say it first so I'm going to. I really, really like you."

His words radiated down my spine and through my toes. My eyes opened, searching his. The truth was so clear in them that it shook me to my core.

"I want to be your boyfriend. A real one."

My world stopped spinning, my heels lightening as if the gravity had been sucked from the room. I couldn't speak. Could barely think. Cole wanted to be with me. My heart felt so full that I was afraid it would burst.

"I have wanted you since I first saw you. You challenged me in every way imaginable. You call yourself invisible but I see you, Bella. I've always seen you."

He took my hand and placed it on his chest. Beneath the hard muscles, I felt his heart beat strong beneath my fingertips. Fast. It was so fast.

His heartbeat matched my own.

"Take what's yours, Bella. What's always been yours."

His words were beautiful. I wanted so much to fall into Cole and never return. But I couldn't. There was too much at stake. It was too dangerous.

One fat tear rolled down my cheek. A tear for the boy that I wanted, but could never have.

"Cole, please don't say things like that."

"Like what? That I want to be with you? Well, I do. I can't eat. I can't sleep. Every waking moment, all I can do is think about you. And then I see you with him and I can't sit still. I begged and I pleaded and I prayed for you to come to me, but you were too stubborn for your own good, so here I am. I want you, Bella. Today, tomorrow, and forever. Just ... please, say that you want me, too."

Little beads of delight burst from my soul and I allowed them to see the sunlight for just a second. Just one second of happiness. Just one second for me to stand here in front of a boy that I wanted more than anything and allow myself to pretend that I said the words back to him. That we'd be safe and in love and together forever.

The second passed.

It was not to be.

I smothered the happiness. Killed it. Happiness was not meant for me. Not anymore.

Cole's eyes turned pleading. Horrified.

"Bella, don't do this."

I didn't want to hurt him.

"Bella."

I never wanted to hurt him.

"Bella, please!"

I had to hurt him.

"I don't want to be with you, Cole."

And with the words that sealed my fate of misery, I ran in to my apartment, closed myself in my room and completely fell apart.

51

Two knocks echoed through my room, followed by Ariel's face peeking through the door.

"Can I come in?" she asked.

I shrugged, curling my knees up to my chest.

She nodded, stepped in to the room and quietly shut the door behind her.

"You're not okay," she said.

I shook my head. "No. I'm not."

"What did Cole say to you in the hallway?"

I shook my head and squeezed my lips together. It wasn't what he said to me, it was what I said to him that haunted me. The lies that spilled from my mouth. Lies that I told with such ease now.

Ariel sat down next to me and put her arm around my shoulder.

"Bella, you're so secretive lately. Maybe if you opened up about what's going on in your life, you'd feel better."

I snorted at the irony of it all.

Opening up would ruin Ariel's entire existence and here she was asking me to do it.

That time would come but I didn't want it to come anytime soon.

It would mean the end of our friendship and I wasn't ready for that yet. Honestly, I didn't know if I would ever be ready.

"Is it about Jake? Did he do something to you? Is he hurting you?"

In more ways than one, I wanted to say. But I didn't. I kept my mouth shut because it was what I had to do.

"So you're going to sit there and not say anything?"

I could hear the anger rising in her voice.

"We are best friends. We tell each other everything and now I'm not good enough for you to talk to anymore?"

"That's not it."

"Did you tell Stephanie what's going on?"

"What? No?"

"Mel? Ursula? Dana?"

"Why would you even say that?"

"Because you seem to be cozy with them lately. Meanwhile, Jasmine and I barely ever see you. I'm here, trying to repair our friendship before it all falls to crap and you can't even tell me what's going on? You can't even look me in the eye."

A tear dripped down my cheek. If I spoke, it would ruin everything. I knew it would.

"Bella, I can't do this anymore. I can't be in a one-sided friendship. You have to decide right now. Tell me what's going on or I am gone."

Another tear dripped in to my lap.

"You're gone anyway," I whispered.

Ariel's eyes went wide, as if I just slapped her. She let out a breath and stood.

It was hard walking away from Cole.

It was even harder to watch Ariel, my best friend, my partner in crime, my heart, walk out of the door and not look back at me. I felt her begin to hate me and I knew that I deserved it. I deserved every ounce of hatred she had because I had lied to her and I'd made Eric lie to her, too. I had made her fall in love with a lie and when what I did comes to light, I was going to lose her forever.

Or maybe I had already lost her forever.

My tears began fresh and I mourned for Ariel and Jasmine as if they'd died. As if I'd never see them again. I mourned for all the jokes we'd never again laugh at. Late night movies that we'd never watch. Gossip we'd never share. I'd never again look at Ariel in science class and make a funny face. We'd never be able to talk without saying a word again. Those times were over.

And I was alone.

Truly, hopelessly, terribly alone.

I'd done that to myself with a lie.

Now there was only one thing to do. I dried my tears and put on a jacket.

I'd lost everyone in my life that I loved. Now, I'd make it count for something. If nothing else, I would see that my school was no longer overrun with Jake's poison.

I had to call Detective Harding and tell him what I'd learned. But I needed to see someone first. I had to say that I was sorry.

52

Mel Pleasant sat in the fading light of her living room. She no longer looked like one quarter of what my friends and I called the evil queens. Her black and purple hair was pulled up into a loose ponytail, her face gaunt, her skin moonlight pale. She wore an oversized jean-colored sweater, black leggings and bare feet. It was the first time that I'd seen her with no make-up in, well, ever.

I stood in the doorway, not sure if I should go in or not.

"You can come in," she said. "I'm not contagious."

I swallowed and stepped into the room. Her mother had told me where Mel was, then disappeared. She was on the phone, talking to someone in hushed, angry tones. I was certain that the conversation was about her daughter.

The room was wide and comfortable. Soft, beige carpet, green cushioned chairs, high windows overlooking Central Park. A fireplace sat at the far wall, unlit.

Heavy sadness hung over the room like a black cloud. Sadness that radiated from Mel. It swirled in my lungs, hung around my heart, oozed within my gut. I coughed to keep from choking on it.

I sank in to the chair closest to Mel, resisting the urge to pull up my legs and wrap my arms around them. I had to be strong now. Mel needed me to be strong.

"I came to see how you're doing."

She turned from the window and looked straight at me. Her eyes looked sunken and she had dark bags beneath them. I swallowed a gasp.

"I'm leaving for rehab on Tuesday so I guess things could be better."

"Rehab? You're only sixteen."

"Apparently, age is not really a factor when you overdose."

I nodded, trying to find something to say that was a bit more cheerful. I failed.

"How long will you have to stay?"

"Long enough for me not to be an addict anymore. Or until I turn eighteen and my parents stop paying for it. Whichever comes first."

I couldn't imagine going to rehab. It was even harder to imagine being there for two years. My hands began to sweat and I nervously rubbed them on my jeans.

"Mel, I came to say that I knew you didn't want to go with Kenny that night. I should have said something. I should have stopped you. I ... I'm sorry."

Her mouth tried to smile but ended up frowning instead.

"Do you think what happened to me is your fault?" she asked.

I nodded. "Yes. I should have said something. I should have-"

"I have been on and off with Kenny for the past two years," she said, her voice rough but strong. "He gave me free drugs and I gave him whatever he wanted. It was a good arrangement while it lasted. We even liked each other from time to time." Her lower lip shook and she sniffled, but didn't cry. "What happened that night was just one mistake in a long line of mistakes. It wasn't your fault."

A weight lifted off me and I let out a breath.

"Thank you," I said.

She looked at me with the same hollow expression, like she was a puppet that someone else was talking for. This was not the lively girl that I knew. This girl was a husk of her former glory. How could her life had gone so wrong?

"You are the first person in school to come and see me," she said. "I've been home for three days and none of my friends came to see if I was okay."

I frowned.

"On Friday, they basically fell apart in front of the entire school. They made your locker into a shrine with flowers and teddy bears and get well soon cards."

She snorted. "I'm sure they did. That's what they're supposed to do. Girls like that, girls like me, we keep our attachments light. That way, if someone goes off the rails, it's easier to cut ties. Popularity is all icy ground. One minute, you have your footing then next, your sliding off into oblivion and no one even asks if you're okay." She shook her head. "Why would you change? Why would you want to be like us? We are empty inside. Hollow. Why couldn't you stay the way you were?"

A tear fell down her cheek, then another. She covered her face with one pale hand and sobbed loudly. I wrapped her in my arms and held her as she fell apart. Her words touched me deeper than I could express.

I'd felt the emptiness that popularity brought me but I didn't believe it. I thought that there was something that I was missing. Some piece of the puzzle that, once found, would give me fulfillment. But there was no missing puzzle piece. There was nothing to fill me up. Just empty words and texts from people who only knew my name because of who my boyfriend was. Mel knew that. She tried to fill up the emptiness with drugs. Who knew what I would have turned to.

"Don't do it," Mel sobbed. "Don't be like us."

"I won't." I wiped away a stray tear. "I promise. And don't worry. I won't let what happened to you happen to anyone else. I'm going to put a stop to it. I swear."

"The only way to stop it is to put Jake in jail and his father would never allow it. You have to face the facts. It can't be stopped. He's too powerful."

Mel's tears soaked into my shirt and we didn't say anything further. After a long while, she dried her eyes and we bid each other goodbye.

Seeing Mel so down saddened me but it strengthened me, too. I'd made a promise to her. I would stop the drugs from coming in to my school. That was my purpose now. It was why I had lost everything. So that I could save my fellow students' lives.

I descended the steps of Mel's building and pulled out my phone.

It rang twice before a familiar voice answered.

"This is Detective Harding."

"Detective, this is Bella French. I have the information you wanted about Jake Winsted but you have to promise me that you won't tell my dad."

❧ 53 ❧

Ariel and Jasmine weren't there when I arrived at the front steps of our apartment. Funny, I thought that we would be even closer once we lived in the same building. Of course, that was before I had ruined everything with my lies.

I rode the subway alone then picked my way through the crowds that herded into school.

Jake could wait today. In fact, he could wait forever. I'd made up my mind. I would no longer be his puppet. It was time for me to remember who I was. I was Bella French. I was strong, I was honest and I was no one's fake girlfriend.

With my new lease on life firmly wrapped around me, I walked up to my locker, only half surprised to see it graffitied with the word Tramp.

Such an old school word and with not nearly enough punch. Maybe Jezebel would have been better, or harlot. Something with some pizazz.

I pulled down the papers, gathered them into a neat pile and walked them to the garbage can.

Along the way, Dana passed me.

"Dana," I called.

She turned and looked at me like I was an annoying mosquito she wanted to swat away.

She wasn't with her usual troop of friends. I'd never seen her alone before but I was too pissed about my locker to think about that now.

"The next time you write on my locker, try using a thesaurus. Tramp is played."

She squinted at me, her annoyance growing.

"What are you talking about? I didn't write on your locker."

I shook my head.

"I know you did. Just fess up and let's call it even, okay?"

"If I wrote on your locker, it would be to call you out on you stealing my outfits or your stupid hair cut or your loser of a boyfriend. I would never call you a tramp. A prude, maybe. Weirdo. Freak. Spaz. Faker. Poser. And especially a liar. But I'm not ninety-seven years old. Therefore, I would never call anyone a tramp. Maybe try looking for someone who cares that you exist."

She flipped her hair and walked away, leaving me speechless.

It didn't make sense. If Dana wasn't writing mean things on my locker, then who was?

54

I was summoned via text after third period. Only, it wasn't by the Winsted brother that I wanted to see.

After enduring English with Cole so close and yet so far away, Jake practically sprinted over to me.

Cole glanced at me and left.

I wished he'd come back.

"What?" I asked, my irritation clear.

"We have to talk."

He took my hand and dragged me halfway across school to the empty chemistry lab. His touch was different from Cole's. Cole's touch left trails of fire that burned in my blood, while Jake's touch left me cold as ice.

He slammed the door behind us and turned to me, his hands on his hips, his eyebrows furrowed.

If Jake was worried, then something must have been wrong. My heart beat picked up in anticipation of his words.

"We have a problem," he said.

"What problem?"

"Eric wants out."

My heart literally stopped beating.

"What? Why?"

This was the worst thing that could happen. If Eric wanted out of the deal, Ariel would be devastated.

"He likes the girl. He said that he doesn't want to keep lying to her."

"Welcome to the club."

"Forget about that now. If Eric tells Ariel, then our secret will be out. Dana will find out that you and me aren't real. I'll be the laughing stock of the school. Do you know what that means for a guy like me?"

"That you'll finally understand what the rest of the school goes through every day at the hands of the popular kids?"

I crossed my arms over my chest. Jake was freaking out but I was surprisingly calm. I had made peace with the fact that when this was all said and done, the three most important people in my life would not want to have anything to do with me. Ariel, Jasmine and Cole would all be gone and I would be alone. The thought brought tears to my eyes but I sniffed them back. It would do me no good to cry now.

His frowned deepened.

"Try to act a little more concerned, French. This is my life we're talking about. My reputation."

"Funny. You had no qualms about destroying my life. My reputation."

He ran his hands through his blond locks. "That's because you didn't have one that mattered."

I glared at him. "You're a jerk. Do you know that?"

He waved the comment away.

"Solutions, French. I need a solution to this very upsetting problem."

I rolled my eyes and leaned on a nearby desk. I had no desire to help Jake out of anything but I was willing to give Ariel as much time as I could with Eric.

"What do we do?" I asked.

"I told him to stall. Just to sit tight and wait it out. Maybe the feeling will pass."

"The feeling to tell Ariel the truth or the feeling of him liking her?"

"Either way, it will work out in our favor."

I sighed. Maybe it was better that he did tell her. The weight that I'd been carrying around on my shoulders was exhausting. And Eric's wanting to tell Ariel the truth revealed the answer to a question that I'd been asking myself for a week now. Eric really did like Ariel. For real. All my lies and half-truths had been worth something. Ariel was happy. Genuinely happy.

I'd do it again to keep her that way.

"I told him that I'd call him tomorrow and see how he was," Jake said, pacing the room.

"Where is he now?"

"I don't know. They've moved on from the weird hand thing to making out around school all day, which by the way, is more than I can say about us."

"We have an agreement."

"An agreement that should have had more clauses."

I rolled my eyes. "I'm going back to class."

"What are you afraid of, French? That you'll like it?"

There was only one boy whose lips I wanted on me but I didn't tell Jake that.

"Jake, this isn't real."

"What if it could be?"

"What's that supposed to mean?"

His pacing left him at the teacher's desk, where he played with a stack of yellow pencils that were sticking out of a *Charlie Brown* mug.

"I spoke to Dana on Saturday after you left. She's done with me. Forever. It bummed me out but then I thought to myself, I have you. You are my work in progress. Under my tutelage, you are growing into what Dana could never be."

"What's that?"

"More than a Queen. A goddess." He began a slow walk toward me, his eyes shining as if he'd just discovered the answer to world hunger. "The kids around here look up to you. You could rule this school. You could have anything you want. Do anything you want. Be whatever you want to be." He paused, standing next to me, his lips only inches away from my ear. "But, you need me beside you."

"No." The strength in my voice surprised me. "I don't want any of that. I want out."

His face turned red, his angry frown deep.

"Out?" His hands rose to my face, taking it between his hands. "No one gets out. Not you. Not Eric. Not anyone."

I narrowed my eyes, glaring as hard as I possibly could.

"Dana got out," I spat at him. "If she found a way, I will too."

His grip on my face tightened, nearly lifting me from my feet. I squirmed. Tried to push him off me. My heart pumped hard in terror. My stomach dropped. I'd never seen Jake so angry before.

"Let. Me. Go." My voice was chocked with my head bent back so far. "Jake."

He released his grip and took a step back, running his trembling hands through his hair. I sucked in a breath, and brought my hands up to my cheeks. Through trembling fingers, I felt dents where his hands had wrapped around my face. I scurried backward, away from Jake, until my back hit the bookshelf behind me.

"You are going to be mine, French," he said, turning back around. His eyes were wild, as if he were battling for control. "Mind, body and soul."

"I will never be yours!" I screamed at him. "Not now. Not ever."

"You will be mine." His eyes were calmer now. Calculated. Evil. "If you refuse, then I will gut him like a fish."

My eyes went wide. He wouldn't. Not to his own brother.

He nodded, answering my question.

"I will wait until he's asleep. I will creep in to his room, put a pillow over his face and slice him from head to toe. There will be nothing left of him for you to love. You'll come running then, won't you?"

Horror froze me in place. I had to do something. I had to warn Cole about his psychopath brother.

My gut raged and my skin felt hot.

"You have until tomorrow."

Jake smirked and yanked opened the door, nearly walking into Stephanie.

She was crouched down, right where the keyhole to the door was.

Listening.

"Hello, Jake," she said, stealing the smirk that he'd given me just a moment ago. "It seems that we have a lot to talk about."

55

"What do you want, Stephanie?"

My back was pressed to the wall, anxiety and fear eating through my gut.

Stephanie had heard everything. She knew about Jake's plan. She knew about Ariel. She'd heard Jake's threats against his brother. What would she do with the information?

My eyes settled upon her, her blonde hair, her green eyes fixed on Jake.

"I want what all girls want," she said. Her voice was smooth, like silk.

"Out with it," Jake said.

Stephanie raised an eyebrow.

"Something small. Something not even worth mentioning, really."

"Say it," Jake bellowed, his patience gone thin.

"I want you, Jake. And all the money that you come with."

A small ray of hope shone through the clouds of my life. This was a good thing. If Jake replaced me with Stephanie, all my problems would be gone. My secrets would remain hidden and I could go back to being invisible. There was still the problem of Eric but I was sure that I could talk him out of telling Ariel the true nature of their first meeting. He was reasonable, after all.

"And," Stephanie continued, "since you're in the business of buying and selling boyfriends, I have a friend, too. Ursula. And wouldn't you know it, she wants Eric back."

My heart sank into my gut.

"Eric Shipman?" I asked.

She nodded.

"No," I said, my voice finding its strength. "Absolutely not."

"Why not?" Stephanie asked. "Jake sold him to your friend. Now, he can sell him to me."

Jake shook his head.

"He's not a joint," Jake said. "I can't just pass him around. He liked Ariel. That's why he said yes in the first place. Eric is off the table. I am, too. End of story."

I stood up, rushing toward him.

"You can't be off the table. Stephanie wants to be with you. Let her be with you. Let me go, Jake."

He looked at me as if I were an idiot. Maybe I was.

"No way. I've put time, effort and money into you. I'm not letting you go that easy."

"But Stephanie wants you."

He shook his head and ran a hand over my cheek. The same cheek that he'd almost broken a few minutes ago.

"I can't control Stephanie like I can control you."

My breath left me and I took a step back. And another. And another until my back was against the wall again. I would never be free of Jake. He'd make sure of it. I'd made a deal with the devil and now I was going to burn for it.

My stomach clenched tightly, and I wrapped my arms around myself.

Stephanie's eyes drifted from me to Jake.

"Well, it's been lovely catching up but it looks like I have some evil gossip to spread. Tah tah." She waved and turned, walking back toward the door.

Jake reached it first, covering it with his own body.

"You can't say anything. I'll be ruined."

"You know what I want. All you have to say is yes."

Jake stood up straight, trying to gain some ground.

"You can't make threats against me, Stephanie."

"With what I just heard, sure I can. By tomorrow, I will be the new Queen of this school with you by my side, of course. Ursula will be with Eric and everything will be right as rain. Or, you can sit at the invisible table for the rest of your life. You're choice. Now, move."

Jake glared at her, challenge in his eyes.

Stephanie smirked.

"If you even think about touching me, I will sing it to every blog, newspaper and TV anchor in New York. By the end of the day, your face will be plastered all around this city. And then, your father's will."

Jake stiffened, the fight going out of him.

He moved from the door and Stephanie opened it wide.

"Til tomorrow, lover."

She sent a sneer at me, then walked out of the room.

I hated Stephanie but I had to admit, she played Jake like a guitar. I wanted to be strong like that. I wanted to move the mountain that was Jake Winsted. To bring him to his knees.

That was when I realized I couldn't. I wasn't evil like her. I didn't go around hurling threats at people. That wasn't me. If I was going to get out of this, it would be in the only way available to me. By telling the truth.

56

Jake and Stephanie sat at their separate lunchroom tables, presiding over their minions.

With Dana gone, Stephanie had taken over as the next in line, laughing and flipping her hair as if she was already a queen.

Jake, on the other hand, was sullen. Red-faced. After Stephanie left, he told me that our deal still stood. I had to agree to be his permanent girlfriend or else I would regret it. When I asked about Stephanie, he said to let him worry about her and left, so I was back in the same place I was before. Too afraid to tell the truth. Sinking in to more lies.

Ariel and Eric were already firmly seated at the popular kids table. Funny. She had taken to her newfound visibility like a fish to water. Popularity suited Ariel. She was beautiful and unique with a kind heart. The invisibles looked up to her, another princess risen from the darkness.

I watched her and Eric watching each other. He had a sort of sadness in his eyes. A glossiness. As if each glance would be his last. He touched her cheek with his fingers, saying goodbye without words. His guilt was just as great as mine. We'd both fallen in love with a girl and then ruined it with lies and manipulations. Each moment was a step closer to her slipping away from us forever.

The thought sat like a stone in my heart.

If only we'd been stronger. If only we hadn't been lured with Jake's deceptions and with our own greed, then none of this would have happened.

I looked around at the dozens of kids like me. The invisibles. The kids who looked up to the popular kids. Who envied us. Who wanted to be us. I couldn't keep silent anymore. I had to do something. I had to tell someone how wrong my course was. Eric's course. Mel's course. I had to warn them against the same fate.

An inner strength that I didn't know that I possessed took over me and I stepped on to the lunch table amidst the gasp of the jocks that surrounded me. They could keep their gasps. I had something to say.

"Hi!" I shouted.

The lunch room quieted and turned. That was the thing about being popular. People were always waiting for some pearls of wisdom to drop from your mouth, as if you were better than them. As if you held the key to life.

If only they knew how stripped bare we were.

"My name is Bella French."

A few cheers and whoops rose form the crowd.

"A week ago, most of you didn't know that. To be honest, most of you didn't know that I even existed until I became Jake Winsted's girlfriend and that's okay, because being his girlfriend, and having all of you know that I'm alive, has made me realize something very important. Popularity is a lie."

A collective gasp rose from the lunchroom. Still, I pressed on.

"It tells us that we have to measure our worth by tangible things. By the number of people who say hi to us in the hallway, by the amount of compliments we get from strangers, by how big our wardrobe is and by how much money our parents make. And, that's all crap. Party invites and friend requests don't give lasting happiness, and the truth is that everyone at this table," I gestured to the table that I stood on, "is empty and alone and shallow and missing out on every good thing that this world has to offer. Like friendship, and love. Simple things like that elude us because they make us a little less perfect and that is unacceptable. We have to be perfect. But, of course, being perfect is impossible, so we fake it. We become these over-sexed, over-dressed, photoshopped robots who try every day to live up to impossible standards that we create for ourselves. It sucks! We're not to be envied. We're to be pitied. Don't be like us. Don't sacrifice yourself to the popularity gods. The truth is, the popular kids are afraid of you. They're afraid that one day, everyone will wake up and see them for what they really are. Just like everyone else."

My heat slowed. My words ran out.

I stepped off the table to absolute silence. The crowd parted for me as I walked out of the lunch room and down the hallway. I planned on hiding in the library for the rest of the period. I wanted to be alone. I wanted to remember the good times that I'd had. To remember my friends. To remember being in Cole's arms. To remember what it was like to feel normal. I had made up my mind. Today was the day that I would tell Ariel everything.

I would finally tell the truth.

I hoped it would set me free.

My steps echoed in the empty hallway. Somewhere in the distance, I heard applause.

57

I was waiting at the table when Cole showed up. He wore the same expression that he'd worn the first day of our sessions. I'd called it piss poor then. Now, I understood. When you wanted something so badly and you couldn't have it, that was the expression you wore. Frustrated. Sad. Alone.

I wondered if mine looked the same.

He didn't sit down. Only stood awkwardly over me, looking at me like I was a dying puppy.

"I came to say that I spoke to Mr. Cogg. He said that you were doing better in French."

I nodded and knew that what he was going to say next was going to break the tiny piece of me that was yet unshattered.

"I told him that I couldn't tutor you anymore. Lucienda Collins is going to take over as of tomorrow."

I nodded, because there were no words to say. We both knew that this was best for the both of us. We couldn't be together. His brother stood between us like a wall.

"I'm sorry," I said.

"Yeah. Me, too."

We stood in silence, looking at each other like we often did. It was comforting to know that some things never changed. I liked looking at Cole. He liked looking at me. It was our thing.

"I'll miss you, Bella," he said. "I'll miss hanging out with you."

"What will you miss?" I asked. My eyes watered but the tears didn't fall. I think it was because I didn't have any left.

"I'll miss calling you Pippi Longstocking," he said.

"I don't remember you calling me that."

"Well, not to your face. I thought it, though. I meant to tease you about it but I didn't get the chance."

I smiled. A sad smile.

"I'll miss how your French accent reminded me of Pepe Le Pew," I said.

"That was deliberate. I knew you'd remember what I said if I did it in a funny accent."

"You're a liar."

"Maybe. I'll miss your red sneakers. Non-name brand, size ten. I meant to tease you about it but we ran out of time." He ran his hands through his hair and sighed. "There was so much that I never got to tease you about. It sucks."

"You can tease the next girl."

"There won't be a next girl. No other girl can match me like you can. You're witty and smart. It's annoying, really."

A lump formed in my throat. I opened my mouth to speak but I couldn't. It hurt to be around Cole and not be with him. Like breathing in glass.

"I know that you didn't want to partner with me at first but I'm glad we did. I'm glad that I got to know the girl that I'd fantasized about for two years. You exceeded my dreams, Bella. You still do. And if you're with Jake, that's fine. I'll stand back and let him have you. But I want you to know that you were everything that I never knew I needed or wanted and the second you have a doubt, you come to me. I'll be waiting for you."

He tapped on his notebook twice, then turned and walked away.

I thought that I had no more tears to shed.

I was wrong.

The final piece of me shattered there at the library table. I didn't bother to hide my tears and no one asked me why.

58

After an abysmal day, I took the subway to the Central Park stables.

Cole emailed me a copy of the report that we had to write on A Midsummer Night's Dream. I emailed him a copy of the dramatic reading. Something I threw together at the end of the day with minimal effort. I was sure that it wasn't five minutes and it was more than likely terrible, but it was all the mental capacity that I could muster.

I checked my voicemails for the millionth time but there was no word from Detective Harding. With Jake still walking free, I wondered if there was something else I needed to do. Maybe my information wasn't good enough. Maybe there still wasn't enough evidence to arrest Jake. Maybe Jake found out what I'd done and had the detective paid off or killed. Would I be next? Would my father? Would Cole?

The weight of the world sat on my shoulders as I entered the horse stables.

It had been such a long time since I was around horses. It made me feel a little better. My mind recalled Sweet Lips, my old horse. She had meant so much to me. I wondered if these horses meant as much to the owners. Were they beloved, prized creatures or just a means to fifty bucks a ride? I hoped not.

Daddy met me at the entrance of Central Park stables, his arms crossed over his chest as if he were still angry at me for sneaking out last week. I knew he wasn't but I understood his need to be a hardcore parent sometimes.

"You're late."

"Sorry. The train was running behind."

"Well, try to keep it to a minimum, all right?" He turned and led me through the stables, familiarizing me with my new place of volunteer employment.

To my great disappointment, there weren't any horses around. They must've all been out, servicing the paying public.

"And here is where you will be working," he said, stopping in front of a row of filthy stalls.

"No," I groaned.

"Yes. You will be mucking stalls."

"Daddy, come on!"

"What? I thought you liked mucking stalls?"

He gave me a teasing grin that I did not return.

"Who wants to clean up horse poop?" I demanded.

He handed me a pair of gloves, some oversized, dirty pants and boots.

"Take solace in the fact that it could always be worse."

"How could this get any worse?"

"You could be on fertility duty."

He winked at me and walked away, leaving me to do the dirtiest job ever.

The stables were dirty. Like, never been cleaned dirty. Who had been doing it before and where were they now?

I sighed, sucking in a deep whiff of the stable through my nose. It was an earthy mixture of poop, hay and cooling metal. I hadn't smelled the gross scent since I last visited my grandparents' farm. It wasn't something that I looked forward to.

After slipping on my oversized, dirty, mucking clothes, I pulled a wheelbarrow over, picked up a shovel and began to clear out the lumps of brown and green earth. It ran across my mind to keep some to deliver to Jake later but I decided against it.

Here I was, working in a horse stable and I couldn't even ride a horse. I was left shoveling crap on top of crap.

I couldn't help but think that this was symbolic of my life.

Just me, doing more crap to cover the crap that I'd already done.

I'd been shoveling, polishing and shining for only thirty minutes when Daddy reappeared, phone in hand. Anger was pulling down his features.

I knew that look. It meant that I was about to face hurricane Maurice. I tried to cut it off at the pass, pasting on my sweetest smile and leaning against my shovel.

"Is everything okay, Daddy?" I asked, batting my eyes.

"That was Jasmine."

My heart thudded hard. Jasmine? Why would she be calling my father?

"Did something happen to her?" I asked. "Is everything okay?" I put down my shovel, ready to run to my phone and if need be, to Jasmine's rescue when Daddy pinned me in place with a look.

"She told me all about the party."

My heart dropped.

"She did?"

He nodded and crossed his arms across his chest. "I thought we had an agreement. You would break up with that Jake kid and stay out of trouble. Now you're sneaking out at night, for the second time in less than two weeks mind you, to go party out at some mansion with this kid? Where is your head at, Bella? What are you thinking?"

I shifted my weight on my feet and looked down at the ground. I tried not to hate Jasmine, but in that moment, I did. How could she rat me out like this? I thought we were friends.

"It's not even the sneaking out part that pisses me off. It's the fact that you know who this kid is and what kind of life he leads and you're still dating him. And then, you lied to me about it. You lied to me about everything!"

I squirmed, wanting to put my hands in my pocket, but they were still covered in stable muck.

"I'm sorry."

"That's all you have to say? You're sorry?"

I bit the inside of my cheek, guilt grinding my insides into powder.

"Bella, I asked you a direct question. I asked if you were still seeing him. You told me no. You lied to me. How am I supposed to trust you again when you are lying?"

"I thought it would help with the investigation," I said. Not a full lie. A half-truth.

"You are not a police officer. You are not investigating anything!"

"I have to. People are suffering."

"Then you let the cops do their jobs. I have half a mind to call that detective's superior and tell him how inappropriate it is to have my sixteen-year-old daughter be a stool pigeon."

"Daddy, please don't. I need to do this."

"Do what? Date this punk?"

"No. I need to do something good for once."

He shook his head.

"Not like this. Not this dangerous!" He ran a hand over his face. "Home school. We are starting home school first thing Monday morning."

I gasped. "Daddy, no!"

"Don't 'Daddy no' me when you are throwing yourself in the line of fire!"

"Am I interrupting?"

Daddy and I turned our head at the same time. There, standing in the doorway, was Ms. Mitchell. My English teacher.

What was she doing here?

I took in her outfit. Jeans. A black coat with a fur hood. A plastic bag.

Red was rising in her cheeks and she looked embarrassed.

"Leah?"

Leah? My father knew her name? We hadn't had parent teacher conference yet. How did he know her?

"I just came by to drop off some dinner," she said, stepping in to the room.

Her warm eyes turned to me.

"Hello, Bella."

I frowned. Something was going on here. Something that I couldn't quite process.

She smiled at my father and that was when I knew.

The cologne. The shaving. The going out at night.

My dad had lied to me. He did have a girlfriend. That girlfriend was Ms. Mitchell.

All the blood drained from my face. I couldn't speak. I couldn't think. I had to get out of there. I had to get some air.

Without another word, I threw down my shovel, grabbed my purse and ran out of the stable.

59

I sat in my room, holding a framed picture of my mother.

She was beautiful. Perfect. How could my father do this to her? To me? To this family? How could he bring another woman here? How could he lie to me about it?

I heard the front door open and slam, followed by Daddy's footsteps approaching my room. He flung the door open, flipped on the lights and stood, arms crossed in my doorway.

"What do you want?" I asked, my hands still gently caressing my mother's picture.

"What you did at the stable was rude and completely unprofessional."

"Unprofessional?" I demanded, my anger exploding. "You're dating my teacher. I could have her fired!"

"You're not going to do that."

"Why not?"

"Because we're not dating. We are just friends."

I rolled my eyes. "You looked mighty cozy to me."

"Is this what I am going to have to deal with the rest of my life? Every time I am interested in a woman, the pictures come out and the guilt trips begin?"

"It's better than pretending like you were never married."

"I was. I was married to your mother for eighteen, wonderful years. Years that I treasure. But it's been six years since Leslie died. Am I never allowed to date again?"

"No!"

He threw up his hands.

"You're being unreasonable!"

"She was my mother!"

"She was my wife! I loved her, too."

"I can tell."

"What are you? Crazy? Do you think I'm just going out with some psycho stranger?"

"It doesn't matter. You shouldn't be going out at all. Mom just died. How are you over her?"

"I will never be over her!" His eyes turned glossy. "I will never be over Leslie but I was married for eighteen years. I'd like to be married again someday."

"And so you've chosen my English teacher?"

"I didn't know she was your English teacher until a few minutes ago when she told me after you jetted out like your tail was on fire."

"Great. Now you know. Dump her."

"I am not going to dump her. We're not even dating."

"Great. Then it will be easier."

He groaned. "You are being ridiculous right now. I love you. I loved your mother when she was alive. I am not an evil person for seeing a woman occasionally."

He said this last line more to himself than to me. I could tell by his tone that he'd said it before. How long had he been convincing himself that this was a good idea before he tumbled head first back in to the dating world?

Not long enough, apparently. And definitely not by informing his only daughter that he was going to be marching a caravan of women through my life from now on.

"We've had a very stressful day," he said softly. "We've both said some things we didn't mean."

"I didn't," I muttered.

"And let's not forget the original issue—that you snuck out of the house and lied about being with that Jake boy."

"I guess it runs in the family."

I saw the hurt in his eyes and ignored it, pulling my knees up to my chest and burying my head.

A moment later, Daddy closed the door.

I turned off my light, sitting in the darkness while Mojo nuzzled my feet.

How could Daddy date again? Didn't he miss my mom?

I'd never thought about Daddy dating before today. Was it so bad that he dated again? Yes. Yes; it was. He was a widower. His wife had just died. He should be focused on dealing with his grief. Not with dating. That came later. Much, much later. And with my consent and approval. After all, I was his closest relative. I should have a say in who he dates. As his only daughter, it was up to me to make sure that the woman in question was right for him.

And that woman definitely was not Leah Mitchell.

I laid down and covered myself with the blankets, my mother's picture still in my arms.

60

It was time to change my life.

I was going to start with my locker.

I woke up early and walked Mojo. He complained about the early wake up time with whines and barks. He got a few dog treats for his inconvenience, which seemed to be enough.

By seven o'clock, I was standing in the bushes that grew out of the front of my school, waiting for the graffiti artist to show themselves.

The old Bella had returned to St. Mary's Academy complete with French braids, jeans and red sneakers. She would never leave again.

At exactly five after seven, a shadow walked along the sidewalk, arms stacked with white papers. Her long brown hair, perfectly cut, gave her away and I choked back the shocked gasp that threatened to spill out of me.

The defacer wasn't Dana or Stephanie or Ursula.

It was Regina.

I watched in shock as she walked up the steps, through the unlocked doors and directly to my locker as if she had every right to be there. She dropped her armful of papers in a neat pile at her feet. I silently stood in the hallway, watching her tape the white background to the metal, then write in big red letters, LIAR.

By the time she had written the R, my anger could no longer be contained. I stepped forward, ready to do battle with this girl who was defacing my locker for no other reason than I was dating her brother against her wishes.

"What are you doing?" I demanded, coming close enough so that I was in punching distance from her.

She turned, saw me and let out a breath, as if I wasn't a threat.

Little did she know, I was the biggest threat she would face today.

"Oh. It's just you," she said, placing a hand over her heart.

"Yes. It's me. The girl whose locker you're destroying."

She shrugged as if it was no big deal, then held out her hands in front of her.

"I guess you caught me. I am the locker painter. Not that you're going to do anything about it."

"Why, Regina? What did I ever do to you?"

"To me? No. Not to me. You have been nothing but kind to me." She gathered up the markers that were splayed around her feet. "My brother, however, is a different story."

"What are you talking about?"

"You, Bella French, are the worst kind of girl. The kind that pretends to like someone, then goes and slinks off with their brother." She took a step toward me, placing the markers in a yellow box. "That's why this sign is so appropriate. You have been lying to my brother for over a week now and I'm sick of it."

Regina's face was calm, as if she were dispensing righteous justice.

My lips twitched. Then I laughed. I laughed so loud that she rushed forward and shushed me.

"What is your deal, spaz?" she demanded.

I took a deep breath to steady myself.

"You think that Jake is the victim here? You think that I lured him to me like a siren?"

I laughed again and looked at her. I wanted to her know that what she was saying was absolutely ridiculous.

She scowled.

"Not only are you a slut. You're crazy. Wait until my brother finds out about all you've been up to. The sneaking around at parties.

Dancing with Cole. Nearly kissing Cole in the hallway at Bree's mansion. If I hadn't told Jake and Stephanie where you were, who knows what could have happened." She came nose to nose with me and bared her teeth. "You disgust me."

"I disgust you? Or do I inspire you to paint?"

She blew out a breath.

"The world has to know what you are. What you call a locker, I call a canvas. It's how I am exposing you and your little secrets, each and every day. I'd hoped that pitting you against Dana would get you kicked to the curb but when that didn't work, I found that there was a sort of peace in waking up early and coming down here to create my masterpieces." She shrugged. "You can expect locker art for many years to come. I think I'm hooked."

I smiled at her. A smile full of pity.

She thought she was so pious. She had no idea what her brother was really about.

"Jake told me that if I went out with him, that he'd encourage Eric to go out with Ariel and make me popular. It was a business agreement. Not a real relationship."

Regina's face squeezed in shock, then disbelief.

"You're lying. My brother wouldn't need to do that to get a date. He could get any girl he wants."

I shrugged. "I was the one he chose. At first, he said that if I told anyone, he would tell Ariel that Eric was only going out with her because Jake told him to. Then, I found out about the drugs. His real name. Your father." The shock turned to anger. Protectiveness. It was a bad idea to tell Regina, Jake's sister, any of this. For all I knew, she was the mastermind of the business operation. But I had to tell her. I had to redeem myself by telling the truth and that started here, with Regina.

"When Jake thought that I would tell the cops about his drugs, he threatened to kill my father and put his body in the swimming pool. When I refused to make our relationship a real one, he threatened to gut Cole."

"You're lying."

"I'm not. Jake, your brother, is a monster. His drugs were the ones that Mel overdosed on. He is what is tearing this school apart. I'm not going to let that happen. I have already called the cops. They are going to take him down."

Regina stepped back, her breath coming in hard.

"I understand why you don't like me, Regina. You don't like me because you love your brother. You want to have a say in who he dates. I get that. But your brother is a heartless monster and I hope he rots in jail for the rest of his life for all of the horrible things that he's done."

Her eyes narrowed and she stomped toward me, spouting off something in Russian that I didn't understand. Her hands went to my neck and I knew what she'd meant.

She was angry. She wanted to kill me.

I'd like to see her try it.

I stepped out of her reach and she had just shifted her weight to lunge for me when a voice called us from down the hallway.

"Girls, what are you doing here?"

Mr. Mann was swiftly approaching us, his eyes sweeping over first Regina, then me, then my locker.

"What on earth is going on here?"

"Take the blame," Regina whispered. "Take it and I will help you get out of your mess with Jake."

I shook my head.

She glared at me. Her words were slow. Calculated.

"If you don't help me now, I will let my brother kill you."

Mr. Mann stepped in to hearing distance just as the Regina spoke her last word. He hadn't caught our little conversation.

"What is this?" he asked, gesturing to the locker. "Who did this?"

Regina looked at me, the threat clear in her eyes.

But I was done lying to cover up my sins. It was time to let the truth set me free.

"Mr. Mann, that is my locker. Regina has been defacing it for a week now."

Mr. Mann's chin tipped up and he crossed his arms over his chest.

"Is that true, Ms. Winsted?"

There was murder in Regina's eyes. She didn't reply.

"My office. Right now."

She sent one last glare at me before following Mr. Mann down the hall.

Telling Regina everything was hard.

Telling Ariel and Jasmine would be even harder.

JAKE WALKED WITH HIS TYPICAL SWAGGER UP TO MY LOCKER, holding a red, shimmering bag. When he saw my outfit, he frowned.

I had ditched the mini-skirts and expensive, too tight shirts for jeans, a t-shirt, a light jacket and my red sneakers. It felt good to be me again. Not who Jake wanted me to be.

"You didn't meet me at my locker," he said.

"No. I did not."

He looked at my outfit, clearly disapproving.

"You look ... different," he said.

"I look like me," I replied. "That's how I am going to be looking from now on."

I frowned at him. No. Not frowned. Scowled. I hated Jake. I hated him with every fiber of my being. Just the fact that he was here made my blood boil.

"This is for you," Jake said, handing me the red bag.

I didn't want it. I didn't want anything from him.

He shook the bag at me and I snatched it, hoping that it would get him to go away faster.

"Open it," he said. It was more of a command than a request.

I peered inside.

There was a pair of shoes. Hot pink and open toe. The bottom of them was painted red.

I gasped. They were beautiful. I reached in to touch the soft material and noticed the size.

Six and a half.

I frowned.

"They're too small," I said.

"What?"

"They're a six and a half. I'm a ten."

He shook his head. "That's impossible."

I handed back the bag. I knew exactly who wore a six and a half. The girl that I wasn't.

I wasn't sure what was more degrading. The fact that he thought that I would magically turn into Dana, or the fact that he wanted me to.

Why were we doing this to ourselves? Jake didn't want me. He wanted Dana.

I didn't want Jake. I wanted Cole.

"I'll have them exchanged," he said, reaching out to take the bag back.

"Don't bother. Just give them back to Dana. I don't want them."

The first period bell rang and I walked away from Jake Winsted, feeling more normal than I had in a long time.

"Meet me after school by my car. We have some business to take care of."

I turned around, facing Jake.

"There will be no business," I said.

"We'll see. Either way, the piper must be paid."

"And our other problem?"

"It's being handled."

"By who?"

"Don't worry about it. Just meet me later."

The bell rang again and I power walked to my class, with Jake's words ringing in my head.

The piper must be paid.

19

I skipped English, because, well, reasons, and hung out in the library. When the bell rang, I got up and walked down the hallway to lunch.

I had no idea who I would sit with. Definitely not Jake. That was for sure. And with Jasmine and Ariel not on speaking terms with me, I supposed that I had to find another table to loiter at while I ate my salad.

The vibe in the hallway was different. Like something had happened. Something terrible. I looked at the faces around me, trying to get a gauge on the situation, when a loud smack had me jerking my head to the right.

"You did this to her!"

The voice had come from Dana. She was standing in front of Jake, his face red where she'd obviously slapped it.

"You and Kenny and your drugs. You did this!"

She rushed at him, fists flying, landing hard punches on his arms, his face, his back.

Two security guards ran to the brawl, pulling Dana off a clearly stunned Jake. They practically dragged her down the hall kicking and screaming. I could still hear her cries echoing down the hall.

"You did this! You did this!"

I turned to the boy on my left. I think we had chemistry together but I couldn't be sure.

"What's going on?" I asked.

He shook his head.

"Stephanie Pleasant overdosed last night. They found her this morning in her house."

I gasped. I'd seen Stephanie take drugs before but I never thought she had a problem. She wasn't like Mel. I thought she was stronger than that.

"Is she okay?" I asked.

"She's dead."

My heart thudded hard. Stephanie was dead? She couldn't be dead. I just saw her yesterday. She had threatened Jake and me. She was going to tell the...

My thoughts trailed off in to a dark place.

When I asked Jake about Stephanie this morning, he said that it was taken care of. He did this. He killed her. Jake killed Stephanie Pleasant.

I had to do something. I had to tell someone.

I turned around, intent on marching straight to the principal's office and walked directly in to Jake.

How had he gotten behind me so fast? I didn't even notice he'd moved.

He put his hand on my lower back and my entire body turned cold. His lips touched my ears and I shivered, afraid of what he might do.

"It's time for us to go."

JAKE DROVE ME TO THE DOCKS WHERE A MID-SIZED YACHT WAITED.

I was absolutely terrified. Was this where he was going to kill me? Would he drop my body in the river? Would he harm my father or Cole?

My thoughts raced, my mind searching for ways to escape, as he led me up the stairs of the bobbing boat.

Shiny wood floors, leather couches, a television and bear skinned rugs greeted me. It looked closer to a rustic living room than a yacht. On the bear skinned rug were several black bags, two wine glasses and covered plates.

A picnic? I grew even more on edge. What exactly was his plan? To feed me then kill me? Was that what he'd done to Stephanie? Did he take her out to dinner first, then kill her?

He led me to the rug.

"Sit."

I did as I was told, sitting cross legged on the floor.

He opened the basket and pulled out a large, black dish. He placed the dish on the floor between us and pulled the top off it. Sushi. I grimaced. I hated sushi.

I sat back on my haunches, leaving my food untouched.

"Dana would have liked this," he said. His face turned sad, like Cole's did sometimes. He put down his bowl, looking over to the side.

I didn't respond.

"She told me that she was never coming back. And now, after Stephanie, I'm sure that there isn't anything I can do to change her mind." His mood shifted, going from sad to unreadable.

His eyes focused on me and my gut constricted.

He crawled across the rug toward me, not stopping until his face was only an inch from mine.

"Let's pretend," he whispered, tilting his head to the side. "Just for a minute."

My heart sped up. Was he asking me to pretend to be Dana? This was too much. This had gone too far. I wouldn't do it.

I shoved him but he didn't budge. He moved closer, his arms on both sides of me, trapping me.

"Just for a minute."

"No."

He bolted forward, his lips slamming into mine.

I let myself drop back to the floor, disengaging us and scurrying away from him.

He was fast. He threw his weight on top of me, wrestling my arms into submission.

"Just relax!" he bellowed. His eyes were furious and wild. "Chill out!"

"No!" I screamed at him again.

He readjusted himself on top of me, balancing on his knees.

"No one says no to me!" he cried out. "Nobody."

I panicked, and threw my knee between his legs.

He let out a curse and fell to the side, gripping where I had kicked him.

It was my shot. I grabbed the keys from the keyring Jake hung them on and bolted out the door.

"Get back here!" Jake screamed after me. "Get back here!"

62

I took his car and drove back to school, my hands shaking on the wheel.

I didn't want to go home and be alone. Not with Jake no doubt coming after me. I had to be around people. I had to be safe. So, I went where I knew people would be. School. It was almost three o'clock. The jocks would be at football practice. Ariel would be at swim practice. People would be around. People who would protect me.

I ran in and went straight to the locker room, looking for someone that I could sit with. Who would be a witness in case anything happened to me. I considered calling the police, then decided against it. Detective Harding still hadn't gotten back to me. Maybe the cops thought I was lying. Or worse, that I was somehow trying to throw off their investigation.

I burst through the locker room doors, only to find that they were mostly empty. No one sat on the benches. No showers ran. I walked past the aisles, looking for someone, anyone.

There, sitting in front of her locker, looking vacant, was Ariel. Her red hair looked tangled, like a red bird's nest. Ariel never let her hair tangle. She was constantly styling it or combing it. It was her pride. Her joy. She turned to me, and my blood ran cold. My heart stopped.

She knew.

"I told him that I never wanted to see him again," she whispered. Her face remained calm. I wouldn't have even known she was upset if her eyes weren't so filled with anger and hatred.

"You know?" I asked.

She nodded.

"He told me what you did. What he agreed to do. How could you do that to me? I loved you. I thought we were friends. How could you humiliate me like that in front of everyone? You knew how I felt about him."

"I ... I'm sorry."

"You're sorry? That's all you have to say?"

"Ariel, I just wanted you to be happy."

"I loved him. Did you know that? I loved him and it was all a lie! A game!" She shook her head, confused. "Did I do something to you? Did I offend you? Did I say something to you that you didn't like?"

I ran to her and took her cold hands in mine.

"No. You were perfect. You were the best friend that I ever had."

"Then why did you do this to me?"

"Because I loved you and I wanted you to be happy!"

"By making me love a lie?" She jumped up, nearly throwing me backward off the bench. "I thought that we would grow old together. That it would be you, me and Jasmine forever. I trusted you with my life and you turn around and stab me in the heart!"

She shoved me and I fell backward off the bench, banging my head against the locker behind me. Pain exploded in my head and I saw stars.

"I trusted you and you took everything from me! I hate you! I will hate you for the rest of my life and when you die, I will write backstabber on your grave." She stood over me, screaming at me. I deserved every hate filled word. "We are done. Do you hear me? Done. If you even look in my direction, you will regret it. You called yourself my friend but you are nothing more than a faker."

She grabbed clothes out of her locker and stomped away.

My worst nightmare had come true.

Ariel had found out and now she was gone. Out of my life forever.

They say the road to hell is paved with good intentions. This was my hell. A life without my two best friends. My good intentions were plastered all around me. My choices were made.

I wished that the ground would swallow me whole.

But there was no time to grieve.

Doors slammed open and Jake's voice bellowed through the locker room.

"Bella, I know you're here!"

He had come for me.

"Come out, come out, wherever you are."

I pressed my back against the locker, trying to gather my scattered thoughts. How did he get back here so quickly? Did he steal someone's car? Did he keep a spare vehicle at the docks just in case? Had he called one of his drug cronies to give him a ride?

Heavy steps echoed through the locker room. Row by row, looking for me. I backed away, keeping as far away from his echoing shoes as I could.

"You're going to pay for what you did to me. I can promise you that."

I could barely hear him over my panting breaths and my banging heart.

I could see the doors to the locker room, still swinging from the force that he'd pushed them with earlier. I had to get out of here. If I stayed, Jake would kill me. I was sure of it.

With a burst of energy that I didn't know I had, I sprinted to the door. It moved closer, and closer. I willed my feet to move faster. It was almost within reach. And then, I ran in to a wall of a man.

Jake. His wild eyes. His strong arms. He'd found me, and I had no idea what he was going to do.

"Looking for me?" he asked. An evil grin stretched his face. "You're going to pay for that little stunt in the yacht. Oh yes. You are going to pay."

I struggled against him, desperate. He was going to kill me. I was sure of it. I had to get away. I had to.

He flipped me around, until my back was pressed to his chest. No chance of my knees finding their way to him now. I squirmed and screamed.

"Let me go!"

"No one is around to hear you, Bella. Scream all you want. It's just you and me now."

Like a lion, Cole's voice roared through the locker room.

Jake froze then released me, turning to his brother. I crashed to the floor, my body weak with fright.

"This doesn't concern you, Cole!"

Is this what you're doing to girls now?"

"I said that this doesn't concern you, Cole!"

"She *is* my concern!"

"Not anymore. You hesitated, and she's mine now. Mine to do whatever I want with."

"She'll never be yours, Jake. Ever."

"If you want her, you'll have to come through me and we both know that you'll never win."

"I will. I will, because she's worth it."

Cole and Jake rushed at each other, their fists and bodies clashing like warring titans.

Cole grabbed Jake by the collar and swung him in to a locker. Jake's back crashed in to the metal with a loud clang.

"Get off me!" he cried.

But Cole didn't let up. He reared back his right hand and punched Jake in the chin. The nose. The mouth. Again and again, he rammed his fist into his brother's face until Jake's body collapsed on to the floor. Cole threw himself on top of him, grabbed him by the collar and readied himself for another swing when...

"Stop!"

An older man walked into the locker room.

Cole immediately stood, leaving his brother woozy on the floor.

I pressed my back against the metal, my body still weak.

Who was this man? He looked to be in his sixties with white hair and pock-marked skin. His body was strong and tall, his face held the look of someone who'd seen more than a few fights in his life. He wore a black suit and shiny shoes.

"Dad," Jake sputtered. "What are you doing here?"

Dad? So, this was Ivan? The famous Russian gangster?

"Watching my sons kill each other," he said a long string of words in Russian.

Cole nodded and walked over to me, standing by my side.

Jake withered beneath his father's hard stare.

"I told you to play your football and stay out of trouble. I told you that this life was not for you. And yet, here I stand with a dead girl all over the news, the police sniffing around my home and my son's very expensive school filled with drugs."

He kicked Jake hard in the side. Jake rolled over with a groan.

"I should ship you back to Russia to live with your grandmother. Would you rather raise goats?"

"No."

"Then why am I hearing reports that my son, my flesh, my blood, has been taking my supplies and selling them to his classmates? Why am I getting anonymous calls saying that my oldest son is a drug dealer?"

"Papa, it's not true."

His father nodded and crouched next to his son.

"That is what I said. So I asked your sister, 'Regina, tell me that these things I am hearing about your brother are not true'. And do you know what your sister, your blood, did? She clammed up like a dead fish. Your sister, the one who can't shut up, was speechless. So, I went to that kid you hang out with. The kid that I said was no good. Kenny. My men held him upside down over the river, and he told me everything. Every bag of coke, every pill, every drop off, every safe house, every dime you made. That punk kid has no honor. He's not blood. He's not family. You are trusting him while you steal from me!"

He stood, sending another sharp kick to Jake's ribs. A loud cry rang from Jake's lips and he rolled over again, groaning in pain and holding his side.

"I told you not to be like me, but you didn't listen. Your brother told you to stop and you didn't listen. You and your sister were in cahoots against your own father."

Jake's eyes went wide.

"No, Papa."

"You do these deals and cut me out?"

"No, Papa!"

"You lie! That's exactly what you did. You stabbed your brother and me in the back. Your poor mother, the saint that she is, is home dying and this is how you repay her?" He picked Jake up and shoved him against the locker.

"You are banished!"

Jake's face fell.

"No, Papa. Please!"

"You and your sister will go back to Russia to live with your grandmother. There, you will learn the true meaning of loyalty. Respect. Family. Only then, will I allow you to return."

"Papa, please!"

"Get in the car before I forget that you're my son and leave you to rot in jail next to your friend."

Jake's face turned red and he fled the room.

Ivan's strong presence turned to me. He had such intense eyes. Eyes that made me want to cower. But I wouldn't cower. Not in front of anyone ever again. I stood up straight instead.

"Who are you?" he asked.

Cole moved a little closer to me.

"I'm Bella French, sir," I replied, surprised at the strength in my voice.

"Are you the girl that sent the flowers to my wife?" he asked.

I nodded. "They always brightened my mother's day when she was dying. I hoped it would do the same for your wife."

His stare softened.

"She says that the sunflowers are good but daisies are better." To my surprise, he gave me a little smile. "French woman."

I smiled back, my body still feeling a little woozy.

Ivan looked from me to his son.

"Is this the girl that you are taken with?" he asked.

Cole nodded.

"Yes, Papa."

Ivan grunted.

"She is a good woman. Not an idiot, like your brother and sister." His eyes fell on me again. "My son is going to assure me that you will never tell anyone that I was here. He will assure me this because he knows that he is the only reason why you aren't in a trunk. Is that clear?"

I nodded.

"My son will also assure me that there will be no further calls to Detective Harding, who is now my permanent employee. Any issues you have with my son will be addressed with me directly."

Cole stepped forward. "Yes, Papa."

"Let her answer."

I locked eyes with Ivan. He was infamous, his name said in the same breath as *Scarface* and *Noriega*. I refused to look away.

"I never saw you," I said. "But you have to keep the drugs out of my school. Promise me."

His chin raised, a smirk on his face.

"Me, promise you?"

I stood strong, my hands fisted.

"I want your word."

He examined me for a moment, then looked at his son.

"French?" he asked.

Cole smiled. "In name only."

"Good enough." His eyes fell back to me. "You have my word that this school will be clean. If it is not, you will call me and I will take care of it. Clear?"

I nodded. "Clear."

And with that, Ivan grunted and turned away, leaving Cole and I alone in the locker room.

It was over.

With everything out in the open, I felt free.

Alone. But free.

And surprisingly, hopeful.

"I'll take you home," Cole said.

I leaned on him, basking in his strength. In his love.

"Yes," I said. "Please, take me home."

63

I slept in on Tuesday. Then that night, I sat down with my dad and told him everything. Everything I'd done, every lie I'd told, every phone call I made, every time I snuck out. He was angry at first. I couldn't blame him for that. But then, after things calmed down, he handed me a chocolate chip cookie, placed a kiss on my head and sat with me on the couch. He held my feet in his lap while I moved between watching television, crying, being sullen and being grateful that I was alive.

He left for work on Tuesday morning, calling hourly to make sure that I was okay. That I was eating. That I was sleeping. That I was taking it easy. I tried to sound strong, but inside, I was dying. A black cloud circled my head, and to be honest, I didn't want it to go away. I had lost so much in the last week. I wanted to sink in to a big vat of oily, inky pity and never come back out.

How would I go on?

Everyone in school probably hated me by now. After all, I was single-handedly responsible for getting the star quarterback shipped off to god knows where in Russia. Granted, he tried to kill me, but they didn't know that. Kenny had vanished, which meant that there would be no more pot Fridays, and definitely no more of the hard stuff that had developed such a devoted following in the school. Ariel hated me. Jasmine hated me. Cole ... I hadn't heard from Cole since he dropped me home on Monday night. No phone call. No text. Not that I was holding out any hope for it. After all, his brother and sister were gone because of me.

And so I ate ice cream, watched *Judge Judy* and *The Price is Right* and after having lost everything, I hid from the world.

64

It was twelve fifteen on Wednesday afternoon when someone knocked on my door.

Odd. Daddy was at work and I wasn't expecting anyone.

I stood on shaky legs— how long does it take for muscles to atrophy? —and slowly pulled the door open.

Dana Rich looked at me in a weird mix of amusement and pity.

"You look awful," she said, pushing past me and walking in to my apartment. "And this apartment smells like spaghetti sauce."

Daddy had been making spaghetti with meatballs and garlic bread for three days straight since he knew it was my favorite. With each tasty bite, I loved him a little more.

"What are you doing here?" I asked.

"Watching you spiral into a pit of social oblivion," she said, sliding an empty tub of ice cream out of her way with her toe.

"Get out, Dana."

She stopped her march of disgust through my living room and turned to me.

"You have to come back to school," she said.

I snorted and rolled my eyes. "Believe me, no one wants me back there."

"Will you stop thinking about everyone else?!" she commanded, stomping one heeled foot. "You know, your little speech got it wrong. Being popular is not about creating some impossible standard of perfection for everyone else to live up to. Being popular is about not caring what everyone else thinks. That's why you feel empty. That's why you feel alone. Because you have been caring what everyone else thinks and not worrying about yourself."

She turned away, looking out of the open window behind the television.

"I was the one that called Jake's father."

I gasped.

"What? Why?"

"Because Jake and Regina were destructive and had to be stopped. Did you know that Regina broke me and Jake up? She sent me fake screenshots and told me that Jake was cheating and I believed her. Stupid. If Jake and me were still together, I could have stopped him. He would have listened to me. But by the time I found out what she'd done, Jake had already moved on to you and I was out of the circle."

"So why call his father?"

"I had no choice. Stephanie was dead. Mel was in rehab. Somehow, you turned my boyfriend into a psychopathic killer. I had to call him. No one else could stop Jake. And now, he's gone. Stuck in Russia somewhere with his sister filling his head with stupid lies." She sighed. "She finally got what she wanted. Her little brother, all to herself."

She sniffled and wiped her nose. She tried to hide it, tried to look like she didn't care but I saw it. I saw the love she felt for Jake in her eyes. I saw the hurt she felt at not being with him. At what he had become.

I wondered if by losing Dana, Jake lost a bit of his humanity, too. Maybe that was why he did what he did with me? Or maybe he was just a kid who'd never been told no. Who thought that no matter how terrible he acted, he was untouchable. Either way, he got what he deserved.

"Anyway, that's not why I'm here. Stephanie is gone, Ursula's mom sent her to boarding school, everything is in shambles. The school needs a leader. We could be that leader."

"We?"

"Yes. You and me can step in and fill the void. We can rule this school together. But you have to come back."

I sighed. The old me would have jumped at the chance to be popular and to have Dana as an ally, no less. But the old me was dead. This was the new me. The me that knew the dark side of popularity. I would never step over to the dark side again.

"Dana-"

"Is this about me punching you in the Stamford Club because I was just doing it in solidarity with Stephanie?"

"No. It's not about that. I don't want to be popular. I'll come back to school but it won't be to fill some void. It will be so that I can be me."

"But you'll be alone. No friends. No allies. You'll be invisible again."

I let out a breath.

"I'd rather be happy and invisible than to be miserable and popular."

"You're joking? I'm offering you the tools you need to make your wildest dreams come true. You can't just tell me no."

I shook my head. "My dreams right now are to pass French and English and to try and get my friends back. Being popular is not going to help with any of that."

Dana squeezed her lips together and walked past me, putting her hand on the door. She snatched it open and walked back out.

I sighed, sat on the couch and looked around at the mess that I'd been hiding in.

I bent down and began to clean it up.

65

I spent one more day at home and re-arrived back at school on Thursday.

I expected that everyone would stare at me. Whisper behind my back. Boo even. But there was nothing. No fanfare. No uproar.

A few people looked at me and whispered, but mostly, they looked through me. I'd been gone from school for three days, and, already, I was forgotten about. A memory.

I tried to go about my day, to be normal, but it was hard. Ariel and Jasmine walked past me. Jasmine looked okay but Ariel looked shell-shocked. Devastated. Her hair was in a single braid down her back and her eyes were glossy. I wondered how many times she'd fallen apart since Monday. Once. Twice. Dozens. Guilt wracked through me that I had caused her this pain but I also felt guilty that I wasn't there to catch her. To help put her back together like she'd done to me dozens of times.

I looked away, grabbed my books from my locker and walked to first period, on time for once.

I dove into my studies, collecting the homework and class notes that I'd missed over the past several days. Jake's seat was empty in English class. Cole's, too. I wondered where they were. Had Ivan changed his mind and banished both his sons to Russia? I swallowed down the sadness that rose in my throat at the thought of Cole and focused on Ms. Mitchell's English lesson.

I ate lunch in the library and during study period, I went to visit Ms. Mitchell.

"Bella!" she said, a half-eaten apple in her hand. "Nice to see you out of fourth period."

I smiled and sat in the middle seat of the front row.

"I just wanted to come by and say thank you."

"For what, dear?"

"For pairing up Cole and me. You said that we would become friends and we did. So, thank you."

She smiled wide.

"Thank you, dear. I have a sense about these things. I've always said it."

"Yes, you have."

"It's a shame what happened with his mother," she said, her eyes turning sad.

"What happened with his mother?"

"She passed this week. They're somewhere in France, I think they are putting her to rest."

I gasped, tears clawing up my throat for Cole. First his siblings, then his mother. He must have been hurting. Broken. I wanted to go to him. To hug him tight and to tell him that he was a good son. That he was loved. But he wasn't here and so I whispered the words as I wrapped my arms around myself.

"You really cared for him, didn't you?"

I nodded slowly. "Yes."

"Did you ever tell him how you felt?"

"No. I told him that I didn't like him."

I closed my eyes, wishing that things were different. But I couldn't change the past. I could only look forward.

"I'm sure he knew. People are odd like that, always reading between the lines and hearing words that no one's ever said and ignoring words that we say outright. Crazy creatures, we are." She gave me a small smile. "I'm sure that it will all work out for the best. Love has a crazy way of knowing what it wants, no matter how much we try to persuade or tame it."

I tried to believe her. I wanted to believe her.

"I know what will cheer you up."

She pulled a book out of her desk. A beautiful, young couple on the cover caught my eye immediately.

"A good book is the best medicine."

She stood and walked around her desk, handing me the book.

"Same time next week?" she asked.

I nodded. "Same time next week." I got almost the entire way to the door before I turned around.

"Ms. Mitchell."

"Yes, dear."

"I'm glad that my dad chose you."

She let out a breath, her cheeks reddening.

"Bella, that means so much. Thank you."

I nodded and left. After Regina's rant, I realized something. You can't hold people so close that they never live. Regina tried to keep Jake all to herself and ended up hurting both of them in the end. I wanted Daddy to be happy. I wanted him to live, and if he decided that it was going to be with Ms. Mitchell, then I was happy with that decision.

66

The English project was due on Friday so Thursday night, I had a mini panic attack. If Cole wasn't back, I was going to fail English. Maybe French, too. A hit like that would seriously affect my GPA. A low GPA meant getting in to college would be that much harder. A low-end college would mean a lower paying job. A low paying job meant that I couldn't pay back my student loans. I pictured myself living with my father for the rest of my life. Or worse, ending up next to that homeless guy in the subway who always held up the peace sign.

There had to be a way to get in touch with Cole. I reached into my pocket and dug out my cell phone. My fingers danced over the buttons and found his number in my contact list. I was about to press the call button when I remembered. Cole wasn't just out on some pleasure cruise. His mother had died. He was probably surrounded by family, being consoled in some French cottage. I couldn't interrupt him. Not now. Not when he was in mourning.

I stuffed my phone back in to my jeans and resigned myself to homelessness.

Meanwhile, Dad moved around the kitchen, pots clanging, making dinner.

We were having pasta again. Daddy seemed to cook pasta a lot lately. Maybe because he was tired when he got home and wanted something quick. Maybe it was because I used to cook dinner on the weekdays but hadn't since our lives turned upside down last week. Maybe it was because he knew that pasta was my favorite.

I left my phone on the couch and walked in the kitchen, realizing that there was someone else that I had to make amends with.

A pot lid clanged to the floor, followed closely by a metal spoon.

Daddy groaned, his brow already sweat-soaked.

I bent down to pick up both the top and the spoon and place them in the sink.

"Need some help?" I asked.

"Only if you're offering," he replied.

I walked over to the table, grabbed a paper towel from the holder and walked back over to my father. My hand raised to his shoulder and he turned to me. Gently, I dabbed at his sweaty forehead and ears.

Our eyes danced away from each other, neither of us knowing what to say.

What could I say? Daddy had raised me, basically alone, for the last six years. He bought me my first box of tampons, knew my favorite conditioner, had sewn buttons back on my shirts and taught me how to French braid my hair. We'd fallen apart together when Mom died and we'd built each other up so that we could keep going. He wasn't the most hands-on dad but he was my dad, and I wanted him to be happy.

"I spoke to Ms. Mitchell today," I said, my voice calm and even. I continued to carefully dab at his forehead, though the sweat was all gone now.

His eyes rose to mine, searching them for reasons why I would talk to his most likely ex-girlfriend.

"I told her that I was happy you chose her." I balled up the paper towel and threw it in the trash can by the door. "I understand that you are a grown man with feelings." I cringed at the thought, but pressed on. Daddy stood tall and still, waiting for my words. "But you're also my dad. You're the last parent that I had left and I guess I was holding on to you so tight because I didn't want to lose you and I didn't want you to get hurt." I took a deep breath. "If you want to date Ms.

Mitchell, that's fine with me. I only ask that you are open with me about what's going on in the relationship and don't be gross with each other around me. Let's start with firm handshakes and go from there, okay?"

I didn't get to finish my sentence. Daddy wrapped me in a bear hug that raised my feet from the floor. He hadn't hugged me like that in years. I held on tight, burying my face in his shoulder.

"Thank you, sweetheart," he said in to my hair.

"I love you, Daddy."

"I love you too, honey."

We stayed wrapped in each other's arms until my nose tingled. Something was burning. Something like...

The garlic bread!

I jumped out of Daddy's arms and ran to the stove. I turned the white dial back to off and yanked the door opened.

The garlic bread was burnt black.

How long had it been in the oven? Where was Daddy's usual timer?

"Well, there goes the garlic bread." I sighed, pulling on a kitchen mitt so that I could dump it in the trash.

Daddy came up behind me and put his hand on my shoulder.

"How about we wrap this up for tomorrow and we go down to Sophia's to get a pizza?"

His smile was warm. Loving. Fatherly.

I loved that smile.

"Fine," I said, dumping the bread in the trash. "On one condition."

"What?"

I threw the oven mitt at him.

"You invite Ms. Mitchell?"

Daddy's eyes widened, a grin spreading over his face. He threw his arm around my shoulder and led me out of the kitchen.

"Not so fast, cowgirl. When I said that Leah and I were friends, I meant that. When we're ready to move to the next step, you'll be the first one to know."

"Come on, Dad. I need her to pass me on my English project. My partner flaked. I figured maybe if I got her some pizza, she'd consider it."

Dad laughed out loud. I did, too.

"Get your hat on, kid." He pointed to the window. "It's snowing out."

I looked to the window, admiring the snowflakes that slid against it. Every one unique and beautiful. Every one special.

Just like Daddy.

Just like me.

67

"Excellent," Ms. Mitchell said, clapping her hands.

Nadira and Kiln had done their short, dramatic piece on *Much Ado about Nothing*. In it, Kiln accused Nadira of texting another guy. He'd searched her phone and found the text. In the end, Kiln discovered that it wasn't even Nadira's phone and he apologized.

Not exactly the spirit of the play, but there was only five minutes and let's face it, they weren't the best English students in the world.

Dana had gone before them. Hers had been a video presentation, which Ms. Mitchell allowed. Apparently, her and Jake had recorded themselves doing a pretty much word for word reenactment of Titania and Oberon's final scene in *A Midsummer's Night's Dream*. The same scene they'd done last year in the school play. Seeing Jake's face again made my stomach ache. I wondered when they recorded it then put the thought out of my mind. I didn't want to give Jake a second more of my time. I was worth too much for that.

My stomach tied in knots as Noah and Cassie went. Cole and I were at the bottom of the list and he still hadn't shown up for school. I had our piece in my shaking hands but without Cole, I wasn't sure that

Ms. Mitchell would pass us. If I failed this class, I was sure that I would cry. So would my GPA.

I gripped the marked up, white loose-leaf pages and studied them. I'd thrown the little play together in less than two hours. At the time, it seemed like a masterpiece but now, the more I read it, the more terrible it sounded. Not as terrible as some of the other kids' plays, but still not my best work.

If only Cole and I had spent more time on it. But it was too late to think about that now. Plus, I didn't regret the time that I spent with Cole. He'd mellowed me out and made me laugh. Our time was precious and I wouldn't change it for anything in the world. Not even a passing grade.

Noah and Cassie were fake stabbing each other with pencils then making out with each other in their weird version of *Romeo and Juliet*. I could tell by Ms. Mitchell's wary smile that she was as confused as the rest of the class. But as a teacher, she had to applaud their effort and so she clapped.

"Thank you, Noah and Cassie, for that ... uh ... inventive retelling of *Romeo and Juliet*. Now, we come to our final pairing. Bella French and Cole Winsted."

My stomach filled with mutant butterflies, all clawing at me. I was an okay public speaker, but it wasn't my favorite thing to do. Especially when I had to do a play with two characters and it was only me. I walked to the front of the classroom with heavy, slow steps. Anything to eat up the seconds.

This was going to be horrific.

"I, uh ... this was supposed to be a two person play, but my partner isn't here, so..."

All eyes in the room were staring at me as if I had a clown suit on. They saw my nervousness and now they were pouncing on it. Last week, these people called me their queen. Now, I was just another loser. I guess what they say is true. Time changes everything.

I cleared my throat and raised my paper, reading off the first line. My line.

"I can't believe that my dad said we couldn't go out, Lincoln. And all because you're not rich like me."

I know. Lame.

My eyes darted to Cole's next line on the page. I considered doing it with a deep voice, then rejected that idea. I would be entirely too embarrassing. My hands shook and broke out into a sweat.

I looked at Ms. Mitchell.

"I'm sorry. It was supposed to be two people."

She smiled softly and nodded. "Why don't you just read the rest, dear? We'll get the point."

I nodded, swallowed and immediately wished for the floor to swallow me whole.

It didn't.

"Why does... Why does..." This was stupid. Utterly and completely stupid. I couldn't read this play by myself. Why didn't Ms. Mitchell just give me a pass? She knew that Cole's mother died. Why would she torture me like this?

"Then Lysander, uh, Lincoln says ... uh..."

Suddenly, the door burst open and Cole rushed in like a man on a mission.

My heart leapt. He was here.

"Sorry I'm late," he said, throwing his bookbag on his desk while running to the front of the room.

"It's okay, Cole," Ms. Mitchell said. "Just start from the beginning."

I was sure that I was grinning like an idiot and my face was red, but I didn't care. Cole was here to save the day.

I mouthed *thank you* to him.

He winked at me. I found that I didn't mind it so much.

"I can't believe that my dad said we couldn't go out and all because you're not rich like me."

"Why does your dad have to be so corny?"

"Because he's my dad. He thinks he controls everything."

Cole put his finger on his temple, pretending to think. He was really hamming this up. A bubbling of laughter rose from the class as the fated lovers, Lincoln and Hermia, planned their escape in to the woods.

"I'm afraid, Lincoln. What if we get caught? What if something happens to us?"

"Oh, Hermia. Even if we only have an instant in time to be together, in that instant, I promise that I will love you with all of my heart."

Yes, it was amateurish, but even as Cole said the words that I'd written, I imagined that he meant them. That he wasn't talking about Hermia, but about me.

Cole had said he wanted me once. He'd even kissed me. A kiss that I still thought about every day. Did he? Could Cole ever forgive me for ripping apart his family? For sending his brother and sister away? For refusing him?

It was a secret wish. One that I couldn't let blossom too deeply within me. My heart was still so fragile. If Cole had changed his mind about me, I decided that I didn't want to know. It would hurt too much. I had my chance with Cole and I blew it. I doubted life would give me another shot.

We bowed at the end of the presentation, even though the only one who clapped was Ms. Mitchell and I was sure that she was just being nice about it.

"Class, you all did such a wonderful job. I am very proud. In fact, this project was so successful that I am thinking about doing it again for the spring."

The class groaned.

"Now. Now. For doing such a good job, no homework this weekend and I will see you all on Monday."

The bell rang, releasing us from English for the next two days.

Just four periods left.

"Class dismissed."

68

I paced the darkened backstage area of the auditorium. The St. Mary's Academy talent show had started a half an hour ago and already there had been six acts.

Margaret Flynn sang opera. Charlene Bloomfield danced a classical ballet. Miles Tanner played the flute. Darcy Simmons read her beatnik poetry (the audience all snapped their fingers at the end of that one). Next was a trumpet player and a piano player.

After Xavier Gaddison finished his magic show, I would be on next.

My heart was on the verge of exploding. I considered myself a pretty good singer but when I envisioned doing this, it was with Ariel and Jasmine behind me. Now, there was only me, singing an eighties song on stage, alone. My breathing turned into pants and my chest tightened. I felt like I was under the water at Bree Larson's party again.

All racing heart and no air.

I can do this, I told myself. But I didn't think I could. What if the kids laughed at me? Or worse, threw tomatoes? What if they booed me?

I gulped in a lungful of air, even though my chest felt like a gorilla was sitting on it.

The crowd applauded and I spotted Xavier holding up a white

rabbit out the corner of my eye. I looked down at the trail of brown pellets on the floor that stretched from the back of the stage to the middle of it. I thought they were some sort of food. Now I knew why they smelled so bad.

Would someone clean up all the rabbit poop before I went out there? What if I tripped in rabbit poop while I sung?

My stomach clenched, then twisted.

"Are you ready for this, French?"

Cole leaned in the doorway that led to the steps. I was so happy to see a friendly face, especially his, that I ran to him and jumped into his arms. He stepped back with an oomph, then wrapped his arms around my trembling body.

"I'm terrified," I admitted. "Ariel and Jasmine were supposed to go on stage with me but that was before everything happened." I pulled back to look at him. "I can't do this."

"You can do it." His gaze bored in to mine. "I believe in you. You just have to make that audience believe in you, too."

"How do I do that?" I asked.

"What are you singing?"

Another round of clapping sounded. Xavier must've been wrapping up. I saw the kid who was in charge of curtains walk to his place and blood rushed through my ears.

"French," Cole said, pulling my attention back to him. "What are you singing?"

"*Sussudio*," I replied.

He wrinkled his nose. "Are you singing it in a towel?" he asked.

"No. Of course not."

"Then I wouldn't. Uh ... what other songs do you know?"

"A million. Not sure how that helps, though."

He thought a minute.

"I think I have the perfect song for you."

He whispered the words in my ear. My heart went into a full-on sprint.

"Do you know it?" he asked.

"Yes, but I don't have the music and I didn't practice it."

He smiled.

"I think you'll be okay."

He turned and jogged back down the stairs.

"But what about the music?" I called after him.

"Don't worry about it, French. Just get on stage!"

And then he was out of sight, leaving me feeling nauseous.

No. Not nauseous.

I felt my light lunch crawl up my throat so I ran behind the blue gym mats leaning against the wall and let it loose.

My stomach immediately settled.

I wiped my hand across my mouth and squeezed my eyes shut.

I can do this, I told myself. I can do this.

"Let me do the rap."

Cole's words hung in the air as he flew past me. Before I could ask what he was talking about, the crowd broke out into applause and Xavier rolled his magic act past me. I squeezed against the mats, hoping that he wouldn't see the mess that I made there.

If anyone asked, I'd blame it on the rabbit.

"Thank you, Xavier, for that amazing magic show. Now, we'll have Bella French accompanied by Cole Winsted on the piano, singing, uh..." She stuttered, paused and whispered something. "Singing *Perfect* by *Pink*. Let's give her a hand."

I took a deep breath and reminded myself to sing the radio edit.

You can do this, I told myself again. You can do this.

Dressed in my *King Kong* T-shirt, jeans, red sneakers and two French braids, I walked through the dark blue curtains. A few drops of rabbit poop still littered the wooden floor as I took my place center stage.

I looked out in to the audience. It was packed. The entire school and their parents stared back at me.

The microphone shook in my hand.

I can do this.

I nodded to Cole that I was ready and began the first verse.

Between Cole's amazing piano playing and my voice, which soared thanks to the million dollar acoustics in the auditorium, the crowd was captivated. I saw their eyes watching me with approval and awe. Me.

When Cole stood up and rapped in the middle of the song, the crowd cheered.

When I sang the last bar, they stood on their feet and went wild.

I was invisible once. Now, with my voice raising and my heart pumping, I felt like they saw me. Not the pretend Bella that Jake had shaped into a popular beauty queen, but the real Bella. The friend. The dreamer. The thinker. The girl who wanted so badly for everyone else to accept her that she forgot about her own happiness. The girl who had sacrificed everything for love and even though she lost, had gained an understanding of herself.

I knew who I was now. I was a strong, loving woman who no longer cared if other people accepted me. I accepted myself. I was a girl who would fight for herself and the ones I loved, even if it cost me everything. I was a girl who loved a boy and who hoped that, one day, he would forgive me enough to love me back. I was my mother's daughter. If she saw me now, I knew that she would be proud that I had finally discovered myself.

And who I was, was glorious.

69

I opened the door that separated the lobby from the long hallway leading to the stage. Parents and friends filled the cavernous room, some with flowers and teddy bears, others with balloons and some with just proud smiles.

There was no one waiting for me, though. I hadn't told Daddy about the talent show. Just that I had to stay after school to finish something up and that I would be home around six o'clock. Honestly, I hadn't even thought that I would make it onto the stage. If it wasn't for Cole, I wouldn't have. Now, as I pushed through the bodies in the lobby, I wished that I would have told my dad. I wished that someone was waiting for me, too.

"Nice job."

Some man I didn't know clapped me on the back. I gave him an awkward smile and kept walking.

"You have an excellent voice, dear." This came from Mrs. Jonas, the assistant principal. She was waiting for her daughter, Alexa, who had done a jazz dance routine.

"Thanks," I replied.

"You sounded like an angel," a tall, thin woman with glasses said.

She clasped her hands in front of her as she said it, her face serene as if I had really just stepped down from heaven.

"Thank you," I replied.

"You sounded great, Bella!" Mrs. Smalls called out. She stood to my right, a buff man with dark black hair and a five o'clock shadow standing next to her. A small child, hers also I presumed, turned to her mother.

"Mommy, can I get her autograph?"

Mrs. Smalls smiled and shook her head. "I'll bring it home to you next time I see her," she said.

I nodded at her. "Sure thing."

I continued to squeeze through the crowd, trying to make my way home. Exhaustion pulled at me. It'd been such a long day. My bed would feel heavenly right now.

A flash of red caught my eye but it was gone just as suddenly. For a brief moment, I pretended that Ariel and Jasmine were here, rooting me on. I envisioned them walking next to me, our friendship strong and unbroken. But they were gone, not returning any of my calls or text for forgiveness. I considered writing them a letter. It's harder to ignore letters. Especially hand-written ones. If they ignored the letter then I'd just have to storm the door to their apartments. Ariel and Jasmine had been my best friends for years and I was not just going to let that slip away. I would do whatever I had to do to win them back. To have them forgive me.

Everything except lie, of course.

I promised myself that no matter how long it took or how much groveling I had to do, we would be friends again. It was a promise that I intended to keep.

I was stopped five more times with accolades. Finally, I burst through the front door and spilled into the outside. A few people were scattered about, smoking cigarettes and talking, but not many. It was freezing and starting to snow. I tugged my jacket closer and began my walk to the subway station.

"Need a lift?"

Cole's voice was a sweet serenade to my ears.

I turned. He was leaning against a blue *Honda Civic*, a grin on his face. His long body was dressed in all black except for the fur around his neck. His blue eyes seemed to glow in the darkness.

He'd disappeared after my song. I assumed that he'd gone home. I was glad he didn't. Just seeing him now warmed my entire body.

"I thought you left," I said, walking toward him.

He shrugged. "I was going to but there was this girl that I knew would need a ride home so..." He gave me one of his teasing smiles. God. I loved his smiles.

"I guess I'd better leave before you find her then. Wouldn't want her to get jealous."

"I wouldn't worry about that."

A soft wind blew and I crossed my arms in front of me, trying to keep the heat in. Yet, I didn't want to get in the car yet. There was so much unsaid between Cole and I. I feared that, if I got in his car and he took me home, that I'd never get to say any of it. I needed to tell him the truth about how I felt. He deserved that much.

"Cole, I need to tell you something," I said.

He nodded. "Okay."

The breath left my lungs in a long sigh and I dug the toe of my sneaker in to the snow on the ground.

"Thank you," I said finally. "For being there for me tonight. And in the locker room. And when I needed you for the English project, and when I needed tutoring, and on the beach, and every other time. Just..." A lump formed in my throat and I swallowed it. Why did this feel so final? Why did this feel like goodbye?

"Just thank you," I said. I swallowed again. It didn't help. The lump bobbed back in place.

Cole shifted his weight against his car.

"You're welcome."

"And I'm sorry about what happened to your brother and sister, and about your mom. I'm sorry that I pushed you away when you told me how you felt. I was confused and scared and just..." I let out a foggy breath and shook my head. Hot tears welled up behind my eyes. Why was this so hard? "I'm sorry, okay? For everything that I did that hurt you." A single tear fell down my cheek and I quickly wiped it away. I felt it's watery trail freeze on my cheek. "I was stupid and dumb and naïve. I hope that one day, you can forgive me."

He nodded, and broke eye contact with me, looking off to his right.

The lump in my throat got bigger and I looked down at the ground. He didn't forgive me. Whatever Cole and I had, was now over. Officially.

I nodded and turned from him, walking in the direction of the train station, hoping that I could make it to the gate without completely falling apart.

"I didn't call you a ninja turtle."

I turned around, frowning.

"What?"

Cole walked toward me, his boots crunching over the snow.

"That day in the hallway when I called you Michelangelo, I wasn't calling you a ninja turtle. I was trying to be witty and tell you that you looked like a work of art but it came out wrong. Every time I tried to say something nice to you, it came out as some stupid joke and I'm sorry for that. I should have told you that I loved you the first day I saw you but I was scared and stupid."

I looked in to his eyes, so blue and warm despite the cold.

"You loved me?"

"From the first time I saw you."

He brushed his thumb over my cheek, smoothing away the icy tears. I leaned into his touch and closed my eyes. Could it be? Could there still be a chance for us?

I opened my eyes and gazed at Cole. He was so beautiful, inside and out. No other boy lit a spark in my soul like Cole did. I knew in that moment that no boy ever would. Cole had loved me once. It was time to stop being afraid. It was time to finally take the one thing that I wanted.

"I love you too, Cole."

My chest tightened, and my body flushed.

Cole looked taken aback and fluttered his eyes.

"Can you, uh, say that again?" he asked.

I took a deep breath, saying it louder this time.

"I love you, Cole. Even if you don't feel the same, I want you to know it."

And there it was. My heart was laid out in the snow, ready for him to receive or stomp on it. I had never been so vulnerable, so open, in my life. It was terrifying but at the same time, freeing.

He closed his eyes and leaned his head back. A little hum escaped his throat. Then, his eyes opened and he looked at me with such emotion that it made my heart race.

"I have been waiting so long for you to say that. I just had to hear it twice. I love you too, Bella. I've never stopped loving you."

And then his lips swooped in to cover mine, stealing what little breath I had in my lungs. My entire body glowed with happiness. With the joy that came from being loved and loving in return.

He kissed me until our toes froze in the snow. Then we climbed in his car and he kissed me some more. Each press of his lips was like pure light. A dream that I never wanted to awake from.

He held my hand and kissed me at every red light and stop sign. I was so happy that I thought I'd burst!

When we pulled up to the front of my apartment, he unhooked his seatbelt, pulled me toward him and kissed me some more.

"We have a lot of time to make up for," he whispered against my lips. "Two and a half years of missed kisses."

"How much time did we put in tonight?" I asked, my smile wide.

"Not even a day." I closed my eyes and fell in love with him a little more. Cole's kisses were quickly becoming my new favorite thing.

"But there's something that I have to ask you first," he said.

"What?"

"Will you be my girlfriend?"

I chuckled against his lips.

"It's a little late for that, isn't it?"

"I just wanted to hear you say it."

"Okay. I'll be your girlfriend, Cole. Forever and ever."

He stilled.

"Say it again."

My smile widened.

"I, Bella French, take you, Cole Winsted, to be my boyfriend."

He smiled against my lips. "I love it when you say it twice."

I laughed out loud and pushed him. He dramatically fell backwards, though he was so strong, I knew it wasn't because of my push. Then, he climbed out of the car and walked around to open my door and to my surprise, walked me in to my lobby.

"Are you going to be valiant and walk me to my door?"

He shook his head. "Nope. I'm going to go upstairs and meet your dad. He'll need to know who his daughter's new boyfriend is."

I snorted. "Seriously?"

He squeezed my hand. "Seriously."

I smiled. I was bringing home my first boyfriend. It was a little nerve wrecking but I had learned an important lesson. With Cole by my side, nothing really bad could happen. He made everything better.

We stepped off the elevator and walked toward my door.

70

The following weekend, Cole and I had our first official date.

A musical called *Dear Evan Hansen*.

Cole didn't usually flash his money but this night he gave me money for a new dress. I picked out a long yellow number with sequins and low shoulders. At seven o'clock, he knocked on my door, shook my father's hand, gave me a kiss on the cheek and walked me to an awaiting limo that took us to dinner and to the show.

Through the entire play, which I loved, he didn't once let go of my hand. Afterward, we went for hot chocolate at a little sweets shop by the water which, I was told, he'd asked to be opened up especially for this occasion.

"This was the best night ever," I said, sipping my drink. "Thank you for bringing me here."

He kissed my shoulder, his smile bright and happy.

"I knew you'd like it," he said.

"The songs were amazing. That *Waving Through the Window* one was fantastic."

"Yeah?"

"Yeah."

"You know, my band is covering that song at our next gig."

"Your band, huh? I'd heard tales that you had a band. I'm not sure that I believed it, though."

He raised an eyebrow. "Why not? I'm musically inclined."

I laughed. "Yes, but I didn't know you were that musically inclined. What's your band named?"

He thought a minute.

"How about you guess?"

I sat up straight. I loved playing guessing games with Cole. It was one of our 'us' things.

"First clue," he said. "It's named after a clothing item."

My brows pressed down as I thought.

"Too vague," I said. "Next clue."

"The item is something you wear on your feet."

"Heels? Sandals? Boots?"

He laughed and waved my guesses away.

"No. You're on the right track, though. Okay. Here is your final clue. It's something that you wear on your feet every day."

I smirked. "Sneakers?"

Cole raised an eyebrow and pulled out his phone. His thumbs glided over the keypad, then he looked at me.

My phone dinged and I pulled it from my purse.

The words were like cupid's arrow to my heart. I read it out loud.

"I love red sneakers."

A lump formed in my throat. I put down my phone, threw my arms around Cole's neck and kissed him long and deep. I loved kissing Cole. It was probably the best 'us' thing we did.

"If I had known you liked the band name, I would have told you a long time ago," he said with a grin.

"What do you play?"

"Lead singer."

"And?"

"Guitar. Piano, if I am feeling so inclined."

"Can I see you play?"

"You've already seen me play."

"No. I mean your band."

He sighed dramatically. "I don't know. Girls usually fall for drummers. Not sure if I'm ready to risk that."

I kissed him again.

"You're the only guy that I could ever fall for," I said when we pulled apart.

"And you're the only girl I could ever fall for."

We smiled at each other, two crazy kids in love.

"I think it's time to take you home before your dad grounds you again."

I rolled my eyes. I didn't want the night to end but I knew that there would be tomorrow and the next day. And the day after that. I wasn't letting Cole go. Not now. Not ever.

The limo drove us back to my building and Cole walked me up the stairs to my apartment, hand in hand, heart in heart. When we arrived at my floor, we spied someone standing in front of my door. The boy turned to us.

"Eric? What are you doing here?"

He shoved his hands in his jeans pocket, his face looking pale and sad.

"Bella. Cole. Hey."

"Uh, hi," Cole said, squeezing my hand again.

Eric's head bobbed and he snatched off his black hat and ran his fingers through his midnight hair.

"This is a little weird but I came here to ask for your help."

"Um ... okay," I said.

"Ariel was the best thing that ever happened to me. I want her back. No. I need her back. Will you help me?"

Eric and I stared at each other. In his eyes, I saw the same pain that radiated through my heart. The loss of a fiery red-headed girl that gave color to both of our lives.

I nodded.

"Okay." I walked forward, putting the key in to the door and let myself inside. "Let's get her back."

To be continued...

Thank you for reading. Please leave a review on Amazon or Goodreads.

PREVIEW CHASING MERMAIDS (BOOK 2)

I've spent most of my life chasing mermaids.

Well, not actual mermaids.

Mermaids as in goals. Aspirations. Ambitions. Things people dream about but never achieve.

Like being a rock star, or a professional athlete, or a billionaire.

Most people will never attain those things.

But I'm not most people.

My name is Ariel Swimworthy, and I'm going to swim in the Olympics. That's my dream. My mermaid. And I'm not just going to chase it.

I'm going to catch it.

I keep these thoughts in focus as I fly through the water, arm over arm, legs kicking hard, body stretched. If I touch the wall in time, I'll qualify to compete in the Tri-State Swim Competition in Orlando, Florida—the first step on my road to being an Olympian. All I need is twenty-five seconds and fifty meters in the blue.

I have to touch the wall in time.

My swim team's loud shrieks echo throughout the gym. Their cheers make me push harder.

One.

Two.

Breathe.

One.

Two.

Breathe.

My arms slice through the water like hot knives through silk. My feet flutter powerfully behind me. My heart hammers in my chest. The wall is almost in reach. I launch myself toward it, swimming harder than I've ever swum before.

Almost there!

My fingers stretch forward, inch by inch by inch until, finally, I touch the coolness of the tiles. My palms press against the flat surface, and my body slows to a stop.

Instantly, a sense of triumph fills my chest.

I've done it! I've touched the wall!

The pride only has a second or two to penetrate before doubt shows up and kicks me in the shins.

Yes, I've finished my fifty-meter freestyle swim. But was it enough?

My heart beats hard. Half of it is from exertion, but the other half is all nerves.

Everything I've done has led me to this moment. I've worked my butt off for it. Sweated for it. Bled for it. If my time is even a fraction over twenty-six seconds, I can kiss my Olympic dreams goodbye.

That thought alone devastates me.

I jump out of the pool, sending white foam splashing onto the tiled floor.

Vanessa Uma is already sitting there, legs crossed at the ankles, feet dangling in the water. She slowly pulls off her goggles and gives me a condescending smile.

I hate that smile. I hate Vanessa. She has what I call a punchable face. She shares this trait with her stepsister, and my cousin by marriage, Ursula Meyers. They have the same dad, my uncle, but different moms whom I've never met.

I roll my eyes and turn away from Vanessa, instead choosing to focus on Coach Fish and his clipboard.

His forehead is sweating, and his warm up suit—complete with

Olympic rings on the back—crinkles as he scribbles words on a scratched and faded brown clipboard.

My heart pounds against my ribs so loud I'm sure people can hear it in New Jersey.

Coach Fish doesn't say anything at first. He simply looks from me, to Vanessa, then back to his clipboard. The silence tightens my nerves to torturous levels.

He has to say I made qualifying time. He just has to!

My eyes drift shut.

Please God, please.

I'm not a religious person. Before today, I was an annual prayer at best. I'm not even sure if God cares about what's happening to me right now. All I know is I want this so badly I'm shaking, and I need to know I've covered all my bases.

I hear Coach Fish's voice, and my eyes pop open.

"Vanessa Uma swam a twenty-five twenty-eight," he announces. "Impressive."

Twenty-five seconds and twenty-eight milliseconds. Olympic qualifying time for the women's fifty-meter swim. Figures. After all, she *is* an Olympic champion. A freaking national hero. That still doesn't negate the fact she's a terrible person who makes everyone around her feel like garbage. No amount of medals can fix that kind of attitude.

"And Ariel Swimworthy swam a..." He pauses. My heart beats so hard I'm sure I'm about to go into cardiac arrest. "Twenty-five twenty-eight."

My heart stops cold. Did I hear him right? No. I couldn't have. It's impossible. Vanessa is an Olympic champion. I couldn't have tied her time. I've never outswum her before. Ever.

"Twenty-five twenty-eight?" I ask.

I wait for him to correct me. To tell me there's been a mistake. That he accidentally read Vanessa's time twice. Instead, he smiles wide.

"Twenty-five twenty-eight. Olympic qualifying time."

A scream of pure joy bursts from my lips. "No Running" signs blur past me as I race to the other side of the pool and join my teammates, who have gone from shrieking to what looks like euphoric seizures.

I've made my time. My dream of being an Olympic swimmer is one step closer to reality. I'm so overjoyed I can barely breathe.

Five girls tackle me, and we all tumble onto the floor in a giggling heap of arms, legs, and swimsuits.

Claire Vonnegut's butt slides down my back and, in typical Claire fashion, she farts. Not a girly, it just slipped out kind of fart either. This thing is loud, hot, and completely unapologetic. Farting has been Claire's contribution to all our victory piles for the last three years. I love her to pieces, but there's no denying that this habit of hers is super gross. I try to move away, but I'm trapped beneath five other people. All I can do is squirm and hope the smell doesn't melt my nose hairs.

Did I mention how classy our team is?

"Yuck! Come on, swamp butt!" my best friend, Sophia Johnson, cries. She squints and pinches the bridge of her nose with three fingers. "That smells like dead raccoons!"

Claire wiggles her blond eyebrows at Sophia, taunting her. "Nope, it smells like cheese pizza. That's what I had for lunch."

"Was it cheese pizza with skunks on top?"

Claire winks at her. "Maybe."

I laugh so hard my stomach hurts. It's amazing to me that Sophia still gets mad about Claire's farting even though Claire does this every day. Literally. Every. Single. Day. It's gross, but funny too.

"Ms. Swimworthy," Coach Fish bellows.

His commanding tone sends us all scrambling to square our shoulders and straighten our spines like we've been conditioned to do since he started coaching us.

"Sir, yes, sir."

Ademar Fish used to be a marine. Then he was a five-time Olympic champion. Now, he's our swim coach/drill sergeant. He runs our team like we're preparing for war. He has a hard edge, but his encouraging words and good nature make up for it. Mostly.

He stands directly in front of me, his hazel eyes taking me in. I look back at him, examining the crow's feet around his eyes, his tanned skin, and his downturned mouth. He takes a single step forward and crosses his arms loosely over his broad chest. For a man who must be in his fifties, he still has a swimmer's body. Strong. Lean. Tall.

"Twenty-five twenty-eight." His French accent is still strong, even though he's been in the United States for nearly forty years. His arms uncross, and he leans on one hip. His clipboard taps against his leg, and the sound echoes through the now silent room like a drum beat.

"You have one of the fastest times of all the girls here. You should be proud of yourself."

I am proud of myself. Even Vanessa's condescending smirk can't diminish that.

"You don't know this," he says, scratching the side of his head, "but I've been talking to your teammates. They've made an almost unanimous decision. One I wholeheartedly approve of."

Decision? What decision?

My brows knit together, and I hold my breath.

What could the girls have said about me?

Coach Fish holds out his hand to me, pride written on his face.

"Let me be the first to congratulate the new captain of the St. Mary's Academy All Star Women's Swim Team."

My breath catches in my throat and my eyes are about to pop out of my head.

Captain? Me?

My head spins so fast I can barely process what the coach has just said. Then, piece by piece, my body rejoices. First my feet bounce off the floor like I'm doing high knees in gym class. Then my stomach trembles with delight. Next, my lungs fill with warm, chlorine-scented oxygen. Finally, my mouth opens wide, and I scream my freaking head off.

A million dizzying emotions explode within me at once. Joy. Excitement. Relief. Disbelief. Before I have a chance to process them all, I'm on the floor again, Claire is farting up a storm, and I'm so full of happiness I can barely hear Vanessa screaming in fury.

"But that's not fair!" she argues.

Sorry, Vanessa. That's life. And, for me, life is sweet.

The five girls on top of me celebrate as if we've all just been pronounced captain. In a way, we have.

Amid my celebration, tingles break out along my shoulders. The sensation runs up my neck and down my back.

Someone is watching me, and, somehow, I know exactly who that someone is.

I frown and, almost automatically, look in the direction of the observation box above the pool.

There he is.

Eric Shipman.

My gut fills with a weird ache, some mixture of hostility and something else I can't describe. The emotions are painfully sharp, but unfocused and confusing. I hate the feeling.

When he catches me looking, he smiles and claps, celebrating my victory even while my heart is still healing from the death blow he gave it just months before.

Eric Shipman is a liar. No amount of clapping or spying will erase that fact.

I loved him once. He said he loved me too.

But it was all a lie.

Just one big lie.

ABOUT THE AUTHOR

Thank you so much for reading The Boyfriend Agreement.

Being a teenager is hard. There's school, tests and classes to think about. Not to mention friends, dating and fashion. It's the time of our lives when we are expected to make mistakes, yet punished for them. We want to love but we're told we're too young to know what love is. We want to be treated as adults but we are still trying to figure out exactly who we are inside. It is from this place of uncertainty, curiosity and hope that The Boyfriend Agreement was born. I wanted to capture that time in our lives where the only thing constant is change. Bodies change. Friends change. Decisions change. Who we were yesterday is not the person that we are going to be a year, a month, even a day from now. Life is constantly in flux and it's absolutely fascinating.

You may be surprised to know that this book started out very differently. In its original form, Cole was a lot more *Beast*-like. Literally. He terrorized the school to the point where the students had signed a petition to have him expelled. Cole was angry. He lived in a terrible neighborhood and had three siblings, a drug addict mother and a drug lord father. His life was, at best, unsteady, and at worst, an absolute nightmare. Meanwhile, Bella was a lot more country. She used her country girl charm, her love and her confidence to peel back Cole's layers and help him to trust again. This original version was a lot more "shoot 'em up". Seriously, there was a drug war, lots of bodies and Jake was ten times worse, if that's even possible. I got through about 75% of the book and I had to stop myself. It was deep. Heavy. In a word, not me. I didn't want to write a novel bordering on Urban Fiction. I wanted something light. Something that celebrated teenage romance.

Something that made people laugh and cry. So, I went back to the drawing board and wrote something that was a lot more me. Funny. Romantic. Honest. Hopeful.

I hope you feel it, too.

Of course, I have to address the *Disney* parallels. They are put there quite purposefully. You see, I was born a *Disney* fan. Back in 1988, my parents purchased a timeshare property in Orlando, Florida. Our annual trips to *Disney World* are one of my most cherished childhood memories. I have seen every *Disney* animated movie imaginable, as well as the not animated ones. My favorite animated movie? *Alice in Wonderland*. My favorite non-animated movie? *The Parent Trap*. I can sing the original *Mickey Mouse Club* theme song, I play *Disney* trivia on car rides, I can beat everyone but my husband in *Disney Scene It*, and I can name all the *Disney* princesses in chronological order. In short, I have a problem. So, it is no surprise that some of my *Disney* mania has crept in to this book. Hopefully, you'll enjoy the little *Disney* Easter eggs as much as I enjoyed writing them.

So, what's next for The Boyfriend Agreement? Well, there is the question of, where's Kenny? The next book will feature Ariel and Eric's story. Be on the lookout for King Triton, Sebastian, Flounder, and Ariel's six sisters. I will explore how far she will go for a dream, and of course, what happens to her and Eric. Do Ariel and Bella ever reconcile? Will Jasmine ever find true love? And what about Sophia Johnson (You remember her from The Beginning of Forever, don't you? You didn't think I forgot about her and Josiah, did you?).

All in all, St. Mary's Academy is just getting started and I hope that you will all come along for the ride.

-Seven Steps

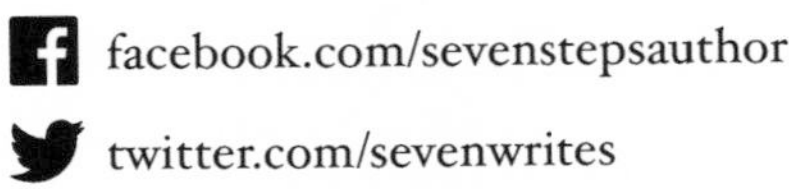

ALSO BY

Adult Contemporary Romance

Peace in the Storm

New Adult Romance

The Last Rock King

St. Mary's Academy Series

The Beginning of Forever

The Boyfriend Agreement (Book I)

Chasing Mermaids (Book 2)

The Golden Boy (Book 3)

Stealing Hearts (Book 4)

The Secret Lives of Princesses (Book 5)

Kissing Frogs (Book 6)

20044161R00241

Made in the USA
Middletown, DE
08 December 2018